The Reach Of Shadows

DI Bliss Book 4

Tony J Forder

First published in 2018 by Bloodhound Books

www.bloodhoundbooks.com

Print ISBN 978-1-912986-01-9

Also By Tony J Forder

DI Bliss Series
Bad To The Bone (Book 1)
The Scent of Guilt (Book 2)
If Fear Wins (Book 3)

Scream Blue Murder
Cold Winter Sun

Praise For Tony J Forder

"Forder didn't spare the horses when writing Scream Blue Murder. This book rockets along, a breathless action-packed ride. Perfect reading for fans of Simon Kernick and Jeff Abbott."
Matt Hilton, author of the Joe Hunter thrillers

"An action packed, twisty thriller. Great stuff."
Mason Cross, author of the Carter Blake series of thrillers.

'The book is well written gripping and gets right into your mind and feelings as you are taken on a fast paced journey through a book it is impossible to put down.' **Jill Burkinshaw – Books n All**

'Degrees of Darkness is an engrossing and haunting thriller!'
Caroline Vincent – Bits About Books

'This is an awesome read that for me that put it on a scare factor alongside Stephen King and Thomas Harris.

The heart breaking opening will make most readers just stand back and take a breath.' **Susan Hampson – Books From Dusk Till Dawn**

'From start to finish I felt I was reading this in the edge of my seat while holding my breath. It really is that kinda read.' **Philomena Callan – Cheekypee Reads And Reviews**

'I read the book in one sitting and was completely enthralled in the story!' **Donna Maguire – Donnas Book Blog**

Chapter One

The curious thing to his mind was how loud his bare feet sounded as they slapped against the sodden pavement, puddles exploding and spattering his legs from the knee down with rainwater the colour of thin gravy. The way the sound reverberated along the quiet streets, he might as well have been wearing clogs. As his legs and arms pumped and the muscles that worked them burned, the thin cotton dressing gown he wore flapped behind him like a superhero's cloak. He was only subliminally aware of these things, because his direct focus remained on the figure ahead. The one he had chased from his back garden, and who was now steadily increasing the gap between them. Much to his disgust.

I'm too old for this shit, Bliss thought.

His body agreed.

Jimmy Bliss seldom slept well during humid, sticky summers, and his slumber that night had not been deep. The fierce downpour that started rolling through the city shortly after midnight hadn't helped, with the constant tip-tapping against windowpanes and the sound of rainwater overflowing from leaky guttering. He woke often, tossing and turning, not knowing which had inspired the other. Remnants of scattered dreams drifted across his semi-conscious thoughts, each of them as unwelcome as the last. Every time his sleep was disturbed, Bliss had considered throwing aside the thin cotton sheet and getting up out of bed.

After all, there was music to listen to, movies to absorb, work to catch up on, exercise to stretch his muscles, or a car to punish hard on the dark and quiet roads around the city. Anything other than this sweaty torpor. But each time, just as he was about to rise like a drowning man surging upward to break the surface for one last breath, sleep claimed him again and dragged him back under.

For a time during the next moment of restlessness, he had lain perfectly still, in tune with the moist air surrounding him, eyes wide open as he considered his options. As soon as he heard the odd sound, Bliss knew it was out of place. He thought hard about it as he leaned up on one elbow, waiting for it to brush against his senses once again. The reluctant noise had not been naturally occurring; it had been… furtive. Not something created by a shift in the building, a breeze blowing through the eaves, the expansion of floorboards, nor any rodent lurking behind the skirting boards. Furtive meant only one thing to his mind.

Human.

Bliss sat up straight, his body slick with sweat. Flaming June had become sweltering June, and had then swiftly moved on to molten June over the past few days, with the nights not becoming a great deal cooler. He had switched off the ceiling fan earlier that night because it dried out his throat, and the moisture that had subsequently coalesced in the air since was overwhelming, an almost physical presence now threatening to choke him.

He checked the digital read-out on the alarm clock beside his bed as he turned sideways and planted his feet on the carpet; saw that it was 3.31am. Every movement he made was as slow and precise as he was able to take. He had turned fifty-six in May, and his joints were not as loose as he would have liked, especially first thing in the morning having spent the past few hours prone and squirming. Bliss slipped into his moccasins, padded across the room then pulled his dressing gown off its hook on the back of the bedroom door, easing into it.

His head jerked up.

There it was again.

A subtle snicking noise. Like the sound adhesive tape makes when being pulled from a roll. Bliss tried to control his breathing. The noise had not come from inside the house, but rather from the back garden. His mind drifted away to a case earlier in the year, when a similar situation had occurred. At the time he had not been at all sure whether anyone had been out there in his back garden in the dead of night; certainly, he had not seen anyone from the bedroom window, and had not gone outside to check. This time he wanted to be certain. As a detective inspector working for the city's Major Crimes unit, he had more than his fair share of enemies. Not all of them villains.

Without switching on any lights or stopping to find a torch, Bliss swiftly moved outside the bedroom, along the landing and down the stairs. Heading into the kitchen, he scooped up his keys from a blue glass bowl which sat on the worktop. Pausing by the living room door, Bliss studied the curtains drawn across the French windows. He felt his chest rise and fall, every breath sounding to his ears like a jet airliner about to climb off the runway. He saw no movement, no light, heard no further sound.

Adhesive tape being pulled from a roll.

If you wanted to drill a hole in glass or break a pane, then taping it first was a good way to deaden the sound and lessen the effect of the shards snapping. A relatively quiet way of breaking in.

Bliss exited the front door and pulled it closed behind him, having set the latch to prevent it from locking. He crept around his car in the driveway, scuttled down the alley that ran alongside the house and cut left into another alley, which spanned the back of all four dwellings in his row. He reached up for the latch on the back gate, slowly raising it with the soft pad of his thumb, and as it disengaged in well-oiled silence, he eased the wooden gate open.

The gap was no more than six inches wide when Bliss felt the weight shift. In that moment, the gate was pulled from his grasp and as he started to stumble head first into his own back garden, a figure barged into Bliss and sent him crashing off towards the neatly trimmed section of lawn. In that instant, both the element of surprise and his own momentum worked against him, and Bliss crabbed sideways two paces before the ground seemed to rise up to swallow him whole.

He picked himself up quickly and immediately gave chase. As his feet sought traction and skated almost comically on the turf for a moment, both moccasins flew into the air. Realising they were lost to the darkness, he ignored them and ran back into the alleyway.

The figure, who wore dark clothing and what to Bliss looked like a baseball cap on his head, sped away around the side of the house. Heading out of the estate, the fleeing intruder ran across several roads, before cutting across a narrow strip of land beside the main street that ran down the hill towards Oundle Road.

As the pursuit continued, the burn hit Bliss quickly. Deep inside his chest at first, coiled heat spread out into his shoulders and thighs. Pain, too, in other joints including hips, knees and ankles. An avid and enthusiastic sportsman in his youth, Bliss knew his running days were long behind him, and his respiratory functions were in no condition for a lengthy foot chase. After only a couple of minutes he started to labour, every breath ragged and bursting from his lungs in short gasps. Bliss wasted no energy on calling out, and as it was approaching four in the morning, nobody was around to offer any assistance.

It was at that point that he became fully aware of how ridiculous this chase would appear if anybody did happen to be looking on.

Refusing to give up, Bliss pushed himself to run harder. While he exercised regularly, little of it involved prolonged physical exertion like this. His body cried out, begging him to stop. But anger fuelled him as he lumbered on in vain.

The younger and fitter man he was chasing ran through another alleyway between two rows of houses, the distance between them increasing all the time. At the kerb on Oundle Road he did not so much as pause, speeding across in loping, powerful strides. Bliss realised he would not catch up, but sheer bloody-mindedness ignored logic and drove him on.

Whether it was the rage he felt at having had his privacy snatched away by the prowler, or the adrenaline-fuelled pursuit itself, he did not know and would never recall. Either way, when

Bliss reached the road crossing his path, he ran straight over without even thinking about the possible consequences.

He was less than halfway across when the car hit him.

Perhaps he sensed it at the last moment. Maybe sheer human instinct and self-preservation took over. Whatever the reason, Bliss was in mid-air when the vehicle struck. It whipped his legs away, sending his body hurtling at an oblique angle towards the windscreen. He slammed side on against the rim of the roof, bounced once and skimmed along its surface, before spinning off the back and tumbling onto the road behind the car. As tyres squealed like an animal in pain, Bliss's mind started to shut down, drowning in a sea of inky blackness.

The last thing Bliss heard that night was the thump of his head striking the warm and hard surface of the road, made slick first by the brief summer storm that had blown through, and now the blood that had started leaking from his scalp. The last thing he felt before losing consciousness was not pain, but a mournful sense of vulnerability, and the gut-clawing fear of dying alone.

Chapter Two

When Chandler arrived two days later to collect him from hospital, Bliss noticed immediately the sour look on her face and a piercing glare that could melt steel. Both cheeks were pinched and hollowed out, mouth a tight slit, and her eyes were coal-black pissholes in the snow. His sergeant was pale and looked as if she had not slept well in a long time.

'Who shit in your handbag?' he asked.

For a moment that went on too long for comfort, Bliss wondered if his partner was going to respond at all. She shook her head from side to side and seemed to be biting down on her tongue. Eventually she relented with a heavy sigh.

'I am royally pissed off. The plan today was to pick you up, drive you home, get you settled. Right?'

'Right. I gather that's no longer happening?'

'No. Ten minutes before I was due to set off, Edwards called me into her office. A new case. Which is fine. We still have a few on the go, but nothing that can't be set aside for a few days. I was expecting to be told to handle it myself until you were back on board, or that they'd be pulling in a DI on loan. But no. Our glorious leader tells me – no, *instructs* me – to collect you from hospital, cracked ribs and all, and take you to the crime scene.'

'What's wrong with that?' Bliss asked.

He had been sitting on the edge of his bed waiting for her to arrive, the plastic carrier bag of essentials that DS Bishop had brought in the previous day now sitting by his side like a faithful pet. He had been in hospital for two whole days while they monitored his concussion and iced his cracked ribs. All he wanted to do was get out of there, no matter where he ended up.

Chandler was giving him one of her looks. 'What's wrong is that your direct superior, rather than order you to a new crime scene, should have made sure you went straight home. Rest and recuperation, it's called. I sometimes wonder whether these people have ever heard of the benefits of recovery.'

Bliss waved it off. 'Don't fret. It's better for me to be working than sitting around at home. I'm clearly wanted for my searing intellect rather than my fitness levels, and that's always been the case.'

'Except that DCI Edwards is constantly preaching about regulations, and here she is flouting them. You should be at home, taking care of yourself.'

Bliss grinned. 'Aww, you're angry on my behalf.'

'I am. And a fat lot of good it did me.' She shook her head again. 'I'm telling you, boss, there's something not right about this one. Something more than just sending you to a crime scene when you should be off work. Edwards could barely look me in the eye. She was keeping something from me, I'm certain of that. And whatever it is, it stinks.'

It wasn't exactly a bundle of laughs leaving the hospital. Bliss had forced himself to take a few walks the previous day in order to stretch his aching muscles, but nothing had prepared him for this. Every movement was both excruciating and exhausting, and he had to shuffle along at barely half his usual pace.

The hospital corridors were unreasonably long, the walk across multiple car parks to where Chandler had managed to find a space, almost interminable. By the time he slumped down into the passenger seat of her Ford Focus, he was drained and dripping with sweat. The damaged ribs were like razors slicing into bone, injecting him with little shots of agonising pain.

Bliss hated being a passenger at the best of times, but he found Chandler's driving in particular something that was best endured with both eyes closed and one hand gripping the door handle. He was not looking forward to the experience.

'You doing okay?' she asked him as she gunned the engine. The sympathy in his colleague's eyes was palpable. 'I'm happy enough to disobey the mighty Edwards if you are. The best place for you right now is at home, with your feet up. I'll take the bollocking.'

'You going to hang around and see to my every need while I'm at home?' Bliss asked, snapping the seatbelt into place, wincing as it tightened across his chest.

'Some of us have work to do. But look at yourself, Jimmy. You're in agony.'

'Right. But I'll be in agony no matter where I go. Don't worry, I won't be leaping tall buildings or chasing runaway trains. You'll hardly know I'm there. And Pen, if I happen to nod off on the way over – which would be a miracle with you behind the wheel – make sure you wake me when we get to wherever we're going. I won't be happy if you leave me sitting in the car with the window cracked open as if I'm a dog.'

Chandler manoeuvred the hatchback out of the car park and hung a right to take them out of the hospital grounds. As soon as the car had straightened, she glanced across at him, shaking her head in admonishment.

'You'd think at your ripe old age you'd learn a few simple lessons. What were you thinking? Running around the streets in the middle of the night wearing hardly any clothes and chasing a suspect all on your own?'

'Stop banging on about my age,' Bliss said, wanting to cough but holding it back in fear of what it might do to his ribs. 'I'm not in my box yet.'

Though I guess I could have been, he thought. And that's precisely what Chandler would have been thinking ever since she was given the news about his accident. Which reminded him about something.

'Hey,' he said, turning to face her. Delving into his personal toolkit, Bliss reached for his most disarming smile. 'Thank you.'

'For what?'

'For giving up part of your holiday and flying home early. For being there when I woke up. For… for caring, I suppose.'

Chandler rolled her eyes. 'You're not getting all mushy on me, are you? I think those drugs they gave you are still in your system. Now shush until we get there.'

He shrugged and allowed himself to relax. New England was one of the older districts of Peterborough, and had once been home to the Great Northern Railway marshalling yards. Chandler drove them to the eastern tip where it merged into Dogsthorpe around the Welland estate. In 1994 the area had become nationally infamous when a six-year-old boy by the name of Rikki Neave was found murdered in woodland, having disappeared on his way to school. His mother was arrested and charged with her son's murder, but was later acquitted by a jury at the Northampton Crown Court. A little more than twenty years later the cold case was thawed open, and Bliss knew that his partner had been involved in the manhunt that followed. He wondered if returning to the area held any fears for her, especially given that the case remained unsolved.

'You find this place a little haunting?' he asked.

Silence followed, and Bliss wondered if Chandler had even heard the question. As he was about to repeat it, she said, 'It doesn't so much haunt me as make me angry. I wasn't on the original investigation, obviously. Now that *might* have thrown up a few ghosts. But we worked bloody hard, and it would have been nice to have got a result after all this time.'

Bliss had thought the same. But in the past week, the Assistant Chief Constable had announced that, while the case remained open, there were currently no active lines of enquiry.

'Was Edwards involved in that op?' he asked.

Chandler shook her head as she hit the indicators and turned left off the main road. 'No, that was DCI Harrison. His last case before he took time out to take care of his wife.'

He nodded. It was Harrison's decision to take extended leave that had paved the way for Bliss to return to the city after a twelve-year absence.

The series of roads that formed the giant rectangle they had entered was a real curiosity. Every home on both sides of the streets was a long, narrow bungalow, part of a series of semi-detached dwellings. The lack of a second storey on either side was peculiar, and played tricks on the eye as if the brain was incapable of processing such a regular formation. It took Bliss a few moments to adjust to the anomaly. As the Ford turned onto the longer stretch, the first responders were obvious among the vehicles mostly parked up on short and narrow driveways.

Police officers were in the process of sealing off the scene with tape, behind which the gawkers did what gawkers do best. The day was bright and hot, the sky unadorned save for a few erratic streaks of cirrus. Those neighbours who gathered on the periphery of the crime scene wore little clothing, and stood shielding their eyes, fanning their faces as they indulged in excited chatter. Bliss asked himself why they didn't just drag out a barbecue and a cooler box, throw some burgers on hot coals, whip out some chilled beer, and have done with it.

Chandler slipped her car in beneath the tape after flashing her warrant card at a uniform Bliss did not recognise. He kept his eyes on the road and away from the crowd assembling rapidly on both sides of the cordon. Bad news spread fast and drew out the ghouls. Even the gamers and tweakers emerged from the shadows.

'Any idea at all what we have waiting for us in there?' Bliss asked, dipping his head in the direction of a bungalow painted grey, unlike others in the row which were a uniform sandstone colour.

Drawing back the handbrake and killing the engine, Chandler replied on a heavy exhalation. 'Not a Scooby. Beyond suspected murder, that is. I told you, Edwards wanted me out of there as fast as my tiny little feet would carry me. I'm lucky she found time to give me the address.'

Milling awkwardly outside the property were six uniformed officers, which accounted for the three patrol vehicles parked up within the cordon. All were in short sleeves and baking beneath the relentless sunshine. There was an ambulance standing by, and Bliss saw two crew members attired in dark green chatting with a female police sergeant. One unmarked vehicle was parked close to the drive, and Bliss assumed this would belong to the on-call doctor who had been summoned to pronounce life extinct or variations of the same.

With the aid of the door frame, Bliss managed to haul himself up and out of the car without asking for help from his partner. His chest had been iced prior to him getting dressed, and he had also taken some heavy-duty painkillers, but the damaged ribs were quick to let him know he should be resting in his recliner at home. His shirt clung to his back as if he had stepped out of the shower. Chandler held back, not looking at him but waiting all the same. He could have kissed her for that. Instead he took a deep breath and made his way across to the uniforms.

'Who was first on site?' he asked, flashing his credentials.

The constable who stepped forward with his hand raised was someone Bliss recognised but could not put a name to. 'PC Virgil, sir,' he said. 'We took the call and assessed the situation upon arrival. A neighbour reported hearing a scuffle and what they believed to be a loud cry. I entered through the kitchen door to the rear of the property. My colleague, PC Irwin, was waiting out front still trying to get attention from the owner. We did knock several times before I headed round back.'

'The kitchen door was unlocked?' Bliss asked, nodding a greeting. He now remembered Virgil as one of the officers involved in a major vehicle chase across the Fens the previous autumn.

'Hanging wide open, sir.'

'So, having received no answer to your previous knocks, you went inside?'

'Yes, sir. I announced myself on the threshold, and when there was no answer, I entered the property.'

Bliss smiled. 'It's okay, PC Virgil, save all the proper terms and procedure for when you make your statement. For now, just give it to me as it happened.'

Virgil smiled. 'Yes, sir. The kitchen was empty. I called out again, but still nothing. I moved through into the hallway, still calling out. Next thing I did was open up the front door to let my colleague in. I wasn't sure if it was better to send him off looking for signs of a potential break-in or clear the house first. I decided it was better to clear the house.'

'You did the right thing,' Bliss told him. Virgil had made a snap decision as to whether to search for signs of a forced entry or check each room inside the property in case the occupier was in distress.

'Thanks. Anyway, I happened to be first inside the bedroom, which was at the front of the property to the right of the front door. I found a body lying on the bed, covered in blood. She was naked, her legs were spread wide and her hands were tied to the metal frame of the bed. I was pretty sure she was dead even before I noticed she wasn't breathing. I didn't want to interfere with the scene, but I knew I had to check her out just in case there was still time to do something to save her. I edged my way around the perimeter of the room, then I spotted a magazine on the bedside cabinet, so I picked it up just with the very corner of its cover and dropped it onto the floor so's I could step on it rather than the section of carpet so close to the victim. That put me in reach of her.

'I didn't want to touch the skin. I guess I was thinking about forensics, although I'm sure I ought to have checked for a pulse instead. Anyhow, I wear reading glasses, so I took them from my shirt pocket and held them just beneath the victim's nose. When they didn't mist, I told Irwin to call it in.'

Bliss was astonished by the officer's composure. His heart had to have been hammering its way out of his chest, with a thousand-and-one thoughts tumbling around inside his head, yet he had kept his cool and done a pretty good job of maintaining the integrity of the crime scene. Though Virgil's intentions were right, using the magazine to step on was not such a good move, as his shoes might have smudged clear prints on the glossy paper. Nonetheless, Bliss was impressed.

'You did very well,' Chandler said. She was standing close by and had overheard the entire exchange. 'Not sure I would have done all that even now.'

Virgil blushed. 'Thank you, DS Chandler.'

She raised her eyebrows. 'You know me by name. Have we worked together before?'

'No. I've seen you around whenever I've had reason to be at Thorpe Wood. I make a point to learn the names of as many detectives as I possibly can. It's where I want to be in a year or so. Major Crimes, that is.'

'Well, you're off to a good start here, Constable,' Bliss told him. 'Some quick thinking inside that bedroom.'

'Thank you, sir.'

Bliss looked at his partner. 'Ready?' he asked.

'Not really,' she replied, shaking her head. Shortly after their arrival on scene she had tied up her shoulder-length hair, and only a few loose strands fanned the air around her. 'But let's do it anyway. How are the ribs holding up?'

'Sore. But I'll survive.'

'I heard you'd been in an accident, sir,' Virgil said, his eyes narrowing. 'I trust you're recovering well.'

'I'm doing better than our victim,' Bliss muttered as he stepped towards the bungalow. He flipped a mental switch and immediately cut off everything except that which lay ahead, blotting out the rest of his surroundings. Fatigue and pain moved with him. He was feeling every one of his years and more, but it was time to go to work.

Chapter Three

According to the documentation they discovered during their initial cursory sweep, the victim's name was Jade Coleman and she rented the property from a local housing association. Bliss stared down at the body for several minutes without either moving or speaking. He wanted to cover her up, but could not. The crime scene manager would be there soon enough, followed swiftly by the team of forensic investigators. He could not disturb the scene prior to their attendance.

Bliss regarded the nightmarish vision before him. *They will be busy in here today*, he thought. Despite the fierce heat of the morning, he felt a chill coming off the room that carried with it much pain and suffering. The sensation would stay with him now wherever he went, circling the drain but never disappearing entirely. Eventually it would filter through his skin and lodge somewhere alongside all the other obscenities he had witnessed in his career.

His own purpose was to get a feel for what had happened. Unlike many detectives of his rank, Bliss opted to visit the scene at this stage, before the CSI and mortuary crews had carried out their work. He had no need for the sanitised version, long after the body had been excised from its place of death. He had rarely been able to get a feel for a victim once their lifeless form had found its way into the mortuary. Here at the scene was where their life had been extinguished – in this case, so clearly snatched away from them in such brutal fashion. So here at the scene was where Bliss believed he had to observe them, if only for a few minutes. He felt he owed them that.

'I bet she was named after her eyes,' he said, more to the room than its other living occupants.

The doctor, a willowy forty-something with a kind face and upturned lips, looked away from the notes she was writing up on her Acer tablet and leaned forward over the bed. Her wavy hair hung down almost protectively over the victim, but she took care to ensure there was no contact.

'I see what you mean,' she said, as she stood up straight again. 'They were a gorgeous colour.'

'They still are.'

The doctor smiled at him and nodded. She had introduced herself to him as Faith McGovern. No pronouncement of or insistence on the use of her title. Bliss liked that about her.

'You're a romantic,' she said to him, a single eyebrow arched.

Behind them, Chandler apparently felt the need to cough, though it did nothing to disguise the harsh snort that had preceded it.

'Hardly,' Bliss responded to the question. 'But even without life in them, those eyes are expressive.'

'You see her killer in them, Inspector?'

'Now who's the romantic?' Bliss gave a thoughtful smile.

'Are you in pain?'

'Why do you ask?'

'I noticed you wincing, that's all.'

Bliss nodded. He hadn't realised.

'That's just his indigestion,' Chandler said, slipping around the other side of the bed, her eyes fixed on the victim. 'Old men tend to get that sort of thing more frequently.'

Bliss stifled a laugh. This was her unique and less than subtle way of suggesting he steer clear of the doctor; that she was far too young for him to chase after. In truth, while McGovern was attractive enough, he had not once thought about her in that way. Perhaps he was finally feeling as old as his partner insisted he was.

Ignoring Chandler, Bliss gave a brief summary of his accident to the doctor. When he was done, and had received the expected sympathetic response, he added, 'So then my sergeant here dragged me out of my hospital sick bed today and brought me straight to work instead of home for a spot of R&R. What do you think of that, doc?'

McGovern shot Chandler a disapproving glance. 'After a concussion, and with cracked ribs, rest is precisely what you need in the first few days, Inspector. I would have signed you off for two weeks.'

Bliss chuckled at Chandler's scowl aimed in his direction.

'Don't listen to him,' she said. 'He wants to be here, that's the truth of the matter. And believe me, it was not my decision to bring him to the scene. If it had been down to me, I would have driven him home, kicked him out without braking and left him there to rot on the driveway.'

'Ah, I see,' McGovern said, head bobbing, a broad smile stretched across her face. 'I've been had. I'll remember that for the future, Inspector Bliss.'

He lifted his shoulders, which sent a spark of pain down his back. 'Just making light of a grim job,' he said. 'That way we don't have to think too much about what this poor woman went through, and how we can't even give her any dignity in death by covering her up. Instead, we have to leave her exposed like this for everyone who walks through that door between now and when the crime scene techs are finished with her.'

The doctor flipped the cover over on her tablet and tucked it away inside a large shoulder bag which she had planted on the floor by her feet. Her eyes remained on him, and he felt himself colour beneath her scrutiny.

'Well, that's me done here,' she said, her voice smoky and low. She hooked the bag strap over one shoulder and started for the bedroom door. 'Life is extinct. She's all yours, Inspector. Oh, and take no notice of your colleague's mocking. There's clearly more to you than you'd have her know.'

McGovern gave a brief wave and left the room. Bliss followed her with his eyes, then turned to Chandler. 'See,' he said, tapping a finger against his chest. 'Hidden depths.'

Chandler grunted. 'Yeah, right. And all of them shallow.'

Bliss ignored her and slipped back into his usual routine. He examined the contents of Jade Coleman's purse, which was lying on the bedside table next to her mobile phone. Along with her bank debit card, Visa, gym membership card and more than sixty pounds in cash, it contained her driving licence, which confirmed her age as thirty-eight. The money and the cards told him this had not been a robbery. In the ID photo her hair was shorter and styled differently, but it was definitely the same woman. Nothing in the bedroom suggested Coleman had not lived alone; there was no men's clothing in the open wardrobe, nor any men's items on the dressing table or on either bedside cabinet.

Other than the volatile tableau presented by the crime, the room looked as if it was usually kept clean and tidy. The bed, its sheets, pillows and duvet, now wore ragged scars of blood. It was dry but had not yet oxidised. Bliss had no doubt that he would still be able to smear it beneath his gloved thumb.

As he stood in place, he snapped his nitrile gloves against his wrists. Bliss had often been told this was a habit of his; yet, had refused to believe it until seeing it for himself on a crime scene video when he was accidentally captured in front of the camera surveying a murder scene.

The victim before him now had been in good shape, he thought, with narrow hips and long, silky smooth legs with excellent muscle tone. She had taken time grooming herself to look good. Bliss wondered if that was for herself or someone else. Perhaps even a special someone.

Bliss counted seven or eight obvious wounds confined between the chest and torso area. The only blood on the woman's face appeared to come from stray spatters, probably resulting from the knife, that had clearly been used, being withdrawn from the body in order to repeat the stabbing motion. On both hands and arms there were what he imagined would prove to be defensive wounds – deep and brutal – where Coleman had initially raised her hands to fend off the attack before being tied up. Crimson spatters of cast-off climbed the walls and window blinds like a poisonous, deadly form of ivy. There were red blotches and scuff marks on the bedroom carpet, leading away out of the door and into the hallway, where Bliss had already seen they faded and then stopped before reaching the kitchen.

Bliss took a moment to reflect. The killer had got some blood on the soles of their footwear, but not a lot. They had been wiped clean in just a dozen or so paces. The attacker must also have had blood on their own skin and clothing at a minimum. Had they exited the bungalow without washing up and changing? Had they worn protective clothing, which afterwards could have been discarded and bagged prior to removal from the scene? Obtaining answers might lead them closer to understanding how much of this had been planned.

Jade Coleman had lived in a quiet neighbourhood, but her sharp cry and the scuffle that ended her life appeared to have been overheard, so Bliss was already thinking that witnesses would be crucial during the early stages of this operation. As if they had been waiting to snag his attention at the most appropriate moment, the horizontal blinds rustled and flapped. The movement indicated that the window behind them was open, which was unsurprising given the hot day. It explained why the sounds emitting from the room were overheard.

As PC Virgil had described, the victim's hands were tied to the wrought-iron bedframe. Bliss noted the use of two leather belts. One was white, the other a pale blue. Neither looked long, both appeared more feminine than masculine, and Bliss was confident they had belonged to the murdered woman.

There was no sign of the weapon. Neither he nor Chandler had carried out a search in any shape or form, and it was possible that the knife was still in the room, perhaps beneath the bed or lying somewhere within the creases in the jumble of bedclothes.

'Check the kitchen will you please, Pen,' Bliss said to his partner. 'See if there's a knife rack with a blade missing. Or a cutlery drawer lacking a carving or chopping knife.'

Chandler edged back out of the bedroom without comment. She would understand as well as he did that if the knife that caused Coleman's fatal wounds was part of her own set, then making a case for premeditated murder would become that much more difficult. On the other hand, if the killer brought it with them, then it was considered a weapon and all bets were off. Bliss would insist they make the murder charge stick in that case.

His mood had become sombre. The earlier gallows humour was history, the time for hard thinking and deduction having taken precedence. Bliss took another sweep of the room and smiled sadly. This supposedly safe space was a physical part of her life, that their victim had put time and effort into: the pastel shades accented with highlights of colour, mostly raspberry in tone; the frills on the linen cloth that ran the length of the dressing table; the matching jars, pots and vases with paper flowers inside them. A tall bookcase overflowed with both hardback and paperback novels, ranging from Jo Watson and Jojo Moyes, to fantasy fiction by the likes of Neil Gaiman and Philip Pullman. Bliss knew little of Jade Coleman's life, but he got the sense that this was where she allowed herself time and space in which to relax. That her life was taken from her in this very same room was immeasurably sad, and was the poignant note Bliss often experienced during an investigation.

'There's a magnetic strip screwed to the kitchen wall,' Chandler said from the doorway. When he turned, she nodded at Bliss with the kind of resigned expression he had seen on her face all too often. 'There are two small knives for peeling or chopping, a breadknife, and space for one more. I'm guessing a decent-sized carving knife. I had a look in the drawers and sink, but there's no sign of one anywhere else.'

'Dishwasher?'

Chandler shook her head.

'Thanks. I guess that means we'll have to work twice as hard.'

Chandler nodded towards the bed and their victim. 'She put up a fight. From the look of those wounds on her right hand she may even have been the one to snatch up the knife first. If so, she might have cut her attacker during the struggle. Some of that blood over there could be his.'

'Yeah. What's the chances of us getting a DNA match after weeks of waiting for the results?'

Bliss could recall only a handful of his own investigations where DNA had proved to be the difference in obtaining a guilty verdict. And of those, all but one had been cold cases. Chandler did not respond, and he had not expected her to. The failings of a creaking system were all too familiar and thoroughly depressing.

'Come on,' he said. 'The house can wait, and the dead will have their time. Let's speak to the living.'

When they re-emerged back into the sunlight, the crime scene investigators and forensics teams had rolled up. They were busy pulling on their protective suits. Bliss caught the eye of the scene manager, a civilian by the name of Brian Finnegan. They each nodded a greeting. Chandler waved a hand. Standing on the grass out of the way of anyone who wished to enter the bungalow, Bliss summoned over PC Virgil with a flutter of fingers.

'What do you know about who called it in?' he asked the enthusiastic uniform.

'All we got at first was that a "neighbour" had rung in, sir. As soon as we knew what we had here I got back on comms and asked for further details. I have a number and address, which is one door down to the left of this building.'

Bliss turned to glance along the street. The call had come from across the alleyway that divided the semi-detached properties. He swivelled another few degrees and saw that only the upper section of the small two-piece window in Jade's bedroom was open, caught on its security latch. Enough to provide an air flow, not enough to attract would-be burglars. If the neighbour also had their windows open at the time – which was likely given the weather – then it was certainly possible for them to have heard whatever took place inside their victim's bedroom.

'Are they at home now?' Bliss asked Virgil. He had noticed that the windows to the front of the neighbouring property were closed.

'I don't believe so, sir. As I understand it, they were asked to remain at home for us to speak to, but said they were going out shopping.'

'Well, can't let a little thing like murder ruin their entire weekend, can we, Constable?'

'I didn't see them leave, sir. To be fair, they may already have gone out by the time we arrived. I suppose I ought to have secured them as soon as I called in the scene.'

Virgil looked distressed, but Bliss shook his head. 'Don't worry about it. You had a crime scene, and that was your first priority. It's always nice to speak to witnesses when the incident is still fresh in their minds, but we can't compel them to hang around. If they want to report a scuffle and a scream and then bugger off to IKEA, there really isn't a great deal we can do about it.'

'Who do you want me to call in, boss?' Chandler asked.

Bliss took a look around at the street and neighbouring properties. The crowd had not thinned, and several people were raising their voices at the uniforms who stood by the flimsy strips of tape barring the way, demanding to know what was going on.

'Everyone,' he told her. 'I'll want Bishop and Short inside the property following up in CSI's slipstream. Everyone else, plus half a dozen uniforms in pairs doing the canvas. Have Carmichael take charge of that. Tell him his first job is to get these people back inside their own properties in preparation to be spoken to.'

'Ian is on secondment, boss. Remember?'

He had a vague memory of DC Carmichael requesting a temporary attachment elsewhere, but recent events were still a little fuzzy around the edges.

'Well, then whoever we have spare. This is a murder scene, not a bloody carnival attraction.'

Clutching a hand to his chest where, if the pain was any indication, one of his damaged ribs now appeared to be ripping its way through his flesh, Bliss paused to draw breath. Beads of sweat dotted his forehead, and he was starting to feel a little light-headed. He suspected dehydration.

'Also, arrange for at least two uniforms to walk this area. I want to identify every way in and out. Canvas questions to include any sighting of any person or any vehicle that doesn't belong in this street, not just today but going back a month or so. And please see if anyone has got a bottle of water they can spare.'

Leaving his partner to it, he turned back to the two officers who had secured the scene. 'Can either of you two think why this call-out may have warranted special attention?' he asked. He took a few deep breaths and took a bite into his bottom lip. As human scaffolding went, ribs were fragile little bastards. 'By that I mean, we were summoned here with greater urgency than even a murder like this would usually warrant. I wondered if you had implied anything untoward when you called it in, or anyone had suggested something to you two when you made the call.'

Virgil shook his head immediately, but his colleague, Irwin, gave it a moment of thought before responding. 'Nothing that was said exactly, sir. But I think I might know why this received an urgent response.'

'Don't keep it to yourself, Constable,' Bliss encouraged him.

'Well, sir, what PC Virgil is unaware of is that this address would have raised a flag.'

'In what way?' Bliss's curiosity was dialled all the way up to eleven at this point.

'Because Miss Coleman had previously reported having a stalker, sir.'

Bliss closed his eyes for a moment. He tried not to wonder whether the day could get worse, because usually that was the precursor to it becoming just that. But the question was out there, spinning around inside his head.

'A stalker. And our victim was spoken to, and by that, I mean interviewed formally?'

'Yes, sir.'

'By uniform? Locally?'

Irwin gave a nod that was more sheepish than regretful. 'I wasn't involved. I only know about it because it was part of a morning briefing we were given a few weeks back. I remembered the name and address, sir.'

'So our murder victim, now stabbed to death in her own bedroom, reported a stalker and all she received in return was an interview with a uniform and a few words over a full-scale briefing?'

'Yes, sir. Well, actually, no, sir. Not quite.'

Bliss closed his eyes again and blew out a frustrated sigh. This was where the day really turned to shit. 'What do you mean, Irwin? What did I not mention?'

'Miss Coleman was also spoken to by two detectives, sir. From Thorpe Wood.'

Chandler appeared as if from nowhere. She handed Bliss an uncapped bottle of spring water and two painkillers already set free of their bubbled casings. He swallowed them down and guzzled back half the cold water in three enormous gulps.

'You all right, boss?' she asked him.

Bliss shook his head. 'You know that scene in *Jaws* where the shark first appears, and Chief Brody turns to the skipper who hadn't laid eyes on it?'

'Ye-es?'

'Well, I think maybe we're going to need a bigger boat.'

Chapter Four

Having returned inside to assess the crime scene more fully, Bliss then hobbled back out of the bungalow to greet the team as they arrived at the scene. He was not exactly expecting a hero's welcome. After all, not only had he not apprehended the figure who had been snooping around inside his back garden, he'd also been stupid enough to run in front of probably the only car on the road at that time of morning. And he had done so wearing nothing more than jockey shorts, a dressing gown and a cold sweat. Even so, he had expected his appearance to warrant more than a casual nod as his colleagues passed by.

Those who did not immediately enter the property stood in a small group to the left of the front door, speaking in low voices as the workload was divvied up. Having pretty much ignored him as they approached the victim's home, his colleagues continued to do so as Bliss stood and glared at them.

He said nothing. He now had a reputation as one of life's great internal fumers. It was a technique he had mastered over a dozen years or more, and for him it beat the volatile explosions of his past. Conquering his temper was an on-going project, but he had made great strides in the right direction. Still, he was finding it hard holding back his annoyance. While a ticker-tape parade in his honour might have been overdoing things, the odd verbal greeting and an enquiry or two as to his condition would not have gone amiss.

Fuck you all, Bliss thought.

He shook his head with obvious displeasure, then moved as swiftly as possible back to Chandler's car. Still blinded by anger at both his colleagues for snubbing him and himself for reacting to it, Bliss yanked the passenger door open only to be confronted by himself.

That was, himself as depicted in a caricature impression flying through the air wearing only a pair of Y-fronts, a cape, and a completely bamboozled expression on his face. The cut-out board stood about three feet high and had been securely buckled into the seat, with an A4-sized note affixed to the front spelling out, '*Our Fearless Leader Cheats Death Once Again*'.

He heard the laughter before turning back to his team, who now stood in a single line watching him, clearly enjoying his reaction.

'You bastards!' Bliss could not keep the smile from his lips, but it felt good snapping at them all the same. 'You complete and utter bastards. Are you all going to cough to this, or was it one of you in particular?'

'I confess, boss,' DS Bishop said. 'But society is to blame.'

DS Short stepped forward and said, 'I'm Spartacus as well, boss.'

Hunt moved alongside her. 'I'm Brian, and so's my wife,' the detective constable said, offering his widest toothy smile.

The line from Python's *Life of Brian* was always worth a chuckle, but Bliss thought he'd had enough film references for one day. He raised a finger to admonish the whole group.

'You're still bastards. Every single one of you. But thank you. Even if that snort of laughter I gave just now did cause my busted rib to shred even more torn flesh.'

'Gul's the one with the artistic flair, boss,' Bishop revealed. 'Maybe you ought to blame her.'

'Oh, believe me, DC Ansari will pay for this. Where is she?'

'Court, boss. I left a message for her to join us as soon as she's free.'

Chandler freed herself from the group of uniforms tasked with searching the area for potential routes in and out of the property and wandered over to the car. Her face radiated delight at him having encountered his cartoon superhero image.

'You knew all about this, I take it,' he said. They both understood it was an accusation, not a question.

His partner feigned shock. Badly. Hand to her chest she said, 'Me, boss? No, boss. I had absolutely no idea, boss.'

Bliss narrowed his gaze. 'They wouldn't have been expecting me to be here at the crime scene. My little surprise would have been waiting for me in my office, probably sitting there in my seat. You told them to bring it with them.'

'I think you'll find that is what's known as circumstantial evidence. Good luck proving it.'

They got back into the car and took off, Bliss having relocated his welcome back gift onto the back seat. He assumed Chandler was now driving him home. But, as she dropped back off the parkway, his partner explained that DCI Edwards had called her while Bliss was busy taking a look around the interior of the bungalow.

'She wants a quick chat. No more than ten minutes. Then you are to go home and put your feet up. For the rest of the day.' The final sentence was said with a notable lack of enthusiasm.

'So I get an entire half day to convalesce. I am honoured.'

'I know. I couldn't believe it when she said that. You don't have to listen to her, boss. You're entitled to sick leave. You could ignore her and take it. Take the two weeks your doctor friend offered.'

He shook his head. 'Let's just get it over with. I'm tired of all the games. Tired of all the nit-picking. Basically, I'm just bloody tired.'

'Well, you were knocked down by a car, boss.'

'I was indeed. On the whole, I don't recommend it, Pen.'

'And I don't recommend chasing someone around the streets while almost naked, but I hear some men will do anything for attention.'

Bliss smiled at her. Chandler always had to have the last word.

Back at HQ, she remained in the car rather than hunt for a parking space. His breathing laboured, stride shortened, Bliss took the lift up to the second floor. Normally he used the stairs, but today they would not be his friend. He found Edwards in her office, door open. He knocked anyway.

She motioned him in, then got up to close the door behind him. He levered himself into the chair opposite her desk, barely managing to contain a groan as the ribs reminded him they were unhappy.

'Thank you for stopping by,' Edwards said, as if he'd had any choice in the matter. She retook her own seat. 'How are you doing?'

'About as well as you'd expect, I suppose. Possibly better, considering how bad it could have been.'

'Indeed. I know about the rib damage and concussion, of course. The abrasions on your face look sore, too.'

He was aware of them, having taken a casual look in the mirror when brushing his teeth that morning. He had also showered, but the simple act of cleaning his teeth took so much out of him that he had chosen not to shave. There were a good few days of stubble to cover up the worst of the damage to his cheeks and chin. The raw friction wounds to his nose and forehead were left uncovered to allow them to breathe and heal more quickly, and some antiseptic ointment soothed and protected them well enough.

'I'll try not to scare any members of the public I happen to encounter,' Bliss said, laughing it off. Other than the ribs, the worst wound was to his pride. He could only imagine what he must have looked like splayed out on that road.

'Well, you take it easy later on, and tomorrow I'll have you on lighter duties for just a few hours.'

'How so?'

The DCI's features took on a worried edge. 'I need you to intervene in something that might later become a problem. When the call came in about this poor victim over in New England, it came with a red flag warning. Not only was the victim listed on the files of the stalker task force, but she was actually interviewed by two of our own.'

Bliss nodded. 'So I heard. How did that occur?'

Edwards blew out her cheeks. 'One of those days that conspires against you, Bliss. For a variety of reasons, including court attendance, holidays, sickness and training commitments, the task force was short-staffed. They asked to borrow two DCs, so I loaned them Hunt and Ansari. This was while you were on holiday, as I recall.'

'Sounds like a reasonable enough request and response.' Bliss was curious now. He wondered where this was headed, and why Edwards had decided to involve him.

'It was. However, I was under the impression that DCI Mulligan, as head of the task force, would be reading the report and debriefing Hunt and Ansari if necessary. Mulligan was under the impression that I would be doing so before passing the details though their system. We were both mistaken. Now, of course, the fear is that if this poor woman has been murdered by the stalker she reported, we have to ask if it could have been avoided.'

'So you want me to do what, exactly?' he asked.

Edwards leaned forward, hands clasped together on the desk. 'We would expect a formal enquiry to occur at some point. However, DCI Mulligan and I believe it would be to everyone's advantage if our two detectives were spoken to informally beforehand.'

'Which is where I come in.'

'Precisely.'

'Why me? I wasn't even here at the time.'

'That's one very good reason why it should be you, Bliss. You won't be regarded as covering your own back.'

'And the other good reasons?'

'Hunt and Ansari will feel less pressurised if you speak with them first. They also work closely with you, and respect you. You can more easily convince them that no one is looking to put them in the frame.'

Bliss tilted his head to look directly at his DCI. Their eyes met, and he thought she knew exactly what he was thinking right at that moment. Which was confirmed when she spoke next.

'I can guess what's going through your mind, Inspector. No matter what our differences in the past, believe me when I tell you that neither I nor DCI Mulligan are attempting to dump this in the laps of two junior detectives. We simply want to get ahead of it before the formal procedures kick in.'

Bliss now knew why Edwards had insisted he be taken to the crime scene, and Chandler's sense of unease over the instruction was explained. 'I'm sorry,' he said, shaking his head, 'but I think that is a really bad idea. I won't do it.'

Edwards sat back as if to regard him more fully. 'What do you have against it?'

'It's too soon, for one thing. You're reacting to this as if the supposed media rumpus had already kicked off. That's a last-ditch move. Also, the risk of calling Hunt and Ansari in at this early stage is that we alienate them.'

'Surely you have the capabilities to persuade them otherwise, Inspector.'

'Possibly. What I lack is the inclination.'

'These are your people, Bliss. I would have thought you would want to help.'

'It's not a matter of not helping, boss. It seems to me that this could easily lead where you would rather it didn't, and I think it's unnecessary at this stage. The last thing you want is for this to leak out to the press. If you start rattling cages, that's precisely what could happen.'

Edwards pushed herself back and rose from her chair. 'It's up to you, Inspector. I really don't see what the problem is. But I'm hoping you will do what you always do, which is your job. And I'll take my chances with that.'

Bliss also got his feet, though more slowly and painfully. He wondered if there had been a compliment buried in that statement somewhere. He nonetheless shook his head at his DCI.

'I will do my job, boss. But I won't go to John and Gul in the way you suggest. Of course I will discuss the issue with them, but I think that has to be part of the natural flow of the investigation, and not by pulling them to one side now and questioning them. It's not only a matter of how they react as individuals. How do you think it will look to every uniform and every suit out there if, at the first hint of trouble, we start circling the wagons? It will look as if you think we're guilty of something. That we have something to hide. In my opinion, the best way to proceed is by backing your own people here and now, and letting them get on with their jobs.'

The silence that followed was screaming with tension. Bliss realised that his relationship with Edwards was never going to be without its troubles. He was not her type of copper, and she was not his kind of leader. In recent months, however, they had found a way to muddle through that was neither disruptive nor corrosive. He wondered now if he had stepped over the line yet again and set them all the way back, perhaps even to the point where it became unworkable.

But then Edwards surprised him. She nodded, and even managed to tease out a small upward curve of her mouth. Something approaching gratitude gleamed in his DCI's eyes as she responded.

'In retrospect, I agree that it's not just about how we react, but how that reaction is perceived by others. What is, in reality, a trifling matter to us, may be regarded by others as something far more incongruous. Allowing the matter to be raised as part of, rather than separate to, the general team discussions will work better. Thank you, Bliss. For your candour. I appreciate it very much.'

Bliss nodded and turned to leave. 'You're welcome, boss. Let's just hope you don't come to regret it.'

And me neither, he thought.

As he walked away, Bliss evaluated the potential fallout for both Hunt and Ansari. He would speak to them about their interview with Jade Coleman, but at the right time and in the right setting. In a perfect world they would both seek him out to mention it to him first. He could not see how his decision could possibly create problems for his team members, but he resolved to keep a wary eye on the situation to ensure that the internal political machinations did not rise up against them. If heads had to roll, it would not be theirs.

Chapter Five

'I love what you've done with the place,' Chandler said as she blew through the ground floor of his house, her inquisitive nose twitching as she sniffed out every aspect of his life drawn from a thirty second observation.

Bliss knew she was making light of a serious point. This house, which he had lived in now for almost seven months, looked pretty much the same as it had the day he moved in, and similar to the house he had lived in during his first posting to Peterborough many years earlier. The furnishings were spartan but functional, walls bare, the entire dwelling lacking any form of personal touch. Other than the essentials, Bliss's home life revolved around the one small section of his living room which housed his TV, Blu-Ray player, and stereo equipment. Beside these stood stacks of DVDs, CDs and vinyl albums. Two armchairs sat facing the media centre and the back garden.

It probably didn't take much more than a thirty second peek through his keyhole to sum him up, Bliss reasoned. It was only when someone else visited that he ever thought about how his home looked to other people. It had everything he needed and functioned exactly as required. There were photos and a handful of framed prints currently sitting inside cardboard boxes which by now he could have found time to put up on the walls. Yet he had always decided against doing so, unsure of the purpose. He had no need of physical reminders when it came to the important people in his life; they remained with him wherever he went, taking up a warm and comfortable spot inside his head.

Bliss struggled over to his favourite chair, easing down into it as gradually as possible. By the time he was done he felt as if he had run a marathon. When he had settled and found a comfortable sitting position, he gave a sigh of relief. 'That's me for the rest of the day,' he said, elevating his feet.

Chandler came in from the kitchen, her quick scrutiny finished for the time being. 'Do you want something switched on in here? Also, what are you going to do about your dinner?'

He raised a small plastic caddy which held a number of different remotes. 'I can switch on anything I need with these because everything is on standby. As for dinner, I might get a takeaway if I fancy it. I'm not hungry right now.'

She laughed. 'At the pace you're walking, you'd have to set off for the front door before you even placed your order.'

Bliss clutched his ribs as he also chuckled along. 'It's pathetic isn't it? Mind you, I keep coming back to the fact that I got run over. I really shouldn't complain about a couple of dodgy ribs and some cuts and bruises.'

Taking the other chair, Chandler wiggled her backside into the cushion. 'This is nice. Comfy. Surprisingly good choice. Look, Jimmy, I can always pop back over and help you out. I'll make some lunch now, knock up some dinner later when I get off work. It's no trouble.'

Friend or not, Bliss was not accepting more of Chandler's help than was absolutely necessary. She was also his work subordinate, and it didn't feel right having her take care of him away from the office. He imagined there was also a hint of macho nonsense about his decision, not wanting to appear weak in her eyes. But even though he recognised it for what it was, he nonetheless declined the offer.

'I'll be fine,' he insisted. 'I'm used to taking care of myself. I'll work something out. But thanks.'

'How about changing your strapping?'

Bliss shook his head. 'They don't do that any more. These days they like you to have room to breathe and expand your lungs. Makes me wonder how many people died of vicious strapping injuries in the old days.'

'It's probably more about saving money than medical thinking.'

'Either way, there's nothing to help me with. I managed to get dressed by myself, and I can get around. In fact, I need to mix up the rest I'm told I need, as well as keeping on the move. No heavy lifting, but I can probably drive in a day or two. Ice and anti-inflammatories are about it when it comes to treatment.'

Nodding, Chandler said, 'I don't suppose you could invite anyone else round to keep you company? I know you and Angie are no longer a thing, but I was wondering about the Bone Woman.'

Bliss had been waiting for her to go there. He admired her effrontery, if not her timing, and when he looked back at Chandler his eyes were narrowed to slits.

'You mean the woman who only became a widow just a few months ago?'

'I'm not saying you should invite her around as a date or anything, but you took her in for a few days when she needed some friendly support. You got on okay with her all over again, so you said. There's nothing wrong with calling her up to tell her what happened. You never know, she might offer to come over without you even needing to ask.'

'It's too soon. Besides, she would feel obliged to help even if she didn't really want to. I don't want to put her in that position. I'll speak to her, let her know what happened, but when I'm feeling a little less vulnerable.'

Chandler hugged herself. 'You men are so bloody stupid. That part of evolution really passed you by, didn't it? How is it you still don't realise that it's precisely when you are vulnerable that you should be asking for help? It's no sodding use afterwards.'

'Look, I had a scare and I'm banged up a bit. I'll be fine for one night, then back to the grindstone tomorrow. It's not a problem. Really.'

He had always been grateful that Chandler seemed to know when the dead horse she was flogging had started to decompose. His partner appeared to take the hint now, throwing her hands in the air theatrically.

'Fine. Whatever you say. But speaking of tomorrow, what did Edwards have to say for herself?'

He took a few minutes laying out the basics of the discussion that had taken place.

'That's very sneaky of her,' Chandler said, her look instantly disapproving. 'She gets early notice of everything John and Gul are going to say if questioned, making you the bad guy for interviewing them in the first place. Then if you give the go-ahead for the stalker aspect to be followed up – which, let's face it, you would have to do – then she can claim later that you did so out of spite.'

'That was exactly how I felt at first,' Bliss admitted. 'But Edwards seemed genuine this time. I suppose you had to be there really. I would never say I trust her completely, but in this instance I do. Even so, I told her I wasn't going to do it. I think it would only make matters worse.'

'I bet that went down well.'

'Astonishingly, she was all right about it. More than all right. She not only agreed, she also thanked me for my honesty.'

'And this is the same DCI Edwards?' Chandler said, sceptically. 'Your boss. The one who has given you nothing but strife ever since you came back to the city last year.'

'The very same. Her reaction took me completely by surprise, but that suits me just fine. It makes for a nice change of pace.'

'You'll be speaking to John and Gul about it at some point, though, won't you? I mean, it won't have escaped their notice that our victim is the woman they both interviewed.'

Bliss nodded. 'I will. Of course. But unless they approach me first, I'll slip it into the conversation when the time is right. I don't want them to get the impression we're making a big deal of it.'

'That sounds sensible. Especially for you. But what about if they come to me this afternoon instead, given you won't be around?'

'Give them some of the old Penny Chandler charm, make sure they're aware they are not in trouble. Let them know they can come and see me as soon as I'm back.'

Chandler smiled. 'Yeah, butter me up first, why don't you? Fine, I'll make sure they get the right message. And only if they mention it first. Meanwhile, I take it you want me to get things moving on the investigation, yes? Incident room, boards, operation name, early actions.'

Bliss told her that was precisely what he wanted from her, but then something else occurred to him. 'If John or Gul do discuss the issue with you, tell them they are not to mention the stalker aspect of this with anyone else until after they have spoken to me. They both had a chat with our victim, and they'll have a good idea where this investigation will lead us. But I don't want it spreading beyond them until I have had a chance to manage it. So yes, get the ball rolling on the case, but steer away from that particular avenue until tomorrow if you possibly can.'

'Will do. It's not looking good for Edwards and Mulligan,' she said with a heavy sigh. 'Now that I know she had a stalker, Jade Coleman's murder instantly makes sense.'

'That's the way I see it, too. No way of avoiding it. Not unless something significant emerges between now and the next briefing that sends us down another path. And if it was the work of her stalker, then Mulligan will come under fire as the head of the unit, but Edwards is bound to get caught up in the mess given she's responsible for loaning out Hunt and Ansari.'

'She must be extremely concerned if she tried to rope you in to do their dirty work for them.'

Bliss agreed. 'I actually felt sorry for her. But I'm more anxious about the potential trickle-down effect.'

'We'll stand behind our colleagues. Just as we always do.'

'Bloody right we will.'

Chandler stood to leave. As he watched her get to her feet, something flashed across Bliss's splintered memory. For a moment he considered leaving it for another time, but decided against it. What he had to say could not wait.

'Pen, you might want to sit back down again,' he said gently. 'I just remembered something I needed to talk to you about. It actually came up on the evening I was knocked down, and what with everything that happened and my memory not being exactly clear at the moment, it went right out of my head until just now.'

'Okay.' She frowned at him. 'Judging by the look on your face, this is going to be serious.'

His partner retook her seat, spreading her hands, palms upwards and fingers splayed. Bliss saw that Chandler was not only intrigued, but openly anxious as well.

'It is. Pen, you remember I had some communication with an agent from MI6 during that murdered airman case?'

'I do. At least, I know what you were able to tell me at the time.'

'Well, despite having backed him into a corner he did not wish to be in, I ended things by asking him for a favour. It was a long shot, and I never expected him to come through. The thing is, he has. And now it concerns you.'

'Me?' Chandler put a hand to her chest. 'Please don't tell me you recommended *me* to them.'

Bliss shook his head. 'No, nothing like that. I hope you're not going to be angry with me, but I asked the man I spoke to if he would look into your issues in Turkey. To see if he could confirm or deny whether your ex and your daughter are still in the country.'

'You did what? You called in a favour on my behalf?'

He could not tell if her expression was one of shock or fury. 'Yes. I'm sorry, maybe I should have asked you first.'

'No, I'm not angry with you, Jimmy. I'm surprised, is all. I can't believe you would do that. So, they have some information? Is Hannah still out there in Turkey?'

'She is, Pen. Not only that, but I now know exactly where.'

Chandler sat forward on her cushion so rapidly that she almost slid right off the chair. 'You do? Really?'

Nodding and smiling, Bliss said, 'I have her current address in Antalya, on the southern coast. And there's more. The man I always thought of as just Six told me that he had someone light a fire under the Foreign Office. They re-opened your case, fed all of the fresh information into their system. They are now prepared to work hand-in-hand with the Home Office plus the SIS out in Turkey in order to apply some leverage to the Turkish side of the political arena. All you have to do is say the word.'

Tears fell from his partner's eyes, as Bliss had known they would. Seventeen years ago, the Turkish father of their then two-year-old daughter abducted the little girl and fled with her back to his home country. Despite all her best efforts, not only had Chandler not seen Hannah since, but for some time she was not even certain that they were still in Turkey. Bliss had attempted to shift both the Home Office and Foreign & Commonwealth Office during his first posting to the city, but his friend and colleague had long since given up any realistic hope of seeing her daughter again. The break she had returned from upon hearing about his accident, was actually her annual pilgrimage to Turkey in an effort to track down her missing daughter.

Bliss grunted and winced as he edged forward, looking up into Chandler's glassy eyes. 'Pen, I know this is a step forward. But it also takes you closer to the point where you have to start embracing the reality of the shifting sands. Hannah will no longer be westernised, she almost certainly answers to a different name now, and has probably forgotten that she ever spoke English. You've always accepted that your ex will have told Hannah her mother is dead. You have to prepare yourself for the real probability that even if you won some sort of case against Mehmet, Hannah is old enough now that visitation rights no longer apply, and she may decide not to even meet with you.'

Using the heel of her hand, Chandler wiped away her tears. She blinked a couple of times before looking directly back at him. 'Jimmy, if you offered me even that faint hope right now, I'd chop your hand off for it. To go from the genuine prospect of never seeing Hannah again, to possibly being able to visit her and spend time with her even a couple of times a year, would mean the world to me.'

'I know. I understand that. But – and I don't mean to seem harsh – Hannah is a teenager now, not the little toddler you knew and loved. The early stages of any reconciliation could be extremely brutal.'

'I'm strong enough to withstand that.'

'Of course you are. I don't doubt that for a moment. But is she?'

Chandler closed her eyes as that sunk in. Bliss hated to be the one to both open a door for his friend and then put obstacles in the way of her walking through it, but he could not allow Chandler to rush blindly into something which might make an horrific situation even worse. She was strong, a mentally tough person who knew her own mind. But to regain contact with a young woman who was now a stranger, only to see that relationship flounder, would be hard to endure.

When she looked back up at him, Chandler's expression was one of single-minded determination. 'One step at a time is how we'll take it,' she said. 'I accept that Hannah may not want to see me. I accept that she's no longer the little girl who was taken from me. But no matter what, she is still my daughter. So, what do I have to do?'

***

After Chandler had gone, Bliss sat in silence for a good while. He had pulled back the curtains and now lost himself in the natural beauty of his Zen-inspired garden. Ignoring his constant discomfort even when sitting perfectly still, Bliss took his mind back to the new murder investigation. Once again, he was drawn to wonder why nothing could ever be simple. The killing of Jade Coleman was a despicable act, and if, as seemed likely, it had been the work of a stalker, then the chances were good that the team would eventually track down the perpetrator.

But the complications put a different slant on the enquiry.

The fact that the victim had previously been spoken to by two of his Major Crimes detectives meant that questions would be asked of them as to whether the murder could have been prevented. Which was bad enough. But to have two DCIs allowing that oversight to fall through the cracks was an impediment Bliss could do without, as it would lend credence to any allegations of collusion. The focus of a murder should never be on anyone or anything other than the victim. But here, as on too many similar occasions in the past, the distractions were never far away.

Bliss turned his thoughts to Jade. The gaudy horror of her death was in stark contrast to the room in which she had lost her life. And here was the first point of pause. This poor woman would now have her life picked apart at the seams, torn this way and that as the team worked to not only find her killer, but to also protect the investigation and its evidence in terms of presenting a winning case to the Crown Prosecution Service at some point down the line. Those who made allegations and sought prosecution had to be prepared for everything the defence would throw at them, which meant the team having to uncover each skeleton and every sordid tiny detail if it existed. Sometimes Bliss felt as if they were brutalising the victim all over again.

He considered the way she had been displayed. There was something a little off about it. As if it had been rushed. Bliss understood how that might happen if the attacker was concerned about the struggle and Jade's cry being overheard, but then why proceed with the binding and positioning of the body? Yet if the binding had taken place first, at what point had the struggle occurred? The timing felt out of sync, and that was a concern to him.

Finding out whether she had been raped was now of paramount importance. Bliss felt it was unlikely that a stalker would go to such lengths only to murder his victim before obtaining some form of sexual release. Unless this particular sick freak got his jollies from penetrating a corpse. Bliss had encountered one or two of those in his time. But given the scream the neighbour thought they had heard, and the frenzied attack that had taken place, it could easily be that the killer had panicked and simply ensured that he could never be identified by Jade. Knowing if rape had occurred was crucial, but Bliss was not certain which conclusions might yet be drawn from the result of the testing that would take place.

Like most men and women involved with police work, Bliss did not like coincidences. He recognised they existed, and that from time to time one would come along to bamboozle an investigation. Here, however, he had to ask whether the fact that a few weeks after reporting a stalker, Jade Coleman's brutal murder was coincidental to that report. In Bliss's experience, it would be unlikely.

But not impossible.

If Bliss had learned anything at all during his long career, it was that absolutely everything was possible when it came to murder.

Chapter Six

Chandler knocked on Bliss's door shortly before 8am the following morning. He had told her he would take a cab into work, but she insisted on giving him a lift in, suggesting they could use the short drive to catch him up on any progress made the previous afternoon. He had relented; it was futile to do anything else once she had made up her mind about something.

What he had seen in the bathroom mirror that morning was downright painful and depressing. Discounting the bruising and scabbed abrasions, the signs of ageing were more pronounced than ever. His hair, prematurely salt-and-pepper twenty years earlier, was now fully grey. As ever he wore it trimmed close to the scalp, and whilst receding and thinning it was holding together much as his father's had at the same age.

The flesh on his face was loose, sagging now beneath both eyes and chin. Deep blue eyes that had once stood out as his best feature were now lost in whites permanently marbled by fierce red lines. Somewhere along the way his old acne scars seemed to have become swallowed up by time – score one for age, Bliss thought.

A slow and painful shave, a good long soak beneath the most powerful shower setting he could find, plus some clean, fresh clothes, made Bliss feel a little more human. He was glad he did not have to bother strapping himself, but he did press a bag of frozen hash browns against the affected area for a few minutes. The pain was remorseless, and he popped another couple of co-codamol capsules. Given that he was already on a daily regimen of medication for his Meniere's condition and high blood pressure, Bliss did not like having to take additional pills. He reasoned that if he could dull the effects of the damaged ribs to a raging ache then it was a risk worth taking.

His Meniere's Disease diagnosis followed a series of tests back in the autumn of 2005. A condition associated with the inner ear, it caused him to suffer from a loss of hearing, constant tinnitus, a loss of balance and some mild mental confusion when fatigued, together with occasional vertigo. Every so often his body demanded a system reboot, and he took time off to recuperate, but mainly it was just a matter of getting on with the changes the illness had wrought upon him. Right now, he was more concerned with his ribs, as his lifestyle changes were helping him manage the disease.

Chandler blasted questions at him about his injuries and whether he was taking care of himself. He admitted that he had not bothered eating anything other than a bowl of dry Honey Nut Cheerios the night before, and had helped dull the pain with a few bottles of Anchor Steam. However, he assured his partner that he had enjoyed a good breakfast and that the pain was under control. Bliss was keen to move the conversation away from himself and on to the case.

He was impressed with Chandler's work so far. Operation Cauldron already had a full complement of Major Crimes team members, plus an equal number of uniforms attached to it. The even spread was something Bliss had always tried to achieve, not only because it made the uniformed officers feel part of something significant, but also because it gave him and his team an opportunity to spot potential future detectives among their ranks. The uniforms who plotted the lay of the land in the neighbourhood the previous afternoon were due to report on their findings at 10am. An hour later, the neighbour who had called in after hearing a loud scuffle followed by a scream, was scheduled to be interviewed in their own home. Chandler had assigned that job to herself and Bliss if he was up to it, otherwise she would take DC Ansari with her. Interviews with other neighbours were currently being collated and entered into the system. Jade Coleman's family, who lived in

Wiltshire where Jade was born and raised, had been informed and had driven up the previous evening to make a formal identification.

In the lift on the way up to their floor, the two encountered Detective Superintendent Fletcher. Bliss noticed that she had recently opted to forego her usual contact lenses for designer-framed glasses, and their stylish mix of colours had softened features which, at times, appeared unintentionally severe. Several weeks earlier, the Super had undergone a complete restyle, including her hair and wardrobe of work clothes. This had triggered the usual spate of rumours around the station. Bliss ignored them, but he thought the changes made her seem more feminine and less aggressive. It was a combination he approved of.

Fletcher got out of the lift with them and detained Bliss briefly, concerned about his injuries.

'I'm doing okay thank you, ma'am,' he assured her. 'It could have been a lot worse.'

'Indeed it could have. Inspector, has anyone briefed you yet on what we discovered about the vehicle that struck you?'

Bliss blinked. His memory remained hazy when it came to the incident itself, though he had been informed that the traffic investigators were looking into it. He said as much to Fletcher, adding that he had received no update since.

'In that case, I have to tell you there is clear evidence that the person you chased and the driver of the car that struck you were working together. The traffic team located CCTV footage, and while their opinion is that there was no clear intent to run you down, the brakes only went on after you were hit, and moments later the figure you had chased away returned to the scene and jumped into the car. The vehicle was found burned out beside a field near Elton.'

'So when the prowler ran, I guess the driver circled around to find them. Then I dashed out in front of them.'

'That's the way it looks, yes.'

'Did either of them check me to see what state I was in? Did they call the emergency services?'

Fletcher cleared her throat. 'There was only one triple nine call. Someone living nearby heard the… bump and the squeal of brakes. They had no clear view of what had happened, but they did at least make the call.'

Bliss thought about that; the intruder he had chased. He was reasonably certain that he had received similar attention from the security services at the start of his previous major investigation. That case had been resolved, so he had no idea why anyone would have been snooping around in his back garden in the early hours of last Wednesday morning. That whoever had run him down had then simply driven away after scooping up their partner in crime implied an underlying malice towards him. Even if hurting or killing him had not been their ultimate intention, they were seemingly indifferent to his fate.

'Any ideas as to who this might have been?' Fletcher asked him.

Bliss shrugged. 'Not one, ma'am. I'm at a complete loss.'

Fletcher tapped him on the upper arm, wished him well and told him to get some rest. Bliss thanked her and slowly made his way towards the Major Crimes area. The place was empty – those on duty away from their desks carrying out their instructions. Bliss sat at DS Bishop's desk opposite Chandler, deciding he would rather be with her when news started filtering in than stuck in his office alone. No sooner had he taken his seat, Chandler thanked him again for everything he had done on her behalf.

'It's really okay,' Bliss told her. 'I took a chance. If the man from Six had blanked it then I figured I would never have to mention it to you. I certainly didn't see the harm in trying.'

'I couldn't stop thinking about it last night,' Chandler confessed. 'I hardly slept at all.'

'Which was precisely what I was worried about. Don't get ahead of yourself, Pen. They may not be able to do anything more.'

'I know. But at the very least I'll be able to write to her. Who knows, Mehmet may even allow her to read it.'

Bliss nodded, but they both knew that was never going to happen. Chandler's only real chance would be if those with some clout in the country could in some way compel Mehmet to allow his daughter and Chandler to communicate. Or at least contact Hannah directly on Chandler's behalf.

It wasn't long before the first updates of the day dribbled in. The report from the officers who had scoured the area around the crime scene was interesting in terms of the most likely route in and out used by the killer. Bliss studied a Google Maps close-up of the streets and followed the key findings of the report. Chandler stood beside him, arms folded across her chest as the map was displayed on the big screen in the incident room. The room was quiet still, with just a couple of uniforms having drifted back after completing their assigned tasks.

Bliss switched to Street View to get a better feel for what he was seeing, and immediately the scale of the problem they faced became clear. If the killer had been on foot or riding a bicycle, the quickest way in and out of the street was via a public footpath that ran along the side and to the rear of the corner property. The path led to a large stretch of open ground containing both a park and playing fields. It also merged with another path that led all the way to the Paston area, broken only by a couple of cross streets before taking a route beneath the elevated Soke Parkway. If they had driven, the attacker could have parked up anywhere in one of those nearby streets and walked through, or cycled in almost any direction once off the street in which they had taken the life of their victim.

Before driving out to interview the neighbour who had called triple nine, Chandler again questioned the merits of Bliss accompanying her. She could not understand why he had not taken the rest of the weekend off, half-heartedly joking that he clearly lacked faith in his team to do the job properly without him. Bliss explained, yet again, that he could not sit back with his feet up at such an early and critical stage of the case. It served no useful purpose as far as he was concerned. He agreed to take the following day off instead, and that seemed to appease her.

He was in no state to follow the path once they arrived on the scene. He did manage to struggle as far as the point at which it broke out into the open land and playing fields.

'This is it,' he said to Chandler, who stood a couple of yards away peering along the pathway that ran through to a point beyond the A47 Parkway. 'Whether he walked briskly, ran, or cycled, this has to be the way he came and went.'

Chandler nodded her agreement. 'Makes perfect sense. Unless he drove in and out, and that seems unlikely.'

Bliss had made his own reference to their killer being a 'he' in exactly the way his partner had – it was merely a shorthand verbal expression at this stage, despite them being uncertain of the perpetrator's gender. It made life easier when talking about the case. He agreed that the use of a vehicle was improbable. In a tight street during daylight, people tended to remember strange cars or vans that did not belong. The other possibility was that the killer was local and had simply melted back into the community, but Bliss was equally doubtful about that.

'Witness statements are going to be more important than I first realised,' he said. 'We need to re-interview everyone and highlight the possibility of somebody heading from and back to the alleyway and footpath, plus extend the search for witnesses to the playing fields, park, and all points along that pathway. I think an appeal on local news would be an advantage here.'

He noted the arched eyebrows and look of doubt that came his way. 'I know, I know,' he said, raising a defensive hand. 'I'd usually prefer to squash my own balls in a vice than go to the media, but I think this is one time when they can really help rather than hinder. It would take us too long to do a door-to-door on this scale, plus we need to reach out to everyone who walked or cycled these paths yesterday.'

They headed back to the bungalow next door to the property Jade Coleman had rented, Bliss carrying himself protectively.

'Try not to get too angry with them, boss,' Chandler said, as she matched his slow and uneven progress.

'What do you mean?'

'You know full well what I mean. I'm as pissed off with them as you are that they buggered off shopping rather than hanging around after calling it in, but I'd rather we avoided a fractious interview if at all possible.'

Bliss grinned. 'Look, provided they don't say anything crass, I'll be as meek as a lamb. And if I do feel the need to vent, I'll save it for the end. Deal?'

'Deal. But I bet you can't keep a lid on it until we're ready to go.'

'A tenner says I can.'

'You're on.'

At the door, Chandler rang the bell and they waited in a narrow porch. Bliss winked at her and said, 'You seem to forget, I'm a changed man these days, Pen.'

'Of course you are. And boss, don't call me Pen.'

Chapter Seven

It was a bet Bliss wished he had not made from the moment he first met Adam and Chrissy Baldwin. The pair were at pains to point out how inconvenient it was for them to be instructed to wait indoors on a lovely sunny Saturday, and Adam Baldwin in particular presented a disinterested figure. For the first five minutes he even kept the TV switched on and the sound at a deafening volume.

'Would you mind please turning that off?' Bliss asked, having swiftly drained the reservoirs of his patience. 'I'm finding it hard to hear myself think.'

'Excuse me for having a life,' Baldwin said, his wife having disappeared elsewhere within the bungalow as if she wanted no part in the intrusion into her busy schedule. He depressed a button on his remote to mute the sound, though he left the set switched on.

'Well, that's more than Miss Coleman has,' Bliss said, hoping his disapproving glare would make some impact upon the seemingly impervious and unfeasibly thick hide of the man who had somehow managed to dredge up some internal strand of humanity when making the emergency call. 'And it is important, Mr Baldwin, for us to gain a clear insight into not only what you heard, but also the moments that followed it.'

Baldwin made an impatient gesture with his hand, motioning for Bliss to continue. Bliss wanted to reach over and slap him, but managed to keep his cool.

'Were you off sick or on holiday yesterday?' he asked.

'I'm between jobs.'

'I see. So, having made the call because of what you heard, it would be only human nature for you to have at least glanced out of your window to see if you could spot the source of the disturbance.'

'I suppose.' The nod Baldwin gave was non-committal.

'So, did you? And if so, tell me what you saw. For that matter, tell me if you heard anything at all either before or after the initial scuffle and scream.'

Baldwin puffed out his cheeks and seemed to give the matter a little thought before responding. 'I heard some clattering about and a crash, as if something had fallen to the floor. Then the scream, although maybe it was more of a yelp than a full-blooded scream, you know?'

'Did you call us before or after you looked out of the window?'

'In between, I suppose.'

Bliss was pleased with the answer. He had sensed the man's reluctance to admit to having twitched his curtain, and so had ensured his next question assumed it had happened anyway. Baldwin had simply followed on from that.

'So you took a look, picked up your phone to call it in, and then returned to the window. Tell me what you saw.'

'Nothing really.'

'That sort of response tends to suggest there was something.'

Baldwin breathed heavily through his nose. He was clearly unused to being put on the spot by anybody, and disliked being questioned in this way. Bliss did not care, provided the answers that eventually came were truthful.

'I might have seen a bike go past. There were kids playing out on the street, so they will have noticed. You should go ask them.'

'And we will. We thought we would begin with the adults, sir. Now, can you remember anything about either the bicycle or its rider?'

'Not really.' Baldwin shook his head. His face was oval with a long chin, the weight of which seemed to pull his mouth into an almost permanent downward arc. 'It was just a flash of something going by. I was looking one way, it went the other.'

'So, you looked out to your right, in the direction of Miss Coleman's home,' Chandler prompted, nodding to encourage a response. 'And the cyclist shot off to your left.'

'That's it exactly.'

'But you didn't see where it had come from? Whether from outside the property next door or from further down the road?'

'No. It was almost by me when I saw it. I noticed it, but never *took* notice of it. If you know what I mean.'

Bliss knew exactly what he meant. He imagined a lot passed this man by. 'So let's focus on the bike for a moment,' he said. 'Can you remember its colour? What type of bike it was?'

Baldwin's shake of the head was firm this time. 'No. I couldn't tell you. And all I can think of now when I try to picture what I saw is dark clothing, possibly a hoodie pulled up around their head.'

'Okay. That's something. Any sense of build? Of gender?'

'I can't be sure. I suppose if I thought about it at all I thought it was a man, but I couldn't explain why. It was just a glance. There and gone. Like I say, I was looking the other way.'

Bliss thought about it. The cyclist could have been anyone, but equally it could have been their killer. The fact that some kids had been outside was a bonus; there might well be more to be gleaned from further local interviews, as he had suspected. He did not believe Adam Baldwin had any more to offer on that specific issue, so he decided to change tack.

'Sir, approximately how long after you heard the sounds coming from next door did you make that call to us?'

'Right away I suppose.'

'So, within a few seconds of hearing the sounds?'

'I suppose.'

'I imagine you must hear all kinds of noises and cries what with the kids playing out on the street.'

Baldwin snorted. 'Too bloody right I do. Noisy buggers that they are.'

'So what made this any different?'

'How d'you mean?'

Bliss kept his gaze even. 'Well, you are used to hearing lots of different sounds, so I'm wondering what there was about this particular set of sounds that made you reach for your phone to call us before you even checked outside.'

The question seemed to perplex the man. 'I... I can't say for sure. It didn't sound right, is all. Especially the scream.'

'What about the scream, Mr Baldwin?' Chandler asked, leaning forward to emphasise the importance of the question.

'I don't know. It was wrong somehow. Proper fear, I suppose. And cut short.'

Bliss nodded along. 'Fair enough. And what did you do after you had made the call and looked back out of the window?'

The man frowned at him, bristling as if indignant. 'What do you mean? What should I have done?'

It was the response Bliss had expected. 'What I mean is, you were compelled to make a call to the police. What you heard obviously concerned you enough that you felt it warranted a police response. I'm wondering what you thought might have happened, and what your own response to that was.'

'You already know what my response was. I called you lot. If I'd known how I was going to be treated I wouldn't have bothered.'

'Treated, sir? How are we treating you, exactly?'

'All these questions. You'd think I'd done something wrong.'

Bliss smiled and shook his head. There was a tenner riding on this. 'Not at all, Mr Baldwin. I don't know where you got that idea from. You must surely have expected to answer some questions, even though you didn't hang around long enough for us to ask them yesterday. And all I am asking you now is whether, having considered what you heard to be serious enough to warrant calling triple nine, you did anything more than peer out of your window again. Did you, for instance, go outside at all? Did you approach Miss Coleman's home?'

Baldwin licked his lips uneasily. 'Look, I made the call. I knew you lot would respond. We had already arranged to go out, and so we did as soon as the coppers arrived. There was nothing we could do about what had happened, so there didn't seem any point in hanging around. As for what I did after calling it in, I looked out of the window until the first of your cars pulled up.'

'I see.' Bliss nodded. 'I find that odd, because pretty much everyone else on the street seemed to be gathered outside when I arrived on scene yesterday. That seems to be the natural reaction these days to a police presence – people wanting to see and hear more first hand. Yet you and your family simply went shopping.'

'We'd done our bit. We had plans. I didn't want to stand out there gossiping. I'm not like everyone else out there.'

'That's fair enough. Mr Baldwin, were you worried at all about Miss Coleman?'

'Of course. I wouldn't have phoned you lot otherwise, would I?' He shook his head as if astonished at being asked such a ridiculous and self-explanatory question.

'Naturally. But not worried enough that you went over there to see if she needed any assistance.'

'That's what your lot gets paid to do.'

'You're right. It is. How well did you know your neighbour, Mr Baldwin?'

'Why? What's been said?'

Bliss frowned. That was an interesting response. 'Nothing has been said… as far as I know, although I have yet to read all of the initial interview statements. No, what I wondered was how long you and your family had known Miss Coleman, how often you spoke, that sort of thing.'

Baldwin took a breath. 'Oh, I see. Well, she's lived next door for about three or four years now, I suppose. We stopped to chat if we saw each other, and she came over for a barbecue we had last summer. That sort of thing. Neighbours, but not close.'

'So what did you think I was referring to, sir?'

'What do you mean?'

'You asked me what had been said. What did you imagine might have been said, and by whom?'

The man shot a look at the open doorway. The living room in which they sat led into the passageway and in turn the rest of the property. He lowered his voice and his head at the same time.

'I think Jade might have been under the mistaken impression that I was interested in her. You know… more than a neighbourly interest. I mean, she would often lie out in her garden on a hot day wearing a bikini and would loosen the straps. A couple of times she caught me looking at her. There was nothing to it. She was a young and attractive woman wearing what amounts to little more than underwear, so I naturally didn't turn away when I happened to catch sight.'

'Naturally. Did she ever say anything to you about it?' Chandler asked. 'When she caught you ogling her.'

Baldwin's cheek pulsed. The grimy nails of his long, thin fingers raked the arms of the sofa he was perched on. 'I never used that word, did I? It's not like I stood there gawping at her. I noticed her. I looked for a second or two. She caught me looking. That was it.'

'Okay. My slip of the tongue. But did she ever confront you about it?'

'No.'

'But you wondered if she might have mentioned it to someone else. Another neighbour, perhaps.'

He nodded. By the flickering in his eyes he realised he had opened up a trap door into which he had fallen. 'Yeah. I think she was a bit too meek to call me on it, but she could maybe have told someone else. It might have seemed wrong from her perspective, like.'

'You mentioned that you found her attractive,' Bliss said, warming to the subject. 'Was your wife aware of this attraction?'

'You're making it sound tawdry. And you're twisting my words. I never said there was an attraction, I said she was attractive. There's a difference, in case you're not aware of that.'

'I'm aware. So, you considered Miss Coleman to be attractive and you admired how she looked in a bikini, but you were not attracted to her in any way.'

Now Baldwin closed his eyes as he took a deep breath. The tip of his tongue seemed to be caught between his teeth for a moment. 'It's not the way you're trying to make it out to be. So what if I was attracted to her? She was a good-looking woman with a great body. I'm a red-blooded male who doesn't think there is a problem in finding the opposite sex attractive. She was pleasant enough, but in fact she wasn't my type. Physically, yes, sure, but not as a person. She was a bit too awkward and shy and quiet for my liking. Not that any of this has a thing to do with her being murdered. You know damn well I didn't do it, because I called you.'

Bliss glanced across at his partner. She gave the slightest of nods, and Bliss took that as a tacit agreement to push the man a little harder.

'Was your wife with you that entire time?' he asked Baldwin. 'Prior to you making the call I mean. For, let's say, an entire thirty minute period leading up to it?'

The crease in the man's brow deepened. A genuine fear settled in his eyes. 'Are you kidding me? Are you actually looking at me for this?'

'I wasn't,' Bliss said. 'We came here today to speak to you purely as a potential witness. But I am now very keen to learn the answer to my question, Mr Baldwin. Was your wife with you in the half hour prior to you making your call?'

'She was here with me, yes.'

'Actually with you? In the same room, I mean?'

'I don't know. I can't remember. She was in the house, and so were the kids. We were planning to go shopping, remember.'

'I do, sir. But what I really need to know is whether anyone can verify your exact whereabouts during the period I specified. Because you must acknowledge how easy it would be to slip next door for ten or fifteen minutes and come back without anyone knowing you had even gone, especially if your wife and children were in other parts of the property at the time.'

Baldwin's eyes opened wide, and his jaw hung open for a second or two. He had started out angry, now he appeared genuinely terrified.

Bliss glanced across at Chandler once again, this time injecting anxiety into his gaze. He had continued pushing this line of conversation more in an attempt to cajole Baldwin into taking the matter seriously, rather than because he genuinely believed the man had anything to do with the murder. But now Bliss realised he had made a serious error in judgement. The questioning had run away from him, leading him to a point where he now had no alternative but to step on the brakes and approach the next stage with far greater caution.

Because the simple matter was that those questions had sparked off a doubt in his mind. Adam Baldwin had swiftly moved from a grudging witness to a suspect without Bliss even being fully aware of it at the time. His mind reeled as he realised what he had to do next.

Rising quickly to his feet, Bliss looked down at Baldwin and said, 'Sir, I apologise, but I'm going to have to ask you to continue with this interview back at Thorpe Wood.'

Baldwin groaned, deep in the back of his throat like an animal in distress. He slapped two hands to his head. 'You have to be fucking kidding me.'

'I'm afraid not.' Bliss turned to his partner. 'DS Chandler, would you please go and find Mrs Baldwin. Make sure she remains elsewhere while I get her husband out to the car.'

'Am I under arrest?' Baldwin demanded. He looked between the two detectives, disbelief etched into a face now leached of blood.

'Not unless you force my hand,' Bliss admitted. Silently he cursed himself for not having predicted this outcome. He had no grounds for arresting the man, and no way of compelling him to accompany them to the station.

He paused while Chandler slipped out of the room to make her way along the hall. When he spoke next it was with great reluctance.

'Mr Baldwin, I have to admit that this interview has taken an unexpected turn. I would much prefer not to continue with it now as we were. I have to ensure that you and your wife cannot collude in any answers to the questions I need to put to you, and the safest way to do that now is for me to talk to you on your own in an interview room back at the station.'

'But why? I don't understand. Because I looked at her when she was wearing a bikini? Because I fancied her?'

'Sir!' Bliss raised a hand and hardened his gaze. 'I strongly advise you to stop talking right now. Let me explain to you exactly what I plan to do, and then you can decide whether to accept what I'm telling you or not. At this moment you are not under arrest, but I do wish to ask you questions relating to the murder of Jade Coleman. You don't have to answer them, and you don't have to come with me. I can only compel you by arresting you, and neither of us wants that.'

'Too bloody right we don't!'

'I would prefer to continue this interview with you under caution but without arresting you. You can have a solicitor with you if you request one, but the fact is that we wandered down a path I'd not previously considered and had no intention of stumbling on. Now that we are here, we have to take the next steps in a more formal arrangement. This is purely in your best interests. Do you understand what I'm telling you?'

'This is what I get for helping. This is what I get for calling the police.'

Bliss hung his head and sighed. 'I'm sorry things turned out this way, Mr Baldwin. But right now, yes this is what you get.'

Chapter Eight

DCI Edwards was not on duty, but Detective Superintendent Fletcher was on site having attended an area meeting in the Thorpe Wood conference room. By the time Bliss called her office, Fletcher was preparing to leave for the day, but she told him to go on up anyway. They sat in the L-shaped meeting area rather than at the Super's desk, but Bliss felt no less uncomfortable as he took Fletcher through the interview with Baldwin.

'I dropped a bollock,' he confessed. 'A stupid mistake. The conversation took a turn and before I knew it things had switched around. As soon as I realised my error, I halted the interview, made sure he spoke to no one else, and convinced him it was in his best interests to come in and answer the remaining questions under caution. The problem being I'd already let it get too far.'

'It happens,' Fletcher said, dismissing the issue with a careless shrug. 'Do you think Baldwin is a genuine suspect?'

Bliss had considered little else since leaving the property in New England. 'I think he is a viable suspect in terms of the questioning that now has to take place. I also believe that either his wife or children will probably provide all the alibi he needs when we get around to them.'

'You think if you had taken things further when you were still back at their home that Mrs Baldwin would probably have remembered where she was at the time, and that she would say she was with him?'

'That's what I'm thinking, yes. It was the next logical line to pursue, only the moment I realised where we had suddenly got to, that I was now talking to him as a suspect, I knew I had to call a halt and part them.'

'You did the right thing, Inspector.' Fletcher nodded as if to emphasise her observation. 'It may look like an overreaction to some, when thirty seconds of questioning Mrs Baldwin would probably have cleared matters up. On the other hand, if he ends up being guilty and that interview had continued without caution, with the possibility of collusion as well, then we would have had a tough case to answer.'

Bliss was relieved. He doubted that DCI Edwards would have been so understanding and forgiving. But with no axe of her own to grind, the Super recognised how easy it was for interviews to slip away and become far more than anyone had intended.

'The thing is, ma'am,' Bliss said. 'Adam Baldwin does meet the criteria for being a genuine suspect. He lives right next door. He admitted to finding Jade Coleman attractive. Admitted to watching her when she was sunbathing in her garden. He could easily have been the stalker she became aware of. And despite his wife and children being in the home at the time, it's not impossible for him to have slipped away for long enough to have committed the murder. That said, it doesn't feel right to me, and it would have been absurd of him to have then called us. On the other hand, criminals are generally no Einsteins.'

Fletcher nodded gently as she took that in. 'You're absolutely right not to discount him. When something like this happens, we usually begin looking at people who were closest to the victim. Geographically, Baldwin fits the bill. And from what you say he had a bit of a thing for Coleman. No, you erred on the right side of caution here, Bliss. So, what's your next move?'

'When we got back with our suspect, DS Bishop and DC Ansari were still around, so I sent them over to speak to Chrissy Baldwin. I made sure they informed her it would be under caution, and that if she wanted a solicitor present they'd have to bring her here. But also, to get the message across that it could all be done and dusted within a couple of minutes sat around her own kitchen table over a nice cup of tea. We really just need to know if she saw her husband in that period before he made the call. It's unfortunate that the first suspect we drag in here is also the person who made the emergency call, but that can't be helped now. As soon as his brief arrives we'll get on with it.'

'But your sense of this is that he's not your man.'

Bliss shook his head. 'I don't believe so, no. But maybe he's a good starting point after all, because prior to this we had all too quickly focused on it being the work of the reported stalker, examining how he might have come and gone from the area. We pretty much jumped right in there without necessarily taking the investigation down its usual paths. We do still need to look hard at Jade's family, friends, and neighbours.'

'You were not exactly helped by this issue over the original stalker complaint. Without that I'm sure everything would have gone more according to plan.'

Grateful for being offered an escape route, Bliss said, 'That's true, ma'am. Even so, with Baldwin suddenly being in the frame, it's a timely reminder for us to concentrate on all possibilities and not have the limitations narrowed for us.'

Fletcher nodded. 'If that's all, I really need to push off. If I were you, Inspector, I would not be overdoing things, either. Make sure you get away at a decent time today, and I don't want to see you here again until Monday – and only then if you're feeling up to it.'

'Thank you. I'll get the rest of this interview out of the way – my mess to clear up – and then I'll call it a day.'

'Good. By the way, how are things with DCI Edwards these days?'

'Improved, ma'am. We're never going to be the best of friends, but I have to say our relationship does seem to have settled down. I take it I have you to thank for that?'

'I don't know about that. I think the Chief Inspector came to understand that we somehow had to find room for you both here, and that when it came to who remained if that was not the case, it would not be decided by rank.'

Bliss read what he was supposed to read between those lines. That Edwards had been told to make nice or run the risk of being the one who was pushed sideways.

The murder of Jade Coleman was the biggest case they had running in Peterborough right now, so the corridors of the station were largely empty. Staff who were off duty were keeping well away and gearing up for a much larger and more significant response after the weekend. The first few days were always critical, but most people had no idea how much of that time was taken up by formalities and structure. The whole operation had to be moulded into shape, and information was the key that usually unlocked the first door leading to the starting point.

Bliss nodded to a couple of uniforms he met on his way down to the ground floor, where he was pleased to discover that Baldwin's duty solicitor had already arrived. Bernard Stillwater was familiar to the interview rooms within Thorpe Wood, and could often be found on call at the weekend. Not because he was junior, more because he needed additional income in order to pay for two failed marriages. Bliss had encountered him only once before, but he had a reputation for being fair-minded and maybe even a little cavalier when it came to objecting to lines of questioning. Bliss knew he would not have to tread too carefully around legal niceties, but was nonetheless wary of allowing the conversation to escape him again.

None of the five suspect interview rooms were large or anything less than grubby, but the room designated for witness interviews was tasteful and comfortable. Baldwin somehow fell between both, but because Bliss sought his cooperation, he had chosen the nicest space in which to talk. They got the formalities out of the way. Bliss sat opposite Baldwin, Chandler faced the solicitor. Bliss got the ball rolling.

'Mr Baldwin. First of all, I would like to thank you for coming in to answer our questions. As I advised at the time, you are here on a voluntary basis, but are also now represented by a solicitor in Mr Stillwater, and hopefully with his help we can clear things up in no time at all.'

Baldwin grunted a response of sorts. Bliss had suspected it would be this way. The man had not welcomed the initial interview when sat inside his own home, so having to come to the police station was hardly going to make him a more pleasant character to deal with. Nonetheless, Bliss moved it on.

'Sir, I want to pick up where I left off really. This is where I hope we can ease towards the right outcome for all of us. All I need you to do is to tell me exactly where you were yesterday during the preceding thirty minutes leading up to you making the triple nine call and asking for the police. In addition, I would then like to know where your wife and children were at the time.'

Baldwin scratched his nose. It was a gesture Bliss did not care for, as it often suggested guilt, but just as often implied anxiety which could be explained away by the stress of the interview.

'As far as I can recall, I was in the living room for most of that time,' Baldwin said, his voice gruff and monotone. 'I might have popped into the kitchen or to the toilet, but if I did, I didn't stop to mark it on the calendar.'

Bliss nodded. 'Thank you. So, to the best of your recollection, Mr Baldwin, where were your wife and children during that same time window? And I don't mean were they at home with you, I mean whereabouts in the house were they?'

'I really don't know,' Baldwin said, gesturing with his shoulders. The look on his face suggested he wasn't trying too hard to remember.

'Then I recommend you think about it more carefully, Mr Baldwin. I do realise a whole day has passed, but, of course, the only reason for that is that you made yourselves unavailable to us yesterday afternoon while we attended the crime scene. The whereabouts of your family would, I'm sure, have been much clearer to you then. As it is, we now have to work with what we have. The location of your wife and children during that half hour period of time could be crucial in terms of what happens next, Mr Baldwin. So please, do try to remember.'

'What do you mean it could be crucial?' Baldwin asked.

'I think this will go quicker if I ask all the questions for now. You'll have your say.'

Bliss glanced at Stillwater, who turned to his client. 'You are here to answer questions, Adam. I would advise you not to ask them. But I think what the inspector means is that if your wife or children were with you during that period and are able to verify that separately, then you will have established a credible alibi.'

'An alibi, yes,' Chandler said, without looking up from the notes she was taking. 'We might debate their credibility later.'

'The thing to remember here, Mr Baldwin,' Bliss said, suppressing a chuckle at what his partner had said, 'is that this interview is taking place in order to establish that alibi. We are not looking to prove either your guilt or innocence at this time, which is why no charges have yet been brought against you. We simply need to know where you were, where they were, and whether you were with any of them during the specified period of time.'

Baldwin took a long, deep breath and let it out slowly. 'Okay. So, if I'm remembering correctly – and I don't want you coming back at me with claims of lying later if I'm mistaken – my son, Jamie, was playing out in the garden. I'm not entirely sure where his sister, Fiona, was, but most likely she will have been in her bedroom. As for Chrissy, she was busy getting ready to go out, so would have been flitting from room to room. The fact is, although I'm pretty certain that at one time or another she was in the living room with me, I can't be absolutely certain. I know she wasn't when I heard the commotion from next door and started making the call, but I can't be definite when it comes to where she was beforehand.'

It occurred to Bliss that Baldwin's recollections were perfectly reasonable. A short period of time in which very little of note happened would be difficult to recall in detail the following day.

He did not find that at all suspicious. The problem for him was that as an account it helped nobody.

Nodding, Bliss said, 'Hopefully your wife will have a clearer memory.'

'And if she does, I can go?'

'That depends. But yes, I think it's likely. Your solicitor can advise you as to procedure, Mr Baldwin, but please understand that just because your wife provides you with an alibi – if indeed she can – it does not mean we are finished with you. There are other matters to cover. We will be providing you with a warrant later so that we can search your home, and we will want to take away with us the clothes you wore yesterday. Before we get there, however, tell me please, were you ever in Miss Coleman's home?'

It was interesting watching Baldwin's features as he digested the question. He was difficult to read because he took his time, seeming to review his response before uttering it. Bliss realised that his dislike of the man was an encumbrance in trying to weigh him up, but he had seen less shifty characters who were nailed-on guilty.

'Never,' Baldwin said eventually. He sat back and folded his arms.

Ironically, given the defensive gesture, it was this response that caused Bliss to become convinced of Baldwin's innocence.

'Are you certain?' he asked. 'You never popped next door to fix or adjust something for your neighbour? Nothing like that?'

'No.'

And there it was again, Bliss thought. It was an easy question to answer in the affirmative even as a lie, both because Coleman was no longer around to contradict it, but also mainly due to the fact that admitting to being inside offering help to a neighbour would explain away any print the CSI team might lift. It suggested Baldwin was either stupid or not guilty and telling the truth, and Bliss had an idea the man might be more slippery than he appeared to be.

'So there is no chance of us finding your prints inside her home?' Bliss prompted, watching the man's response closely.

'None whatsoever.' For the first time, the rigidity in Baldwin's face loosened its grip, and Bliss could almost feel him relax.

There was a knock at the door. Chandler went to answer it, had a whispered chat in the doorway, and then returned to the table. 'We have some news resulting from a brief chat with your wife, Mr Baldwin.'

'Oh?' He edged forward and rested his arms on the desk.

'Unfortunately, your wife's recollection is no sharper than your own. Pretty much as you described, she says she was there and moving from room to room, is sure you were both in the same room at some point, but she cannot be certain of precisely when. She is, however, convinced that it would have been no more than ten minutes before you made the emergency call, as she does remember asking you specifically about lunch.'

Baldwin snapped his fingers at the two detectives. 'Yes! Yes, I do remember that. We talked about where we might eat while we were out.'

'But you can't tell us for sure what time that conversation took place?' Chandler asked.

'Well, not for sure, no. Like she says, couldn't have been much more than ten minutes or so before I heard the noise from next door.'

'Sadly, Mr Baldwin, that all lacks the sort of precision we were hoping for.'

The man waved both hands across his face as if tearing at ribbons of fog obscuring his vision. 'So what you're saying is that you think I waited for my family to be elsewhere, then ran next door, knocked off Jade, and then came back indoors and called for the police. Is that really what you think happened?'

'What we think happened is not up for debate right now,' Bliss replied. 'We have to ask ourselves what could have happened. And the scenario you just described is not beyond the realms of possibility.'

'So what did I do about the blood, then?'

Stillwater jerked out a hand and lay it on Baldwin's forearm. He shifted sideways in his chair and lowered his voice to a whisper. 'Adam, it really would be best if you either answered only the questions which are put to you or respond that you have no comment to make. It does not help your situation when you volunteer your own questions in that way.'

'But since he did,' Chandler said, grinning and staring pointedly at their suspect. 'Tell me, Mr Baldwin, who said anything about blood?'

Chapter Nine

It was a cheap shot neither of them expected to work. Baldwin blew it off as the kind of comment anyone might make when they already knew the victim had been stabbed to death. Chandler saved face by insisting that he could have worn some kind of coverall, which was just one of the reasons why they wanted to search his home. Bliss hoped the warrant came in before the man exercised his right to leave whenever he felt like doing so. He still did not rate Baldwin as a prime suspect, but the man was coming across as a creep, and Bliss was convinced there was more to his fascination with Jade Coleman than he was admitting to.

It was the voyeurism that bothered Bliss most. Not the act itself, but what it might mean. There was not a huge leap between spying on a neighbour in the way Baldwin had admitted to, and the significantly more perverted actions of a peeping tom. Secretive actions and lustful thoughts were triggers for stalkers, and to Bliss, the man gave off bad vibes. Baldwin was not exactly unhinged, but neither was he entirely stable.

Baldwin was informed that the police would prefer it if he did not go back home until the search had been completed, and he was asked to remain in the interview room in case there were more questions to be answered. He complied, albeit with his habitual grumble. If he was a killer, he was the least nervy one Bliss had ever encountered.

As they left the interview room, Bliss turned to Chandler and stuck out a hand. 'That'll be ten quid, please.'

His colleague came to a juddering halt. 'You what? I think you mean you owe me ten pounds.'

Bliss shook his head vigorously. 'No. I won the bet. I didn't lose my rag with him.'

'You bloody well arrested him!'

'I didn't do any such thing.'

'Okay, so you didn't arrest him. But you dragged him out of his home and brought him here. How does that win you the money?'

'Because it was a voluntary interview. And the bloke would hardly have volunteered if I had lost my temper with him.'

'Semantics,' Chandler insisted.

Bliss rubbed his thumb and forefinger together. 'Come on,' he said. 'Hand it over. I won, fair and square.'

She shook her head and continued walking, calling back over her shoulder, 'I don't have it on me at the moment. You can have your blood money later!'

On the way back to his office, Bliss encountered DS Short, who welcomed him back with a broad grin and a happy gleam in her eyes. 'Glad you made it, boss,' she said. 'And it's good to see you wearing more than jockey shorts this time.'

'Be thankful I wasn't going commando.'

'We all are, boss. Believe me. How come you're not resting up at home?'

'Stupid question, Mia,' Chandler chipped in as she appeared from the stairway. 'Have you ever met DI Bliss before?'

Short frowned. 'Boss, I don't mean to step out of line, but you really ought to take some time off. I understand why you felt the need to attend the scene yesterday, and I realise we have a murder on our hands, but we can hold the fort for a couple of days without you.'

Bliss was touched. His colleague was genuinely concerned. She was a rising star among the ranks, and although Chandler had revealed to him that she personally was currently happy remaining at her current rank of sergeant, Short was aiming for the very top. She would achieve her objective, and he believed she would be a fellow inspector within the year. Unfortunately, that might mean her having to move on to another area in order to progress up the ranks if a slot became available, but she was bright and keen and deserved her opportunity.

'Mia, I've already been through this exact same conversation with Penny. It's not that I don't trust my team, nor do I have a hard time delegating, this is strictly a selfish act on my behalf. It would drive me crazy sitting at home licking my wounds while there was a murder investigation on the books. I'll rest when I need to rest, but when I can work, I will do so.'

'You're the boss. Only you know how you feel after what happened to you.'

'Thank you, Mia.'

'For what?'

'For not trying to mother me.' He gave Chandler a baleful sidelong glance. She held up both hands in surrender.

Chandler had intended to run him home after the interview, but Bliss asked if they could stop off at the Woodman pub just a couple of minutes up the road. He enjoyed their stack burger; it came with barbecued pulled pork and smoked brisket, though Bliss always asked for the final ingredient of mac and cheese to be left back in the kitchen. Preferably in the bin where it belonged. The restaurant had long been revered for its coffee, which was always one of his main requirements. Reluctant at first, because it was so close to work and therefore the station became too easy to slip back to, Chandler eventually decided she was hungry enough to tackle their surf and turf.

'I'm taking you home right afterwards,' she told him, with a narrow gaze that felt like a Venus fly trap had snapped closed. 'No questions, no whining, just back home to rest.'

'Once I have a meal inside me I'll need to put my feet up, so don't worry about that.'

'By the way, about what we discussed yesterday, I've decided to call the Foreign Office first thing Monday. If there is some momentum on this, I want to make the most of it.'

He nodded his head. 'Good. I'm pleased to hear it.'

She smiled at him. 'Are you? I know you worry about this giving me even more false hope, and that even if I get the opportunity to see Hannah again she may decide she doesn't want to. But I need you to know that's fine with me, Jimmy. I would rather feel that sense of loss all over again than to fear it so much I do nothing. I'm going to take it as far as I can. And it's all down to you.'

'Actually, it's all down to the mystery man from MI6. Just shows how people can surprise you.'

They had just ordered drinks and were studying the menus when a large shadow fell across their table. 'Jimmy? Jimmy Bliss, is that you?'

Since moving back to the city, bumping into people from his previous posting had become a regular occurrence for Bliss. But this man went back further than that. Much further. Back to a time long before Bliss had stepped foot in Peterborough. He was large and loud and a real presence. Someone Bliss had never cared to run into again. Without waiting to be asked, he squeezed his way into the booth at which they were sitting.

'Jimmy bloody Bliss,' he said, nodding away to himself as if stunned by the sudden and unexpected meeting.

Bliss scowled. 'To give me my full title.'

'Aren't you going to introduce me to this lovely little thing?'

'This is my DS, Penny Chandler. Penny, this is Gerry Quinn. An old colleague of mine.'

Quinn stuck a meaty hand across the table, leaving Chandler no option but to shake it. 'DI Quinn,' he said. 'And I am very pleased to make your acquaintance, darling.' His fingers lingered longer than necessary, and when they finally slid off her hand, Chandler shuddered. Bliss did not know whether to laugh at her horrified reaction or smack the newcomer in the mouth.

Quinn slapped him on the back. 'You're looking good, Jimmy. Too bloody good, if you ask me. You don't change at all.'

'Whereas you do, Gerry. You've put on a shit-load of weight and lost a shit-load of hair.'

Bliss searched for any sign of anger in the man's face, but there was not even the slightest tic. Instead he laughed. Said, 'Same old Jimmy Bliss. Always were a straight talker. You ain't wrong, though. I've piled on the pounds, and my barnet and me parted company years ago.' He rubbed his smooth dome of a head. 'So how's it going, pal?'

'It's going fine, thanks. How's life treating you, Quim?'

The DI wagged a finger. 'Now, now, you know I always hated that fucking nickname.'

Bliss smiled. 'I know. That's why I always used it.'

If the exchange failed to burst the man's bubble, it did appear to sober him a little. 'You didn't seem at all surprised by my rank, Jimmy. I could have been running the show these days for all you knew.'

'No, inspector was as high as you were ever going to climb, Gerry.'

'Same as you, then.' Quinn gave a knowing wink.

'Yep. Same as. Difference is, it's where I choose to be. What the hell are you doing up here, Gerry? I thought you got a nosebleed if you ever went north of Watford.'

Quinn nodded. 'I'm having exploratory talks about getting myself posted here in the city. My ex-wife and my two kids now live just outside Huntingdon. I'd like to be closer to them.'

'London's not that far away, Gerry.'

'It is when you live south of the water, pal. Plus, the place is dragging me down. London's a fucking zoo these days, run by politically correct wankers. Years ago we were jumped on for all the stop-and-search being aimed predominantly at the coloureds. Then when all the so-called black-on-black killings began it suddenly became okay to do it again. Then as the Yardies backed off that all changed, and we were all back to being racists for stopping them on the streets. All that *driving while black* cobblers. Now the fuckers are stabbing and shooting each other again, and they want us to do more. Do less I say, let the blacks kill other blacks and leave the streets for decent people.'

'I'm going to the bar to get those drinks,' Chandler said, rising to her feet. She did not so much as glance at Quinn as she stood. 'Why don't you two catch up. Jimmy, perhaps you'll introduce your old mucker here to the twenty-first century.'

Bliss apologised with his eyes. It was his misfortune to run into one of the few colleagues he had ever truly despised. He knew how gangland crime in the capital was viewed by those who had to police it. They did feel they were having to do their jobs with one arm tied behind their backs, and to an extent Bliss sympathised. They were damned if they carried out street searches and damned if they did not. Yet some officers took things way too far, and Bliss had long ago recognised Gerry Quinn as being one of them. The man's mind was a cesspool of resentment and irrational hatred.

He wondered why Quinn had sought him out having spotted him here. Bliss had rarely bothered sharing the time of day with him when they worked together, usually giving him a wide berth. The man loathed being called Quim – a nickname his proper surname clearly lent itself to – and so Bliss had always made sure he used it as often as possible. The two had been far from friends. If he had noticed Quinn first, he would have been at pains to avoid him, and as he was pretty sure Quinn felt much the same way about him, Bliss wondered if there was more to this than a chance meeting. If the DI was seriously looking for a move, he might just be seeking a recommendation from an ex-colleague already working in the area.

'She's a bit of a sort,' Quinn said, eyes feasting on Chandler's backside and legs as she walked away. 'I like them bolshie. You thrown one up that yet, Jimmy?'

Bliss cut him off with a tight glare. 'Gerry, why don't you stop all this false bonhomie and tell me why you came over to speak to me. Is this the chance meeting you claim it to be, or did you ask around about where I enjoyed having lunch? Whatever you're here for, get it over with. You're a racist and a misogynist, and I can't abide either. Let's not pretend we ever liked each other. It's insulting.'

The smile withdrew from Quinn's face in an instant. It was replaced by an indignant scowl. 'I thought maybe the past was the past. I thought that if I might be working up here shortly it would be good to have a friendly face around. That's all. I know what you think of me, Jimmy. You were never really the sort of bloke to hide it. You always walked the fringes, without ever really diving in. I suppose I was stupid enough to think bygones could be bygones. After all, we were never enemies. Not friends, maybe, but we had the common bond of being detectives going for us.'

Bliss regarded Quinn thoughtfully. He wondered if he had misjudged the man, had perhaps dismissed him too easily. But then he thought of the casual racism in Quinn's manner when talking about the gangs in London, and the way he spoke about Chandler. The sexism was something Bliss himself could have been accused of at one time, but he believed he had long ago conquered that way of speaking, much of his banter having been misunderstood. He was old school and wasn't always aware of the politically correct changes in society. He doubted he would ever wrap his head around gender fluidity or declarations of being non-binary, but neither would he go out of his way to offend a person who claimed they were. Bliss had always been aware of the thin line he bestrode and had no time for those who did not care if they went beyond it. Quinn following Chandler's backside with his eyes was one thing, the leery comment that followed quite another.

'What are you now, Gerry – fifty-odd?' Bliss asked.

'Not far off.'

'And you want to see out your final years in the job up here? A bit of a wrench leaving London. It was for me, and I was much younger. You really think you can make it away from the bright lights, Gerry?'

'I reckon so. If I'm given half a chance.'

'You won't be if you bring that personality or mindset up here with you. They won't stand for it, Gerry. They take the service part of modern policing very seriously. I'm as old as dirt, but I won't tolerate it, either.'

'I wouldn't have thought that would suit you, Jimmy. You were never shy of breaking a few rules.'

'It doesn't suit me entirely. I admit that. But I reached the conclusion that if it came down to me bending or them bending, it was going to have to be me. I still don't like all the petty-minded bureaucracy, all the softly, softly new legislation, and I love nicking villains. But even back in the day I knew the difference between right and wrong. I'm not sure you ever did.'

Chandler returned to the booth. She slipped in next to Bliss, putting a bottle of Budvar on the table in front of him. She made no apology to Quinn for not buying him one.

'Me and your boss were just chatting about old times,' Quinn said, seemingly not put out at all by the snub. 'We had some crackers back down in London. Jimmy, you remember all those old jokes about villains having to visit the flyover supports over at Bow if they wanted to find missing mates?'

'I do.' Bliss nodded and despite himself gave a thin smile. 'And then one cracked open and when a team of workmen went to repair it, they found four bodies inside.'

Quinn roared with laughter and slapped his knee. 'The look on everyone's faces. Everybody thought it was an urban myth, yet there they were – human flyover supports. What was left of them, anyway. They had to do scans of all the other supports and they found three more bodies. What was it they started calling the Bow flyover afterwards?'

'The Boneyard Flyover.'

Another roar. Another slap. Bliss glanced at Chandler and shook his head, hoping she realised he was simply playing along.

'Then there was that job down in that factory on the Isle of Dogs. Do you remember that tosser's face when he was interviewed, and he was told that we'd found fifty grand in a hidey-hole in his office? Instead of denying knowing anything about it, he screamed at the interviewing officers and claimed there should have been a quarter of a million quid.'

This time Bliss laughed. He remembered it well, mainly because of the uproar the claim caused. 'Yeah, it was funny at the time but not so much later. We really got looked into.'

'You did?' Chandler said, looking up.

Bliss nodded. 'Afraid so. There were twelve or fifteen of us on that raid, and we were all inside the warehouse at some point, so we were all questioned.'

'Did they ever find the missing money?'

'There never was any,' Quinn said, a look of disgust twisting his lips. 'The wanker made it up just to fuck with us.'

'I don't know, Gerry,' Bliss said. 'If he was making it up, he was a bloody good actor.'

'I suppose.' Quinn hiked his shoulders. 'Still, that was a better result than some. The number of times we went on raids only to find the place empty. Someone was minting it by tipping them off.'

Bliss was surprised by the comment. At the time, he had suspected Quinn of being one of the officers thought to be earning money from villains by providing them with tip-offs. But it seemed odd for him to have raised the issue if he was actually guilty. Bliss wondered if he had misjudged Quinn simply because he did not much like the man.

'You ever wonder about those days?' Quinn asked, lowering his voice. He sneaked a wink at Chandler who visibly recoiled. 'Seriously, Jimmy, the number of man hours we wasted on raiding empty places drove me insane. Did you ever suspect anyone?'

'Other than you?' Bliss smiled as he asked the question.

Quinn laughed. 'Yeah. That's why I never had a pot to piss in. You had to have wondered about some of the lads, though. You remember Tubby Brown?'

'I do. Short arms and long pockets.'

'That's the one. Tight as two coats of paint. Never liked to get a round in, yet always seemed to have enough money to dress in expensive clobber. And you remember the motors young McNeice used to flash about in? Never could figure out how he managed that.'

Bliss shook his head. 'Brown's wife was a banker, and she came from money. I got the impression she dressed him. As for McNeice, he only had his cock to keep. Lived at home still and indulged his love of cars.'

'So who then? Which of those bastards fucked us over on a regular basis? Who was on the take? Who pocketed what should have been evidence?'

'I don't know, Gerry. To tell you the truth, I don't think about it any more, and I don't want to think about it any more. Those were different times, and we were all different people.'

Quinn blew out a long breath. He made a show of checking his watch. 'I ought to be going. Maybe we can do this again, Jimmy. Go out on the lash and talk old times.'

'I've only just landed this murder case, Gerry. Plus, I have to rest up my ribs.'

'Of course. Nasty business, that.'

'What was?'

'Getting knocked down. Could've been worse, of course. But makes you think, I bet.'

Bliss eyed the man suspiciously. 'So this wasn't a coincidental meeting after all, was it? If you know about my accident, then that means you've been sniffing around.'

Shrugging, Quinn said, 'Can't blame a bloke for trying. I thought it might be nice to have someone in my corner is all. Can't have too many mates, Jimmy.'

'I'm not so sure about that.'

Quinn smiled and patted Bliss on the arm. 'We'll see. I'll be in touch. It was good seeing you again, Jimmy. Good meeting the other half as well.' His eyes slipped across to Chandler, whose return glare was icy.

The two men shook hands. Chandler dropped her eyes to the table so that she would not have to either shake or refuse if Quinn offered his hand again. When he was gone, Bliss rolled his eyes, sat back in his seat and took a long gulp of his drink straight from the bottle.

'Sorry about that,' he said.

'Not your fault. We all have old mates we'd rather not talk about.'

'Believe me, Quinn was never a mate. A colleague for a while, so we spent some time together, but we were definitely not friends.'

'Please just tell me you were never as bad as him when you were back down with the Met.'

'I would hope you know otherwise. No, Quinn was an abomination even back then. I can't believe he hasn't changed one iota in all this time. Most of us steered clear of the man. He's a racist and a buffoon, but worse than that, he's loud about it. He gave us all a bad name.'

'Perhaps because you all stood by and let it happen.'

Bliss glanced up, eyes narrowed. 'Is that a criticism of me? If so, then you don't know what you're talking about.'

Chandler stood her ground. 'But that sort of attitude can only thrive if it's allowed to. He should have been reported to your superiors.'

'Like I said, you don't know what you're talking about.'

'Jimmy, I–'

'No, leave it there, Pen.'

She did. For about ten seconds. 'Jimmy, I can't not have this out with you now. It's impossible. I know you. Or at least, I think I do. I need to know what you mean when you say I don't know what I'm talking about.'

On a heavy sigh, Bliss said, 'You have no idea about how things were back then. I'm not suggesting that sort of attitude was rife, but it was hardly uncommon. You go to one of the bosses today, Pen, and you'll find all the support you'll ever need when it comes to things like intolerance, bullying, race hate and sexism. But not back then. You'd be lucky to get someone to listen to you. And even if they did listen it was ignored anyway, so then the whispers started, and before you knew it, you'd be a pariah inside your own nick.'

'So what… nobody even bothered to try?'

'Of course they did!' Bliss slapped a hand down on the table. He choked down on his anger, managing not to raise his voice. 'Why do you think those bastards turned their backs on me when I needed them most? When Hazel was murdered, and I pointed the finger at a fellow cop, the only case they ever tried to build was against me. They seemed almost desperate to nail me for murdering my own wife. After that I was regarded as a leper, and every time I dragged myself up off the ground, they knocked me back down again. Why do you think I ended up here in the first place?'

Chandler had closed her eyes and hung her head in the face of his passion and raw emotion. Now she looked up at him and lay a hand upon his. 'I'm sorry. I shouldn't have said anything.'

'It's all right.'

'No. No, it really isn't. I should never have pushed you like that.'

'It's okay. Honestly. Seeing Quinn again got my engine cranked. He dredged up all kinds of emotions that I've had buried away for years. Him and people like him are the reason all of us in the job today are targeted and branded.'

'I have to be honest, if he'd touched me again I think I would have chinned him. That or thrown up.'

Bliss smiled. 'Yeah, he has that effect. You think I'm forever stuck in the eighties, I'm nothing compared to that Neanderthal. He was tough to work with sometimes, mainly because beneath all that crap he carries around with him he was actually a decent detective. Just a liability when he opened his mouth.'

'I am surprised you didn't send him off with a flea in his ear much earlier.'

Bliss tapped the side of his nose. 'You know me, Pen. I accept that coincidences exist, I just don't trust them. Him turning up here like that was just plain wrong. I'm not sure what it means, but it can't be good.'

'I hope he doesn't try for our squad if he's serious about moving up here.'

Bliss laughed. 'Actually, I do. Can you imagine him interviewing with DCI Edwards? She thinks I'm bloody Fred Flintstone, so Gerry Quinn would blow her tiny mind.'

Chandler joined in with the laughter. So much so she started weeping and holding her stomach. 'That would be hilarious. Especially if he called her "darling".'

Bliss roared, almost spitting out his drink. Their spat was over, and he was glad of it. His partner called him out on his shit when she had to. He hadn't liked it when Chandler questioned him about his past, or the potential comparisons to Quinn, but he thought he might have overreacted. She had meant nothing by it.

They finished their drinks. Bliss no longer felt hungry, and Chandler did not care either way. He wanted nothing more than to return to HQ and spend a few hours getting to grips with operation Cauldron. But he also realised that he had good people around him, who would get things in shape, so that by the time he arrived back at work on Monday morning he would have a much clearer view of their objectives.

He fended off his partner's offers to come over and cook him some dinner that evening, as well as take him out for a carvery Sunday lunch the following day. He thanked Chandler and was appreciative of her concern and willingness to help him out, but all he wanted to do was lie back in his recliner, keep a cooler of beers close to hand, and to put on a little music while he stared out at his garden.

Waving Chandler off, his thoughts turned to Gerry Quinn once more. The man was a mess, and it had been an embarrassing encounter, but Bliss could not help wondering why the DI had sought him out only to not go ahead with a request for a recommendation.

Chapter Ten

Bliss slept right through Saturday night, having closed his eyes just to rest them shortly after 11pm and woken in his recliner with the fierce glow of the morning sun cutting shards of light through gaps in the drawn curtains; dust motes idly coiling and spiralling like insects trapped within the warm beams. He stretched out, feeling stiff and irritable but rested. Even his ribs were not gnawing at him as they had been the previous day.

Sunday turned out to be one of the laziest he could remember having in years. He caught some colour sitting out in the garden, his contemplative thoughts occasionally accompanied by a chilled bottle of beer. Bliss had somehow managed to ignore his phone, forgetting to switch it on during the day because he had forgotten he had switched it off the night before.

Not that his relaxed mind had entirely prevented itself from wandering. The investigation had yet to be pulled into shape, and there were a number of items in need of crossing off his list before they could either make some headway with Adam Baldwin as their main suspect or move forward beyond him.

There was also the stalker angle to consider, and how affected the task force would be if this proved to be the work of someone whose very existence they had apparently ignored in terms of following up on Jade Coleman's statement and Hunt and Ansari's subsequent report. Developing that lead further was of paramount importance.

As for Gerry Quinn, Bliss hoped never to lay eyes on the man again and felt indignant that his old colleague had inflicted his poison upon Chandler. Then there was the voicemail he had received on Saturday afternoon from Sandra Bannister, a reporter from the local *Peterborough Telegraph*. Her message simply asked him to call her as soon as he could, and he thought he knew why.

Bliss was feeling a whole lot better when he presented himself at his front door after Chandler rang the bell at 7.30am on Monday morning. During the short drive to Thorpe Wood, she related what had been achieved in his absence.

On Saturday afternoon the search of the Baldwin home had taken place, a magistrate having eventually granted the warrant. Although Bliss had yet to arrange a promised interview with the reporter, Bannister, it was the Baldwin intrigue he thought she had called him about. The eager but professional journalist would be looking for an inside scoop as to why the family who had made the emergency call had been questioned and their property searched.

Bliss decided she could wait. Little of interest had been uncovered during the examination of the Baldwin home and, so far, the forensics unit had found nothing to suggest Adam Baldwin had ever been inside Jade Coleman's house. He had been allowed to return home late on Saturday afternoon, threatening to sue for wrongful arrest until he was reminded that at no point had he actually been arrested. Coleman's parents had carried out a formal identification and had been briefly questioned in relation to their daughter. The victim's social media history, emails, correspondence and friends were in the process of being wrung out to see what spilled across the floor. As he had predicted, her life was being torn asunder and violated all over again.

Safely ensconced in his office by 7.45am, Bliss began preparations for a briefing in the incident room. No sooner had he sat down and logged onto the network system than his desk phone rang. It was Bannister calling from her desk at the *PT*.

'I was sorry to hear about your accident, Inspector,' the reporter began. Bliss thought she came across as sincere. 'I trust you are recovering well?'

'Thank you. Yes, it's coming along. Early days, and ribs just heal in their own time. I'm a bit raw and scuffed up, but a day basking in the sunshine helped. Are you calling about the interviews?'

During his last serious case, Bliss had liaised with Bannister over the placing of two stories, only one of which went on to be published. Part of the trade-off was that he'd accepted her request to be interviewed for a book she was writing about one of his previous cases. Initially Bliss had refused to take part, but he had eventually needed her help and knew it was the price he had to pay. With Superintendent Fletcher's blessing, three hour-long interviews had been agreed upon, though Bliss had yet to arrange the scheduling of them.

'I think you know I'm not, Inspector. I'm wondering how serious a suspect Adam Baldwin is in connection with the Jade Coleman murder.'

Bliss imagined her frown deepening. She had an earnest face which could be pretty when not pinched with either interest or suspicion.

'Every suspect is a serious one, Miss Bannister. However, we are looking further afield, and Mr Baldwin is, as I'm sure you know, back home with his wife and children. As soon as we have anything more concrete we will issue a press release, because the moment Mr Baldwin is no longer on our radar we want the local public to be made aware of that. I must insist that he was spoken to while under caution, but at no time under arrest, and was helping us with our enquiries.'

'Whatever that means.'

'It means exactly that. We had questions, Mr Baldwin answered them for us. He lived next door to the victim, he made the triple nine call, it would be a dereliction of duty if we didn't have questions for him.'

'Agreed. But to also search his home… what was that all about, Inspector?'

'Nothing untoward. Unfortunately, people read the worst into what for us is mere procedure. The positive spin would be that, having been interviewed, and having had his home searched,

Mr Baldwin is not sitting in a cell right now. That should surely indicate something to your readers.'

'Fair enough. I'll see what I can do as an update to this morning's online feed. You'll keep me informed?'

Bliss shook his head. She had some nerve. 'Let me be clear about something, Miss Bannister. Our arrangement was for me to provide you with three interviews, each with a very specific focus. Those will be your payment for helping me. We never once discussed my feeding you critical case information.'

'We didn't? Are you sure?'

Now he imagined her smiling down the phone, and the day seemed to brighten with it. 'I'm positive. I'll get back to you about those interviews.' Bliss killed the call before she had a chance to shoot anything else at him.

Less than thirty seconds later, DCI Edwards slipped into the office and closed the door behind her. She declined to sit. 'You're looking better today, Inspector,' she said, nodding appreciatively. 'Some of those grazes are already fading.'

'Thank you. Yes, I sat out in the sun much of yesterday and I have to say the vitamin D has done me the world of good. Amazing how much a bit of sun, a shower and a shave can re-energise a person.'

'And the ribs?'

'Score another one for the recuperative powers of the sun. Or maybe I just dulled the pain with beer. The ribs let me know they're still angry with me every now and then, but I've adjusted how to move and walk with them damaged, so they're not giving me many problems.'

'Good to hear. I just caught up with DS Chandler. She appears to be coping admirably.'

'I never doubted it for a moment. She's one of the good ones, boss.'

'I wanted to ask you about Hunt and Ansari. How are things looking there?'

'As far as I am aware from DS Chandler there are no issues at all. Their visit to Jade on behalf of the stalker task force came up during the Saturday afternoon briefing. They did what they were sent to do at the time. Neither thought there was much to it. The log was updated, the report written, and that was left with one of the task force officers. They've nothing to rebuke themselves for. And with respect, boss, neither do you. If anyone made an error on this, it came from inside the stalker task force. At first glance, however, I don't think anyone should catch shit for this. According to Chandler, Jade Coleman's statement to Hunt and Ansari was flimsy at best. She admitted that her fear was based on a sense of being watched, a sense that maybe someone had been inside her home. There was simply nothing concrete to work with. If it had dropped on my desk, I doubt I would have spent too much time with it.'

Edwards nodded, but she was clearly concerned. 'The fact remains, if it turns out that Miss Coleman was murdered by her stalker, a stalker we dismissed, then nothing will prevent that from leaking out to the media. It won't matter how lacking in substance Coleman's statement might be. Somebody will have to pay for it.'

'Then it will have to be DCI Mulligan.'

'I'm not so sure.'

'Boss, I realise he delegated to you, but the thing about delegation is that the responsibility for following up on it is his. I don't want to see him suffer because of this, but it shouldn't be you, either.'

Edwards appeared fazed by what he had said. Even a little embarrassed. 'Thank you, Inspector. I'm not sure what to make of this new-found… support for me.'

'Fair's fair, boss. We're jumping the gun here, because the murder may have nothing to do with a stalker. But even if it has, in my opinion neither of you are to blame. On the other hand, if somebody has to carry the can then it should only be the man who made the request.'

'I think in this case, "should" is the operative word.'

'Always has been. I suppose it always will be.'

Bliss smiled to himself when Edwards left. He realised his vocal support of his boss would throw her off kilter. He did not like his Chief Inspector much, and in the past, she had been more than willing to throw him under the bus. But at his core he thought of himself as a fair man. Credit where it was due, but also when the shit hit the fan it was only right that it ended up smeared only over those who deserved it. On this occasion, Edwards had not made any errors. Bliss was prepared to back her in those circumstances, just as he would any other member of the team. He checked his watch and cursed. Time he had set aside for other matters had been eaten up.

The morning briefing overran. It took time to get going from the outset while Bliss accepted the warm greeting of welcome from the assembled full squad. He took the barbs about him running down dark streets in his underwear in good humour and gave as good as he got in response. He had to be a good sport about it, because it was a ridiculous thing for him to have done, and ridicule was what he deserved in return. Afterwards, the team ran through operation Cauldron and brought everybody in the room up to date.

'Evidence suggests there was no break-in,' Bliss concluded. 'So there is every chance that Jade Coleman knew her killer and simply allowed him to enter her home on Friday. Either that or it was someone she had been expecting to call, perhaps for an appointment. There's nothing on her calendar, and we are still waiting for access to her online mail, diary and social media accounts. Jade was a Facebook user and there's nothing obvious from that to suggest that she was waiting in for anyone on Friday. But we may find more luck from her electronic diary.'

'Why was she not at work?' a uniform by the name of Snelling asked.

'Good question. We need to arrange for interviews at her place of work.'

'Uh, boss,' Short said, raising her hand like a reluctant schoolkid. 'I was the one who went through her Facebook postings. Jade quit her job about eight or nine weeks ago. That's all I could glean from her posts. No reason why, no clue as to what she was doing currently.'

'Thank you, Sergeant. I must have missed that update in the log. Apologies, folks.'

'Ah, boss. It was actually my error – I haven't yet updated the logs.'

Bliss grinned. 'I realised that, Sergeant. I was trying to save you some embarrassment.'

That spread some gentle laughter around the room. Bliss was pleased to hear it. Briefings and discussions in the incident room tended to veer between great highs and depressing lows as the investigation in hand altered throughout its duration. One moment you were despairing of hearing any positive news, and the next came the breakthrough you had been waiting for. The dynamics changed constantly, and Bliss endeavoured to keep things as upbeat as possible.

'We do still need to follow up with the employer to try and find out more about why Jade quit,' he said, looking around at some very tired faces. 'But also, who she was close to while she worked there. Any enemies she may have made, too. DS Chandler, if you could contact them when we're done here, perhaps you and I could take care of that. Meanwhile, we need to zero in on a possible boyfriend, carry on with the neighbours, and look more closely at this stalker connection.'

There were groans all round. Bliss raised his hands. 'I know, I know. By now I'm sure you are all aware that Jade Coleman previously reported being stalked, but that both her initial account and eventual statement were lacking in detail. They were not taken seriously at the time, and so ended up on the back burner. The task force has a genuine problem with stalkers at the moment, with on average two reports per day, and therefore we have to reconsider the statement and give it the attention it now warrants. I'd also like somebody to take a closer look at Adam Baldwin. DS Bishop, would you please find out when the post-mortem will be and then arrange the actions for the day, including attending it.'

Bliss returned to the squad room with Chandler and Short. On their way through, a young, clean-cut detective with dark brown hair and a slim build approached him. To Bliss he looked like an insurance salesman.

'Can I help you?' he asked the man.

'DC Gratton, boss. We met last week. I'm filling in while DC Carmichael is on secondment to the Cambridge counter-terrorist unit.'

Bliss blinked a couple of times. He recalled Carmichael being intrigued by the CTU during a prior major crime investigation following the torching of a young RAF airman. He also remembered being a bit put out when the secondment came through suddenly and swiftly, taking everyone by surprise. But of this young detective standing before him, he had only a hazy, distant recollection.

'I'm sorry, Constable,' he said. 'My mind is still a little bit fuzzy in terms of what happened last week. I'm sure it will all come back to me in time. Long- and short-term memory appears to be okay, just not the day of my accident, nor a day or two either side, it seems.'

'Understandable, boss. I just wanted to say that I chose this squad because of you. I realise it may be for just a few months during DC Carmichael's absence, but I want to learn as much as I can from you. And your great team, of course.'

Gratton was keen, and Bliss wasn't about to knock that out of him. 'Well, you've landed on your feet with operation Cauldron, Constable. Stick close to Hunt and Ansari, learn from them. Sergeants Chandler, Bishop and Short as well. Each about as good as it gets.'

While Chandler was on the phone, Bliss spoke to Short about Coleman's social media presence. 'How did she come across?' he asked. 'In general, I mean. Was she a keyboard warrior? You know the type, get all bolshie because they are online when in reality they'd say nothing. Or was she just… ordinary?'

'Oddly enough, I'd say she was a bit of both. Most of the time her posts were yawn-inducing. Standard Facebook stuff detailing what she ate and where she ate it. She was a member of some reading groups and a lot of fitness groups. Also, a fair few anti-nuclear groups. The difference being that she never once contributed a single post on those, whereas she was pretty active about her reading and fitness.'

That explained the physical conditioning and the bulging bookshelves. 'You said most of the time, and hinted at some uncertainty.'

Short tugged at her hair, a gesture Bliss had come to recognise that she made whenever she strayed into areas relying on impressions rather than facts. 'Recently she had started to come across as a little... not unbalanced, but certainly unravelling. She loved any posts that even hinted at conspiracy theories. I got the impression she felt things were going on which were being covered up.'

Bliss looked up at that. 'This have a tie-in with work at all? Perhaps why she left her job?'

'Possibly. Her manner online seemed to change shortly before she stopped working.'

'Which is my cue,' Chandler said, having put the phone down and turned her attention back to them. 'I have Jade Coleman as working for a company called Esotere-UK. What I wasn't aware of until just now is that Esotere-UK was previously known as Whittlesey Energy Disposal. And by 'Energy' that mostly meant nuclear waste. Campaigners battled against them for years, right up until around four years ago.'

'I remember it all very well,' Short said enthusiastically. 'My family live in and around Whittlesey, so it's all very familiar to me. The campaign group called themselves Citizens Against Whittlesey Energy Disposal. There were several investigations into alleged fire-bombings of homes associated with workers and suppliers. The CAWED activists were regularly investigated, and the whole thing caused a lot of fuss locally.'

Bliss folded one arm across his chest and cupped his chin with the other hand. 'I actually worked on one of those investigations. It never came to much, but we were pretty sure the local protestors were involved. So, Jade Coleman worked there until recently despite belonging to anti-nuclear groups on Facebook. That's an intriguing path to follow.'

'Activity from that particular group ended four years ago when the group lost their final court appeal, boss. It's unlikely to have a connection.'

'Agreed. But let's keep our eyes and ears open. The group may have gone away, but the ill feeling built up over those years may not have.'

'I've got us a meeting there at 1.30pm,' Chandler confirmed. 'For what it's worth.'

'Even if it closes a door, it's one less we have to consider later. Mia, would you please speak with the stalker task force for me. Tell them I'd like to arrange a briefing with them before our own one later this afternoon. I'd like to get a feel for what they're doing and what their suspect pool looks like.'

'Will do, boss,' Short said. 'Though I think they would be very happy if our investigation moved away from the stalker theory right now.'

'If you get any blowback, just tell them we are looking at absolutely everything at the moment. My mind is wide open on this one.'

As Bliss cut back through the corridor towards his office, he happened to notice two figures at the far end having what appeared to be a heated exchange. He recognised DCI Mulligan, and was dismayed to see the large man standing toe-to-toe with Ansari and looming over the young officer in what to Bliss looked like a threatening manner. Guessing what the disagreement was about, Bliss marched down the corridor as fast as his ribs would allow him to move. As he grew closer, Mulligan's voice softened, and as he approached, the Chief Inspector turned to face him.

'I was just tearing a strip off this dozy article,' he explained. He smiled, but there was no humour in it. Mulligan's florid nose and cheeks spoke volumes.

'And I was just explaining that I did nothing wrong,' Ansari said, standing her ground. Her own cheeks were tight with fury.

Mulligan rounded on her. 'Well, if that was true then that woman probably wouldn't be dead, would she?'

'Hey!' Ansari cried. 'That's not fair.'

'Well boo-fucking-hoo, sweetheart. Life is not fair.'

'That's enough,' Bliss said, shifting closer towards his team colleague. He glared up at the taller man. 'You have no right to speak to DC Ansari that way. You have a problem, you go through the channels. And by that, I mean me. What you don't do is bully one of my detectives.'

Mulligan reared back. 'Oh, is that so. Let me remind you, Inspector, I may not be your DCI, but I am *a* DCI, and that means you show me some bloody respect.'

Bliss moved to stand directly between Mulligan and Ansari. 'I'm showing you all the respect you deserve right now, sir. I'm telling you to back off. And if you are at all worthy of your rank you will do so, and apologise to DC Ansari before you walk away. Because from what I overheard, right now she would have a good claim for bullying and sexism in the workplace. I suspect the detective constable here is big enough to accept your apology and let it drop. But that's up to you. Sir.'

Mulligan stared hard at Bliss. 'I've heard about you, Inspector. All about you. And I can't say I like what I hear.'

'Whereas I've heard absolutely nothing about you, sir, which says a lot really. But I call it as I see it, and to be honest with you I am not impressed. Now, you can do as I suggest, or we can both go and find the Super and ask her which of us is a prick and which of us is an even bigger prick.'

Bliss noted Mulligan clenching and unclenching his fists. All the while the colour bled from his face as his temper cooled and the reality of the situation seeped in. Bliss made allowances for the fact that the DCI was probably under enormous pressure and looking to find a scapegoat, but it wasn't going to happen here and now with a member of his team. He met the larger man's gaze full on, hoping his expression revealed his resolve. The silence hung between them like a block of ice, but Bliss thought he detected the first sign of thawing on Mulligan's side. A moment later, the DCI glanced sidelong at Ansari.

'I think I may have been a little hasty,' he said. 'I meant nothing by it.'

Bliss looked at him for a moment, then turned to his DC and said, 'I think that's as close to an apology as you're going to get. Chalk it up as a win and move on is my advice.'

Mulligan did not wait around to find out if he was off the hook or not. Bliss and Ansari watched him go. 'Thank you for that, boss,' Ansari said. She flashed a vague smile and breathed out heavily.

Bliss raised his eyebrows. 'Actually, you should be kicking my arse. I know you could have handled him on your own. You were doing a pretty good job of it before I rocked up. You know me, Gul, I occasionally act before I think.'

'Occasionally?' Ansari's smile grew broader.

'Hey, you've been spending too much time with DS Chandler.'

'Boss, you're right when you say I could have handled it myself. On the other hand, I'm sure I would have done so badly and ended up suspended. You saved me from that.'

He nodded. 'Then all is right in the world.'

'Except now you're the one he's angry with.'

Bliss looked back down along the now empty corridor. He shook his head. 'No, I think his problem was and is that he's angry with himself. If he's a decent DCI then right now he'll be angrier still, and will seek you out to offer a proper apology.'

'And if he's not? A decent DCI, I mean.'

'Then I guess I'm off his Christmas card list,' Bliss said. He winked at Ansari. 'Come on, Constable. Let's get back to some real police work.'

Chapter Eleven

'Let's go for a drive,' Bliss said to Chandler, as he swept into the Major Crimes operations room. 'And don't get too used to having this power over me. I'll be back behind the wheel before you know it.'

He was restless, and when he got that way he liked to get away from the office. Occasionally he needed a different setting in order to provide some inspiration, and he had such a place in mind.

Chandler shook her head at him as she slipped out from behind her desk. 'It's been less than a week, Jimmy. You won't be cleared to drive for ages yet. And you bet I will make the most of being the nominated driver.'

'Get over yourself.'

'I'm your chauffeur on sufferance, but it's also necessary. You have damaged ribs, remember? You need to rest, remember?'

Bliss waved her away. 'You're like a broken record.'

'Yeah, well, even a broken record is right twice a day.'

Chandler gave him a look as if to suggest she had outfoxed him. He rolled his eyes and said, 'That's a clock, Pen. Not a bloody record, you dozy mare.'

She had to think about it for a second, but eventually Chandler flushed and shook her head. 'Oh, yeah. Well, same thing.'

'Of course they are. A timepiece and a recording are often mistaken for each other.'

'You know what I meant, you pedant.'

Bliss laughed this time. Chandler joined in a moment later. Several of the team members were now at their desks, and those who had overheard were chuckling.

'The last time someone called me a pedant, I clocked them one,' Bliss said, smiling at the memory. 'I thought that was the same thing as being a pederast.'

Chandler shook her head. 'One way or another, you were a pretty dumb kid, weren't you?'

'This was just last year.'

They enjoyed the moment together. Before they left, Hunt asked him if he could spare a couple of minutes. Bliss nodded and stepped out into the corridor. Ansari arrived in Hunt's wake.

'What is it?' Bliss asked, hoping he already knew. 'An intervention?'

It was Hunt who stepped forward. 'Boss. I realise that you're aware by now that Gul and I were given a stalker team job while you were away on holiday. We were the ones who spoke to Jade Coleman after she reported a possible stalker. We wanted you to know that, as far as we are concerned, we did our jobs. But we wanted to clear the air with you, just in case you weren't sure what to do about it.'

'I take it Gul told you about her run-in with DCI Mulligan?'

'She did, yes.'

'Good. For the record, then, I was asked to have a chat with you both on Saturday morning. An informal debrief, if you like. I declined. DS Chandler has since seen both the report and the statement, both of which she and I discussed at length. As I later informed DCI Edwards, you two did your jobs and had it been my task force I would have put it somewhere near the bottom of my list. You did nothing wrong. There's no air to clear. But I appreciate you both coming to me.'

The conversation put him in a happier mood as he and Chandler left the building. He had known from the beginning that Ansari had the right stuff, and now it seemed that Hunt was also growing into it.

Chandler's Ford Focus was a dark blue automatic and only four years old. Bliss sat quietly in the passenger seat as she drove, offering directions as necessary but otherwise not speaking.

Eventually they came to a little pull-in near the end of Lincoln Road where it ran alongside Bourges Boulevard. The pull-in was actually part of a road that had once been a side street, before the bulldozers came in to run a tarmac backbone through the city. Chandler snapped off the engine and they sat in silence for a few moments. The sun was high and hot and bathed the car in its warm embrace, glinting off clean glass and a high-sheen waxed dashboard. Bliss thought about his own car, whose interior only ever got cleaned when it was serviced.

'You mind telling me what we're doing here?' Chandler asked.

'See that alleyway,' Bliss said, nodding across the road to their right.

The alley was wide enough to take vehicles and ran between two sets of terraced houses. Halfway up the alley stood a pair of iron gates, which were closed and looked padlocked. Beyond the gates was a series of shuttered lock-ups. They were too small for garages, but ample for either small works or storage. There was a time when they had provided shelter for market stalls and security for the wares sold from them. Bliss had often wondered what treasures might be hidden away behind one or two of those roll-up shuttered doors.

'One of those pods was once the less than swanky HQ of CAWED. That's the anti-nuclear group Mia mentioned earlier. They moved to bigger and grander premises later on in Whittlesey itself, shortly after money started drifting in from the Anti-Nuclear Action Group and other like-minded organisations. But this was where they first plotted how to demonstrate their outrage. And believe me, they were angry people at that time.

'The year before, planning permission for the disposal business was granted and the local paper ran a piece on it. That was when the CAWED group was first formed, and they demonstrated daily outside the building site and then the business that it later became. The campaign never really gained much traction nationally. Not until it became violent, that is. The organisation was supposedly a co-operative, but in reality, they were led by two people: Marvin

Cooke and his then girlfriend, Ellie Simms, whom he later married. They were the ringleaders and planners.'

'I have to say that before I became aware of the kind of attacks they were making, I had some sympathy for them,' Chandler said, squinting at the lock-ups. 'Nuclear energy scares me, and the thought of its radioactive waste being so close to us was, and still is, terrifying.'

'It's an emotive subject. The very mention of nuclear has people running scared, but that's often due to a lack of understanding. These companies use landfill sites for low-level waste only, saving the nuclear industry billions. Low-level waste used in the atomic industry includes clothing and plastics as well as metal and building rubble. It makes up an extremely high proportion of the UK's radioactive waste, but supposedly contains minimal radioactivity. But at the end of the day it still is radioactive nuclear waste, so if a young firebrand has the balls to go for it, and they protest peacefully and make lives difficult for the right people, then my sympathies might also lie with them.'

'I suppose you're about to tell me that's not always the case.'

'I worked one of the firebombing investigations. It was one of my first jobs after moving up here, and you and I had yet to be thrust together as partners. I had to visit the temporary shelter provided to a family of five who found themselves burned out of their home in Bretton.'

'That can't have been a pleasant experience.'

'It wasn't. You know what the husband and father worked in, Pen? He was in IT. He was no expert on waste, and certainly had nothing to do with the place being built and then operating. Worse still, he wasn't even at home the night those people firebombed his family home. His wife was, as were their three children, aged between three and seven. I knew even before I spoke with them that these people should never have been targeted.'

'So why were they?' Chandler asked.

'The protest group claimed their victims were complicit because they helped run the place, and the hardened activists could not have cared less that three little kids were now too terrified to close their eyes and go to sleep in case the fire came for them again. The frustration of those CAWED people I could understand. Their targeting, however, left a lot to be desired. But what I couldn't stomach was their self-righteousness, their arrogance, their inability to understand the different perspectives of others. I loathed each and every single one I met.'

'It's not as if there wouldn't have been better targets,' Chandler acknowledged with a nod. 'It's okay to agree with their cause but not their tactics, isn't it?'

'Of course. I was very torn, until I looked into the eyes of those shocked children and saw the misery that had been brought into their lives. Then, of course, I reminded myself that things could have been so much worse. They might not have escaped the fire.'

'I wasn't involved with any aspect of how this city dealt with the campaigners. But a friend of mine, a fellow uniformed constable at the time, was caught up in a major skirmish with the CAWED group. She was trampled on at one point. Kicked and stamped on, too. Had her leg and knee busted, ligaments damaged. She loved the job, but she had to leave. And all because those bastards couldn't control their own people.'

'Oh, I think they were controlling them only too well.'

'You do? They always claimed the trouble-makers had come from outside the organisation.'

'I know. And I didn't believe a word of it.'

'I guess you'd know better than me, boss.'

'I found the whole CAWED thing a bit cultish if I'm being honest. I came to regard them as a bunch of zealots who seemed to care more about their vision, bringing others into the group, and achieving notoriety, than the actual people and property they were supposedly trying to protect.'

Chandler shrugged. 'So what's this potted history lesson all about?'

'I wanted to get out of the office, for one thing. Plus, you'd do well to bear in mind what these people are like if we do have to dig deeper into their lives. Many of them did some time, mostly on charges of disturbing the peace, aggravated assault, and fraud rather than terrorism. I think the fraud presented the prosecution service with an easier win, as they seemed to have evidence relating to campaign money being misappropriated. Plus, terrorism charges would have led to some sympathetic protests, whereas them being exposed as crooks pretty much put an end to their cause.'

While he was running through all of this, Bliss had snagged hold of an idea. He took out his mobile and tapped in a number. Moments later he was speaking to the journalist at the *Peterborough Telegraph*.

'Miss Bannister. It's DI Bliss. I was wondering, what would it take for me to get your deep background on CAWED mailed across to me, and how long would I have to wait?'

'That's an interesting leap, Inspector. What's the connection?'

'You'll find out eventually, so no harm in telling you now, I suppose. Our victim worked for the energy disposal place in Whittlesey. Esotere-UK.'

'Ah. During CAWED's reign?'

'No. I'm not saying we're looking into them just yet, but it may go that way and I'd like to know if you would send me what you have and if so, how long I would have to wait.'

'If I decided to send it to you, I could have most of it cobbled together within a few hours. What's in it for me?'

'A sense of civic duty?' Bliss suggested, winking and smiling at his partner, who was listening via the open speaker.

'I'm a reporter, Bliss. We don't have a conscience, apparently. I seem to recall a certain DI who told me that at one time.'

'That's shocking. An awful slur on a noble profession and a terrible thing to suggest. Okay, so how about if it takes us anywhere, I'll give you a head start on national media.'

'All media? Local TV as well?'

'All media. Time enough to knock up a few thousand words and plaster it all over the Internet before they even get a sniff.'

'Then you have yourself a deal, Inspector. I must say, your own media people are playing this Jade Coleman murder very close to their chests. Those statements they are releasing say virtually nothing. Barely warrants a mention in the nationals.'

'We're trying to avoid the usual frenzy. Wild speculation only interferes with what we're trying to do, so we have to limit it somehow. That's why they won't let me anywhere near your lot these days.'

'Sensible people.'

'Now that we can agree on,' Bliss said.

'What was that all about?' Chandler asked him when he ended the call. Her face was a picture of astonishment. 'Jimmy Bliss cosying up to a journalist? Has the whole world gone mad?'

'Bannister is okay. I have a whole thing going on with her. Professionally, that is. Don't ask, but suffice it to say that my darkest secrets will be revealed in what you may shortly find on sale for fifty pence in a charity shop bargain bin. Anyhow, she's a pro and she understands the two-way street we both travel.'

'We must have our own data in connection with CAWED. Why go cap in hand to the *PT*?'

'It's easy to dismiss them, but we would all do well to remember that they are also investigators. Journalists ask different questions to those we need answers to, and often over a much longer period of time than we can afford. They also have different objectives. So, they tend to gather a lot more information than we do, and use only the pieces they can make headlines out of. I admit I'm a hypocrite in both despising them and using them, but I reckon we have to exploit that usefulness as and when we can. Besides, we could do with having a friend on that side of the fence.'

His phone rang before he had an opportunity to slip it back into his pocket. It was Nancy Drinkwater, the city pathologist. 'Just letting you know there has been a delay on the PM you're waiting for,' she told him.

Bliss was unperturbed. He did not imagine any surprises awaited them. 'Thanks for letting me know. You backed up down there?'

'That's a bit personal, Inspector.'

He laughed. 'I mean work-wise. I have no interest in your bowel movements.'

'It's not that. Jade Coleman's parents are orthodox Jews. They have appealed against the autopsy, and have volunteered instead to pay for the body to be scanned and additional blood tests taken in order to find out the true cause of death.'

This was by no means unusual these days. Back in 2009, allowances were made in law for people of all faiths to appeal on religious grounds. Some faiths fought against the further desecration of a body, demanding it be kept intact. Only in special circumstances would a pathologist and the justice system fight such an appeal. Bliss felt sure this one would be granted.

'I don't suppose you have a TOD for me, do you?'

'Time of death was somewhere between 6am and 10am on Friday morning.'

Bliss knew that dropped right within the timeframe they already had. The call from Adam Baldwin had been logged at 9.07am. Which meant they now had to extend the man's alibi, as he could easily have murdered Coleman earlier than he had placed the call. Not too much earlier, Bliss reasoned. He could not have allowed the body to become too cold, otherwise it would have been obvious that the murder had occurred much earlier. More thinking to do on that one.

'Any chance you can narrow that down further?' Bliss asked.

'Probably. If you pushed me on it right now, I'd say closer to 9am.'

'Thanks, Nancy. So regards to the different method of PM, you'll MRI her and work from that, right?' he said.

'We will. It's not ideal, but in this case I think it's simply a matter of deciding which punch with the blade delivered the killer blow. If any single stab was indeed responsible. It could easily have been the trauma resulting from the volume of penetrations. Perhaps even a vital organ was punctured.'

'Doctor McGovern seemed to be on the ball.'

Drinkwater laughed. 'She spoke very highly of you, too. I think you may have a fan there, Ray.'

'Behave, will you.'

'No, I mean it. She mentioned you often.'

'Yeah, well I think my days as an old letch are done, Nancy. There was a time when I would have been all over her, but I'm at the point when I know I'm batting way out of my league. She probably thought of me as a father figure.'

'Hmm. Now that you mention it, I think you could be right. Grandfather figure, even.'

'Thank you, Nancy.' Bliss cut the connection.

'Ray?' Chandler said to him, peering at him curiously.

Bliss chuckled. 'She says from some angles, especially side-on, I look a little like Ray Winstone. It's become a running joke.'

Frowning, Chandler shook her head and said, 'No, I don't see it. He's quite an attractive bloke in a brutish sort of way.'

'Thank you. Charmer.'

'So if you're Ray Winstone, who am I?'

'She's never said. But to me, I would say you're easily a Claire Goose.'

Chandler pursed her lips. Nodded and said, 'I can live with that. It might even be a compliment.'

He grinned. 'Very nearly.'

The phone in his hand rang once again. 'I might as well never put this bloody thing away again,' Bliss complained, before answering it. This time it was DS Bishop. 'You heard about the autopsy delay,' he began. After Bliss explained who he had just been speaking to, Bishop continued. 'There's a suggestion that Jade Coleman may have been seeing somebody at her fitness club.'

'Ah. So she did have a boyfriend.'

'Not quite, boss. The person she was seeing is a woman. An older woman, at that.'

'We talking a romantic relationship here, Bish?'

'It certainly seems possible, boss.'

'Where did this suggestion come from?' Bliss asked.

'Mrs Baldwin. The neighbour. Apparently, she and Jade occasionally chatted. At one point during one of their chats a woman showed up. Mrs Baldwin got the impression the two were close. Something about the way they behaved when together. It came out at some point further down the line that they worked out together. She remembered the woman's name, and we followed up on it.'

'Good work, Bish. That's genuine progress.'

'You want me and Ansari to speak to her?'

Bliss thought about his schedule. He and Chandler were not due in Whittlesey for almost four hours. Even allowing for a lunch break they had time. 'No, let me have her details. Work and home, all phones.'

Bishop rattled them off, and a moment later Bliss heard his phone chime as the same information came his way via email. Bliss admired the sergeant's ability to multitask. 'One more thing, boss,' Bishop said. 'This Mrs Lancaster you're seeing… it may be best to reach her at work first, because as well as apparently being hooked up with our victim, she is also married.'

Chapter Twelve

Bliss had never heard of the Rebound Trampoline Park, let alone seen it before. RTP was tucked away inside what had once been a frozen food warehouse in Bretton, whose car park backed onto the railway line, the other side of which lay the light industrial Mancetter Square complex. An overhead pedestrian walkway provided an easy route between the two. To Bliss's mind, these estates dotted around the city seemed to consist of businesses which came and went in the blink of an eye, and he wondered how long it would be before the trampolines were replaced with electronics or spare parts. Judging by the car park, it would not be long. But they quickly found out why theirs was one of only three vehicles outside.

'What kind of business opens its doors only from noon?' Bliss asked, eyeballing the poster on the glass door which listed coming attractions, features, and opening times.

'The kind that relies on the sort of clients who stay in bed until lunchtime,' Chandler suggested, shielding her eyes as she put her nose to the reflective pane and peered through the door.

'Well, there are two cars parked up, so someone has to be inside.'

'Yeah, and judging by the white soft-top Merc, I'm betting one of them is the boss.'

Chandler shoved the door, then pulled it. It remained solid and unmoveable. Then she used her knuckles to rap on the glass. Seeing nobody emerging from the dark interior, Chandler turned and used her boot heel to kick the metal plate at the foot of the door.

'We can always come back,' Bliss said.

'We're here now. I don't want to come back.'

'Who would have thought you would turn out to be the impatient one?'

'I know. When did I become you?'

'It's your age. You reach a certain point when you realise that all those years you spent living through a filter were simply wasted.'

Chandler gave a yelp of surprise as the door behind her was yanked open. The woman who stood there jabbed a long and bony finger at the poster on the door. 'I assume you can't read,' she said brusquely. 'We're not open until midday.'

Bliss slipped his warrant card out from inside his jacket pocket and flipped it open. The woman was somewhere in her late forties, had a shapely chiselled face and a trim, wiry build. Thin lips carried the air of superiority on their glossy surface. Sky blue eyes which flickered in alarm when she saw his credentials, drew attention away from the wrinkles which bracketed them.

'Major Crimes,' he told her. 'Detectives Bliss and Chandler. I don't suppose you are Mrs Lucy Lancaster by any chance, are you?'

The irritability and contempt vanished from the woman's face like a tablecloth disappearing from beneath a china tea service with one quick snap of an expert's wrist. 'This is about Jade, isn't it?' she said softly, her taut mask slipping to reveal the crestfallen reality beneath.

'It is. May we come in, Mrs Lancaster?'

The woman nodded and stood to one side, still holding open the glass door. 'There's only a trampoline tech in at the moment other than me, so we can talk in my office.'

They moved through into the belly of the building. The office Lancaster led them to along a narrow and featureless corridor was surprisingly bright and cheery, despite being constructed of plain breezeblock. A number of prints and framed photos adorned the walls, including one of Lancaster standing alongside the city mayor as they shook hands. It was a promotional photo opportunity, announcing the grand opening of the business. On the far wall, Bliss's attention was snagged by a black and white photo of Lancaster dressed in a clinging black leotard as she held a gymnastic pose on a balance beam.

'So what can you tell me about what happened?' she asked, taking a seat on the far side of an oval wooden coffee table to the left of the room. Bliss and Chandler sat opposite, settling themselves.

'I'm afraid it doesn't work that way, Mrs Lancaster,' Chandler said curtly. 'We need to be the ones asking the questions.'

Bliss had suggested she take the interview, that he would chip in as and when he thought necessary. They agreed that this might work well, but would largely depend on whether Lancaster regarded the judgement of a fellow female to be a comfort or punishment.

'Let me save you some bother, then.' The woman's cheeks flushed as she regarded them without guile, and Bliss found himself instantly admiring her inner strength. 'Yes, Jade and I had a relationship. We met at the gym, and often found ourselves working out alongside each other. Drawn together as females in an overtly male environment, perhaps. One day we were side by side on the cycle machines and I had forgotten my MP3 player. Jade asked if I would like to share hers and offered me an earbud. That was all it needed to cement our relationship, really. A little musical glue.'

'You sensed Jade was gay?'

'Oh, yes. Despite the fact that Jade had not, and now will never, come out as gay. I knew, though. Those stolen sidelong glances. The way she fluffed her hair as we spoke. As for me, well I am bi, although my husband is not aware of it.'

'So you're telling us your husband was unaware of your relationship with Miss Coleman?'

'Entirely. I doubt he even thought I might be having an affair. But if he ever did, he would never have considered it being with a woman.'

Lancaster crossed her legs and smoothed down her black stockings. The movement drew Bliss's eye, and he could see why this woman would hold an appeal over just about anyone. Her clothes were of good quality, she oozed charm and elegance, spoke well, and clearly took care of herself. She wore a simple skirt and jacket suit that appeared effortless, yet anyone who noticed it would know it had been chosen with great care.

'What do you do here, Mrs Lancaster?' Bliss asked.

'This place? I own it, Chief Inspector.'

'That's just Inspector.'

'Oh, I doubt you are *just* anything. This is one of three businesses I have on the go. My husband has his own empire to run. We keep odd hours, which made life easier for me and Jade.'

'Where did you and Jade… meet up when you felt like seeing each other?' Chandler asked.

'It's okay if you want to say have sex. It is what we did, after all. Ours was not a relationship that would ever, could ever, have been more. I felt a great deal of affection for Jade, and I like to believe she thought a lot of me. But we were both in it for the physical side more than the emotional.'

'So you never… dated? Never went out to restaurants together? Nightclubs?'

'No, no and no. We spent quality time together in the gym. I occasionally visited Jade's home. At other times I booked a room at the Riverside hotel in Stamford. We arrived separately, left separately, and spent no time together either in the bar or the restaurant there.'

'How often did you book a room?'

'I have a standing arrangement. Every Wednesday. At times I added to it if we were feeling particularly frisky that week.'

'How did you hear about Jade's murder?' Bliss asked. He decided to knock the woman from her comfort zone in which she seemed to enjoy trying to shock them.

'Sadly, from the TV news on Saturday. A local report. Later I read about it more fully online.'

'When did you last see Jade?'

She smiled as she peered at him. 'Ah, the softening up process is over, is it? Time to provide an alibi for myself. I last saw Jade on Wednesday night. And before you ask, of course nobody can verify that because we were never seen together.'

'And you did not visit Jade on Thursday or Friday?'

'No.'

'When did you last speak with her?'

'When we said goodbye on Wednesday night.'

'No calls? Texts?'

'We were not the texting types, Inspector. I rarely called Jade, other than to perhaps ask if she felt like another night at the hotel. We saw each other pretty much every day at the gym. I realise it probably comes across as a quaint idea these days, but Jade and I actually enjoyed speaking to each other while we were in the same room.'

'But not last Thursday or Friday?' Chandler pointed out.

Lancaster blinked quickly and lowered her chin. 'Sadly not. I missed out on Thursday due to a business commitment, and Jade wasn't there on Friday when I went for my session.'

'Which was at what time?'

'Our sessions coincided, obviously. When we first started meeting up it was of an evening, but recently that changed around to early morning. We had a 7am start.'

'Why the change around?' Bliss asked. 'Evening to morning, I mean.'

'Something to do with work, I believe. It was at Jade's request.'

Chandler sat forward on her seat, which let out a gentle squeak. 'Were you aware that Jade no longer worked at Esotere? That she hadn't for over two months?'

'I was not.'

For the first time, Bliss thought Lancaster appeared vulnerable. Disappointed, he guessed. Something significant had altered in Jade's life, yet she had chosen not to inform her lover. The older woman was hurt by that.

'That would have been around the time Jade asked you to arrange morning sessions at the gym instead,' Chandler went on. 'Did you never ask why?'

'As I said before, she mentioned something about work. Changing the session time really wasn't an issue for me, so I confess I may not have been paying much attention at the time.'

'Tell me,' Bliss said. 'Had Jade changed in recent weeks and months? Had she become more distant? More relaxed, perhaps? Was she worried about anything as far as you know?'

Lancaster paused before responding. The first time she had done so. 'Now that you mention it, Jade was less… in the moment. She seemed to drift off, as if her mind was on other things. I wasn't concerned by it – we all have our times wallowing in the blue.'

'In the blue?'

'When we're feeling down, Inspector. Not quite the black dog of depression, just in the blue.'

'You speak from experience?'

'Of both.'

Bliss saw it in her eyes, and the way her bearing temporarily lost its rigidity.

'And you never asked your friend – your lover – why she was feeling low?'

'We didn't have that kind of relationship. If we were troubled, we dealt with it outside of our time together.'

'Tell me, did Jade have any enemies that you knew of? Anyone who might want to harm her?'

Lancaster shook her head firmly. 'I can't imagine anyone even disliking Jade, let alone being her enemy or wanting to hurt her. She was the sweetest person, with a wonderful nature. Naïve at times, but rather that than a cynic.'

'Would it surprise you to know that Jade believed she was being stalked?' Chandler asked.

'Now that I didn't know. That would not surprise me at all. In fact, it would be typical of Jade to keep it from me. As for being stalked, I can't say if it surprises me or not. I've never really been sure what drives such people on.'

'Mrs Lancaster, where were you on Friday morning. Specifically, where were you between six and nine-thirty?'

The woman gave a thin smile. 'I've been waiting for you to ask that. I woke just before the alarm at six, got ready, went to the gym for seven, left the gym just before eight, and was in my office on Park Street within fifteen minutes.'

'What gym would that be?'

'We use David Lloyd. Not far from your station at Thorpe Wood, actually.'

'Anyone verify you were there between those times?' Bliss asked. It was routine. Jade Coleman had been murdered shortly after 9am, at which time Lancaster had been safely ensconced within her office, where he was sure more than one person would vouch for her whereabouts.

'There were plenty of people there. There's also a security feed. As for my office, at least four staff members would have seen and spoken to me, and I made several phone calls during that timeframe. I was in the office until shortly before noon, when I drove over here to speak with the manager.'

'Any idea why Jade didn't go to the gym that morning?'

'No. After I found out what had happened, I assumed it was because she was… murdered.'

'Any idea where your husband was between those same times?'

Bliss had been intrigued by the differing emotions he had seen flash across Lucy Lancaster's features throughout the interview. She certainly had no shields where they were concerned, her every reaction entirely transparent. But for the first time since they had started talking, he now saw fear brush against her.

'I told you he had no idea about Jade,' she said, a tremor in her full lips.

'That you know of.'

Lancaster closed her eyes for a moment. Then she sat forward, shifting herself to the very edge of her seat. Her eyes implored Bliss for understanding. 'Please don't involve my husband. He and I are happy together. We love each other. Just because Jade was able to provide me with something my husband is no longer interested in, nor is capable of, since he is not a woman, does not mean our marriage is a sham. Nor is it under pressure. But if he learns about

Jade, it will break him. Inspector, please tell me you have no need to involve him.'

Bliss took a beat to breathe deeply and push it out slowly. 'Mrs Lancaster, you're an intelligent woman. You will understand why our investigation would be interested in our victim's lover. You will further understand why we would also be interested in that lover's spouse. I don't enjoy wrecking marriages, Mrs Lancaster, although I usually find the couple have somehow managed to do that themselves. The thing is, we have to be certain that your husband was unaware of your relationship with Jade Coleman, and we have to be certain that he did not put a stop to it on Friday morning.'

'I understand that, Inspector. Of course I do. However, if I can provide you with substantiated evidence that my husband was elsewhere and therefore could not have murdered Jade, would you accept it without necessarily having to quiz him directly?'

Bliss glanced across at his partner, who gave a slight shrug. He returned his gaze to Lancaster, who now appeared even more fragile. This saddened him for reasons he could not explain.

'That would largely depend on what evidence you provided. This is a murder investigation and I won't cut corners. I would have to be completely satisfied.'

Lancaster nodded and said, 'He got up shortly after me, but we left the house at the same time. Paul has a driver because he lost his licence last year. They were going out to a site on the other side of Northampton at which Paul's company was breaking ground. I'm sure that his driver could be persuaded to provide you with all the information you need, but he must never mention it to Paul.'

Bliss had been truthful when he told the woman he had no intention of ruining her marriage if he did not need to. He saw that she had now provided them with a way in which this might be achieved so that her husband did not become aware of what was going on around him. It was not a deceit, he decided. It was a kindness.

'Let us have the details before we go and we'll see what we can do,' Bliss told her. He had paused enough to allow Chandler to respond, but for some reason she had held back. 'Meanwhile, last couple of questions for you, Mrs Lancaster. Firstly, did Jade ever mention any issues she might be having with family, friends, a neighbour, perhaps?'

'Not really.' The woman shook her head. 'I mean, there was the perv next door. He always somehow managed to be standing by his garden fence when Jade was sunbathing. She once told me she thought he might be playing with himself whilst ogling her. But we laughed it off together. She even teased him a little by lowering her bikini top straps. I dared her to go topless, but she drew the line at that.'

'So this neighbour didn't worry or frighten her?'

'Not at all. She said he was a harmless perv, and if he got his kicks by checking her out then so be it.'

'Jade sounds very enlightened,' Chandler said. 'A lot of women today would have been furious. Possibly even started an online campaign. You know the sort of thing I mean – I have a hashtag and I'm not afraid to use it.'

'And perhaps the neighbour deserved exactly that. But it was not Jade's style at all.'

'Finally, then,' Bliss said, steering them back on track. 'Did Jade ever mention a run-in with any anti-nuclear activists?'

'Anti-nuclear?' Lancaster gave that some serious thought before briskly shaking her head. 'Not that I recall. And I'm sure I would. Though, I seem to remember Jade once having a friend who was an activist.'

'Is that so?'

'Yes. I'm pretty sure that she used to exercise in the same gym as Jade in those days. I believe this friend was also even a member of that group known as CAWED at one time.'

Bliss looked across at his partner. What had seemed only seconds ago to be an interview going nowhere, had now taken an extremely interesting turn.

Chapter Thirteen

Bliss suggested they stop off for some decent coffee before heading back to HQ. There was a Costa's at the nearby Bretton shopping centre, so Chandler drove them there. It was a nice-looking place, with plum-coloured accents to complement the various wood laminates used throughout. Up at the counter he ignored the variety of cakes and pastries on offer, bought a medium latte for his partner, and settled for his usual black with no sugar. Why these places insisted on forcing him to confirm he meant an Americano he had no idea, but he was just happy to be sipping it down and enjoying the light breath of chilled air wafting around the room.

'So what did you make of her?' he asked Chandler. Bliss narrowed his gaze. 'I got a sense back there that you were not entirely happy at our agreement.'

'You mean about keeping the husband in the dark?' Chandler screwed up her face. 'Neither happy nor unhappy. I was surprised you went for it, if I'm honest.'

'Why? Because I'm a man, and a man was cheated on by his wife?'

'Pretty much. Or doesn't it count if the cheating takes place with a lesbian?'

Bliss laughed. 'You know, it sort of doesn't. For most men it's an ego thing. If their wife has been sleeping with someone else, they hate to feel they might be smaller and less good in bed. It's the comparison they fear most. That doesn't come into it when the lover is another woman.'

Chandler shook her head. 'You really are Barney Rubble, aren't you?'

'It was Fred Flintstone, actually. And I'm just telling you how it is, not that I endorse the view. Besides, does Paul Lancaster really need to know his wife was cheating on him with another woman if that woman is no longer around to cheat with?'

'Perhaps not. Mind you, it didn't sound to me as if there hadn't been other women before, nor that there wouldn't be more in the future.'

'Then that's for another day. A marital problem, not ours. We'd be doing them both a favour if we can keep this quiet, believe me.'

'So you don't think Lancaster is our killer?'

'No. Not even without what looks like a pretty solid alibi.'

'And the husband?'

'I'm not as convinced, but she was. I think all we've stumbled into is a sorry little affair that our victim was involved in. That's what happens when you deep mine a person's life. Would a trawl of yours come up smelling of roses, Pen? I know mine wouldn't.'

'To say the least. But yes, I think you're probably right. I'm more interested in this friend of Jade's. The anti-nuclear demonstrator. Ex-member of CAWED, no less. That can't be a coincidence.'

Bliss thought Chandler had it right. Coleman had joined Esotere-UK after the protest group had disbanded, so at what point had she become friendly with one of its activists? He wondered if it were possible that Coleman's relationship with both the friend and the group had somehow inspired her to start working at Esotere. Had she been a plant, he wondered, placed there to work undercover and report back? And if so, to whom did she make those reports to, and did it somehow tie in with her murder?

The coffee was good, just the right side of bitter. Bliss had always meant to try their beans and grind them himself at home, but once again had forgotten to buy a bag when making the drinks purchase. The place wasn't busy, and they were free to discuss the investigation in greater detail. It beat being stuffed inside the incident room back at Thorpe Wood.

Bliss set his mug down and said, 'I'm starting to think there is much more to operation Cauldron than first meets the eye. I'm not seeing all the connections just yet, but I am getting a feel for it now. Say our victim was not wrong when she made her stalker report. Only it wasn't so much a stalker as a watcher. Something compelled Jade to leave her job. Then she feels like she's being stalked, that somebody has been inside her home. She has a friend who was an activist for the very group that terrorised her employers. There's something that links all these things together, and we have to find out what it is.'

'Hopefully we'll move a step closer to that when we speak to the CEO of Esotere later today.'

Bliss was doubtful. In his experience, people that high up within large corporations either had no clue as to what was going on or had all the power and authority they needed to quash it. Still, it was a necessary meeting. Perhaps more so now than before Lucy Lancaster's revelations. Bliss had yet to decide how to play that interview, but he would certainly be keeping some things close to his chest.

'How're the ribs?' Chandler asked him.

'Doing well with the appropriate level of pain relief. My breathing is a bit ragged, but I'm fine otherwise.'

'Not that you'd say if you weren't. Have you told your mother yet?'

'What's to tell? Why worry her? It happened, I recovered. No need for her to find out. I'm just glad no one at work thought to contact her.'

Chandler inclined her head. 'Do they even know how to? Did you ever bother to inform them that she was living in Ireland now and not Spain?'

He blinked a couple of times, mind racing. He had intended to make the next of kin change, but now that his partner had mentioned it, Bliss thought that perhaps he had never got around to updating the form when his father died. He shrugged and chuckled at Chandler's look of complete disgust and incomprehension.

'Hey, I'm only human,' he complained. 'I can't remember everything. I'll catch up with it as soon as this case is done with.'

'Of course. Why do today what you can put off until tomorrow? Or the day after. Or the day after that.'

'I get it. You made your point. And you don't forget to make your own call. You regenerate interest at the Home Office, they will work their charms with the Foreign Office.'

'You think I could ever forget that?'

Bliss shook his head. 'No. I imagine not.'

Chandler's love for her abducted child had never waned in all the time he had known her. Stoicism was one of his partner's many admirable traits, and whilst outwardly you would never know she was hurting, Bliss knew that Chandler carried around a pain that gnawed away at her inner core, consuming hope, aspiration, and expectation.

But not love.

Never love.

Hannah had not become some kind of cause célèbre for Chandler; there were no online campaigns or hashtag armies fighting for her rights. There was simply the quiet and ceaseless devotion to a daughter she had not seen in seventeen years, the sincerity of love a mother has for her child despite having come to terms with the dreadful, agonising facts of Hannah's abduction.

'You're a step further than you were,' Bliss said. 'At this stage, every single step counts for something.'

'Thanks to you.'

He made no reply.

'Jimmy, what exactly transpired between you and MI6? I know it had something to do with the Bone Woman, I also recall it had something to do with her dead husband. My powers of deductive reasoning lead me to conclude that somewhere in the midst of all that lies a story involving little Miss Reporter at the *PT*. I'm intrigued by all the strands, but nowhere near as much as I am by the fact that you refuse to discuss any of them.'

The mere mention of the Bone Woman caused his thoughts to shift to Emily Grant. Or, Emily Curtis as she now was. Not so much the one who got away, as the one who almost was. A fledgling relationship tossed upon the rocks of a career nosedive that took him all the way back down to London. In the spring of this year she had come to him a newly widowed woman seeking to clarify what had happened to her husband. Every sign had pointed to a suicide, but she was convinced – and in turn had convinced Bliss – that her husband would not have killed himself. Emily had been right about that, but wrong about so much else.

'It's not that I don't want to tell you,' Bliss said to Chandler now. 'It's just not my story to tell, and I don't have permission to reveal even my part in it. All I can say is pretty much what I have said before. Emily needed my help, and I gave it. At one point I was used by MI6, and then I used them in return. Miss Bannister – or little Miss Reporter if you prefer – played a part in that. There was a price to pay for her help. Part of that debt has been repaid, the greater part is yet to come.'

'And what did you get out of it all, Jimmy?'

Bliss looked up from the dregs of coffee he was staring at in the bottom of his mug. 'What do you mean?'

'Well, it seems to me that the settlement from MI6 is that I get the opportunity to find out where my daughter is and possibly arrange to see her again. Little Miss Reporter at the very least gets an interview with you as her reward. The Bone Woman clearly got to find out the truth about her husband's death, irrespective of whether or not it was what she wanted to hear. That sounds like a lot of time and effort you put into achieving all those positive outcomes for others, and yet I'm not seeing the upside for you.'

'Then perhaps my upside is that you and Emily both have an upside,' he explained simply, not even having to think about it. 'I certainly didn't do any of it for reward.'

Chandler shook her head. Her eyes held his. 'Of course not. And I know you're not seeing Emily as such, but have you seen her at all since the spring?'

'One time. I drove over to her house to give her some news about her husband's inquest. We had a chat over a cup of tea, but to be honest I felt more than a little bit awkward. Emily did not really find what she was looking for when she asked for my help, and it was clear to me that she needed time to come to terms with it all. Plus, when push comes to shove, we've both moved on. Our time was a long time ago. We are different people now, changed by our circumstances and experiences.'

'And there's been nobody since Angie Burton? You two should get over yourselves and start seeing each other again. So you had a falling out. Couples do. Then they talk it over and make up.'

'We weren't ever a couple, Pen. Angie and I are friends. Or at least, we're friend*ly*. If we see each other at work we talk, we laugh and joke. We're mates. The truth is, there was never anything between us worth holding onto.'

'How about Robbie Newman? Now I know you liked her. Have you even bothered to call her since we got back from the States?'

Bliss sighed and raised a hand as if warding Chandler off. 'What is it with you? I know you've always felt as if you can poke around in my love life whenever you feel like it, but ever since you came to my house the other day you've been itching to pair me up.'

'I just… Jimmy, I want you to put down some roots here. I keep wondering whether you'll stick around, especially with all the aggravation you get from Edwards. And then when I saw the place you laughingly refer to as home it seemed to me that you're determined not to settle. I came back here to be on your team, and I can't do that if you're no longer here to run it.'

He looked at her for a moment, then risked a half-hearted grin. 'So, your interest is purely selfish? It's all about you, how it affects you?'

Chandler put both hands to her head. 'Aaghh! You drive me insane, Jimmy Bliss. Yes, let's say it is all about me. It's all I give a damn about. So tell me what your intentions are. Why does your house look as if you're passing through? Why are you not putting your feet under the table and claiming this city as your own?'

Now the grin became a chuckle, and Bliss could not help himself. 'Penny, you're drawing major conclusions from minor, obscure reference points. In terms of my love life, it is currently non-existent because I have neither the time nor inclination to do anything about it. As for my home, the lack of a personal touch has absolutely nothing to do with my long-term plans. The truth is, I have none. I genuinely don't look beyond the next day, the next case. Bare walls and no wardrobe add up to exactly what they are – a means to an end. I have what I need. I live how I want to live. When that changes, you'll be among the first to know.'

'I don't mean to nag.'

'Yes, you do.'

'All right, I do. But I don't mean to intrude.'

'Yes, you do.'

'Okay, I do. I just… Jimmy, I just got a bit scared. When I left your place on Friday, I had the awful feeling that you were on your way elsewhere. That's how it felt to me; as if you're waiting for a call that will see you up sticks and leave us without a word.'

Bliss could tell Chandler was serious. He frowned and shook his head. 'Pen, do you really think that little of me? You honestly believe I could walk away from here without saying goodbye? To you, of all people.'

Wearily, Chandler shook her head, a resigned look on her face. 'No. You wouldn't do that. I know you wouldn't. I'm sorry.'

'What if I told you I was considering retiring?'

'Are you?'

'Considering it, yes.'

'How seriously?'

'Seriously enough that I'm mentioning it now.'

'I'd say great for you. If I thought it would stick.'

'What d'you mean?'

'Only that I find it hard to imagine you without this job. It is you and you are it, Jimmy. I don't see you sitting on the side-lines while all that crime is carrying on around you out there.'

'It'll be carrying on long after I'm in my box, Pen.'

'Yeah, but you make a difference. And it makes a difference to you.'

That last statement rammed its way home, because Chandler was spot on. It made a huge difference to him. Bliss shrugged and said, 'Like I say, just a consideration at this point.'

'Will you stay here if you do?'

He smiled. 'Will it help if next time you come over I have walls covered in artwork, photos on shelves, unpacked boxes, and more than my basic furniture requirements?'

'Actually, yes. It may seem stupid to you, but it will tell me you're here for a while, if not for good.'

Bliss winked at her. 'I'll get it done. It may take a while because I have these busted ribs, but I promise you I will do it.'

'I could help,' Chandler suggested, a little too eagerly. 'I could come over at the weekend, you could tell me where you want things and I could go around doing it all for you.'

'Will that make you happy?'

Chandler hiked her shoulders. Her smile was genuine. 'I don't know about happy, but happi*er*, that's for sure.'

He puffed out his cheeks. 'Then it's a deal. Sunday.'

'I'll hold you to that.'

Bliss's phone rang. He took it out of his pocket and thumbed the receive button. It was DC Gratton. Bliss spoke for a minute or so and then ended the call. 'The CEO's personal assistant at Esotere called and asked if we could make an earlier meeting. I agreed, so drink up and let's go.'

'What's the hurry all of a sudden?'

'Not sure. Didn't ask. Gratton didn't say. What do you make of him, by the way?'

'Who, Gratton? I hardly know him. I was on holiday when he started, remember. Since I've been back we've been swept up in this case. He seems all right.'

'I wonder how Ian is getting on with the CTU.'

'DC Carmichael and the counter-terrorism unit were made for each other. He was fascinated by them and the work they do.'

'Yeah. It might not seem quite so idyllic on his fifth day of a stakeout during which absolutely nothing happens.'

Chandler laughed. 'If he obtains a posting there, will you keep Gratton?'

'He's extremely keen.'

'You say that like it's a bad thing?'

'No. But you know something, in all my time as a DI he's the only DC as far as I can remember who has stopped by to introduce himself. He didn't say that's what he was there for, but it was. I didn't even remember him; my brain was still so fuzzy from that heady cocktail of concussion and medication. But he made a point of seeking me out.'

'Again, is that such a bad thing?'

Bliss shook his head. 'No. But it's just another unusual moment in what feels like a cluster of unusual moments lately. Did you ever get the impression that things were happening all around you and you were either too blind or too dumb to see it?'

'Too blind, maybe. But never too dumb.'

'I'm feeling a little of both right now,' he admitted. 'And I don't like it one little bit.'

Chapter Fourteen

The meeting at Esotere-UK took the investigation no further. By all accounts, Jade Coleman had been a respected and valuable colleague working in the large admin department, had been considered shy and a little timid, and had formed no lasting relationships with other members of staff. She was friendly enough when involved in discussions, but attended no after work drinks, staff functions, or parties. To Bliss it felt as if Jade had left little lasting impression on those who worked alongside her.

The nuclear waste disposal site in Whittlesey was a twenty minute drive east of Peterborough, and Bliss used that time on the way back to mull over everything he knew, or had seen and heard about the place and the protests it had provoked. The campaigners who had, for many years, stood outside the entrance to the site, were now long gone. Bliss wondered about them as he exited. All those years and they gained not a single thing other than celebrity. Had they considered it a waste of time, or a triumph of the soul?

Back at HQ, Bliss gathered the team and asked for updates. They were pretty much all back in the incident room, and he was feeling edgy. The case had been his for three days now, and it felt as if little progress had been made. Unlike many of the more senior officers, Bliss understood that investigations often took time to launch themselves. The information-gathering process, and the sifting that followed, was an integral part of any operation. But it took time.

His first DS, a friendly man by the name of Barry Tudor, had insisted that the initial thrust of an investigation could be split down into three individual components and days: the first twenty-four hours the team gathered information, the next were spent sifting through that information, with the final third devoted to breaking the potential leads down into solid ones. Only then did a case take on a life of its own, the pace of it usually increasing rapidly after that point. Tudor lost his life in a car accident two days before he was due to be promoted a rank. Bliss remembered him with a great deal of affection, and had never forgotten the lesson. As edgy as he felt, he also knew that the shift in gear was closing in on them.

Jade Coleman's neighbour, Adam Baldwin, remained on the board as a suspect, but was considered by most members of the team to be low grade. As for the cyclist mentioned by Baldwin, several children and another adult living opposite the Coleman property confirmed the details laid out in his statement. None had provided better descriptions, but all were convinced that the individual was not local. Of those witnesses, only one of the children thought the rider had emerged from in or around Coleman's front path. The others had no opinion to offer. The cyclist had been noted and then dismissed from their minds. Chandler then outlined the work she and Bliss had been doing, and it was agreed that Jade's ex-employer was a dead end.

'There are still some other checks I want running alongside my own,' Bliss told them. He drew a hand down his face. 'Lucy Lancaster's alibi has to be verified, although I'm betting she was not involved. Same goes for her husband, Paul. Let's also do some sniffing into their finances; I'd hate to find out later on that one of them paid somebody to kill Jade for them. Who has been liaising with the stalker task force?'

DC Gratton, who had been sitting at one of the desks, got to his feet. 'I have, boss. DS Short tasked me to have a word. I fed them the description of the cyclist – such as it is. They are piecing it together with their own investigation to see if there is overlap, but it wasn't ringing any bells. Also, regards the meeting you wanted with them, they can't make time until tomorrow morning.'

'Okay. Thanks. Get back to them for an update before evening briefing.' Bliss surveyed the room and said, 'Whoever was looking for a boyfriend in Jade's past now needs to add a possible girlfriend into the mix.'

'That's me, boss,' Hunt said, with a wry smile. 'I'll go back over it. I've also had word from Tech-Ops that there's nothing worthwhile on Jade's mobile. How about the parents? You want me to speak to them about her personal life?'

Bliss chewed his lip thinking about that one. This was one of those times when an investigation bumped up against compassion. Given the raw grief and sense of loss Mr and Mrs Coleman would still be experiencing, the very last thing they needed was to be told that their beloved daughter had kept a significant secret from them. He hoped they were the kind of people who could digest such a revelation without thinking less of their child, but perhaps not when their minds were unbalanced in mourning. Yet, this was still a murder investigation, and Jade's sexuality may have played a part in her death.

There was another reason why Bliss stalled on his answer. He was not convinced that Hunt had the right amount of tact and diplomacy required for such a sensitive interview. He knew it was his job to ensure everyone in his team obtained those skills, but he regarded the DC as a slow learner with a mind that did not quite latch on to the need for an approach requiring both sympathy and empathy. It would come in time, but this was not the right moment to unleash him.

'Tell you what,' Bliss said finally. 'Find out for me if they are still staying locally. If they are, I'll go and see them myself. I want to ask them about their daughter's time at Esotere, and specifically if they knew why she had resigned. As for the Lucy Lancaster connection, and other related issues, I think I'll wing it. If Jade kept from them the fact that she was a lesbian, then of course they would not be aware of any current or recent love interests. However, it's possible that they were aware of a *special friend* of Jade's.'

'I'll check on their whereabouts, boss,' Hunt told him, without complaint.

Bliss nodded his gratitude. Detectives did not take kindly to being taken off an action they had been working hard on, but in this case, Hunt had obviously seen the sense in Bliss's decision and had made no objection.

'Listen up then,' he said. He indicated to the whiteboards as he spoke. 'We have four clear strands here. Neighbour. Stalker. Work. Personal life. By the time we next meet, I would like to see at least one of those erased from the board, and our focus less splintered. My guess is we'll be able to drop the neighbour. Jade's personal life is another I can see us being able to dismiss very soon. It's possible that the stalker and work strands may become a single item. So, DS Bishop, before we're done here, do you have anything more to offer?'

Bishop remained seated. Gratton had been the only one to stand in order to deliver his update. 'Boss, I would agree that Adam Baldwin is looking less and less likely. He clearly enjoyed getting an eyeful of Jade Coleman when he could, but nothing has yet been found to suggest he was ever in her home. The kids playing out in the street were asked whether they had seen anybody at all going into or coming out of Jade's property that morning, but they saw nobody. It's possible that Baldwin accessed the next door bungalow from the rear garden, but it would have been too easy for his wife or children to have spotted him as they came and went between rooms. I have to say I like the stalker theory so far, and I get the impression that's where we'll eventually find our impetus. However, I'd really like to know why Jade left her job recently.'

'As would I,' Bliss muttered. 'And why she started working there in the first place. If her parents don't know, then maybe this friend of hers does. The one mentioned by Lancaster.'

'Although, it has to be said that nothing quite fits,' Chandler observed. 'None of Jade Coleman's colleagues knew why she had quit. None of them believed her to be unhappy there, and she apparently never mentioned it to anyone. The woman she was sleeping with didn't even know, which tells us something. It seems highly unlikely that her parents would be aware if those she spent the most time with weren't.'

'Family ties,' DS Short said. As usual she was hammering a notepad to death with her pen. 'Supposedly they are the ones you go to when no one else will do. If those closest to her genuinely knew nothing, then maybe the parents are the only ones who would.'

Chandler nodded, puckering her lips. 'You make a good point, Mia. We can't know what kind of relationship Jade had with her parents, so as you rightly suggest, they may well be the most likely candidates.'

Bliss took a breath. Decent paths to follow, but none that gave him the feeling they would find answers at the end. He gave Bishop the nod to divvy up the actions once again, reminding him that if the parents were still local then he wanted to be the one who visited them. Before he had a chance to say anything to Chandler, his mobile rang. It was Sandra Bannister's number. Bliss hated the fact that she probably now had him on speed dial, but knew it was part and parcel of selling your soul.

'Is this important or can I call you back later?' he asked, having thumbed the accept button.

'And hello to you, too, Inspector. Not important, no. I was calling to ask if you were any closer to releasing a statement about Mr Baldwin.'

'Closer, but not quite there. Expect a call after our evening briefing.'

'I appreciate that.'

'There will be a formal statement, but that probably won't come until tomorrow morning.'

'Any other suspects?'

'None that I am willing to share with you, Ms Bannister.'

'I do wish you would call me Sandra. And why so hostile? I thought we had an understanding.'

'I assure you that's not hostility, Miss Bannister. That's my *get off the phone I'm busy* voice. Hopefully you'll never experience me when I'm feeling hostile.'

No sooner had he ended the call than the phone rang again. This time it was a summons from Superintendent Fletcher. Her office. Ten minutes.

'Wonder what that's all about,' Chandler said after Bliss told her.

He shrugged and rolled his eyes. 'What can I say? I'm a popular bloke.'

'Hmm. Usually for all the wrong reasons.'

'Not this time, Pen. I'm wounded and therefore a protected species.'

'I wouldn't bank on it, boss.'

'No,' Bliss agreed. 'I wouldn't, either.'

***

It was not unheard of to be asked to speak formally with the Super without first having been through DCI Edwards, but it was extremely unusual. All the way up to the third floor, Bliss asked himself what might lie behind this particular summons. His conversation with Edwards earlier in the day had gone well, so he was certain this was not about any fallout resulting from that meeting. By the time he reached the office and was nodded in by the Super's PA, Bliss had come to the conclusion that the meeting had to be about the stalker and the undercurrent surrounding the visit of Hunt and Ansari to Jade Coleman.

It was obvious from Superintendent Fletcher's preoccupied greeting that he was there for more than a catch-up chat. The two arranged themselves either side of Fletcher's desk. Bliss thought he detected a reluctance from the Super to meet his eye, and all at once a heavy feeling of dread landed in the depths of his stomach.

'How have your injuries stood up to the day so far, Inspector?' Fletcher asked him, looking up at him finally. There was a look of genuine concern and sympathy in her eyes.

'Pretty well, thank you, ma'am. I'm a little tired, but that's to be expected.'

'No further signs of concussion?'

'No. I'm alert to the symptoms.'

'Can't be easy, what with your other medical condition.'

Bliss shook his head. He had been managing his Meniere's disease for over a dozen years, and thought he had a decent grip on it.

'I'll be as right as rain in a few days,' he insisted now. 'Thank you for your concern.'

Fletcher nodded absently, then leaned forward to address him. 'Inspector, putting yourself in the shoes of both DC Hunt and DC Ansari, how would you have felt if you had been approached to essentially be grilled about your work, albeit informally?'

This was a turn in the road Bliss had not anticipated. Now he wondered if Edwards had complained about him after all.

'Ma'am,' he said, spooling the words out in his head before he spoke. 'It wasn't that I felt interviewing them was the wrong thing to do. I did, however, believe it was the wrong time to do it.'

'I'm unconcerned about your decision not to go ahead, Inspector. For now, humour me by answering the question I put to you.'

'Yes, ma'am. Well, if I had been approached the way it was intended, I would have been grateful that my bosses had elected to keep things off the books at that stage and not gone straight for a full disciplinary hearing. It would have suggested to me that they believed I had done nothing wrong, and that the matter was best handled discreetly.'

The Super breathed out through her nose. Now Bliss was convinced that Edwards had made a complaint.

But he was wrong.

'I'm very glad to hear you put it that way, Inspector,' Fletcher said. 'And I hope you retain that viewpoint when I tell you why you are here. The fact of the matter is that I have been approached by two officers from the IOPC who wish to speak with you about a number of investigations in which you were involved. As I understand it, these date as far back as your first years as a detective, and run right up to the last serious operation here in the spring. I can tell you at this stage that I have been provided with no details, and neither have I requested any. It was my feeling that if this could be handled in an informal setting, completely off the record, then I had no need to know what was being discussed, nor why. I want you to know that I regard this in the same way you just described the proposed meeting with your DCs. That is to say, you have my full confidence, and I am keen to have this dealt with here and now, after which we speak of it no more.'

Bliss was struggling to take it all in. The words were taking longer to process than usual. He reached up a hand to finger the small scar on his forehead, recognising the habit immediately and snapping his hand straight back down again.

The Independent Office for Police Conduct had replaced the old and somewhat misappropriated Independent Police Complaints Commission. Word funnelling down had it that the IOPC was little more than an old dog with a new bone, but that the changes had allowed a few things to slip through the net which gave that same old dog new and sharper teeth. In particular, when it came to past allegations of misconduct, or fresh ones concerning historical cases.

His heart clunking away so stridently he thought his boss must be able to hear it, Bliss eased himself back in the chair and formed a suitable response. 'Thank you, ma'am. For those last few supportive words, I mean. As for the rest, I have to admit to being stunned right now. I genuinely believed I had left my past behind me. And while I have never accepted that I did any wrong, other than matters of a personal nature which clearly overstepped the boundaries expected of a DI, I suppose I now have to accept that I was naïve to believe I would be allowed to get on with my job without any of that history dragging me back down.'

'Just because they want to talk to you, Inspector, does not mean they have anything to say.'

He understood exactly what Fletcher meant. Whoever these two officers were, they might simply be on a fishing expedition, with allegation and innuendo as their only bait.

'Nonetheless, it's my past which has put me in their sights. Still that same shadow intruding on my life again now.'

Fletcher spread her hands. 'If I were you, I would focus on the positives. We all know how a new broom likes to work, and unfortunately it seems as if you have been caught up by those fresh bristles. However, if they were serious about this right now they would have come with a warrant, you would now be on desk duty or worse, and we would be calling in your rep. I don't know what they want of you, Jimmy, but please don't react to any provocation. You know you can be your own worst enemy at times.'

Bliss nodded and tried to take deep breaths, looking to clear his head. He appreciated Fletcher's use of his given name, which suggested to him that she was very much on his side and seeking to both calm and support him. That knowledge was helping him regard the news with the kind of clarity he needed. The Super was right. If they had anything on him, they would not have agreed to an informal arrangement. They had travelled up from London, which meant they felt it worth their while, but even so, his focus had to remain positive. It would do him no good to dwell upon the possible ramifications.

This day had been coming. Bliss accepted that now. He had been foolish to assume otherwise. He said, 'Thank you, ma'am. I am grateful to you.'

Fletcher tapped both hands on her desk. 'I will inform DS Bishop and DS Chandler that you are busy and that you are not to be disturbed until you report back to them yourself. Before you do that, you come and find me again. Whatever I am doing, no matter how long you may have to wait, you do so. You talk to nobody expect me after you are done. Do I make myself clear, Inspector Bliss?'

'Yes, ma'am. What about DCI Edwards?'

'She is out of the office for the rest of the day. Let's see how your meeting goes, then I'll decide what information to pass on.'

'Thank you, ma'am.'

'Good. As for your visitors from the IOPC, I've put them in my conference room. Now, go wipe the floor with them.'

Chapter Fifteen

Bliss did not recognise either of the two men who introduced themselves as DCI Batty and DS Lee. As far as he could recall, he had not heard of them, either. Their handshakes were perfunctory, and both men regarded him with what felt like openly hostile looks. Batty was a large man – a Devonian if his accent was anything to go by – with the same kind of physical stamp as Bishop. With his suit jacket fully buttoned, he looked like an over-ripe fruit about to burst free of its skin. The number two buzz-cut made his huge round head appear larger still, and Bliss's attention was drawn to the man's huge ears with long lobes.

As for DS Lee, he wore what Bliss assumed to be a permanent sneer, and his high-pitched Liverpudlian accent drilled through the room when the man gave his rank and name. He was half the size of his colleague, but his eyes looked cold and combative from the off.

'You had off-the-record interviews with two members of your team recently,' Batty said after they had made themselves comfortable at the conference room table in the centre of the room. Bliss had spent some time there earlier in the year, but with a very different group of people. 'How did they go?'

'They didn't take place.' Bliss wondered where that information had leaked from, but he understood where this was headed and rode with it. 'What about them, anyway?'

'Nothing much. Just that my colleague and I were wondering whether you were the kind of copper who could dish it out but not take it. To be honest with you, Bliss, both of us bet against you.'

'I don't have a clue what you're talking about.'

'What I'm saying is that we would like an informal chat with you about one or two things, in much the same way as you were supposed to have had with your DCs Hunt and Ansari. Nothing official, you understand. No rep sitting there blocking every avenue we decide to follow. Just the three of us having a natter about old times.'

Bliss nodded. 'I'm game. Up to a point.'

'And what point would that be?'

'I'll let you know when we get there.'

Batty stuck a tongue in his cheek for a few seconds before continuing. 'Fine. Good. As I am sure you are aware, the IOPC has a new policy which sets aside resources to look into certain cases, certain officers, certain incidents, or a combination of any or all of those things. We spun the wheel and your name popped up.'

'Lucky old me. Do I win a prize?'

'Yes, you do win a prize. This meeting. With us.'

'Like I said, lucky me. By the way, does he speak, other than providing his rank and name?' Bliss glanced across at Lee, who had stared almost unblinkingly at Bliss since they had all sat down.

'He does,' Batty said. 'And he will. If he feels the need.'

Bliss shrugged, saying nothing further. Detective Sergeant Lee's role of attack dog had been established.

'Okay. So, what we would like to do, Bliss, is go through some matters of... interest to us. At this stage, as you can plainly see and as I have already mentioned, this is entirely voluntary on your part and this chat is also unofficial. We would appreciate your co-operation. Before we start, would you mind if I recorded this meeting?'

Batty was already removing his phone from the breast pocket of his suit jacket.

'Yes,' Bliss said.

'Yes what?'

'Yes, I do mind you recording this meeting.'

Lee scowled and said, 'Oh, come on, Bliss. We just want to make sure we have an accurate account for transcribing if necessary.'

Bliss turned his attention momentarily back to the man who had finally spoken up. 'For the terminally hard of understanding in this room, let me point out the problem with your request. You cannot have an off-the-record discussion if there is actually a record made of that discussion. Even you should be able to work that out for yourself. And second, it's *Inspector* Bliss when you address me.'

'But not necessarily when I do,' Batty said, smiling at Bliss and shooting a look at his colleague. The DCI had tiny teeth, Bliss noticed. Yet still they filled his mouth when he smiled. 'I take your point about the recording, so I won't press the issue. Let's get back to me asking most of the questions. Starting with the very exciting and newsworthy op you had here in the spring, which looked for a while as if it could have been terrorists at work, and which eventually turned out to be something quite different. That ring a bell... Bliss?'

'Of course.'

'Our interest today lies with one particular aspect of that investigation. Namely, the point at which you suddenly disappeared down to Essex to join a joint task force raid on a farmhouse. A failed raid as it turned out.'

'What about it?'

Batty leaned forward, clasping his hands together. Bliss noticed the DCI did not refer to notes. 'Two things. First, what led you to attend that raid? Second, where did your sudden interest in it spring from?'

Bliss had known from the outset that one day he might be called upon to answer that very question. The truth would not do. Only a good lie.

'I'm sure the case files mention that I consulted with my old colleagues down at the NCA. My Major Crimes team were looking for a drug connection to our victim. Not finding one locally, I put some feelers out.'

'And so, one of your old National Crime Agency colleagues told you about an ongoing joint task force operation they were involved with and you shot down to Essex off your own bat, not mentioning the lead to your team or your superiors. Is that an accurate description of events, Bliss?'

'It wasn't quite like that, no. I was given two names. One was a villain by the name of Darren Bird, and the other an Essex DI. Nobody mentioned the task force at that time. When I called him to discuss our op, DI Pursey extended an invitation to join him and his team that night, and I accepted. I think that point is worth repeating: I was invited by the DI, I did not initiate that invitation. When I drove down there, I did so alone because it was in my own time, on my own initiative, and therefore not wasting anyone else's case time if the potential lead proved to be unconnected.'

Batty nodded as if he knew better. 'Interesting. Your old colleague at the NCA made no mention of either the task force nor the raid planned for that very night – and how convenient that was, by the way. So it clearly could not have been Sergeant Hanna Jez who provided you with that information. Otherwise she would surely have mentioned both of those critical issues to you, bearing in mind that she was involved in setting it up. And for its failure, as it turned out.'

'Is there a question in there somewhere?'

'No. Just a few observations. We're talking here, right? Chewing the fat. You want questions, I'm happy to oblige. Which of your old NCA colleagues provided you with that information?'

'I wouldn't want them to get into any trouble for talking to me, even though we're all supposed to be on the same side. Well, some of us are.'

'So you're refusing to give me the name?'

Bliss cleared his throat before responding. He knew he was stumbling into dangerous territory here but believed he could clear a way through for himself… and those who had assisted him.

'I am. This is an informal chat, after all. Informally, I'm telling you to move on.'

As if prepared for the erection of this protective wall, Batty immediately sought to overcome it. 'Very well. When the smoke had cleared following the failed raid, investigating officers found it very interesting that not only did your old mate Hanna Jez screw her own task force by tipping off their main target, but that this all happened while you, her old boss DI Bliss, was right there alongside her. What do you have to say about that?'

'Not much. Hanna's family were threatened, she felt she had no choice but to comply. She did the wrong thing, but for the right reasons. I felt more sorry for her than angry with her.'

'So sorry for her that you spoke up for Jez at her subsequent disciplinary hearing.'

'That's correct.'

'And what if I told you that we have since found substantial sums of money paid into an offshore bank account in Jez's name, and that we can tie those payments to Darren Bird, the very gangster she claims was threatening her family?'

'I would have to question the veracity of this chat due to severe doubts about your integrity, DCI Batty. I would say you were baiting me with a lie. I wouldn't have believed that of Hanna even if I had not looked into her eyes when she recounted her story to me.'

'Perhaps you're really not such a good judge of character as you seem to think you are, Bliss,' Batty said, recovering well from the pushback. 'We'll circle back to that. How about we move on to the Thompson case. Now that was something, eh? Rapist of young girls, killer of old women. You must have been thrilled when the mother topped herself in prison?'

'I wasn't exactly unhappy.' Bliss kept his tone even. He had an idea in which direction this would go. Two areas of weakness, both of which these men were bound to exploit.

'No, indeed. I hear Marjory Thompson was a complete bitch. As for the son, I guess we'll never know what drove him. Malcolm Thompson is no longer around for us to question.'

'Ultimately that was down to his actions and some bad luck.'

'That's pretty much what it said in the report. Shame he's not here to verify that version of events. Your partner did, though. DS

Chandler. The same DS Chandler whom Malcolm Thompson abducted and was going to both rape and kill, apparently having been egged on by mummy dearest. What a sick couple of freaks they were. Still, how fortunate it was that you intervened and neither of you had to go through the inconvenience of a trial afterwards.'

Bliss batted it away. 'As enjoyable as this trip down memory lane is, I'm not really hearing a question again.'

'You're right. I'm a bit of a rambler, Bliss. Sorry about that. So, tell me, Inspector, why is it that you and DS Chandler were the only police officers at the scene on the edge of that cliffside that morning?'

'Because I chose not to call for help.'

'Because you chose not to call for help. And why was that?'

'I was instructed by Malcolm Thompson not to bring back-up. But in all honesty, it was also a question of too many cooks. I felt I would have a better chance on my own.'

'And how did that work out?'

Bliss smiled. 'DS Chandler is alive and well. I'd say it turned out great.'

'Not for everybody,' Lee shot back.

'I'll cry me a river someday.'

'Judge, jury and executioner, Bliss,' Batty said, frowning. 'Is that the way you prefer to handle things?'

Lee was busy writing notes. Bliss pointed and nodded toward the ring-bound notebook. 'You forgot tinker and tailor, among others. Can we move on? I've told you what happened.'

'And DS Chandler will presumably back up your version of events. Hark at me, what am I saying? Of course she will. You two are close, so I hear. Extremely so. She was the abductee, you her saviour, so I'm guessing she doesn't really care how it actually went down. I expect DS Chandler is very grateful to you, Bliss. How does she express her gratitude, I wonder? How often?'

If Batty was looking to provoke a rise, Bliss was not about to give it to him. If he reacted, they would know Penny was a weak point for him. He did not want her dragged into whatever this was. Even so, it took every ounce of willpower he possessed not to hurl himself across the table to throttle the man. Bliss settled himself before responding, cooling the hot blood in his veins.

'DS Chandler was in a state of complete shock both at the time and in the immediate aftermath. But yes, she saw everything that happened that morning. It's all in her statement.'

'It is indeed. And you found out where Thompson was holding Chandler how, exactly?'

Despite himself, Bliss admired the DCI's swift change of tack. He was ready for it, though. 'I had Marjory Thompson's phone. He sent a text to it.'

'Ah, yes. The phone. Which really ought not to have been in your possession, but we'll revisit that another time. See, there's a very interesting snippet in your interview with the mother. Oddly enough, yet again you were the only detective in with her at the time. That appears to be a common theme. At one point she tells you to stop the tape and video recording, after which she might give you something. Shortly afterwards, you call an end to the interview. Tell me, Bliss, what did Marjory Thompson say to you before you left that interview room?'

'I can't recall.'

'Fair enough. I expected that response. We'll come back to that operation at some point, I'm sure. So, I would prefer to remain in Peterborough for now in terms of looking at your previous cases, Bliss, but to be fair I think they deserve a meeting all of their own. The autumn 2005 one in particular. But let me just touch on the one which preceded that. The one for which you were suspended.'

'On full pay, with no loss of rank. It was gardening leave.'

'There is no such official term, Bliss. You know that. It's listed on your record as suspension.'

'While I was being cleared. I was not under investigation myself, nor were there any disciplinary allegations to answer.'

'That was how it turned out, yes. But no matter what the official record states, you were being investigated. We all know that, so let's be adult about it. This was a most unsavoury series of events. A young boy originally believed to have been abducted, a number of racially-motivated arson attacks, discovering that the young lad had actually been co-opted by a wealthy right-winger to set the fires and was then murdered by the man. And somehow the boy's grieving father finds out who this wealthy man is before the police can arrest him, at which point the father hunts the man down and kills him. Some might see that as true justice, Bliss. Others might consider it corruption if that poor father was fed crucial information by a police detective. An investigator such as myself or DS Lee would definitely see it as their job to take a long, hard look at that one.'

Bliss nodded. 'Which you are perfectly entitled to do. Examine the records, speak to colleagues and witnesses. It was all investigated at the time. We have nothing to hide.'

'Maybe. But do you, Bliss? Personally?'

'I was questioned, accused of passing on information. I was eventually cleared. I suggest you move on. There's nothing there for you.'

'Interesting choice of words. Nothing there for us. Implies there may be something elsewhere.'

'That is your inference, DCI Batty. It was not my implication.'

The DCI stretched out. His huge frame became enormous. Bliss wondered if the intent of the movement was to intimidate, but he had an idea Batty would know better. That even if it had worked in the past, it was not going to work on this particular day with this specific target.

'Is that it?' Bliss asked. 'Have I answered all of your questions?' He was aware that they were not finished with him. They had mentioned a number of items they intended coming back to. And they had yet to even touch on his past back in London. Even so, Bliss thought it was worth the nudge. He sensed they were only warming up.

'Not by a long way,' Lee scoffed. 'Like the gaffer says, you screwing over your own people back in 2005 needs its own meeting. That's without your Met cases to consider.'

Grinning, Bliss leaned forward slightly and met Lee's narrow gaze. 'The word irony means nothing to you, does it? I mean, you sit there and talk about me screwing over my own, when that's what you two do for a living every day.'

'Look, you!' Lee snapped, baring his teeth and raising a curled finger. 'I don't have to sit here and take that shite from the likes of you. The job we do is–'

'Take it easy, Sergeant,' Batty said, holding out an arm to prevent Lee from taking matters into his own hands. 'No need to rise to such obvious bait. I'm sure the inspector here intended no offence.'

'Oh, believe me, you have that completely wrong,' Bliss said, releasing the pressure just a little. 'It was absolutely my intention to offend you pair of tossers.'

'Really? And to include a DCI in that statement, as well. I could have you for insubordination, Bliss.'

'Yes. You could. If only it weren't for that pesky informality and off-the-record agreement we made at the beginning.'

There was a subtle shift in Batty. Bliss sensed it immediately. A hardening of the eyes, loose skin becoming taut across the cheekbones. Batty had so far played along with a semi-jocular approach oozing sarcasm at every juncture, but the man now seemed angered by the exchange. *I do hope so*, Bliss thought. *You need yanking out of your comfort zone.*

'Please understand me when I tell you we are at the preliminary stage of our investigations,' Batty said. He had turned sullen, and Bliss felt pleased with himself. Now he felt as if he might actually learn something valuable. 'We will be speaking with you again, Bliss, that, you can bank on. And when we do, don't expect this same comfortable arrangement.'

'That's exactly what I will expect if you want to keep it informal.' Bliss kept his focus on Batty now. 'In fact, I will demand it. And, by the way, if you're going to try to sneak in a little rat to feed you snippets of information, use someone with a little more awareness than Gerry Quinn.'

'I don't know what you mean,' Batty claimed, shifting in his chair.

Bliss knew better. 'I wondered why he'd shown up the other day like a bad smell. It seemed odd and out of place. Now you're here. It doesn't take a genius to work it out. I reckon even DC Lee here could if he tried really hard.'

He caught the sidelong glances the IOPC pair threw at each other. Bliss laughed. 'Oh, I get it now. You sent him ahead to sniff around, find out what he could about me, but you didn't actually ask him to seek me out. Well, he did. And he was bloody obvious about it, too. But thanks. Because, frankly, if you're having to resort to using pond scum like Quim, then the IOPC must be really scraping the bottom of the barrel. In fact, that's probably why you two have jobs at all.'

Batty coloured up. He leaned further across the table and said, 'We will be meeting again, Inspector Bliss. And like I say, you won't get such an easy ride next time.'

Bliss pursed his lips. 'When you have enough on me to make it any other way, then you get to set out the ground rules. Actually, not even then, because it's the system you'll be following, not your own initiative. Because that takes real police work from real police officers. Until then, until you're ready to take me down, we do things my way. In my time.'

'Don't push me, Bliss. You would be best advised not to try taking me on.'

'And you would be best advised to make sure you come fully loaded when you do come for me.'

Batty rose from his chair. The movement was slow and filled with thoughtful menace. 'You'd better believe I will, Bliss. The more I learn about you the less I like.'

'Well, I'm all broken up about that.'

'You'd better be prepared to answer my questions more fully next time. About anything and everything. What we've touched on today, your actions in tearing this local service apart all those years ago, some early dubious cases concerning missing goods and money, raids being aborted or failing. It's all there waiting to be picked apart. And then, of course, there's what you did to your own wife.'

This was the attack Bliss had been waiting for all along. He stood. No threat in his stance. He simply glowered at the DCI. 'Do not waste your breath,' he hissed. 'If I can fit you into my busy schedule, DCI Batty, then you and I will talk again. But I'm warning you now, you so much as mention my wife and I will walk away, and we'll be done.'

'You're what?' Batty snarled. 'You're warning me? Me?'

'Yes. Just of that, Chief Inspector. Just of my walking away from any meeting at which my wife is mentioned. That's my only warning. For now.'

Batty's jaw had become so rigid that Bliss thought it might snap in two as his teeth ground their way through it. 'You just made a big mistake, Bliss,' he said in a harsh whisper. 'One you will never survive.'

Bliss nodded and started to walk away from the table. He stopped and pointed a finger at the man. 'So did you. You gave away your end game. Now I know what you're really after. What a piss-poor copper you must have been.'

Whatever response either Batty or Lee had was lost on Bliss as he walked out of the room with more alacrity than he had felt in days.

Chapter Sixteen

Bliss took a few minutes to gather his thoughts. His favourite spot inside the station was on the staircase landing, staring out of the window that overlooked the car park, Thorpe Wood nature reserve, and the parkway traffic hurtling by up on the A47. As he stood with his nose pressed to the glass, he drew deep breaths and thought back over the meeting.

Overall, Bliss thought he had gained more than he had given up. The IOPC pair were both obvious and insufferable. Batty's attitude seemed more calculated, whereas Lee came across as a naturally unbearable character. Bliss agreed that the police needed policing, but it was generally the manner of the officers investigating their own that most fellow cops objected to. Too often they appeared overjoyed at the prospect of taking down a colleague.

His own off-the-books investigation into murder and corruption inside the Peterborough force thirteen years earlier had been a painful wrench, something he had endured in order to seek justice for his long-dead victim. There had also been a genuine need to rid the job of a disease which had infected its heart to the core. Bliss had taken no pleasure in bringing down his fellow police officers and detectives, but he instinctively knew that both Batty and Lee would revel in his own downfall should that time arise. He did not understand the desire that drove them, nor the satisfaction they derived from their job.

Feeling his temperature rise once more, Bliss winced as the damaged ribs reminded him they were there and not doing too well. He placed a hand over them, feeling a little heat beneath the skin. His mind flashed back to the night of the incident. The figure he had chased had been in his back garden. At the time, Bliss's only thought was that the man had been looking to break into the house. Now he asked himself if there might have been an entirely different reason for his presence. Was the timing of the IOPC visit purely coincidental? What if the intruder had been working for them, and had intended planting listening devices?

He also knew there was a chance it ran deeper. Back in the spring, Bliss had been convinced that another unwelcome visitor in the early hours of the morning had been working for MI6. His mind now fashioned a possibility in which the newly formed IOPC had been investigating him all along. The thought caused him to catch his breath, which in turn kicked off the nagging ribs one more time. It was a stone he had to kick over, but now was neither the time nor place.

Fletcher was free and ready for him when he recovered his equanimity. Bliss had half expected the Chief Super to be in attendance as well this time, but the office held just the two of them as it had earlier.

'Tell me as much or as little as you like,' she instructed him. 'Just give me enough to work with.'

Bliss found himself relating everything to Fletcher. He had not intended to, but there was something about the Super that earned his trust. As he spoke, she made notes on her laptop; mini bursts of keys clacking, accompanied by almost imperceptible nods. Every so often she would punctuate the moment with a firm shake of her head, to tut at what she was hearing, or nod with vague enthusiasm.

'You did well,' Fletcher insisted when he was through. 'You got to the bottom of why they were really here. The rest is just window dressing for the main display.'

'Some pretty powerful window dressing when inspected with a jaundiced eye,' he pointed out.

'True. But equally, I'm positive you can be creative enough to ensure that all remains under control. However, they could not have chosen a more powerful weapon to use against you, Jimmy.'

Since the spectre had been raised by Batty, Bliss had struggled to contain thoughts about his wife. Over the years it had become increasingly more difficult for him to conjure up Hazel's image in his mind when thinking about her, but the second he placed her in context with an event, or a moment captured in memory, that beautiful face swam back towards him out of the gloom and hung just in front of him. Tantalisingly out of reach, but so very welcome.

'I agree. Using my wife's murder against me is purely a ploy. It's also the most obvious weapon they could have chosen, ma'am.'

'True. But you overlook its effectiveness at your peril.'

'I'll be fine, ma'am. They can't hurt me on that.'

'That's not true, and you know it. They may not win, Inspector, but they will most certainly cause you great harm. Perhaps even irreparable damage.'

'With respect, ma'am, it's my battle to wage, and I can take care of myself.'

'Inspector,' the Super said, those three syllables carrying the full weight of her authority. 'I've made my mind up as to how this will go from this point on. You will disagree with me; you will not like what I have to say. Nonetheless, you will argue with me over nothing. Not a thing, mind. This is the moment I step in to wrestle control away from you, to take up that burden on your behalf.'

'Ma'am?' Bliss said, uncertainly.

'Today, Inspector Bliss, you will call an early evening briefing, after which you will return home. Tomorrow morning you will call in sick. The ribs ought to be enough, but a mention of the concussion will do the trick if not. You will insist on seeing the Thorpe Wood Occupational Health doctor, in addition to your own GP, and between them they will sign you off work for ten days. A minimum of a further five will be available to you should you need them. Later today, I will be contacting OH psychological therapy and making an appointment for you to speak with somebody, starting sometime early next week. During your twice weekly therapy sessions feel free to discuss the murder of your wife and any other relevant aspects of your career that might fit in with anything the IOPC may want to discuss with you now or in the future.'

Bliss felt his initial frown become a tight V-shaped wedge of anger. It felt like he was being punished, and he could not imagine why. As if reading his mind, Fletcher said to him, 'Inspector, hear me out before you respond. The ten days R&R have a dual purpose. First, it sees you at home resting and starting to recover from your injuries. Second, it keeps you out of the firing line. If you are absent, unfit for work, the IOPC cannot interview you again unless they do so whilst you are under arrest. As for the psych therapy, if you are in sessions with a therapist then nobody can compel you to talk about anything currently being discussed within those private sessions. Not while they are ongoing, at least. Now, I am sure the IOPC will find a legal way to get around that little ploy, but it will buy you some time.'

'Time for what?' Bliss asked, perplexed.

Fletcher leaned forward and said softly, 'To fully prepare yourself. Those two idiots from the IOPC just declared open warfare on you. They were not fully prepared for it, they were not armed sufficiently for it, and they certainly were not ready for you striking back in the way you did. But they will return, Inspector. And they will be coming hard next time.'

'How can you know that, ma'am?'

'Because I am detached, and you are emotional. You would see it for yourself if you were not the subject of the investigation. Inspector, you know they are looking hard at you in connection with your wife's murder. Ask yourself why? Why now? You were previously investigated and cleared. So what has changed? What do the IOPC have that their predecessors did not? I can't answer those questions for you, but it's obvious to me that their interest has been renewed with purpose and vigour. They came here to rattle you, but they also came to fire the first salvo. It will not be their last.'

Bliss nodded, forcing a half-hearted smile. 'I genuinely appreciate everything you've said, ma'am. You're right, of course. Yet it changes very little in terms of how I need to proceed. The murder of Jade Coleman has to come before my own concerns. I was allocated that case by DCI Edwards, and I don't intend to let go of it until we have someone banged up for it.'

Shaking her head and matching his weak grin, Fletcher sat back in her chair and took a long breath before responding. 'Did you even hear me when I told you there were to be no arguments, Inspector? Look, your sickness absence and your therapy provide you with time to build your defences. And they will need to be tall and wide, from what I can gather. As much to prevent you from getting to your attackers as the other way around.'

'I understand what you're saying. But what good is time if I'm sitting on my backside at home worrying about when the knock might come at my door? Also, what will it look like if I'm pulled off the investigation at this stage?'

'But you're not being removed from the op, Bliss. You are unfit to work due to injuries sustained in a road collision – there's a significant difference. As for the time you have been given to recuperate, just because you are not at work does not mean you have to stop working. I think you know what I mean by that. I can't tell you what to do, Bliss. That's entirely up to you. But if it were me, I might just spend that time trying to find out what they have, where it came from, why it has come now, and then work out how you might best defend yourself when they come at you next time.'

Bliss regarded the Super with a new-found appreciation. From day one she had been nothing but fair with him, and now Fletcher was actively encouraging him to take matters into his own hands. If he was buried beneath the weight of investigating Jade Coleman's murder, he would have found little time for himself. Now his own boss had given him a way out. She was telling him to take this opportunity to put to rest once and for all the rumours that had been dogging him for the past seventeen years.

'I don't know what to say,' Bliss muttered, hanging his head. He used his left thumb to worry the small scar on his forehead. 'Other than thank you, of course. Though that seems so inadequate.'

'Jimmy, the only thanks I need is you emerging from this and continuing to lead my Major Crimes team in the way you have been doing. Besides, what are you even thanking me for? All I have done here today is instruct you to take time off to heal your physical wounds, and to speak to somebody about the emotional ones.'

'Well then, I thank you for not asking me.'

'Not asking you what?'

'If I murdered my wife.'

Fletcher's gaze narrowed, her perfectly sculpted eyebrows converging. 'Why on earth would I?'

Bliss blinked and nodded. 'I'm sorry, but I'm not used to that level of trust, ma'am.'

'Inspector, I'm not about to insist that you are always the easiest person to get along with. Your cursory acceptance of rank is an irritant, and your mistaken belief that orders are merely suggestions can increase the blood pressure on occasion. That said, I understand why you are the way you are. I understand that it comes not from a position of self-advancement, but for the benefit of your victim or victims at any given time.

'As a high-ranking officer I find your approach to leadership from above both archaic and frustrating at times, yet the leadership qualities you demonstrate with your own team are commendable. You put your loyalty to the victims and your team above all else, and the larger part of me admires you for that. I am therefore able to accept the pros and ignore the cons which come as part of the overall package – up to a point. You're a bloody good detective, Jimmy. And beneath the thick veneer and rough edges there is also a good man. I am not so high and mighty that I cannot appreciate both.'

Bliss was almost loss for words, but he felt the need to voice his appreciation. 'For what it's worth, ma'am, I don't think I've ever had as much respect for someone of your rank as I do for you. I am extremely grateful to you. And I will take advantage of what you have suggested here today. I am still concerned about the murder case, however.'

'Naturally. But you have an excellent team, Inspector. Use them. However you wish. But use them.'

Looking into her even stare, Bliss thought he knew what Fletcher was telling him. That her words were not related only to the Jade Coleman murder, but also to his own personal pursuits in the days to come. He also knew that he could not let her down. The faith the Super had shown in him had to be repaid in full.

***

The Argo Lounge on Bridge Street was a popular bar and eatery in a busy part of Peterborough. Less than a century ago, the broad pedestrianised street was not only the main thoroughfare into the centre of the city, it was also home to many slums which huddled together in the vast shadow of the Anglo-Saxon cathedral. Bridge Street had been split into two distinct sections, prefixed with the words 'Broad' and 'Narrow'. The high-density housing had been built for labourers in yards behind the shops, but by the time it was demolished in the 1930s it had fallen into severe neglect. Now the shops and cafes that stood in its place ensured that visitors and local inhabitants alike were drawn to the beating heart of north Cambridgeshire. Many sat at tables outside, breathing in the hot evening air whilst doing their level best to appear cool.

Bliss had invited his closest and most senior colleagues for a drink after work, which was why he, Chandler, Bishop and Short were gathered at a table in the basement with drinks in front of them, and several plates of tapas occupying its centre. They were deep into their second round of drinks, and the conversation was lively.

The early evening briefing had taken the investigation no further. The lag was unfortunate, but it was not for want of trying. The effort from everybody involved had been overwhelming, but sometimes an operation took on a pace all of its own and required only one minor breakthrough in order to release the brakes. Bliss had a sense that this was just such a case.

Two of the competing strands were now tied off. The neighbour, Baldwin, had been dismissed as a suspect and Bliss had texted Sandra Bannister ahead of the official media release, providing her with the opportunity to make that information on the *Peterborough Telegraph* website available before anyone else had it. The alibis for both Lucy and Paul Lancaster had been verified, the husband's driver confirming Lucy's version of events. The peek into their finances was on-going, but Bliss thought it likely that the couple would be cleared entirely within the next day or so.

Security footage concerning the cyclist in the hoodie was still in the process of being gathered and analysed. If the cyclist had ridden in and back out as far as Paston, then CCTV cameras close to the Paston Ridings and Topmoor Way junction would be the only feeds available. There was a road camera ahead of the roundabout just as the path gave way to the pavement. DC Hunt had also suggested the local primary school might have an external camera pointing in the right direction, although its view was likely to be obscured by trees. Hunt had taken it upon himself to stay with that lead.

This now meant the focus of debate that evening could be narrowed down to Jade's parents, and the possibility of her having had a closer friend, whose identity was currently unknown to them, at the time of her murder.

'My money is on the parents being a dead end,' Bishop said. 'It feels at the moment like a game of Patience. You know how you can turn the cards for ages and seem to be getting nowhere, then all of a sudden you lay down one high card which leads to a whole bunch of other cards being freed up. My gut still says Jade was killed by her stalker, but we're waiting for that one card to allow us to break the dam and flood through.'

Bliss thought about that for a moment, before making a phone call. He had to put a finger in one ear so as to hear in the busy bar.

When she answered, Lucy Lancaster sounded wary. 'I'm contacting you with good news,' he said, hoping to initially allay any anxiety she might be feeling. 'Your alibis check out. I apologise for some of the questioning, but it was necessary to rule you both out. I hope you understand.'

'I do,' Lancaster said. Her voice on the phone betrayed a weakness she had not displayed in person. Bliss guessed she had not enjoyed the best of days. 'I expect you can't tell me any details, but have you made any progress, Inspector?'

'You're right. I can't tell you. Details or otherwise. But I would like to ask you a question. Actually, to repeat one. I was wondering whether you had given any more thought to Jade's friend. The one who you knew to be an anti-nuclear campaigner. I don't suppose you remembered any more about her, did you?'

Bliss knew he was taking a chance. Lancaster was by no means a slow-witted woman. She would realise that this unnamed friend might also be considered a suspect, and Bliss had to trust her not to reveal the name to anyone else if she knew it. He felt it was worth a shot. After all, the woman wanted Jade's killer nailed, so was unlikely to do anything which might harm the police investigation.

'I'm sorry, Inspector. I've given it a great deal of thought, but I really don't know any more than what I have already told you.'

'How about the conversation you had which revealed the friend to be associated with CAWED. Can you recall how that information emerged?'

There was a brief pause before the hesitant response came. 'I'm really not sure, Inspector Bliss. I think perhaps we were discussing the subject of nuclear disarmament, CND, that sort of thing. Jade was such a gentle soul, but this was a topic which fuelled her passions. Perhaps a news item sparked it, but I'm only guessing. Jade told me she wished she could be as involved in the same sort of activism as her friend.'

'And Jade never mentioned the name? You never asked?'

'No. It was an aside, not an in-depth debate. At least, not that I recall. I distinctly remember Jade mentioning the friend was a woman. Well, to be precise, she used the term her, but for the life of me I cannot remember in what context.'

Bliss sucked on his teeth. He felt they were close, but as Bishop had suggested, still that one crucial card short.

After thanking Lancaster for the information and asking her to call him if anything occurred, Bliss turned back to his team, trying – and failing – not to appear despondent. He drained his pint glass and went upstairs to fetch another round. The Argo Lounge clientele were mostly young and loud, the bar constantly busy, and it took Bliss the better part of ten minutes before he was able to carry a tray laden with full glasses back down into the basement. In his absence the conversation had switched to Jade and her sexuality.

'Given there is currently no intelligence in relation to Jade having a current or recent girlfriend,' Bliss said, 'what does everyone think about my approaching her parents directly when I meet with them later on?'

Mr and Mrs Coleman had remained in the area but were not available until 8pm later that evening. When a female is murdered it is a standard strategy to look closely at the husband or boyfriend. Bliss saw no reason to deviate from that simply because in this case the partner was a female.

'It's a tough call,' Chandler said, sympathising with his dilemma. 'Clearly we have to pursue that line of enquiry. On the other hand, dropping that bombshell into their laps at a time of such emotional turmoil could be devastating.'

'I agree with Penny,' Short said. She sipped from her glass of Southern Comfort and lemonade, in no hurry tonight to rush home to her twins. 'Earlier you suggested you might just play it by ear.'

Bliss nodded. 'I know. I just felt I ought to have a more definite plan than that. It feels a bit like sitting on the fence.'

'You could just feel them out, boss,' Bishop suggested. 'Drop a few hints into the conversation. If they know anything, they'll pick up on it. After all, you only have the word of Lucy Lancaster that Jade was in the closet. Jade may have shared the information with her parents but kept it from Lancaster. If they don't take the bait, then you could opt to leave it there.'

'True enough. It would be expected of me to ask about boyfriends, which would provide them with the opportunity of opening up.'

'I can go with you if you want,' Chandler told him. Her own drink had already disappeared without trace. Bliss thought that his friend's drinking had kicked up a notch or two in recent months, and he made a mental note to keep an eye on that. He shook his head in response to her offer.

'No, you get off home when we're done here. Which we will be as soon as I've told you all why I invited you here this evening.'

'I thought we were here to thrash out the case,' Short said.

Bliss shook his head. 'Not entirely, no.'

'You mean you have an ulterior motive?' Bishop said.

Bliss swallowed thickly and took a deep breath. 'I do. I have something to tell you.'

'Is this about why you were called away earlier, boss?'

'It is. I need to tell you what it was about. After which I also need to ask you all for your help.'

Chandler beamed one of those radiant smiles of hers at him, and said, 'You had me at "I do".'

Chapter Seventeen

It was a five minute walk from the Argo Lounge alongside the cathedral and into New Road, to the Travelodge where Tony and Joan Coleman were staying. Bliss had the receptionist alert them to his presence before he took the lift up to the second floor and walked down the corridor to their room. It would give the couple a few minutes to prepare themselves and perhaps tidy the small space as some people prefer to do when receiving guests.

When you've seen one budget hotel room you've seen them all. This was one of the city's more recent hotels, so at first glance it still looked clean and fresh, and with no smoking anywhere on the premises it also smelled better than some Bliss had stayed in over the years. After the introductions, Mr Coleman sat down on the edge of the bed, allowing his wife and their visitor to sit at the narrow wooden desk-cum-dressing table. Jade had clearly taken her looks and trim build from her mother, who was tall and lithe still, upright as she sat in her chair looking at him with both sadness and expectation glinting in her eyes. Tony Coleman was above average height, but he carried a portly belly around with him, his clothes seemingly either too baggy or too tight as befits a man who probably fell between sizes in just about everything.

'Is your Family Liaison Officer nearby?' Bliss asked. It was customary for newly bereaved families to have an officer with specialist training at hand in order to alleviate the more formal and procedural activities associated with a murder or serious crime.

Tony Coleman nodded. 'She's in a room just along the corridor, Inspector. She's been extremely kind and helpful.'

Bliss began by outlining his role in Major Crimes, with a brief description of the efforts the team had put in so far. He felt he owed it to the couple to be as honest as he could be, so he also informed them that he would be taking more of a back seat in the coming days, due to injuries sustained in his one-sided meeting with a speeding car. Seeing the couple glance at each other, and a flicker of concern pass across Joan Coleman's face, Bliss swiftly reassured them both that he would be remaining close to his team and that it was only his physical presence that would be lacking.

'Three days on, are you any closer to finding out who murdered our daughter?' Tony Coleman asked. His hands were resting palm down on the bed, fingers splayed as if he were about the leap into action at any moment. The shock was palpable in every line of his face, and the man's glazed eyes told Bliss that so much grief was yet to sink in. It was looking at faces just like this throughout his career that caused Bliss to take his cases personally. He never forgot a murder victim, but it was the expression on the faces of those they left behind that haunted him most of all.

'In all honesty,' he replied, 'that depends on the way you look at it. Whilst it is true to say that we have no good suspects or solid leads at the moment, it is also a fact that we have been able to rule out various people.'

'Like the neighbour, for instance.'

'Yes. I regard that as progress, but if I were you, I probably would not draw much comfort from that. We are at the end of day three, and in terms of an average murder investigation we are where I would expect us to be. The workload in the first seventy-two hours is immense. I won't bore you with the details, but there is so much information to gather that our extended team are working all the hours possible. Unless we're lucky and get a decent break, such as a cast-iron witness or CCTV footage, then this is how investigations tend to pan out. I think if we are going to get that genuine break this time, then it will come in the next day or two.'

'Really?' Joan Coleman's eyes beseeched him.

Nodding, Bliss said, 'It's the point at which we have the majority of information and evidence we are likely to obtain during the operation. What we glean from that will more often than not guide us first to and then along the path we need to travel.'

'And if at the end of a further two days you still can't see a way forward?'

'To be blunt, Mr and Mrs Coleman, after that it will become more difficult, simply because we will have less fresh data to work with. Difficult, but not impossible. Every murder investigation is different from the last, every murderer different from the last. We have our protocols and procedures, and we follow them to the letter, but we can never know when the penny will finally drop.'

Jade's mother sobbed for a few moments, dabbing her eyes with a balled-up tissue. 'If it ever does,' she said in a hushed voice.

Bliss hated this part of the job more than any other. He had known some colleagues who would offer platitudes at this point, even lie and insist on a positive outcome. Bliss did not believe hope was always a good thing. In his view it often destroyed people from the inside out. Hearing the truth could be painful, but not as much as broken promises and sleepless hours expecting something which was possibly never going to happen. Bliss had no desire to point out that the couple having delayed the post-mortem on religious grounds had hardly helped speed things up. Not that he expected any surprises when the result finally came in.

'I realise these past few days must feel like a lifetime to you both,' he said gently. 'But believe me when I say that nothing about this is simply routine for us. I expect the hours to drag at times like this, though I am always disappointed when they do. But I refuse to tell you we have leads where none exist, that we have prime suspects when in fact they are merely people of interest. For me, safe harbour comes only when we have the truth. And my job here tonight is to see if you can help us find our way to it.'

'Us?' Joan Coleman touched a hand to her chest as if the notion itself shocked her. 'Inspector, we enjoy a quiet existence down in Wiltshire. Jade had her own life here which we knew very little about. We spoke every few weeks with our daughter, and she would drive down to visit us a few times a year. But our Jade was a private person and shared with us only those things she was comfortable discussing.'

Bliss nodded his encouragement. 'Nonetheless, you probably know more than you realise. Things we may not be aware of. Things which might be helpful to us. There are two things in particular that I would like to ask you about, and I'm hoping they are parts of her life that Jade will have shared with either one or both of you.'

The couple exchanged glances once again. Each nodded through their misery.

'Before I get into those specifics, were either of you aware of any enemies Jade might have had? Perhaps someone who disliked her enough to do this to her?'

'Of course not,' Mr Coleman shot back instantly. 'Our daughter simply wasn't the kind of person who had enemies, Inspector.'

'Very well,' Bliss continued. 'What can you tell me about Jade's boyfriends? Past or present.'

The look that passed between the Colemans this time was telling. It was obvious to Bliss that Jade's parents knew, or at the very least suspected, more about their daughter than she had given them credit for.

'Inspector Bliss,' Tony Coleman said, moving his hands together now and interlocking the fingers in his lap. 'The last boyfriend Jade ever brought home was when she was back in secondary school. They made for the most ill-suited pair you could possibly imagine. Jade never once spoke to us about her… preferences, but I suspect you will not find a boyfriend on your list of suspects.'

Bliss was relieved. Judging by the man's tone there was a lingering pain over his daughter's decision not to confide in them, but Bliss admired the fact that they had clearly never compelled her to. Nor did they judge her sexual proclivities.

'Would you like to know anything about that aspect of your daughter's life?' he asked. There was not a great deal to share with the couple, but he thought that perhaps even a little insight might offer them some solace at this most awful of times.

Jade's mother looked up sharply. 'Was she happy, Inspector Bliss?'

He thought about Lucy Lancaster. The older woman had used a warm tone when speaking of Jade, and despite describing their relationship as purely sexual, Bliss had the feeling there was more to it, that emotion had also played a part.

'Yes,' he said. 'Jade had been seeing someone for quite a while. From her ex-colleagues – each of whom liked your daughter very much – we learned that Jade was precisely the private person you describe, yet always warm and friendly. If they suspected anything, they did not let on. I think that is a measure of the respect they had for her. As for the woman Jade was seeing, there were only kind words and evident grief expressed at her loss.'

Bliss was happy to paint this picture of Jade Coleman for her parents. It was close enough to the truth without revealing every personal decision, and if it gave them even a modicum of comfort then he was content to leave the thought with them. No further discussion on that specific subject was necessary, so Bliss moved on.

'The other thing we're hoping you can shed light on is why Jade left her job at Esotere UK.' He had already decided not to mention the stalker lead. If their daughter had spoken to either of them about it, Bliss felt sure it would have been mentioned by now. He assumed they had avoided the news in its many forms since Friday and had no clue when it came to Jade's report.

'Left her... sorry, Inspector, left her job at where, did you say?' asked Tony Coleman.

'Esotere. Jade may have used its old name, which was Whittlesey Energy Disposal.'

The man frowned as he looked across at his wife. Mrs Coleman shook her head and shrugged. When he next spoke, Jade's father did so with a large measure of bemusement.

'I have no idea what you're talking about, Inspector Bliss. As far as we knew, Jade worked for the local authority, and had done so since moving here. That she apparently left to start another job comes as a huge surprise, I have to admit. And needless to say, if we were not aware of her having worked there, neither of us can offer any reason as to why she later left.'

It was only a small thing, perhaps, especially when compared to Jade not sharing details with them about her sexuality, but Bliss had the feeling this was different. This was about how she earned a living, not the way she lived her life. Changing jobs was certainly high up on the list of topics to discuss with your parents. The fact that Jade had not done so intrigued Bliss.

'Jade always said her job was going well whenever we asked,' Joan Coleman offered, another emotional wound lining her brow. 'Her work was mostly confidential, so she couldn't reveal too much. We accepted that, of course. Now I'm wondering if I ever really knew my daughter at all.'

The woman managed to finish speaking before becoming convulsed in sobs, tears spilling freely down both cheeks. She bent almost double in the chair, the pain becoming physical and too much for her not to yield to. Her husband sprang forward off the bed, knelt by his wife's side and wrapped both arms around her. He ran his fingers through her hair as she continued to moan and weep, seeking to expel the misery from every fibre of her being.

Bliss got to his feet. 'I'm so sorry,' he said, uncomfortable now and not wishing to intrude. 'The part of this I thought would not upset you is the one that has ended up hurting most of all. I'm done with my questions. I'll see myself out. Please accept my deep condolences, and know that I will do everything in my power to find out who did this to your daughter.'

Joan Coleman's flow of grief continued unabated. Her husband looked up at Bliss and nodded. It was all either of them could manage as they wrapped themselves together in order to ward off the tragedy threatening to engulf them. Bliss hoped their combined strength was enough to shut it out, even for a few hours at a time. Because he knew from experience that just when you believed you were through the worst, the darkness became as black and as dense as it could possibly be.

Bliss felt as if he were carrying jagged shards of glass inside his chest as he set off for the taxi rank, so he stopped walking and called for one instead. He met it outside the city centre library on Broadway. The old red brick and white stone building had looked like a place of learning and quiet reflection, whereas its modern and stylistic replacement, which also housed the John Clare theatre, could have been mistaken for the main offices of a major corporation.

The ride home took ten minutes, and Bliss somehow extricated himself from the back of the low-sprung Japanese saloon before paying the driver and opening his front door.

Before settling himself into his favourite recliner, Bliss slipped out into the garden and looked hard at the area immediately in front of the sliding glass doors. He remembered that on the night of the accident he thought he had heard the sound of adhesive tape being unwound from a roll. The snicking noise was such a familiar one that he did not think he was mistaken. At the time, he was convinced that the tape was being used in preparation of breaking a window out back – it had to be either the downstairs toilet or the study, as nobody in their right mind would choose the large glass panes of the doors. Now, thinking back, Bliss wondered if the intruder had been looking to tape something to, or close to, the living room doors.

Such as a bug.

He found nothing suspicious near the glass doors, nor at either the study or toilet windows. The area was paved, so there were no footprints. There was no sign of any discarded tape, and certainly nothing resembling a listening device. He found it hard to bend forward or even squat down and, as the ribs protested, he began to think of his actions as those of a somewhat paranoid man. Yet it wasn't paranoia if they were really out to get you, and in his case they actually were. Whether that had extended to them sending in an advance team to bug him, Bliss could not answer. He only knew for certain that he would not put anything past the IOPC if they thought it might help their case.

Bliss heard his mobile ping as a text came in. It was from Sandra Bannister. In it she apologised for the delay, but informed him that she had sent him a mail which included information and articles relating to CAWED. He sent a reply, thanking her for her efforts and saying he would get back to her for clarification if any were necessary.

The mail itself was hefty, with several attachments. Bliss spent more than an hour sifting through them and arranging each in order of priority. Some he cast aside as being irrelevant or because the information covered nothing more than that which he already had access to. When he was done, he was left with around a dozen items which he thought warranted further investigation. Deciding to leave them until the following day, Bliss turned his thoughts away from the task.

Feeling somewhat melancholic and emotional after visiting with Jade Coleman's parents, he slipped his *Steve McQueen* CD into the slot and sat back with a bottle of chilled Peroni listening to Prefab Sprout at the very summit of their musical genius. The classic single 'When Love Breaks Down' was released in 1984, by which time Bliss had been a serving police officer for two years. He was living in a rundown three-storey house split into individual rooms, grandly and optimistically described as studio apartments, having to share a bathroom with two other occupants on his floor. It was difficult to know why he had ever considered them to be the good old days.

Trying to take his beer slowly, Bliss eased himself back into the recliner and sent his mind in search of something positive. He was supposed to have taken things easy, but the day had been long and busy, and he was feeling the ache of it deep inside. He had chased his own tail, getting nowhere fast. There had to be a way of preparing himself for the impending IOPC attack whilst also overseeing operation Cauldron at the same time, but both would be difficult without access to colleagues and computer systems.

Each required his full attention individually, but so far as he could tell, he had no way of avoiding being torn down the middle.

In terms of physical graft, the donkey work was pretty much over when it came to the murder case. An eye for detail and some logical thinking was now called for. Bliss thought back to his senior team meeting in the eatery and wondered if he could stay on top of things by calling for further meetings right here inside his own home. He did not think any of his colleagues would object, and their reaction to his confession back in the basement of the bar gave him much cause for optimism.

All three had been consumed with rage at the IOPC, especially when they learned of the end game. As far as they were concerned, Hazel's murder was out of bounds, having previously been investigated, and both Batty and Lee were overstepping the mark by a long way. Bliss had been touched by their show of allegiance, and now felt it might be possible for the same small group to help him deal with it.

As for the IOPC approach, Bliss did have an idea where to begin in his search for answers, although doing so required him to take a significant step back into a past he wanted no part of. Bliss contemplated his next move over two more beers before turning in for the night.

He woke up shortly before three, sensing he was not alone in the house. He spent the next ten minutes walking from room to room, switching on lights, opening cupboard doors, checking every space. There was no sign that anyone had been inside.

Returning to bed, Bliss lay on his back, hands clasped behind his head. The greyness of the ceiling swirled above him. Although he readily admitted to being haunted by various aspects of past jobs, there were no ghosts in his life. Hazel was a presence wherever he went, but she had seeped into his pores and become a part of him. The feeling of someone else being in the house had nothing to do with his ex-wife.

Bliss put the blame on an overactive imagination.

Or was it that DCI Batty and DS Lee had got beneath his skin after all?

Chapter Eighteen

Chandler rolled into HQ the following morning determined to prove something to herself. Bliss clearly believed in her, as he had asked her to take charge of operation Cauldron in his absence. Not in terms of making hard decisions – that remained the job of the DI, or DCI Edwards if Bliss could not be contacted. There were procedures to attend to, however, and he had tasked her with steering the team through them to the point where command might need to take over.

Dawn had come early, but Chandler was already wide awake by then. She took her time showering and getting dressed, applying the usual meagre amount of make-up afterwards as she sat at her bedroom dressing table, and decided this was a hair-up day. She had selected a simple skirt and short-sleeved blouse to wear; no power dressing. After spending a little more time than usual checking out her appearance in the full-length mirror, Chandler nodded at the confident woman she saw reflected back and decided she was ready. The roads were still pretty empty, and after arriving at the station, she caught herself up with the case logs and trawled through the most recent statements. As colleagues began to dribble in, she took a deep breath and prepared for her day.

First up after a shortened briefing was a meeting with two detectives from the stalker task force. It was the meeting Bliss had requested, but Chandler was filling in for him. She asked Ansari to join her, and the two were already seated together when DS Spencer and DC Brown entered the incident room. They all knew one another so Chandler got straight to the point.

'For the time being the issue of whether the report made by Jade Coleman ought to have been taken more seriously has to be put behind us. People higher up the pay scale will pass judgement on that. Our priority here and now is to analyse what we know about the murder, and to ascertain whether any of it fits in with current theories or investigations being made by the task force.'

The DS, a stout and steely-eyed Yorkshireman, was the first to speak up. 'When it comes to stalkers, we cast a wide net when we trawl. But we've been able to narrow the search down by using various parameters specific to your murder. Most stalkers are known to their victims, for one thing – about ninety per cent, in fact.'

'I had no idea the figure was so high,' Chandler interrupted, then apologised for doing so. Spencer waved aside the apology and gave a sober nod.

'These are usually ex-husbands or boyfriends, of course. Then there are the close friends who would like to be more than that. I realise we're dealing with an unknown factor here, but in this case I think it's reasonable to hypothesise that your vic did not know her attacker. It was certainly an approach we agreed upon back up in the task force. So, by removing that criteria we were able to considerably filter down the database. However, none of the remaining reports have so far included violence, and all of the stalkers within that ten per cent or so have specific targets. There are no multi-target names in our lists.'

'Which led us to broaden the search again,' DC Brown chipped in. Chandler did not know him well, but he sounded local. 'We included the dark hoodie and then a bicycle. As you can imagine, the hoodie was quite common, the bike somewhat less so. Once again, we came up short because those previously identified are single target stalkers known to their victims.'

Chandler had known from the outset that it was a long shot. 'I take it there are none known to us in the immediate vicinity of Jade Coleman's home?'

'No. We did take a look at acts of violence, specifically those where a blade was used, but once again these were men stalking their ex-girlfriends or wives. As you probably know, many of those men who appear on our list would not so long ago have been accused of harassment rather than stalking. If you offend more than once you now elevate your crime, so the list has swollen considerably in recent years.'

Including acts causing alarm or distress emerging from email or social media contact, Chandler thought. These days your average stalker didn't even have to get up out of bed to frighten women. Which was frightening in itself.

Spencer turned his attention to Ansari. 'You were one of the detectives who interviewed Coleman. What was your impression?'

'Of her? Or of how she was treated?'

Chandler gave an approving nod. She admired her colleague's thoughtful approach.

'Well, both,' Spencer said, leaning back in his chair. 'You were there. You tell us.'

The DC nodded and cleared her throat. She did not glance at her sergeant for moral support, which earned her another favourable tick in Chandler's mind. 'The problem for us was that Jade never actually saw anybody. Her report was all based on feelings. Senses. She *sensed* she was being watched, had the *feeling* that someone had been inside her home. There was no overt threat, only those niggling sensations.'

Spencer grimaced. 'Still feels like one we missed. So, DC Ansari, what overall impression did you take away of Miss Coleman herself?'

'Jade was calm and collected. She talked us through her concerns methodically, without any emotion. Her demeanour suggested concern rather than fear. Only when she mentioned the possibility of someone having entered her home did she crack. And even then, only a little. I got the feeling she was reporting it more because it felt like the right thing to do than because she felt truly unsafe or insecure.'

'But would you say she felt reassured by your visit?'

Ansari had to pause to think about it. A moment later she shook her head. 'That's not how I'd describe it, no. Certainly Jade would have believed we were taking her report seriously, and that we did not consider her to be a time-waster. Both DC Hunt and I made that absolutely clear to her. But I'd say she seemed more relieved at having got the whole thing out of the way than reassured by anything we did or said.'

'The whole report came across as vague because it was,' Chandler said. She kept her focus on her fellow DS. 'Frankly, I don't care whose desk this might have fallen across, nobody reading that report could possibly have anticipated such an escalation. Not to a brutal attack and eventual murder. It's just not there.'

'So maybe it isn't,' DC Brown suggested. 'Maybe her murder had nothing to do with her concerns.'

'Are you happy with that level of coincidence?' Chandler asked him, switching her gaze.

'They happen. This reported stalker was a shadow, a feeling, a sensation that she was being watched, that perhaps someone had been inside her home. Moving from that to a frenzied assault ending in murder just doesn't seem realistic. You said so yourself.'

'Unless Jade caught him in her home this time,' Ansari suggested. 'It's possible that he entered again, only this time she came home unexpectedly or was even already inside when he thought she was out. Her own knife was missing remember, so she could easily have pulled it on him and he reacted out of sheer panic, in fear of getting caught.'

'It's a possibility,' Brown conceded. Beside him, DS Spencer nodded in agreement.

Chandler thought likewise but did voice one qualm. 'The calm and placid woman who reported the offence, and whom we've come to know a little more about, seems at odds with somebody who would snatch up a large carving knife to defend herself against an intruder.'

'Snapping point,' Spencer said, confidently. 'Anything could have been said or done to make the victim feel as if her only defence was to confront him with a weapon.'

'True. But it's looking increasingly unlikely that we'll be finding him on your task force database.'

They were done, but as he got to his feet, DS Spencer regarded Ansari. 'A word of advice,' he said. 'You keep calling the victim by her first name. That's not best practice. You do that, and you only make it more personal.'

'It is personal. For the victim.'

'Where did you learn that? University?'

Ansari shook her head. 'No, Sergeant. From my boss.'

Spencer rolled his eyes. 'I didn't realise DI Bliss was so touchy-feely.'

Ansari gave the man an almost withering glare. 'He's not. Far from it, in fact. He simply believes our victims deserve our respect. I would agree.'

Chandler hid a smile behind her hand. The young DC was showing a real backbone. Disappointed that the meeting had taken them no further, she thanked the two task force detectives for their time, then she and Ansari headed back out into the general Major Crimes open-plan work area.

Hunt, Short and Bishop were all there, along with the other members of the team drafted in for the investigation. The new DC, Gratton, was on the phone with somebody. Chandler felt a little hollow sensation in her stomach. Seeing the space so full meant the cycle of information-gathering was slowing down. And still they had so little to work with.

'Anything?' Bishop asked as Chandler walked past behind his desk.

'Not a bloody thing.'

'Well, we're getting nowhere fast as well. Still chipping away at who isn't responsible and what isn't happening. We need some forward momentum on this one soon.'

'I wish I could provide something, but I'm all out of ideas.'

He shrugged. 'Let's hope the boss has had a lightbulb moment, in that case.'

Chandler nodded. Bliss had called her earlier, tasking her with carrying on in his absence and asking her to speak to her colleagues about regrouping later that evening at his home. Both Bishop and Short had readily agreed. She had hoped to forge ahead this morning so that when they all met up with Bliss later in the day there would be something worthwhile to report. Now all she could wish for was that he was having a better day than she was.

***

Through an alleyway into Regent Quarter, a short walk from King's Cross railway station, Bliss found Gareth Wigg sitting in the courtyard outside Camino. The tapas bar lay off the beaten track, but was well known to those who lived and worked in the area. Wigg had been fortunate enough to snaffle a table beneath a canopy which shielded whoever sat there from the worst of the sun's long, hot reach.

The man Bliss had travelled down to London to see looked up from his newspaper, gave a wide grin and folded the broadsheet in two before setting it down on the table alongside a tall glass of clear liquid garnished with a slice of lemon.

'My dear, Bliss,' he said with great veneration. 'How the devil are you, old boy?'

The voice was suited to the seventy-year-old ex-army officer who had now also retired from the Metropolitan Police Service at the rank of Assistant Chief Constable; though Bliss recalled how out of place it had seemed when he first heard it a couple of decades earlier, when Wigg had been a humble DCI in the east end of London.

'I'm good thank you, Wiggy,' he said, sliding into a chair opposite. As he did so a waitress happened to be passing by. Bliss caught her attention with a smile and a raise of the eyebrows. 'I'll have a pint of San Miguel, please. Plus whatever he's drinking.'

'Gin and tonic and a slice, please,' Wigg ordered. He turned back to Bliss. 'You're looking well, old boy. Despite your obvious injuries and discomfort. The rarefied air up in Cambridgeshire must suit you.'

'You too, Wiggy.' Bliss meant it as well. It had been a while since the two had met, but the older man appeared lean and sharp and had a healthy colour. Bliss knew that his old boss wintered almost exclusively in the Algarve and enjoyed a round of golf, which looked to be doing him the world of good.

'I'm a pampered old man put out to grass,' Wigg said. He shrugged. 'Someone has to be, I suppose.'

'I envy you.'

'Oh, I doubt that, Bliss. They'll have to beat you out of the job with a stick. What would Jimmy Bliss do without a crime to solve?'

'I may find out soon, Wiggy.'

'Which is why we're here, I assume.'

Bliss smiled. With the previous night's thoughts still raging through his head, Bliss had called Wigg shortly before 8am. They arranged to meet at 11.30, and with a fast and direct train thundering south, Bliss was in London less than an hour after setting off. During his journey, Bliss had ignored two calls from Sandra Bannister. He hoped that the journalist was looking for an update, but he also feared that news of his meeting with the IOPC had leaked. He decided to call her when he was done here.

'So, what is it you think I can do for you, Bliss?' Wigg asked, one eyebrow arched in his best Roger Moore pastiche.

'I need that enormous brain of yours, Wiggy. That and, possibly, your contacts in high places.'

'Might as well make use of the old noggin while I am still compos mentis, old boy. I fear the ravages of time have debilitated the cells somewhat. From what you told me on the blower, the sharks are cruising around you sensing blood.'

'They are. But what I am struggling to work out is why they would be doing so now. Also, I had a not-so-coincidental visit from Gerry Quinn the other evening.'

'That scoundrel,' Wigg said with a harsh sneer. 'Only ran across the man on a couple of occasions, but I took an instant dislike to him.'

Bliss inclined his head. 'Yeah, he had the same effect on my DS.'

'So what did that reprobate want?'

'The man was clearly searching me out, but doing his usual piss-poor job of it. Took a trip down memory lane, only it had a few twists and turns in it. Lots of chat about old raids that went bad due to tip-offs. That sort of rubbish. Then came the informal chat with the IOPC.'

'So, not a coincidence at all, then. Names?'

'Batty and Lee.'

'Batty is familiar to me. A DCI to be reckoned with, by all accounts.'

'I can understand why. He led the discussion. Various cases were mentioned, with threats of more to come, and while there is a decent amount of muck to rake up in each of those investigations, what they are really excited about is Hazel's murder. At the time that it happened, I understood. I had to be their number one suspect. But now? All these years on? Something has clearly rattled their cage, and I don't think it's just a matter of a new department looking to justify their hefty budget.'

The waitress came back to the table with their drinks. Bliss paid with cash and gave a decent tip. He drank from his glass as Wigg responded.

'Could this be a vendetta?' he offered. 'Someone who suffered as a result of your actions back in 2005? A copper who lost their livelihood, or perhaps a relative of someone who did?'

Bliss took another swallow before putting his glass down. Nodding, he said, 'That was my line of thinking. Has to be someone inside the job who kick-started this whole thing again, right? Someone who saw the new parameters at the IOPC as a way of launching a fresh investigation. But to do that they would surely have to have had some new information to go along with it. I don't see how that's possible, but without it why would anybody authorise this? Whatever *this* is.'

'Personal, then. Not professional.'

'And from high up.'

'Which brings us to my contacts.'

Wigg took a breath and gave that some thought. Bliss waited for him to work it through. His old boss was one of the Met's most highly regarded officers in his time, and rumour had it that he was often asked to chair various committees despite having retired. His counsel was sought by the high and the mighty. He was a man with influence. And a man Bliss knew he could trust implicitly.

Eventually, Wigg sipped from his glass and nodded twice. 'I see the way your mind is working, old boy. It so happens that I do have a finger in one or two still-warm pies, including the IOPC. I could not be certain of discovering precisely what they have up their sleeves, but I imagine I would be able to find out why they have taken this decision to search you out.'

Bliss let go of some pent-up air. Knowing you were innocent of something was of little comfort when you also knew how easily evidence, witness statements, and even known facts could be manipulated through a haze of smoke and glimmering mirrors to slant things for or against an individual. If he had a fight to prepare for, then having Wigg in his corner and looking for answers could only be a positive step in the right direction.

'Thank you, Wiggy,' he said, realising just how anxious he had been. 'That is a huge weight off my mind. I know I've made enemies during my career, on both sides of the legal fence. I learned from a source a few months back that my own DCI is predisposed to loathing me because her family hold me responsible for costing her uncle a job back in Peterborough. I can handle being demonised up there, because I stick by my decisions despite the seismic outcome at times. I also have few concerns regarding my other cases. But, of course, I am vulnerable when it comes to Hazel's murder simply because of the emotions it stirs up. I think they may be counting on that putting me off my game.'

'Well, you were definitely thinking clearly when you contacted me, Bliss. I may not be quite as useful to you as I perhaps would have been when I was still in the job, but I like to think my reach remains long and effective.'

'I'm sure it does.'

Wigg then asked how things were going outside of the looming shadow of the IOPC interest. Bliss elaborated more about being knocked down. He no longer considered it an accident, and for that reason felt himself fortunate to still be around. They then moved on to discuss the operations Bliss had led since returning to Peterborough the previous autumn.

'That was a pretty horrendous affair with that RAF officer,' Wigg said, wrinkling his nose and pulling a look of utter distaste. 'You did well there, old boy. The security services are not the easiest of people to appease when they sense mayhem about to break loose. That could have gone awry at any moment. The ripples would still have been spreading across your fine city.'

'It still left behind a nasty taste,' Bliss said.

'The sort of rubbish you were up against act out of greed and are therefore always vulnerable, and not exactly the sharpest tools. We won't ever see the back of them entirely, but at least we're getting to grips with them. People were watching you there, old boy. Some waiting for you to slip, others for you to be trampled on by the full weight of the security services. You made an impression when you turned things around.'

'Yeah, for all the good it did me,' Bliss scoffed. 'I drew the attention of arseholes like the IOPC and gave both MI5 and MI6 a bloody nose. Not the best of career moves.'

Wigg laughed. 'Your career is right where it ought to be. Getting your shoes dirty as a DCI and stirring things up.'

'Provided I still have a career at the end of this nasty business.'

'Then it's our job to ensure that happens, Bliss.' Wigg winked and took a long swallow from his glass.

As Bliss drained his own, he could not help but feel a little better. When you were under attack, it helped to have good support. There was no one better than Gareth Wigg.

Chapter Nineteen

Bliss received the worst possible news when he eventually returned Sandra Bannister's call. It was not the request for an update he had been hoping for.

'I was wondering if you would care to respond to a story we are discussing here at the paper concerning yourself and a couple of officers from the IOPC,' the journalist said.

'That depends on what the story is,' Bliss replied. There was no hint of malice or satisfaction in her voice. This was her job and she was doing it to the best of her ability.

'Simply that you were interviewed by them at Thorpe Wood police station yesterday afternoon. A private interview.'

'Forgive me, but where's the story in that?'

'You mean a senior city detective being interviewed by the people who police the police? Sounds like a news item to me, Inspector.'

'I don't think so. There's no filling in that sandwich, Miss Bannister. You have me, you have them, but you have no details. You're fishing.'

After a moment of silence, Bliss heard her chuckling. 'It was worth a shot. I should have known better where you are concerned.'

'Yes, you should. And I suppose I should know better than to expect you to reveal your source.'

'Absolutely.'

'Are you sure? Doesn't sound like much of a source to me. They gave you me and the IOPC in a room together. That amounts to bugger all. Pass them to me on a plate and I'll make sure they never bother you again.'

'Now, that sounds like a threat, Inspector.'

'Not at all. I'd simply make sure they were quietly moved on. I hear the Outer Hebrides is a fine place during storm season.'

Bliss ended the call with yet another promise to get back to Bannister with some dates for his promised interviews with her. But before that she took a chance and asked about the Jade Coleman case, on which he politely declined to comment. He was smiling as he hung up, but the smile quickly slipped from his lips as he thought about the leak at HQ. He puzzled over who, other than the Super and those closest to him, knew the IOPC were even in the building yesterday, let alone that they had met with him.

The first part of the conundrum was easy to solve. Both Batty and Lee would have had to sign in, and Bliss guessed one or perhaps even both of them had made it clear which department they were from and who they were there to see. No quicker way of spreading gossip than telling whoever was manning reception or had responded to their summons via the buzzer on the desk. In his own favour, it would be an equally simple task for him to find out who was on duty when the pair arrived. Not that it would do him any good. It was out there now, the mill regurgitating rumours and in full swing.

The short journey back to Peterborough allowed Bliss to take stock. Having Wigg as an ally was a great start, but despite his own handling of the two IOPC detectives, Bliss was more than a little apprehensive about taking them on in the formal setting of a disciplinary hearing. They would have to do better than Lee, but DCI Batty appeared capable of being a formidable opponent.

Bliss focused on him now. Had he witnessed the interview from a neutral position, Bliss would have said that Batty was more than professionally repulsed by a fellow detective thought to be both bent and a murderer. It had felt personal at times, an affront to Batty outside of the remit of his job. He wondered if that might simply be a case of the DCI trying to get beneath his skin in order to provoke a mistake or even a physical attack. Or was there perhaps more to it than that?

Shrugging it aside, Bliss next addressed his own physical condition. Other than the damaged ribs, he was feeling no long-term effects of being mown down by a car. None of the symptoms associated with concussion, such as headache, nausea, confusion or forgetfulness. No dizziness, either. No more than usual, that was. His ongoing medical condition had a similar vein of symptoms running through it like marble. Meniere's Disease could often cause each one, including ringing in the ears. Even so, none of them had worsened, and if he ignored the sharp teeth his ribs seemed to have, Bliss judged himself to have recovered well.

Jade Coleman plucked at his conscience throughout. Being less than fully involved was not yet harming the investigation, but neither was it helping. By this point, four days in, his commitment would usually have been complete. It would have seen him working late at the office or out on the streets conducting interviews. Sleep would have been elusive, and he would have snatched food and drink whenever he remembered. Now all he felt was a curious sense of detachment. He had put himself out there, headed briefings, issued instructions, and discussed the operation with the team, but despite this he knew he was far from being in charge of it. For his own sanity, and for Jade Coleman, Bliss knew he had to do better.

His thoughts turned to the crime scene once more. The nagging doubts persisted. Bliss wondered about the stifled cry and sound overheard by the neighbour, Baldwin. The attack on Jade Coleman had been vicious and powerful, yet not prolonged. In all likelihood, it had lasted between fifteen and twenty seconds. The most obvious point for the victim of such an assault to cry out, and for sounds of a struggle to occur, were at the outset. The initial alarm and panic would have created that exact reaction. Yet Bliss was unable to picture this murder in the way logic suggested it had played out.

The slice marks across Jade's palms tended to support the theory that it was she who had initially been armed with the knife, the thin and shallow cuts occurring as the blade was ripped from her grasp by the handle in a downward motion. It was possible that she had grabbed at it after being attacked, but the lack of wounds on her fingers suggested otherwise. Even so, a woman confronted by a stranger in her own home, who was fearful enough to snatch up a carving knife for protection, would surely have shouted out or even screamed long before any attack began.

There was another thing bothering Bliss. If the victim took the knife from its place in the kitchen, why were the only signs of a struggle found in the bedroom where she was eventually murdered? No matter how many times Bliss ran it through his head, it did not scan.

There was a beat missing, and he thought it might be crucial.

The obvious solution was that Jade had heard the intruder while she was in the kitchen, had laid her hands on the closest available weapon, and had then walked into the bedroom to confront the man. Obvious, perhaps, but to Bliss it did not ring true.

As he was prone to telling less experienced detectives, when you deliberated and questioned one line of thought, you had to open up the channels to another at the same time. So, if the scenario he had been considering was incorrect in some way, he now had to ask himself what the alternatives were.

It took him only a few seconds to arrive at two possibilities.

Either Jade Coleman had calmly and collectedly approached a stranger in her bedroom, the knife in her hand a last resort and a gleaming, obvious deterrent, when the situation unexpectedly spiralled swiftly out of control.

Or the killer was known to her.

The former required a degree of confidence and courage that belied everything the investigation had unearthed so far about the kind of person Jade was. The latter was one Bliss decided he and his team had to consider strongly. If Jade had recognised her attacker, she might well have picked up the knife merely in order to deter, but had allowed herself to be backed into a corner in the bedroom. It was entirely possible that he was misreading the scene at this stage, perhaps overthinking it because he was pushing too hard for answers. On the other hand, it felt right to question every assumption.

Bliss was snatched from his reverie by the sharp trill of his phone. He noticed the odd raised eyebrow from one or two fellow commuters, but the first-class carriage was where people often carried out their business. This was his, so he answered the call. It was Chandler.

'Boss, I have some news for you. It's a new lead, but there's been another cock-up.'

Closing his eyes for a moment, Bliss drew in a deep breath. The one thing he could not allow was the pressure to build up to the point where stress took a grip. It was not good for his health, and it was certainly not good for the investigation.

'Okay,' he said, injecting a soothing tone into his voice. 'Tell me about it.'

'Ten days before the murder of Jade Coleman, a woman was attacked in her home in Woodston. She was hurt, but not badly. The thing is, boss, she was interviewed in hospital by a uniform, who failed to react to the victim telling him she believed she had been stalked. This was only noticed in his report first thing this morning, and so today was the first the task force heard anything about it.'

Bliss was focusing on the potential positives. 'So we have a survivor. Presumably the victim was able to provide a description. Any chance that it's the same man?'

'The description is vague, boss. She never actually saw him during the attack. However, when it comes to the stalking, she mentions a man dressed in dark clothing, wearing a hoodie, and riding a bike.'

'Okay. I want to interview her myself.' Bliss felt the churning excitement in his stomach, like moths fluttering in anticipation. 'I'll be back in the city in twenty minutes.'

'Do I need to remind you that you are officially off sick, boss?'

He had yet to visit his GP, but he had called in his absence earlier. However, there was nothing to prevent him from recovering early enough to still get some work done today. 'Pen, please get hold of this woman. Tell her it's imperative that we speak to her right away. And would you pick me up at the station, please?'

The pause told Bliss his DS was reluctant and trying to think of a nice way to voice her objections. 'Boss, I'm pretty sure the stalker task force will want to speak with the victim. And perhaps they already have.'

'I don't care. I want to interview her myself. Not at HQ, though. At her home, work, wherever she happens to be today.'

Chandler agreed to making the call and collecting him from the railway station. Her clipped manner told Bliss she was not happy to do so. He decided he could live with that. The conversation he was about to have would be considerably harder.

Bliss stood up and walked to the enclosed space between carriages, both in order for his conversation not to be overheard, and so as not to irritate his fellow travellers even further. He made a call to Detective Superintendent Fletcher's PA, who put him through immediately and without question.

'I gather you were expecting to hear from me today, ma'am,' Bliss said.

'Put it this way, Inspector, I made it known that you might be communicating with me during your enforced absence.'

'Thank you for that. There are a couple of things. I wanted to let you know that I have spoken to an old friend. An ex-colleague, actually. At this early stage it's perhaps best you don't know who, exactly, just that he is a man who retains a good deal of influence despite being retired. I'm hoping that bears fruit later today or tomorrow, that it will provide me with a lead as to what the IOPC are playing at. Regards to operation Cauldron, I think you will agree with me that the less you know about my own influence there the best it will be for us both.'

'I'm happy to hear that you have someone else in your corner,' Fletcher said. 'As for the murder investigation, I would agree. With one proviso.'

'Which is?'

'That if things get… sticky, shall we say, then you come to me before digging any deeper holes for yourself. Remember what I said about relying on your team to do the groundwork for you.'

'I will, ma'am. And DCI Edwards? How much of a lead might she be looking to take while I'm off work?'

'For the time being, very little. Alicia and I have agreed that a combination of Chandler, Short and Bishop will suffice for the time being. Should your absence continue, then we will have to look at bringing in a higher ranking supervisor. DCI Harrison may return to work shortly. I'm not sure if you were aware, Inspector, but Harrison's wife passed away recently. Given the reason that he was on extended leave was to care for her, he may well be back. If not, there's always DCI Mulligan, given his extensive knowledge of the stalker task force.'

'I'm sorry to hear that about DCI Harrison's wife, ma'am. I never met him, of course, but I hear he was a good man and a good detective.'

'He was. He's much missed around here, I can tell you. Nothing against you, Bliss, but Harrison was the go-to DCI when it came to Major Crimes. You have filled his shoes admirably, but I think you will understand what I mean when I say he was politically… sensitive as well.'

Smiling to himself, Bliss gave a nod even though the Super was not around to witness it. 'I know exactly what you mean, ma'am. Well, if the DCI does return, I'll look forward to working with him. Oh, and there is one other thing. There may be a break in the case, and I will be stepping in to interview someone who looks to be both another victim and a witness.'

Fletcher did not miss a beat. 'That sounds terribly official to me, Inspector. It was my understanding that your continued involvement would be the very opposite of that.'

'And it will be, ma'am. I called in sick this morning as agreed, but as I'm feeling a little perkier right now; I thought I would make the most of it and get the interview over and done with before going back absent tomorrow.'

'Does that sort of nonsense work with DCI Edwards, Inspector?'

'Not usually, ma'am.'

'Am I wrong in thinking we had an agreement in place?'

'Not at all, ma'am. I'm simply suggesting we delay it by a few hours. I'll do the interview and go straight home. It won't even be noticed.'

Bliss heard the heavy sigh as if Fletcher were standing alongside him. He thought he'd make one final push. 'Ma'am, we did agree that the less you were aware of the better it would be. We could pretend this conversation never happened.'

'And what conversation would that be, Inspector Bliss?'

'Precisely.'

As he went back to his seat for the final few miles of his journey, Bliss was comfortable in the knowledge that Fletcher was not only being supportive above and beyond all expectations, but that she was also making the right calls. He hoped when he met with the team later on that something positive would have resulted from their efforts so far.

Chapter Twenty

The village of Eye is one of those curious ancient homesteads that has formed part of three different counties in its history. Until 1965 it was part of Northamptonshire, then fell within the Huntingdonshire borders, and only seven years later became a district of Cambridgeshire. Until the 1980s, clay was quarried for the local brick pits in Eye, since when quarrying has continued to take place for both sand and gravel. It was at the quarry that Chandler managed to track down their potential stalker victim, Mandy Vickers.

As Bliss and his partner stepped out into bright sunshine outside the main admin block, which was a large Portakabin situated at the end of a long driveway, the heat hit the two detectives like a physical blow, and the noise levels rocketed. The quarry was heaving with activity. There was a constant rumble of diesel engines in the background, punctuated by the tortured high-pitched shrieks and deeper groans of machinery in action.

Vickers was an administrator, so they did not have to wait for her to be fetched off the site. Instead, they were shown through to the office space she shared with three other people. Chandler approached the woman, produced her warrant card, and suggested they speak elsewhere. The anxious-looking Vickers seemed to root herself deeper into her chair as she asked what it was about, but Chandler convinced her it would be better to have the discussion away from anyone who might be able to overhear.

In a room usually reserved for breaks, the two detectives sat opposite Vickers at a scarred wooden table whose surface was marked with interlinking circles left behind by mugs and cups. Against the far wall there was a sink, a small fridge and several cupboards mounted on the wall. An open window overlooked the car park. Other than nodding at Chandler to close the window in order to block out the ever-present noise of the quarrying being carried out across the site, Bliss never allowed his focus to stray from the woman who offered the real possibility of providing the breakthrough they needed. Mandy Vickers could be DS Bishop's fabled card that broke the game of Patience wide open.

'If this is about what happened to me the other week,' Vickers said, her voice shrill with anxiety, 'then you're too late. I already spoke to two detectives this morning. That got me all in a flap having to relive everything that happened, so I don't know what more I can say.'

Bliss sympathised. It was never nice for a victim to have to recall one of the worst moments of their lives. But he had a murder enquiry to pursue, and so the niceties had to be held in abeyance. The woman looked to be in her late twenties, and although currently pained, she had a kind face that suggested a good nature. Bliss noticed there was some discolouration beneath her eyes, which seemed to spread out across her nose and cheekbones. Vickers wore foundation and eye make-up, but she had not been able to entirely disguise the remnants of her assault.

'Miss Vickers,' he said, offering a nod of understanding. 'Earlier today you would have spoken with the stalker task force, their focus I'm sure on that specific aspect. DS Chandler and I are with Major Crimes, and we are investigating a murder. It is our belief that whoever attacked you may well have gone on to do the same thing to another woman less than two weeks later. Only she was not as fortunate as you, Miss Vickers. She did not survive.'

The woman's eyes widened, and whatever colour had been in her cheeks drained away as if someone had pulled a plug on her blood. 'You're talking about that murder over at Welland,' she said in a hushed voice.

'New England. But yes. Now, before we discuss the connections that we think exist between the two attacks, I would like you to describe for me what happened to you. I realise it must still be very painful for you, both physically and emotionally. I wish I did not have to ask you to put yourself through all this again. But as I mentioned previously, this is a murder investigation, and Jade Coleman was not afforded the opportunity of recovering from her ordeal. I'm sure you will support us in doing everything possible to find the man who murdered her. The same man who may have beaten you, Miss Vickers.'

The reality of what might have been now sank in. Vickers's clasped hands were trembling, and she blinked rapidly as she fought back tears; tormented as much by the fresh agony of knowing how close she might have come to being murdered, as the hideous recollections of the attack itself.

Chandler moved around the table, pulled out a chair beside her, and laid her hand upon the other woman's.

'Is it okay if I call you Mandy?' Chandler asked, ducking her head to peer up into her face.

Vickers nodded, but made no reply.

'Mandy, I know better than most how much you would like to push us away and never have to think about what happened ever again.'

'How can you possibly know how I feel?!' Vickers snapped, heatedly.

'Because last year, I was abducted and attacked by a man who had both raped and killed on several occasions, and who threatened to do the same to me. I'm an experienced detective, Mandy, yet still I fell apart afterwards. I went into my shell, trapped all that pain inside me, believing all the while that it was the best thing to do. As it turns out, it was the very worst thing I could have done. If you allow it to, such a personal and violent event can poison you from the inside out.'

'But I don't want to even think about it any more. I can't bear to.'

'And I'm not about to tell you that it won't hurt, having to recall your ordeal for us right now. But what I can assure you is that the more you speak about it, the less power it has over you.

Eventually, you take control of it, as opposed to how it is for you at the moment. Helping us will ultimately help you, Mandy. I'm not telling you this just so will talk to us today. As someone who has been where you are right now, I would not do that to you.'

Vickers was panting, trying to control her breathing which had become ragged as she started to panic. As it slowed, Bliss read her eyes and her body language, and he knew Chandler's empathy had done the trick. A few moments later, the woman expelled a long breath and nodded for them to continue.

'In your own words, then,' Chandler said, still holding Vickers's hands. 'Please tell us what happened on the night of your attack.'

One more deep breath and the woman was ready.

'I'd come home from work that Tuesday evening. I made myself a cup of coffee, had a smoke in the kitchen, and then went upstairs to change. My bedroom door was open as usual. As I stepped through, something smashed me on the nose. My eyes began to weep, and I put both hands to my face.'

'The blow wasn't hard enough to cause you to fall?' Bliss asked.

'Not that one, no. My head was reeling though, and like I say, my eyes were filled with tears. It was painful. Then I felt two more blows. Harder this time. Much harder. The first made me stagger back against the door. I felt the second one land, then my legs gave way.'

'You were knocked unconscious?'

'For a moment. I know it was only a moment because I came around in time to hear him dashing down the stairs and then letting himself out.'

Bliss let that sit for a few seconds. Had Vickers interrupted a killer in his embryonic state, before his first kill, but at the point at which he was exploring his desires and the possibilities open for him to explore? If so, what had compelled him to take such a huge step the next time, just ten days later? Bliss's guess was the knife. He would come back to that.

'Mandy, from what you say, you never actually saw the man who attacked you. Not clearly, at any rate. Were you able to see anything at all through the tears that came from that first blow to your nose?'

Vickers shook her head. Adamant. He thought it likely that she had replayed that moment over and over again. The attack was a surprise, and her senses were not given the chance to recover before her attacker had fled.

'How about an overall impression?' he asked. 'Did you get a sense at all about this man? By that I mean, was he short or tall, strong or not particularly so? Black or white, British or foreign? Did you notice any specific or unusual odour?'

Vickers was shaking her head. 'I'm sorry. I wish I could tell you what you want to hear. But I got hit three times. Between the first and the third, my eyes were streaming and my head was all over the place. I can't remember a single thing about him, I'm afraid.'

Chandler glanced across at Bliss and shook her head. There was nothing to be gained from continuing this line of questioning. If they did, they would lose her completely. Bliss nodded back.

'How about the stalking you reported?' he asked. He kept his voice low and even, not wishing to exert any undue pressure.

Vickers sighed and lowered her head. 'I can't believe I didn't report it at the time it was happening,' she said, her voice weak and cracked. 'It's just… I suppose at the time I didn't think there was anything to complain about.'

'Explain it to us now. Describe what happened and how it made you feel.'

After a momentary pause to gather herself, Vickers said, 'I think I had noticed him before I became aware of noticing him. If that makes sense. I remember seeing him circling around the car park at the shops, and then thinking that I had seen him before. Same dark clothes, hoodie, and riding around on a bike. The hoodie was what drew my attention, if I'm remembering it right. It was hot. Well, you know how hot it's been recently, so someone with their hood pulled up catches your attention. Rightly or wrongly, you automatically think they're up to no good. I watched an American cop show on Amazon where there was a street robber who turned killer, and he rode about on a bike throughout the entire series.'

'So you clocked him, knew you'd seen him before, and that triggered an alarm, yes?' Chandler prompted.

'Yes. So, when I saw him again, I started to think it wasn't a coincidence. I mean, some people do seem to spend their time riding around aimlessly, but I'd never seen him in the neighbourhood on anything other than the bike, never seen him stop to talk to anyone. Then when I caught sight of him close to here where I work, rather than where I live in Woodston, I started to feel anxious. I got the feeling that he was, you know, sizing me up for something. Not attacking me – that never occurred to me at all. But having seen the TV show I did wonder if he was looking for an opportunity to rob me.'

'But you decided against reporting it to the police,' Bliss observed. 'Why was that, Mandy?'

She shrugged. 'What was I going to say? That I'd seen someone riding their bike? Someone who had made no threats against me. Someone who scared me because of what I'd seen on TV.'

Bliss smiled. 'I can understand your reluctance. It wasn't a lot to go on.'

'Right. And the thing is, I don't even know if the cyclist is the same man who beat me. I only mentioned him because I was asked if I had noticed anything suspicious lately, had seen anyone lurking around. I still can't be sure if it's the same man.'

'Have you seen him since? The cyclist, I mean.'

Vickers jabbed an upraised finger in the air. 'No. And that's what convinces me it had to have been the same man. The fact that I haven't seen him since. But I don't actually know for certain. How can I?'

'I think it's likely. But you're right, there's no way of knowing for sure at the moment. Mandy, I take it your only description of the cyclist is restricted to what you've already told us. Dark clothes. Hoodie. Bicycle.'

When she nodded, Bliss continued. 'Then let's try and fill in a few of the gaps. Tall or short?'

'I'm not sure. I'd say average height.'

'Fat or thin?'

'Average.'

'Colour?'

'I'm not sure. His head was always lowered, the hood up.'

'How about his hands on the cycle handles? What colour were they?'

Vickers raised her eyes upwards. 'White,' she said then. 'Definitely white.'

'Too white?' Bliss asked.

'I'm not sure what you mean, Inspector.'

'Could they have been gloves?'

'Ah. You know, now that I think about it, they could have been white rather than flesh coloured.'

'Any impression of age?'

Sighing, Vickers shook her head. 'Not really. I suppose I would say young, but that's probably due to the cycle and the hoodie more than anything else.'

'That's fine. You're doing well. So, let's focus on the bike. Think about how he rode it. Was he hunched over the handlebars? Was he in a more natural position, arms outstretched? Or was he upright, arms raised? Each of those suggests a different type of cycle.'

Bliss noticed a flash in the woman's eyes that suggested something had sparked in her mind. 'Yes,' she said, nodding enthusiastically now. 'He was riding tall in the saddle. His arms were quite high.'

'How about the colour, Mandy? You saw him on several occasions riding that thing around. What colour was it?'

'Black. Absolutely certain of that.'

Initially, when Vickers confirmed the riding position, Bliss had thought of a Chopper style bicycle. Now he realised that was the kind of bike which would stand out these days, making it an unlikely choice for somebody wishing to go largely unremarked upon. The chances were that it was a standard touring bike with converted handlebars to make the ride more comfortable. The colour was something that would not draw attention to it, either.

The interview had given them little more to work with than they had before. Even so, there were further questions to answer as a result. The intruder had been waiting for Mandy Vickers inside her bedroom when she arrived home from work. That tallied with what they believed had taken place in the New England bungalow on Friday morning. So how had the man gained entry? In Jade Coleman's case, the team could not be certain whether Jade had been at home and had left her back door open because of the increasing heat, or if she had come home and discovered the intruder inside. With Vickers they had certainty.

Bliss also wondered why the stalker had struck Vickers three times and then fled. For her attacker not to be the cyclist was too much of a coincidence. Yet, having surveyed his prey and decided to act upon whatever desires compelled him, he had merely beaten her to the floor and run. No sexual component, no theft, just the punches thrown. Vickers had arrived home at her usual time, so there could have been no element of surprise to disturb him. This was another crime scene that was not quite adding up for Bliss.

Deciding to end with one final question, Bliss asked, 'Mandy, do you have any idea how this man who attacked you gained entry to your home?'

He assumed this would have already been asked and answered and reported, but he did not want to wait until he had returned to Thorpe Wood to access the case file.

'That's just about the one thing I do know for sure,' Vickers told them. 'The security catch on one of my downstairs windows is broken. He didn't break it, it's been like that for a while. I'd fully opened the windows first thing that morning to let some air in after a horribly humid night, and when I closed them over again the catch failed to… well, catch.'

Bliss knew that a crime scene team would not have attended. There had been no theft, and the victim was unable to describe her attacker. The need for a full forensic search would have been deemed unnecessary and not cost-effective.

'Mandy, when the other detectives spoke to you earlier, did they ask you if they could send in a team to look for evidence?'

'No. Nothing like that.'

'Would you mind if I ordered it? I have to assume that if your attacker elected to wear gloves when he was riding around, he kept them on when he broke into your home. But I never like to put my faith in any assumption. I'll keep it short, have them check the window you mentioned, plus your bedroom if that's okay.'

The forensic follow-up was agreed, and Bliss understood the huge sigh of relief Vickers gave when she knew the interview was at an end. But he had one final question for her.

'Last thing, Mandy, I promise. I realise this will seem like an odd question, but do you now, or have you ever, had any involvement with CND or any similar anti-nuclear organisations?'

'No. Never.'

'Okay. Thank you. We're done here, then.'

'Thank goodness. I hope I was helpful.'

'You were,' he said to her as they all stood up from the table. He smiled and nodded. 'You never missed a step all the way through that. I could see you were uncomfortable, but you did brilliantly. There's no way you're going to let that piece of trash ruin your life. Right?'

Vickers smiled for the first time. 'Right,' she said.

And Bliss was confident she meant it.

Chapter Twenty-One

When she picked Bliss up at the railway station earlier, Chandler was still annoyed with him. She had not said as much, but his partner had a way of letting him know when she thought he was in the wrong, and so their drive over to the quarry in Eye had been largely made in silence. By the time the interview was over, Bliss sensed the cooling-off period had worked in his favour.

'How did it go with Mr and Mrs Coleman last night?' his DS asked as they hit the Frank Perkins Parkway at Newark.

'Tragically.'

'You had to tell them their daughter was gay, then?'

'No. We were all spared that, at least. They had worked that out for themselves many years ago, apparently. Jade wasn't aware of it, but yes, they knew. What did come as surprise, however, was discovering that Jade quit her council job three years ago and went to work for Esotere-UK. She simply hadn't told them.'

'Oh, shit!'

Bliss noted the pained wince. 'Yes,' he agreed. 'Oh, shit! That left its mark, especially on the mother. Ultimately, they had nothing worthwhile for us.'

'Another dead end. We're slowly running out of paths to explore, boss. Right now, I would have to say that the stalker angle looks the most likely contender.'

Chandler then went on to tell him about her meeting with the task force detectives, offering a hearty chuckle after outlining DC Ansari's response towards the end of the discussion.

'Good for her,' Bliss said. 'Looks like we may have a winner there, Pen.'

'I think we might. Gul is up for a scrap, that much is obvious. But why do you seem so deflated? You sound as if you found a quid and lost a fiver.'

Bliss thought about it for a few seconds, then explained the doubts he had about the crime scene at New England, and how the conversation with Vickers had done nothing to allay those concerns.

'I get the feeling we're missing something,' he told her. 'That itch you can't scratch is back, Pen. Something too obvious to see. But possibly something critical to our case. I'm too close to it at the moment, and feel as if I should take a step back. But even that doesn't seem like quite the right thing to do. I need time to think about it more. I'm convinced there is something staring us in the face and we're just too blind to notice it.'

'Then let's talk about other matters,' Chandler suggested. 'You say you need time to think about it some more, whereas what you probably need is a distraction. You were on the train home from London when you called earlier. Want to tell me what you were doing down there?'

Bliss decided he had nothing to hide. He rattled off the broad strokes for her.

'You think your friend can help?' Chandler asked, skilfully manoeuvring across lanes as vehicles swept up from a major junction to join the flow of traffic.

'I think he's willing to. That's half the battle.'

'And how does the Super feel about you being back on the job so soon after you went on sick leave?'

Bliss smiled to himself. It had not taken her long to get back onto this subject. His partner was like a dog with a very tasty and extremely juicy bone. He knew how that went.

'I told her it was purely temporary. She was fine about it. We agreed that the less she knew the better it would be when things become official. It's for her own protection, actually. She has been so understanding and supportive, and I don't want her being touched by the shitty end of this particular stick.'

'And when exactly do you intend on grabbing the rest you need?'

'I have what's left of the afternoon, and then the entire night to sit around and do nothing, Pen. Look, if the IOPC have their way I may not get to be a copper for much longer anyway, so let me ride this one out, eh?'

Bliss sensed Chandler staring across at him long before she responded. 'You really think it could go that far? That you could lose your job?'

'Pen, I've seen how easy it is for a miscarriage of justice to occur. I know that innocent men have gone to prison. I've not ruled out that possibility yet. So losing my job is the least of it by comparison.'

'But you said yourself there is no way they can convict you for your wife's murder. You have an alibi. A rock solid one, if I remember correctly.'

'I do. But what I can't prove is a negative. I can't prove I didn't pay someone to kill Hazel on my behalf. Just because they believed me seventeen years ago doesn't mean they will do so now. If I'm right, if they are looking at me again for her murder, then there has to be new evidence. I know it can't be legit. I know because I didn't do it. But will I be able to prove it?'

They drove on in silence for a few minutes. Bliss regretted being as open with his partner as he had been. Chandler didn't need to take on his own fears. He knew that she would, no matter what he told her now. He decided to give it a try, nonetheless.

'Penny, don't take any notice of me,' he said with a deep sigh. 'That's the negative side of it. Worst case scenario. I do have the benefit of being innocent. I also have a lot of support on my side and a great team around me. I'm confident that between us we can work it like any other investigation and find the holes in whatever case they present against me. Because there have to be holes. Whatever so-called evidence they may have dug up is clearly false, and we'll prove it.'

For a moment he did not think Chandler was going to respond. When she did, it was with a complete lack of conviction. 'You're right, Jimmy. You didn't do it, so there's nothing to worry about.'

The discordant tone made lies of her words. Bliss cursed his new-found and alarming tendency to want to share. He yearned for the days when he would bottle everything up tight inside. At least then his worries were restricted to him and him alone. The moment you involved others you took on the responsibility for how it affected them. If he could, he would have taken it all back. Anything so as not to burden his partner with worries that were not of her own making.

His mobile rang, and Bliss was relieved to have something else to think about. He was surprised to see the call was from Wigg.

'That was quick,' he said. 'I didn't know you still had it in you, Wiggy.'

'Never in doubt, dear boy,' Wigg responded in his somewhat offbeat cheery way. 'It was never in doubt.'

'So you have something for me already?' Bliss was exhausted by the events of the day so far, but now felt a renewed vigour.

'I don't know what it is exactly, nor where it may lead. But one name does keep cropping up. I take it you remember Gary Pemberton?'

The name was more than familiar, and the face came rearing up out of the darkness of Bliss's past. Pemberton was not only an ex-uniform, but also a family friend from back in the days when Bliss still lived with his parents in Bethnal Green, east London. His father and Pemberton had briefly been colleagues, and Bliss knew he was the kind of copper who bestrode both sides of the criminal line. Just like Bliss's father, Pemberton had a wide circle of acquaintances who were either thieves or cohorts, small time villains with big time ambitions mostly.

'Your silence speaks volumes,' Wigg said with a gentle chortle.

'Yeah. Sorry about that, Wiggy. The past tapped me on the shoulder there for a moment, and I got a little distracted. Took me by surprise, too. Gary Pemberton must be in his late seventies by now, and for the life of me I can't imagine how his name could have come up on this.'

'He still runs a boxing gym in Stepney. Must come across all sorts in that job, I imagine.'

Bliss didn't have to imagine. In his late teens he had been trained by Pemberton. He wondered if it was the same gym. Bliss had been a promising welterweight, with a decent amateur record. His heart had never really been in the game, and he lacked either the will or the ambition to take it on with him once his career in the police took off.

'So you don't know why his name is flashing up on the radar, only that it is?' Bliss said, seeking to either clarify or eke out a little more information.

'Yes. It's all rather mysterious. As if Pemberton is looming large somewhere in the background, but not exactly the most influential player.'

'So, acting on behalf of someone else, perhaps.'

'That's a possibility, old boy. A silent partner. Or so it would seem. Thing is, I know your father walked a fine line, but then I always had the utmost confidence that he would never be tempted to cross it completely. I did not know him well, but enough that I believed he understood where right ended and wrong began. I can't say I ever thought the same about Pemberton.'

Bliss took a breath. He thought about what Wigg was saying, and what he might be suggesting. 'So Pemberton was bent. Or had it in him to be.'

'I rather imagine he was. Whether that amounted to much more than taking a backhander here or there, I really could not say. All the same, it's disturbing to see him featuring so prominently in the current climate. You may need to watch your back rather more than we had imagined, dear boy.'

'I will, Wiggy. And thanks for the heads-up. By the way, you don't happen to know the name of that gym he runs, do you?'

'Yes I do. But you don't need it – the gym is the same one you used to go to. You wouldn't be thinking of paying him a visit now, would you, Jimmy?'

Bliss smiled to himself. 'Perish the thought, Wiggy. I'd have to be stupid to try something like that.'

'Hmm. Take great care, old boy. My advice, for what it is worth, is that you avoid Gary Pemberton like the plague. If your time in the force is being delved into, you want to keep as far away from him as possible. The man is toxic.'

'You make him sound like Reggie Kray, Wiggy.' Bliss's smile became a laugh, though even to his own ears it sounded disingenuous.

After a slight pause, Wigg replied, 'Pemberton is no criminal mastermind, I grant you that. He has no enterprise to run. But if he is involved, and by all accounts not on the highest rung of the ladder, then you have to wonder who stands above him at the top.'

Bliss was still going back over the phone call long after Chandler had dropped him off at home, where he pulled a beer from the fridge and took a seat on the old wooden bench he kept out in his Zen-style garden. He drank and watched his Koi fish basking in the heat of the day, contemplating the concern he had heard in Gareth Wigg's voice at the end of the conversation. In doing so, Bliss started thinking about his father.

Dennis Bliss had not risen above the rank of sergeant, and had never wanted to; he liked the balance the rank gave him. It afforded him a measure of control and some authority in situations where a clear, cool head was required. But it did not come with the overbearing burden of paperwork and bureaucracy that stepping up to the next level would heap upon him. Bliss remembered his father being the kind of man who enjoyed pulling on the uniform and doing his bit for the community, serving others, and trying to make the streets safe and secure for those whose ambition it was to go about their lives unmolested by criminals and the crimes they committed.

Not that his father had completely ignored the implied hypocrisy; Friday nights out down some local pub, or Saturday nights spent partying in someone's house, saw the Bliss family rubbing shoulders with all manner of faces and villains. For every copper there was a crook, but nobody seemed to care too much. If you lived within the community you policed, it was difficult to avoid, and better to embrace the situation than fight against it.

'You hope to have some influence over them,' Dennis Bliss had told his son on one occasion after a family friend had been given a five stretch inside. 'But at the very least you know that while they are in the boozer with you, or twisting away to a Beatles or Stones track on the stereo, they're not out there thieving.'

A simple philosophy for a much simpler time, Bliss reflected. His father had been gone for nigh on three years now, and Bliss missed him as much today as he had in the first few weeks that followed the non-faith ceremony which took place in Spain. Since then, his mother had taken the old man's ashes with her to Ireland, where she enjoyed a solitary life on the west coast, and he resided beneath a City of London rose bush in the front garden of her well-appointed bungalow.

Bliss knew he had made his father proud when he followed his footsteps into the police force. They had never been stationed together in the same building, but had worked jointly on a case shortly after Jimmy had made detective. An old lag, just out of prison after completing his third stretch in two decades, had met with a grisly end following a hatchet attack. Word had it that the ex-con was a grass, and it was anyone's guess as to which hard-nosed gangster had put a price on the man's head. Jimmy's father had put the word out on the street, and his own specific grapevine fed back some juicy treats. Within hours, the CID unit which Jimmy had been posted to in Whitechapel had pulled in their killer. They sweated him for as long as they could, but he never gave up who had put out the hit. He knew all too well that a hatchet or some other weapon would cut short his own life if he did. But for Jimmy Bliss, his father's involvement somehow enhanced his own reputation, and he was regarded by his colleagues with a new-found respect afterwards.

The warbling sound from his mobile shook Bliss from his musing. It was Chandler.

'I just thought you should know that I've heard back from the FO. The little dance has begun. The HO contacted the FO, who in turn contacted the Turkish Embassy and both arms of our security services. It's in play, Jimmy. No turning back now.'

Bliss was reassured. His arrangement with the man from Six seemed to have had little negative impact on the situation. He felt Chandler's excitement, knowing she was a step closer to her daughter.

'Munday from MI5 warned me against trusting anybody,' he told her. 'But I don't believe he meant it entirely. I won't go as far as to say the man from Six is on your side, but I get the impression he's not against you, either.'

'I got the same feeling. They don't appear to be going through the motions this time.'

Bliss thought about that. Those employed by the Home and Foreign and Commonwealth Offices seldom took a breath without good reason. The fact that they were all in communication with both MI5 and MI6 suggested to him that the wheels were spinning. Prior to returning to Peterborough, he had encountered many individuals working within each of those departments, and they were a force to be reckoned with once they put their minds to something.

'I hope they resolve this in the way you want, Pen. My suspicious mind can't help but wonder what's in it for them, but if it gets you closer to Hannah then perhaps it doesn't matter.'

'That's precisely how I feel right now. Thanks again, Jimmy. See you later.'

'Yeah. How's it going back there at the ranch?'

Chandler laughed. 'Oh no you don't, Jimmy Bliss. I'm not that easily had. You wait for your briefing this evening. Until then, you know what you need to be doing.'

'Would that be putting my feet up and chilling, by any chance?'

'However did you guess? Bye, boss.'

Afterwards, Bliss made himself a snack, took a second beer from his fridge, and decided a call to his mother was long overdue.

Chapter Twenty-Two

Bliss showed the team into his dining room. Naturally it contained not a single item of furniture, only a stack of boxes, plus his guitar flight case leaning up against one wall.

'Nice place,' Short said, nodding enthusiastically. 'When are you moving in?'

She, Chandler and Bishop had all arrived at the same time. Bliss knew immediately that Chandler had prepared her two colleagues on the drive over, and that the three of them had devised a plan. He wagged a warning finger in the air and shook his head.

'Don't even try it. I know Pen put you up to it, so any pre-prepared comments about my gaff being empty, unlived in, bare, undecorated, charmless… forget about them. I made a deal. By the time Pen and I have finished with it on Sunday it'll look like Laurence Llewelyn-Bowen has had his way with it.'

Short rolled her eyes and groaned. 'Ugh! I do hope Penny has more taste than him.'

Bliss laughed. 'I wouldn't bank on it. Have you seen the inside of her flat?'

Chandler ignored him. Instead she glanced around the room and said, 'What, no whiteboard? No coloured markers? How on earth will we function?'

'I thought we might try something outrageous like using our memories.'

'Well, I think we three are safe, but are you sure about that elderly brain of yours? You don't want to overload it.'

'Unlike the dormant organ that rattles around inside your skull, my mind expands infinitely.'

'As far as you can recall.'

Bliss nodded. 'What were we talking about?'

He left the room momentarily, returning with four garden chairs which he proceeded to pull out and situate around the floor.

'Are you serious, boss?' Bishop said, scowling at the fragile-looking seats.

'Don't mock,' Bliss shot back. 'You're lucky I didn't leave you all standing.'

'I was more concerned it might not take my bulk.'

Short patted him on the stomach and laughed. 'Lay off the pies then, porky.'

Bishop wrinkled his nose in distaste. 'Just because you can eat your own bodyweight in cakes and still look like that, doesn't mean we all can. Mine is a genetic problem.'

'To be fair,' Bliss interrupted. 'Mia is right. I think we can all agree yours is a pie problem, Bish.'

This caused them all to chuckle.

'You play?' Bishop asked, nodding towards the guitar case.

'When I find the time. Which is rare enough these days.'

'I used to dabble with a harmonica.'

'Nice,' Bliss said, admiringly. 'I love a bit of blues harp. Jimmy Reed, John Mayall. Great stuff.'

'Jerry Portnoy is a particular favourite of mine.'

'Good choice. He did some nice work with Clapton.'

'Maybe the boss will give us all a tune later,' Short said with a wicked glint in her eye.

Bliss was firm with his response. 'Not a chance. I'm strictly an empty room player these days, and that's how it will stay.'

He made them a hot drink each, and when they were settled Bliss asked Chandler to deliver her update. She took him through everything the team had discussed at the evening briefing, and he made bullet-point notes in his head as each item was touched upon. First up was Mandy Vickers. The forensic search had been ordered for the following day, with the crime scene manager liaising with Vickers directly. At the briefing, the team had talked about obvious areas requiring follow-up activity.

'Both crime scenes bother me still,' Bliss admitted. 'I keep coming back to why our stalker was inside their homes. What was his purpose for being there? All he did was punch Mandy three times.' He shook his head. 'I say "all", but I don't mean it that way. Three blows were awful enough, but I'm wondering why it wasn't any worse.'

'That does seem a little odd,' Chandler agreed. 'You wouldn't think it would be anywhere near enough for whoever did it.'

'Was she his first? Did he panic? Did that experience toughen him up when he encountered Jade? Even then, I come back to motive. With the husband or boyfriend stalker dynamic, it's often all about control. They want their punch bags back, they want to dominate the lives of the women they stalk because they see them as their property. The stranger stalkers are different.'

Short nodded and said, 'The fact that Mandy Vickers was beaten without warning tells us this man is not looking for intimacy, acting out on some fantasy that he's found his soul mate. The fact that he's gone after two women that we know of suggests it's not based on some personal vendetta, either. I think we're looking at the predatory type, the kind of stalker who spies on women in order to eventually attack them.'

'Except there's no sexual aspect to either attack,' Bishop remarked, reflecting on news they had received earlier from the pathologist.

'True, but that doesn't mean there won't be one in the future. There has been an escalation, so perhaps that's the next stage of his evolution. Maybe next time he'll follow through with the full range of whatever it is his sick mind wants to do to these women.'

'We need to focus on the crossing point,' Bliss said, pausing to take a sip of his tea. 'Where did our stalker first spot these two women? How did their paths cross? Let's look at the minutiae of their lives and see if there is any sort of overlap. We have little description of the attacker himself to work with, so for now we keep our attention on the victims and work backwards if at all possible.'

There was general agreement that this was the best way to proceed. They then switched back to the earlier team briefing.

'So, after discussing Vickers, we picked up on the remaining strands,' Chandler continued. 'The scan and bloodwork PM gave up nothing of consequence. Drinkwater's examination of Jade's body confirmed that she was not raped, thankfully, and that the fatal wound punctured the heart. A forceful blow, probably while the victim was already lying on her back. The MRI scan revealed chipped ribs, hence the power required.'

Bliss reflexively touched a hand to his own wounds, then silently chided himself. Compared to Jade Coleman he could have no complaints. 'So Jade was dead before our officers could possibly have arrived on scene,' he commented.

Chandler nodded. 'It would have been a few minutes at most. As for how Jade's killer accessed the property, either the kitchen door found open by the first officer on the scene was also open when her attacker arrived, or Jade let him in. He certainly did not break in.

'We've looked at text exchanges between Jade and Lucy Lancaster, and they are consistent with Lancaster's story. All very casual, and the last was from Lancaster to Jade on Friday morning saying she had missed her at the gym and asking why Jade hadn't been there. Nothing suspicious in the Lancaster finances, either, so I think it's another thread we can stop pulling at.'

'That's not a great surprise,' Bliss observed. 'The woman was clearly upset about Jade's death, and her husband was always only a vague possibility.'

'Agreed. So, before we settle our attentions more fully on the stalker factor, there is one aspect of what we have learned about Jade that has not yet been investigated. Lancaster claims Jade had a friend who was a member of CAWED. We have no timeframe, nothing relevant on social media, no texts or mails, either. We have no name, although we do know the friend was female. The only reason we know about the friend at all is because Lancaster mentioned it. But we have no confirmation from a secondary source. If this friend actually exists, then despite Jade starting work at Esotere a year after CAWED disbanded, I think we have to ask ourselves if there is a connection between the two.'

Bishop jumped in on that. 'How confident are we that this Lancaster woman is remembering correctly? Or telling the truth, for that matter?'

'Why would she lie?' Short responded. 'She appears to have nothing to hide.'

'Mistaken, then?'

'We can check that easily enough,' Chandler said. 'I'll have a word with her myself. See if she knows more about this friend than she was willing to let on when the boss and I spoke with her first time around.'

Bliss thought it was worth pursuing. 'I did wonder whether Jade's friendship with this activist was the impetus behind her getting a job there. From what I understand they have a pretty high turnover of staff, so perhaps Jade took the first genuine opportunity that came along after the campaign fell apart.'

'You mean to spy on them? An insider, all of their own?'

'Why not? It would explain Jade's sudden change in direction regarding work. She never told her parents about switching jobs, so there may be a meaningful reason for that. Which reminds me about something. Jade's parents told me their daughter worked for the council. I think it's worth having a conversation with someone over at the town hall, hopefully tracking down some close colleagues there at the same time. Maybe one of them knows more about Jade's involvement with the anti-nuclear movement and this friend of hers.'

'So we look even deeper into Jade's life,' Short said, sounding a little dismayed. 'Poor thing. It's not enough that she gets murdered like that, she now has us taking bites out of her.'

Chandler flashed her a look of empathy, but said, 'They're potential leads, Mia. Maybe even decent ones.'

'I know. Sorry, it just always feels so… grubby. Rooting around in someone's private life is bad enough at the best of times, but when they are the victim it makes it seem as if they are suffering twice.'

'I think we all know what you mean,' Bliss said. 'But it comes with the territory. It's a lead we need to follow up on. We have to find out who this friend was, talk to her. Perhaps even approach the people from CAWED.'

'Yeah, they're bound to welcome us with open arms,' Bishop scoffed.

'That's never stopped us before, Bish.' Bliss gave a wry smile. 'Even the people we're helping don't really enjoy talking to us.'

'Which brings us back to the stalker angle,' Short said. 'From what Penny told us, we've got our work cut out for us there because he doesn't really fit any known subjects. We're getting no joy with CCTV footage. The public appeal from the media has come up with all the usual rubbish calls concerning just about every young man in the city who has ever ridden a bike or owned a dark hooded sweatshirt. And now that we know for sure he's taken an interest in more than one target, we just have to hope that the sick bastard doesn't focus his attention on some other poor cow.'

Bliss blew out his cheeks. 'Bloody hell. I can imagine the grief I would have got if I'd used that term.'

'Yeah, well I'm a woman so I'm allowed.' Short laughed and shook her head. 'Sorry, but I despise these tossers. They intimidate, humiliate, and degrade women. And why? Because they are without exception poor excuses for men.'

Holding his hands up, Bliss said, 'You'll get no arguments from me. So, we've pretty much narrowed it down to just the two approaches for the moment. Jade's CAWED friend, and the stalker. Speaking with Jade's council employers and colleagues may overlap either or both of those lines of enquiry. We find the friend, maybe we find out more about the stalker.'

'You think the stalker knew Jade?' Bishop asked.

'I do.' Bliss nodded.

'How about Mandy Vickers?'

'I'm not so sure. I wonder if she was in some way his dry run. I can't get over the fact that he had her where he wanted her. Sparked out on the floor. But instead of finishing her off or sexually molesting her, he runs off. To me that implies Mandy was not his real target.'

'But how do you get from there to the stalker knowing Jade?' Short asked.

'For me it's all about the crime scene. My guess is he was fascinated with Jade Coleman, and somehow confronted Jade in her home. I think Jade pulled a knife on him. I reckon she believed it would force him to back off, that she felt she had time to maybe talk him out of whatever he had come to say or do. I don't see her having that opportunity with a complete stranger, someone whose desires and reactions and purpose she had no clue about. I may be wrong, but it's bothered me from the beginning. It's what makes the most sense to me given the few clues we have to work with. Occam's razor. The simplest theory is also the most likely.'

Chandler nodded. 'So what do you want us to do in terms of actions?'

Bliss considered the question for a moment. Finally, he said, 'The team should focus its attention on the stalker. Have a look and see if perhaps there are two or three who come even close on the task force's lists. Pay them a visit. Rattle a few of these scumbags. Recanvas the neighbours, specifically in terms of the hooded cyclist. Make sure every useful CCTV camera feed has been double-checked. Find out from that Baldwin bloke next door if Jade was in the habit of leaving her back door open on warm days. Ingress and egress are the critical aspects at this stage. Leave the CAWED people to me. I have a personal history with them, and I know where their old leaders live.'

There were nods of agreement all round. Chandler suggested she accompany Bliss if he intended visiting the activists, which he agreed to only because he was still wary of driving, and despite his partner's heavy right foot it was better than taking a taxi.

'And we'll just forget about the fact that you're supposed to be on sick leave,' Chandler piped up.

Bliss grinned. 'I do wish you would, yes.'

'Okay. So now let's talk about you and the IOPC.'

'What about it?'

'How can we help?'

Bliss remained genuinely appreciative, but had decided earlier that evening that it was better for their careers if his colleagues distanced themselves from whatever the IOPC were about to throw at him. He shook his head.

'How about I treat you all to dinner instead? The Windmill is just around the corner and they do a decent meal. There's nothing to help me with at the moment, and I'm not sure there will be.'

Short threw him a look of absolute disgust. 'Is that really what you think of us?' she demanded to know, getting to her feet and staring down at him. She was an impressive sight in full flow. 'That we'd rather be kept at arm's length when the professional shit has hit your personal fan?'

Bliss tried to laugh it off. 'Nice turn of phrase, Mia. Look, it's got nothing to do with what I think of you, nor what I expect from you. I know you're all in my corner, and I appreciate it. The fact is, I've had one meeting with them so far, from which I think I've gathered their intentions. But there's nothing formal to defend myself against, no official allegations made.'

'Not yet,' Bishop argued. 'But they're coming, right? So why wait until they decide to trample all over you? If you have a good idea of what they are going to aim your way, it's surely better to take a look at it now rather than later. If I know you half as well as I think I do, Jimmy, then you'll already have people sniffing around on your behalf. We want in on that.'

'Yeah, and a refusal is liable to offend,' Chandler insisted.

Bliss regarded them: three faces creased with genuine resentment at being side-lined. He relented with a lopsided grin. 'All right. I surrender. But in doing so I also think I need to address the elephant in the room.'

'Blimey, boss,' Short said, settling herself back into the garden chair. 'I know Bish has put on a bit of weight, but there's no need for that.'

Bishop gave her the middle finger of both hands. Their laughter echoed around the room.

'You don't need to do that, Jimmy,' Chandler said, when they had quietened down. 'None of us needs you to.'

'Then maybe *I* need to. I know the rumours, and I know the kind of talk there has been. I want to be up front about it all and get it out in the open before you hear the worst of it out of context.'

Bliss paused to sip from his mug before ploughing on. He felt his hand shake. It was the last thing he wanted to discuss, but his team needed to know who they were supporting and what exactly they were dealing with. He swallowed thickly, before clearing his throat and allowing his friends and colleagues to peer beyond the barriers he had erected around himself.

'Hazel and I were so-called swingers for all of four weeks, and on only three occasions – the first of which was purely voyeuristic. We were young, foolish, indestructible, and looking for new experiences. We tried it on for size and quickly decided it didn't fit. This will be the only time I talk about this, so if you have any questions, you'd better get them out of your system now.'

'I have one,' Bishop said, his brow furrowing. 'How was it that when it all came out, you managed to continue working serious and major crimes?'

Bliss smiled. 'Thanks for making it a practical question, Bish. Of course, in doing what I did, no matter how briefly, I made myself vulnerable to blackmail. I should have been sent to sit behind a desk in some isolated spot in the wilderness. The swinging thing only came out into public record when Hazel was killed, and that, plus the aftermath of what happened between me and a fellow cop, shone a harsh light on things the top men and women wanted snuffed out. They decided to focus on the bigger picture instead, which ultimately saved my neck.'

'I can't imagine me and Paul doing what you did,' Short said softly, shaking her head at the prospect. 'I'm not being judgemental, I just can't even contemplate being involved in something like that. But it's a lifestyle choice, so I think the job should be mature about it and apply modern thinking. Personally, the thought of Paul with another woman makes me feel sick.'

'It's not for everyone,' Bliss admitted. 'And we rapidly decided not to continue, because it wasn't for us. I have to say it was nowhere near as sordid and seedy as it may seem from the outside, but we were both more jealous than we imagined ourselves to be. We chalked it up as a mistake, one we could move on from because we were both involved. It wasn't like either of us had been having an affair. So we tried to move on and forget all about it. Which brings me to the second issue I need to clear up.'

Bliss blew out a long breath and moistened his lips before continuing, conscious of the silence in the room.

'The stories you heard about me and the other cop are true. He slept with Hazel once during our first ever session, but refused to take no for an answer afterwards. Even after we walked away from the scene. Long after. You could say he stalked her, and I am absolutely convinced it was him who murdered my wife. So, yes, I did vent my anger on him. I did beat him so badly he spent time in hospital. In truth, I wanted to kill the man, and I sometimes think it was only the thought of how that might affect my parents that prevented me from doing so.

'That is who and what I am. That is the man you say you want to stand alongside, to support now that the IOPC are gunning for me. I felt you had the right to know for certain what until now had only been hearsay. And if any of you want to take a step back, then please know that you will only ever have my utmost respect.'

The room was quiet for a second or two. Then Short got to her feet for the second time that evening, her fine blonde hair swirling around her shoulders. She looked around at the others. Taking a deep breath, she said, 'Well, I'm going.'

'You are?' Chandler said, staring up at her in amazement.

'I am. To powder my nose. And don't any of you stare at my arse as I leave.'

Chandler chuckled. 'Hey, even I sneak an envious glance at that occasionally.'

The spell was broken. Nobody was leaving. Bliss had laid it all out there, and not a single back was being turned against him. He put his head down for a moment to reflect on his good fortune at having such characters around him. He waited for Short to return from the toilet before pressing on.

'First of all, I want to thank all three of you. I'm humbled by your friendship, and so happy that you can overlook my weaknesses.'

'We were all young once, Jimmy,' Bishop said, his broad shoulders shrugging. 'There was a time when the kind of thing you're talking about was all the rage. Nobody really thought twice about it.'

'Is that the screwing around or the beating someone up you're talking about?' Short asked, a smile twisting her lips.

Bishop laughed. 'Either. Maybe both.'

'So where do you think we are with this?' Chandler prompted.

Bliss raised his eyebrows. 'The way I see it is, I'm weak in several areas of recent cases, but nothing that can hurt me as much as the IOPC appear to want it to. My time at SOCA and the NCA were pretty much dismissed, which leaves my distant past to examine. Again, there's the odd wrinkle, but nothing I can't handle. Even if they wrap up all of those weak spots into a single bundle, a good brief will see me through.'

The dozen years he had spent first with the Serious and Organised Crime Agency, which subsequently became the National Crime Agency, had led to Bliss making numerous connections which might be examined in an authorised search for signs of malfeasance on his part. However, the scrutiny he and his colleagues had operated under during those investigations had been greater than any he had known before or since. He simply could not accept that the IOPC would go digging there unless they were unable to find anything else on him first.

Bliss shook his head and said, 'I believe it's all about my ex-wife and her murder. I've always known I'm vulnerable there, but equally I've also known I'm clean. They can't have any new relevant information because there's none to be had. So I suspect a frame job. Why, and from which direction, I have no idea. But that's where I think this is coming from.'

'Could it be the ex-copper?' Bishop asked. 'The one you put in hospital?'

'Anything is possible. But he was pretty much ostracised even before he was forced out, and has no clout left inside the service. To me this feels more like someone with a new grudge using something from my past to get at me.'

'So, once again,' Short said, 'how can we help?'

Bliss took a breath. Thought about it for a while. Nodded. 'I have one lead which I will follow up on my own. No arguments there. It would be useful if one of you took a look at my past cases. I can give you a list of the more recent ones to check out, plus a few from the old days back at the Met. You might spot something I've overlooked or forgotten about entirely. In addition, I don't want to be played for a mug, so even though they skipped over my SOCA and NCA record, I'd feel better if that was given the once over. Working organised crime comes with its own temptations, so I can't see why they would ignore it entirely. Then there's Hazel, of course. To be honest with you all, I'm really not sure where to start with that one, but it has to be my priority.'

Bishop got to his feet and rubbed his hands together. 'Right. Let's allocate the division of labour over some grub. I'm bloody starving and the boss is footing the bill.'

Bliss caught Chandler peering closely at him. He gave a small nod of gratitude. He knew without asking that she had stirred up her colleagues, and that their willingness to help him had been spurred on by her pleas on his behalf. Right now, he felt chastened, but more grateful than it was possible for him to express.

Chapter Twenty-Three

Having picked him up at 8.30am on the dot, Chandler had first driven Bliss to his GP surgery at the Botolph Bridge Community Health Centre. He was in and out in five minutes, fit-note in hand. All he had been required to do was explain to the doctor that he had been hospitalised with concussion, and she had printed off the sheet of paper for his employers without argument. Doctor Regis asked him a few follow-up questions in relation to his subsequent health, but Bliss was eager to get away so he made his excuses and got out of there. It was his first GP appointment since returning to the city the previous autumn.

They had some time to kill, so Bliss suggested they go for a coffee, which turned into a full breakfast because he decided he was hungry. They discussed the previous evening's meeting and meal before setting off for Ramsey to interview the couple who had run CAWED, deciding that Bliss would head down to London on his own later that afternoon while Chandler continued to oversee the investigation back at HQ.

Bliss was both surprised and thrilled that DCI Edwards had so far been conspicuous by her absence. Chandler revealed that Edwards had spoken to her only once in two days, a conversation that amounted to little more than a cursory chat and general update. Bliss thought he knew why their DCI was behaving strangely. His guess was that she was aware of the IOPC interest and had decided to steer clear of him, and the investigation he still technically led. No taint that way, and for once he did not hold it against her.

The small market town of Ramsey was less than fifteen miles to the south-east of Peterborough city centre. The only thing Bliss knew about the place was that the last person to be executed at the Tower of London, the German spy Josef Jakobs, was caught in Ramsey having broken his ankle parachuting into England in January 1941. As claims to fame went, Bliss thought it was an interesting one.

Chandler drove there via Pondersbridge, then took some narrow back roads criss-crossing rich farmland, skirting the northern tip of Ramsey itself. On its outskirts she located the Bill Fen Marina, which was spread over thirty-one acres of land and still expanding and developing.

Chandler pulled up at the marina entrance and spoke to the proprietor, a cheerful ruddy-cheeked woman who asked no questions after she saw the warrant card. The two detectives followed the simple directions and found a space in a small parking bay reserved for boat owners and their visitors. The fifty-five foot traditional style narrow boat belonging to Marvin Cooke was permanently moored close to an inlet fed by the High Lodge waterway. Bright sunlight glinted off the water's surface, floating slicks of oil creating multi-coloured islands bobbing gently beside the boats. The *St Francis*, as the Cookes had named their home, was a gleaming dark shade of green, with yellow trim around the edges of the deck, doors, windows and side panelling. Bliss had never yearned to live on a houseboat, but this was a beauty.

It was a little before 10am on Wednesday morning. Marvin Cooke was relaxing on the deck of the boat and looked up as Bliss and Chandler approached. He used a hand to shield his eyes from the sun, and what he saw caused him to frown.

'It's all right, sir,' Bliss called out as they reached the gangplank which ran alongside two thirds of the *St Francis*. 'We're not bible-bashers.'

Chandler snapped her head around. In a low whisper she said, 'Behave yourself. If it weren't for your cracked ribs, you'd be feeling the sharp point of my elbow right now.'

'What? I'm breaking the ice.'

She shook her head in apparent despair and moved ahead of him along the narrow gangway. Cooke rose from his chair, setting aside a pristine copy of a John le Carré paperback. A man of average height, Cooke's slenderness gave him the appearance of being a little taller. He wore a navy polo shirt, dark grey cargo shorts, and his feet inside deck shoes were bare. He came across to greet them. *More to prevent his unexpected visitors from climbing immediately aboard than to welcome them,* Bliss thought.

'May I help you?' Cooke asked, as if he were trying to think of a way he could convince them he was too busy to receive visitors.

Bliss produced his credentials and introduced himself and Chandler. 'I'm hoping so, sir,' he said. In contrast to Cooke's glum expression, Bliss raised his broadest smile. 'Is it okay if we join you on deck?'

The pause was long enough to tell Bliss that the man did not want to speak with them. He decided to give Cooke a nudge, raising his voice loud enough so that it could be overheard by anyone currently aboard the closest neighbouring boats.

'If it's not convenient, Mr Cooke, you can always come over to Thorpe Wood nick in Peterborough. I presume you still know the way?'

The man sighed and folded his arms across his slight chest. 'I see. It's going to be like that, is it?'

'It needn't be. All we want to do is ask a few questions, that's all. Ten minutes of your time. No strings.'

Cooke swept his hand backwards in a grand gesture. 'Then please do join me, detectives. Ten minutes is all I can spare you, mind.'

'Of course,' Bliss acknowledged. 'That sunbathing won't get done by itself.'

Half turned away, Cooke pirouetted and jabbed the air with a pointed finger. 'I know you, don't I?'

'If by that you mean to ask if we've met before, then the answer is yes. A good few years back. I was part of an interview team.'

'I thought so. Would this conversation be better taking place below deck, Inspector Bliss?'

'That depends on how well you are known to your neighbours, sir.'

'In that case, why don't we get out of the sun? I can probably rustle up a cold drink if you like.'

Chandler was helped on deck by Cooke, who then left Bliss to his own devices. The three headed down a short flight of steps into the living quarters. Bliss immediately felt claustrophobic. Though lengthy, and larger than seemed possible from the outside, it remained a narrow and confined space. Cooke led them into the lounge area, in which there were two leather sofas arranged in an L shape close to a small widescreen TV. It was simple living and quite tasteful, but Bliss preferred the deck. Cooke neglected to offer them the drinks he had mentioned, instead slumping down into one of the sofas. Bliss and Chandler took the other, which was a two-seater and left them squashed together.

'I take it this is about CAWED,' Cooke said, pronouncing the acronym in a single word, exactly as Bliss had done when speaking about the protest group. He crossed one leg over the other and lay an arm across the back of the sofa. He appeared perfectly relaxed.

'To a certain degree, yes,' Bliss replied. 'Though, of course, the organisation itself is well known to us.'

'And what exactly is it you think you know about CAWED, Inspector?'

Bliss did not have to consider his response, as it had been on his mind all morning. 'The basics are that it started back in 2000 after plans for the disposal site were first put forward. The campaign received a lot of media attention locally, but also resulted in some violent acts being carried out in its name. It ended four years ago. Prior to that, you and your wife were jailed having been convicted of fraud, while one of your members, whose name escapes me, did serious time for conspiracy to cause harm to the company staff and its suppliers.'

'You have a good memory, Inspector. Those planning meetings were rigged from the outset, and we know that bungs were offered and taken. It was in the wake of that breakthrough in the paper and on the local TV news that CAWED was formed.'

'You were known to be the group's leader.'

Cooke shook his head, his smile a thin slash of contempt. 'Wrong. One of the main tenets of CAWED was that we were a leaderless resistance.'

Bliss choked off a laugh. 'Which everybody knows was your way of absolving yourself of all responsibility. It was also the only reason you avoided a much longer prison sentence. In reality, you were CAWED's leader, albeit one who refused to be accountable for the actions of your members.'

The smile vanished. In its place there was a rigid sneer. 'That's tantamount to libel, Inspector Bliss.'

'Actually, I think you'll find it's tantamount to slander. But it's all moot. Whatever you think you heard was never said.' Bliss turned to his partner. 'Did you hear me say anything slanderous, DS Chandler?'

'Not a word, boss.'

'How about if I did?'

Bliss turned his head towards the far end of the boat. Ellie Cooke stood there wearing a flimsy peach-coloured robe unfastened over a pale blue swimsuit. She was standing in the galley, one hand resting on the counter by the sink. Bliss recognised her immediately, though in his previous encounters with the woman she had worn more clothes. Even without his suit jacket, Bliss was starting to feel decidedly overdressed.

'Hi, sweetheart,' her husband said. The smile was back now, and he had set it to full beam. 'You feeling better?'

'Fabulous.' She moved towards them, barefoot, gliding silently into the living area. Lithe, silky movements. She made no move to cover up. Bliss made no move to avert his gaze.

'The police are here to speak to me about CAWED, darling,' Marvin Cooke said.

'So I heard. Sounded terribly slanderous to me.'

Bliss shrugged. 'Unless you've got a third person tucked away back there, I'd say we were at an impasse on that subject.'

Slipping into the seat alongside her husband, the woman twisted sideways and rested her legs across his lap. Casually she toyed with her hair, using slow, deliberate movements. Bliss thought she was trying too hard. At what, he had no idea, but too hard at whatever it was she was attempting.

'It's fair to say we have opposing views on the merits or otherwise of CAWED,' he admitted. 'But we're not actually here to discuss the organisation itself. We'd like to ask you some questions concerning specific members.'

Marvin gave an exasperated sigh. 'Still can't leave them alone, can you? You people continue to hound them four years after we folded. What are they supposed to have done now?'

'Well, one of them may have got herself murdered.'

That chilled the room nicely.

'Does the name Jade Coleman ring a bell?' Chandler asked.

Cooke took a moment to compose himself. He had not expected this line of questioning, it seemed. 'It does. And yes, we heard about what happened to her. But Jade was not a member of CAWED.'

'Then how do you come to know her?'

'She was involved, but that was the extent of it. I would describe her as a bit of a hanger-on. Spent some time with us on the periphery of things, attended a few meetings, helped raise some money. She was all for nuclear disarmament and intent on getting rid of the disposal site, but not committed enough to become a full-time activist.'

'You sound as if you didn't care much for her.'

'I prefer people who are fully committed rather than campaigners as and when it suits them.'

'Can you think of anyone from the group with whom Jade was particularly friendly?' Bliss asked. 'A female member, or perhaps another hanger-on, as you referred to her.'

'I can't think of anybody. We never knew her well, though it always struck me that she was a bit of a loner.' Cooke turned to his wife. 'Anyone come to mind, sweetheart?'

She shook her head. 'No. Nobody. Jade attended a few meetings and helped out as and when she could. As Marvin told you, she was a figure on the fringes of the movement. And I certainly don't remember her being friendly with anyone in particular.'

'So she didn't go to meetings with anyone, leave with anyone?'

'Not that I recall. She was just there. And not often. She barely registered on the memory, but her name is distinctive for some reason.'

Disappointed, Bliss tried to think of another approach. The relationship Jade had with Lucy Lancaster was as close to a loving one as any they had discovered so far, and if the woman who had shared a bed with Jade was convinced that she had a friend who was a member of CAWED then Bliss was inclined to believe it. Certainly more than he was willing to accept the word of the pair sat in front of him now.

He understood that neither would wish to draw further attention to their activism now that they appeared to have found a peaceful existence away from the media headlines. But this was about the life of a woman snatched away in the throes of a violent and terrifying struggle.

'I imagine that if I asked you for a list of members you would refuse to hand it over,' Bliss said. 'That's what you did last time you were asked. But from what you say that wouldn't provide us with the full picture anyway. Were there a lot of people like Jade? Followers who did a bit here and there but never signed up to the cause?'

'No list exists any more,' Ellie Cooke clarified. 'But yes, there were a number of people who supported us from the side-lines. We could not possibly remember them all.'

She slid her calves together with a sinuous movement. As Bliss looked up, she ran her tongue over her lips. He realised now that she was attempting to act flirtatiously. Despite the fact that she wore little more than a swimsuit and had retained a good figure, he was not aroused by her. Truth was, he felt embarrassed on her behalf. It made him think of beer-bellied older men sucking in their guts whenever pretty women came near. It was all a little obvious and sad.

'I don't suppose you happen to have any photos or film footage from the old days, do you?' Chandler asked.

It was a good thought, but it also slid open a doorway into an area Bliss had forgotten about. He made a mental note to discuss it with his partner as soon as they were done with the Cookes.

'Those days are behind us. Whatever we had back then is long gone. We are very different people now, and don't need such reminders.'

'That's the truth of the matter,' Marvin Cooke said, nodding and running a hand along his wife's forearm. 'Whether you choose to believe it or not.'

Bliss did not, but left it out there unspoken. 'Just so as we are clear, our interest is not with either of you two. Nor the bulk of your old members and supporters. We're looking for one woman. Someone close to Jade Coleman. If anything occurs to you, if you happen to remember anything about her, you will contact me, right?'

'Of course.' Cooke got to his feet, effectively ending the discussion.

Bliss stood, Chandler rising by his side. He couldn't resist one parting shot. 'You ever lie awake at night thinking about those poor frightened children whose homes went up in flames while they were at home in bed?'

Rather than answer the question directly, Ellie Cooke responded with one of her own. 'Do you ever think about the suffering we humans have caused with nuclear power and radioactivity, the horrific weapons we are stockpiling, or the threat to our own lives and that of the entire planet?'

'Actually, I do,' Bliss replied, meeting her gaze. 'But the difference between us is that I also see the hypocrisy in being willing to terrify and harm people by way of a response. See, when your fight concentrated on the issues and the developers, you had my sympathies. When you indulged your frustrations by selecting easy and wholly innocent targets, that's when our philosophies parted ways. You went from doing something admirable to something criminal... and inhumane.'

Bliss stared them both down for a moment. 'If your conscience eventually pricks you,' he said, 'pick up the phone and tell us who that woman is. But don't worry, I won't be holding my breath waiting for either of you to do the right thing.'

'You're speaking to us as if we are monsters.'

'And in the eyes of the children you terrorised, that's exactly what you are.'

'You would be wise to modify your tone, Inspector,' Marvin Cooke said then. Something had shifted in his eyes. The false friendly expression in them was gone, replaced by a hard glint. 'Both of you, in fact.'

'Why is that, then?' Bliss asked, facing him down.

'Because although CAWED no longer officially exists, and that world is no longer a part of our lives, the anti-nuclear movement is far from finished. We still have powerful friends, people with both money and influence. Believe me, they don't waste too much time with words when they get a bee in their bonnets. There are still plenty around just itching for some action.'

'If I didn't know better, I'd say that was a threat.' Bliss turned fully to stand almost toe-to-toe with Cooke. 'And if I thought for one second that you meant it, you would see a very different side of me.'

'Is that so, Inspector?'

'It is. I realise you don't do your own dirty work. You never did. You had your minions around you for that sort of thing. But I hold you personally responsible. So you might want to think about that. You and I will never be friends, Mr Cooke, but believe me when I tell you that you don't want me as your enemy, either.'

As they headed away from the marina, Bliss sent himself a two word email. Chandler noticed, and asked him who he was contacting.

'Myself. Speaking to those two arse wipes reminded me that Sandra Bannister from the *PT* sent me a load of files and links relating to CAWED. The Cookes might claim not to have kept any memorabilia relating to their glory days, but that's not to say it doesn't exist.'

Chandler laughed. 'You don't like them much, do you? You think there's anything to the veiled threat he made?'

'You mean, do I think he might order a firebombing of my home, or have some of his old affiliates turn up at my door carrying baseball bats? To be honest, I really don't know.'

'I told you about my friend. They gave her a real kicking. Nasty bastards some of them.'

'Hopefully they've grown up and seen the error of their ways.'

'Didn't feel to me as if Marvin and Ellie Cooke had.'

'Did you see her? Preening herself as if she were something precious and exotic. The woman thinks she's still sexy. She made my skin crawl.'

'He wasn't any better. Thinks he's God's gift, but he's just a small man with a tiny mind.'

Bliss shook his head. 'I never did see the attraction. It was more like a cult than a genuine organisation, aimed at protesting against nuclear waste disposal in landfill sites, with those two somehow luring in followers with the force of their personalities.'

'Perhaps that's what it was behind all the anti-nuclear stuff. A cult, just as you said. Maybe Marvin Cooke was their David Koresh.'

'The Waco bloke? What was it they called themselves?'

'Branch Davidians.'

'Yeah, that's it. How do you remember stuff like that?'

Chandler grinned. 'I watched a TV series about it last year.'

'I'm not saying Marvin Cooke put himself out there as the second coming or anything, but I do think his driving force was all about the power and control rather than the disposal of contaminated waste.'

'You think they were lying? You think they know who Jade's friend was.'

'I do,' Bliss replied. 'And I aim to clobber them with evidence of that just as soon as I can.'

Chapter Twenty-Four

Bliss was not quite four years old when gangster Ronnie Kray entered the Blind Beggar pub saloon bar and shot George Cornell to death; he had been an associate of the Kray twins' south-London rivals, the Richardsons. If you believed all the stories about that murder, virtually every Londoner within five square miles was in the Blind Beggar that evening in March 1966.

Bliss's father never made that particular claim to infamy, but he was one of the officers who attended the aftermath of the shooting. Cornell received one bullet to the head from a Luger pistol and was taken to a nearby hospital, where he died from that single fatal wound in the early hours of the following morning. Bliss's father had run the uniformed presence in and around the pub that night.

The Uppercut boxing gym was called The Stepney Hook in those days. It was where Bliss had first learned to fight using the Marquis of Queensbury rules as opposed to the street brawling he was familiar with. His father had insisted that if he was going to keep getting into fights, he might as well learn how to throw a proper punch.

And avoid them.

The gym stood on a side street less than half a mile from the Blind Beggar, and it was in that notorious pub that Bliss and his friends often spent their evenings from the age of around fifteen. It was a popular place, and West Ham footballers Harry Redknapp and Bobby Moore could often be found in there after training. Moore even went on to own the place at one point.

For old times' sake, Bliss drove by the pub that afternoon on his way to the gym. It occurred to him that it was only much later in life that he had given any real thought to that grim moment in the Beggar's past, because to him, his family and closest friends, it was simply the place in which they congregated for an evening on the lash.

Police officers and their families would not have been welcome in the mid-sixties, but as the pub recovered from that dark night, so the owners and landlords became less inclined to welcome gangsters as local celebrities.

The old place looked brighter now than he remembered it, with a fresh coat of paint and the red brick and stonework cleaned up. It brought his early life in this part of the capital into sharp focus, and Bliss wondered if he would ever be that happy and carefree again.

He did not recognise the gym at all. Its soot-stained brick exterior had been rendered over, the old metal sash windows replaced with modern uPVC double-glazing. Below the new sign the old one had been retained in its original condition, which Bliss thought was a nice touch. Most of the east London fighters had trained in The Stepney Hook at one time or another, and it was nice to know that its history had been acknowledged in this way.

Bliss stepped inside and saw that the interior of the gym had received a makeover as well. It was clean with modern fixtures and fittings, but the one thing that neither refurbishment nor the passing of time could ever change was the smell. The sharp tang of cowhide or goatskin leather gloves and the sour reek of sweat and body odour, together with the acrid stench of bleach at its core, made for a heady concoction which could never be removed or forgotten. It seeped into the walls and canvases and refused to let go, becoming as much a part of the past and future as it was the present.

A cacophony of noise greeted Bliss as he entered: grunts of exertion that made their way up from the gut, the thud-thud-thud of punches hitting bag gloves, underlying allegro rhythms of speed bags being caressed, harsh squeals of rubber-soled footwear on polished hardwood floors, and urgent voices echoing around the vast hall.

Memories sneaked up on him like a sucker-punch on the break, and for a moment it halted his breath. Bliss stood in place for several seconds, both afraid to breathe and terrified he might not ever again. A loud cackle of laughter close by shook him out of it, and he felt his cheeks flush a little.

Bliss recognised Gary Pemberton the moment he laid eyes on him. A quarter of a century had slipped by since the two had last been in the same room together, but the ex-uniform's diamond-hard features and concave left cheekbone made him easy to identify. Pemberton was standing to the side of one of three rings, his arm around the shoulder of a black youth whose dripping forehead told Bliss his workout had been intense. The trainer spoke with animated gestures and emotion, and the fighter nodded along as he listened. That was one of the things about boxing: you either learned discipline and respect, or you were out the door, and fast.

In another ring there was a pretty aggressive sparring session going on between two heavyweights. The speed and ferocity of the punching was impressive, and more than a little daunting. The boxers moved like pendulums in their twelve-twenty stances, jabs setting up the power shots that began in the soles of their feet. Bliss knew that just one of those punches would put him down, and probably out, if it connected just right. He watched the fight unfold until a deep and booming voice hurt his ears.

'Fuck my old boots! Is that Marley's ghost or Jimmy Bliss I see before me?'

Bliss turned. Gary Pemberton strode awkwardly towards him, an old hamstring injury still affecting his gait. His hand was outstretched, and he wore a smile on his face, but there was also an impenetrable darkness in the man's eyes which were as dull and cold as pebbles. It was all Bliss needed to see to know that Gareth Wigg's information was accurate, and that Pemberton was somehow involved in whatever investigation the IOPC was building against him. Bliss bit down on his rising anger. He needed this to play out as much as possible.

'Hello, Gary. How's it going? The old place is looking good.'

They shook hands, Pemberton nodding enthusiastically. His grip was as firm as it had ever been. 'Well, I'm still breathing, which is better than the alternative. And yeah, the gym has never looked better.'

The young kid who had been on the receiving end of either a bollocking or a guiding hand, had wandered over with him. The grizzled old trainer turned to him now. 'Mark, when you next have a butcher's at the trophy cabinet, check out the late seventies section. You'll see the name James H Bliss, this is your man right here. A bloody good amateur in his day. Could have been another Stracey if he'd kept his weight down.'

The young black fighter regarded Bliss with respect. Nodded and smiled. 'I had a good corner man, Mark,' Bliss told him. 'You'll go far with this old geezer by your side.'

Pemberton winked. 'Like I say, Jimmy boy was a decent amateur. Never had the stomach to take it further, though. Not like you, kid. You've got the hunger inside you.'

He turned away and chuckled at Bliss. 'Don't mind me, Jimmy. I didn't mean you never had the guts. One thing about you was you never knew when you were defeated. I've seen you turn bouts around when you were out on your feet, old son. Nah, in your case you just never had the drive. You didn't want it enough.'

Bliss regarded the man closely for a moment. The phrase he had used about not having the stomach for taking his boxing to the next level had stung for a brief moment, and he did not believe Pemberton had said it accidentally. There was an undercurrent to the man's feigned enthusiasm at seeing an old friend, and Bliss thought he knew precisely why.

'You're not out until the count reaches ten,' he responded. 'That's what you and my old man always taught me. Ain't that right, Gary?'

'Well, that or when the towel comes in.'

'I never had a towel to throw.' Bliss hardened his stare. 'Still don't.'

Pemberton nodded and lost all pretence from his features. He flashed a smile that was all gleaming dentures. After instructing the young boxer to go and work the bag, he turned back to Bliss.

'Just happen to be passing by, Jimmy? Thought you'd come and check out the old place out of pure nostalgia, did you? Or was there something more specific on your mind?'

'There's always something on my mind, Gary.'

'That's true enough. And you'd hardly be passing by these days, would you? You've got no family around here any more, and the way I hear it, you're up in the Fens now.'

'Near enough as makes no difference. I think we both know why I'm here, Gary. And it's not to chat about the good old days.'

Pemberton gave a slight nod. He seemed to consider how to play his hand. 'Tell you what, how about we continue this little chat in my office?'

Bliss shook his head. 'Now that I'm here and I've actually seen you, Gary, I'm wondering if we really have anything to discuss.'

'You know we do. It's why you're here. No other reason for you to have come back to your old manor.'

'Just us, Gary? Or should someone else be joining us?'

The man stiffened, eyes widening. 'Ah. So you know.'

'I know something,' Bliss replied. The sounds and motions of the gym went on around them, but he felt as if the two of them were somehow stuck in time. 'As you rightly pointed out, Gary, that's what I'm doing here. It's certainly not for the bullshit pleasantries. I don't know the who or the why, though. And I'd also really like to know how come you're the one who stepped up to put my name in the frame.'

Pemberton studied him for a few seconds. Bliss felt the man's deep scrutiny. The tension between them was now tangible, though so much remained unspoken.

'You're very much like your old man, Jimmy. Thought you were so much better than the rest of us. When it suited, of course. Never asked where the gear came from that was sold for peanuts in the boozers. Nor the cheap fags and spirits that somehow avoided the tax man on their way into the country. But when the rest of us looked to make a bit of cash on the side, you turned your backs on us.'

Bliss wrinkled his nose. 'That's not even close to being true. There was doing what you could to help out, going along to get along and turning a blind eye to the petty stuff. And then there was doing the right thing when it needed to be done. When someone crossed the line. Small time stuff could be overlooked, but some people never knew when to stop.'

'And it was the great Bliss family who said where and when that line should exist, right?'

'Did we have standards? Too bloody right we did. I'll never apologise for that, and my old man never did, either. Most people could handle that, Gary. They knew how the game was played. But you always resented it. And over the years that resentment burned its way through your stomach like acid. There was plenty of opportunity to front up back then, back when my old man was around. You didn't seem to have the stomach for it then, though. You want to get your own back on me and my family after all this time. Is that what this is all about?'

Pemberton looked around to make sure they could not be overheard. He leaned in and lowered his voice anyway. 'Why come down here poking around?' he asked with a snarl, lips twitching. 'It's not as if you're going to do anything about it, Jimmy. You ain't got the spherics for that.'

'You really want to find out if that's true, Gary?'

'You're way out of your league, old son. Out of your depth, and out of your comfort zone. Look around you, Jimmy. You ain't got any friends here now to back you up.'

Bliss took a step closer. 'Maybe I don't need them. Maybe all I need is me.'

With a shake of the head, Pemberton said, 'I wish it was that easy. If it was down to me alone, I'd welcome the chance to set you straight.'

'Then do so in a different way. Tell me what this is all about.'

Pemberton took a deep breath, giving himself time to consider his response. 'You want me to make a call? Get a certain someone here who can give you all the answers you're looking for.'

'Why not? Let's get it out in the open.'

'You want to wait in my office while I give him a bell?'

Bliss gave that some thought. Pemberton was right about one thing: this was no longer his stomping ground. It was not even neutral territory any more. His name, and more so his father's name, was once widely respected in the area. But those days were long gone, and Gary Pemberton had remained. The last thing Bliss wanted was to feel trapped, or worse still actually *be* trapped inside the gym, with no friends in his corner. He opted for caution and shook his head.

'I'm going to grab a bite and a drink. How soon can you get them here?'

'Thirty minutes. Maybe sooner.'

Bliss nodded. 'Do that, Gary. I'll come back. But before you make the call, tell me your side. I know there was plenty of unfinished business between you and my old man, but I can't think of any reason why you would want to hurt me now.'

Pemberton leaned closer. 'It's not always about who you want to hurt, Jimmy. Sometimes it's about not being hurt yourself.'

'So what do they have on you? Whatever it is, I bet you didn't need too much persuading. My old man never saw it, Gary, but I always knew you were a wrong'un. He always thought the best of you, and I could never understand why. You'd all be sitting there around the card table or in the boozer, everyone laughing and joking and telling their stories. But I'll always remember the day I happened to clock you when my dad was talking about some crazy escapade or another. You were chuckling away, your shoulders heaving, just like everyone else. But there was a look in your eyes that was pure bile. It was as fake as that dodgy Rolex you've got on your wrist right now.'

'I loved your dad like a brother.'

'Yeah. Right up to the point where you didn't. Then you were Cain to his Abel. I tried to warn him about you, Gary. But he refused to listen. Wouldn't hear a bad word said about you. And this is how you repay him? By coming after me.'

'Like I told you, I don't really have a choice.'

'And if you did? If you *could* choose? Whose side would you come down on?'

Pemberton growled and flapped a hand.

It was answer enough for Bliss. 'Go on and make your call now, Gary. Become the rat I always knew you to be.'

'Fuck you, Jimmy! What do you know about me or my life? You fucked off out of here as soon as you found your feet. Some of us stayed. We had no alternative. This was where we were born and raised, and it's where we'll die. Your old man thought he was the father of this community, but he never wanted to stick around to see it through to the end.'

Bliss was outraged. Somehow managing to keep his voice low and even, his temper under control, he spoke through teeth almost clamped together.

'My dad served every day of his working life in and around this area, you ignorant prick. He never thought he *led* the community, he thought he *policed* it. He wasn't your fucking gang leader, Gary. He was your colleague. And he was also your mate. At least, that's what he thought he was. I knew better. I saw your true face revealed that day, and I knew you were a fucking Judas.'

'Fuck you!'

Bliss took a breath, panting now as undiluted rage threatened to overwhelm him. He raised a finger and pointed at Pemberton. 'Walk away, Gary. Walk away and make that call.'

'Or what?'

'Or you'll see a side of me you've never seen before.'

Turning on his heels to leave the gym, Bliss's thoughts were in turmoil. As he had grown older, he realised for himself that the family friend and fight trainer had always held a little jealousy in his heart where the Bliss family were concerned. Remarks he had taken as jokes when he was too young to understand otherwise, came back to prod his memories and paint them in darker hues. Yet the remark from Pemberton about not wanting to be hurt himself implied there was more than an envious grudge turned septic in play here; that the man had perhaps been compelled somehow by another to become involved in clawing at Bliss's reputation. That a threat had been made.

Bliss shook his head as he burst through the gym doors back out into the daylight. It didn't matter. His retort had hit home. Pemberton may well have been threatened and coerced into contacting the IOPC with fresh allegations concerning Hazel's murder, but he was not the most reluctant of victims. The man saw a way of hitting back at a family he still regarded with envy, and was happy enough to take it.

Bliss had found a parking space across the road close to the gym, and from inside the car he would be able to see whoever came and went. The drive down had been better than he had anticipated it would be. He had dosed himself up with both pain killers and anti-inflammatory medication before setting out, but even city driving, all gear changes and making turns, caused little reaction from the ribs. His right shoulder and hip still hurt, but they were sending out low-level grumbles rather than excruciating waves of pain.

As Bliss sat and watched the gym entrance, he saw an equal flow of people entering and exiting the building. Looking on, Bliss saw a scruffy white van with dents in the side and rust bubbles around the wheel arches shuffle into a tight parking space but thought little of it. Until he spotted the driver stepping out and locking the door. All at once there seemed to be no air to breathe, and the confines of his car became claustrophobic. For a moment, Bliss wondered if he might be on the verge of a panic attack. But he talked himself down, took deeper breaths through his nose and let them loose through his mouth until his lungs were drained, repeating the process several times. Finally, he managed to control himself, though his pulse raced and his head felt as if a railway spike had been driven into it.

It wasn't simply that the person he had seen leaving the van and entering the gym was the last person he had expected to see that day. It was more about what the man's presence suggested in terms of who and what was driving the IOPC investigation, and the degree to which Bliss now realised how much trouble was coming his way.

Chapter Twenty-Five

'So, who was it?' Chandler asked.

While navigating back out of London in the slow crawl of steaming metal, Bliss had called Chandler and asked her to meet him for a drink prior to everyone gathering in his living room later that evening. Overlooking Gunwade Lake, the Lakeside Kitchen and Bar offered one of the most picturesque views of any café or restaurant in the whole of Peterborough. As part of the Nene Park estate which was currently celebrating its fortieth birthday, the café and bar benefitted hugely from being the social hub of a beloved tourist attraction. The fact that it was a stone's throw away from the site of a gruesome murder the previous autumn – Bliss's first case back in the city – had done little to stem the flow of happy customers.

The fine June weather hadn't hurt the celebrations, that was for sure. A deep orange sun continued to blaze fiercely as it slid back towards the horizon and, despite being a working day, the park was choked with people gobbling up their annual dose of vitamin D.

A stiff breeze caressed those who sat outside, as a pleasant evening began to develop nicely. Bliss had managed to snaffle a table out on the boardwalk overhanging the lake, and he was well into his first pint when Chandler arrived straight from Thorpe Wood. She was hot and bothered, her appearance somewhat bedraggled compared to earlier that day. He got up to fetch her a non-alcoholic drink and came back with a second pint for himself as well. A plague of wasps, which had been busy and excited when he arrived, seemed to have settled elsewhere for now.

Over their drinks, Bliss had fed Chandler the broad strokes about his trip down to London and the visit to the boxing gym, including how intimidating it had felt despite the area being a Golden Oldies hit machine for his memories. He also mentioned how much more unsettled he had become the moment he recognised the figure he now assumed was behind his current problems. His partner had been intrigued.

'His name is Nick Nevin,' Bliss told her. The name tripping off his tongue made him want to scrub his mouth out with a wire brush. 'Ex-DCI Nevin, actually. The man who I still believe murdered my wife.'

Chandler gasped, her mouth falling open.

'Bloody hell, Jimmy.' Her voice was soft now, the look on her face a terrible mix of incredulity and horror. 'That just sent shivers down the back of *my* neck, so I can't imagine how it must have been for you. Seeing him again must have been a dreadful moment. But what can he possibly have to do with what's going on with the IOPC now?'

Bliss took a steady sip from his tall glass of Stella. He'd thought of little else since leaving Stepney, coming at the question from all angles. The answer was clear to him now.

'Everything. I did briefly consider him a possibility at one stage, but dismissed the idea because he's been out of the business for so long and has no friends anywhere near the top. I could hardly believe my eyes when he stepped out of that van. My guess now is he is the one who first set the wheels in motion and is using Pemberton to do his dirty work.'

'But why not do it himself?'

'Nevin's name was blackened by what happened back then, and no serving officer who gives a damn about their career would listen to him. He left on bad terms with the job, and the job was equally disapproving of him. But then I think he somehow found a line on Pemberton, who, despite being as bent as a nine-bob note, managed to retain his reputation. He would still have a way into people with influence, just as I have with the likes of Gareth Wigg.'

'But what could they possibly have to say that would spark an investigation into you after all this time?'

'That I still don't know. I think it has to be something offered up by Nevin.'

Chandler took a hit from her glass of lime and soda water. She shook her head and said, 'But why wait until now? It doesn't make any sense. What would be the impetus?'

'No, it doesn't.' Bliss shrugged. 'And I suppose any number of things could have kick-started Nevin. He may have been out of sight, but he's never been out of my mind. Maybe he feels the same way. But I know Pemberton is involved, and seeing Nevin strolling into the gym when he did was no coincidence. Gary called him, and he came running, expecting me to walk back into it later on.'

'So, you didn't confront him at all? Nevin, I mean.'

'No. Pen, if I'd got out of the car, I don't know what I might have done to the man. Last time he and I were together, I put him in hospital. A lot of years have gone by since that night, but I know he holds me responsible for the loss of his career, and his eventual decline. Time has not allowed me to forgive or forget, either. It just reminds me of all the years with Hazel I never managed to have. The promise of a future together that was stolen from us. A life taken, another life ruined.'

'I can understand that. Jimmy, I hope you don't mind my asking, but after the beating you handed out, how was it that you managed to remain in the job at all, let alone working serious cases?'

Bliss did not even have to pause to consider his response. 'If it weren't for Hazel's murder, and the subsequent accusations against me, I would at the very least have been moved well away from front-line policing.'

'So it was because of something about those accusations against you that they eventually did a deal with you?'

'Kind of. It wasn't so much that they accused me of murdering Hazel, because that was an obvious lead to follow. No, it was more the way they went about it. They crossed a number of lines when they tried to wash their hands of me without any good cause. True, if they could have proven anything against me over

Nevin's hospitalisation, then I would have stood no chance. But they couldn't.'

'So all they had was Hazel's murder.'

'Yep. And at no point did they play that one straight. It was eventually decided that there was never going to be any more promotions in my future, and I suppose they reckoned I would quit rather than remain at my current rank. It never occurred to them that I had no ambition to step up any further. My brief persuaded them it was in their best interests to leave me be, although it was also agreed that I was done at the Met.'

'Their loss was Peterborough's gain.'

Bliss grinned. 'Perhaps. I wasn't exactly desperate to stay in London, either.'

'What was it like visiting old haunts earlier today?'

'Good and bad. It always is. It provokes memories, but the place is always smaller and grubbier than I remember it being when I was a kid. Seeing Nevin again was the poisonous icing on a toxic cake, I suppose.'

'What do you think he and this Pemberton bloke were planning to do in that gym when you came back?'

'Nothing physical. More intimidation, but that would be it. If I'm right, and Nevin has cooked up something against me to suggest I killed Hazel, or at the very least put me back in the frame for it, then he would want that to play out as far as it could possibly go. I imagine he would have used my presence at the gym as a stick to beat me with later. He could have claimed almost anything with Pemberton there to back up his story. You know the sort of thing I mean – my threatening him, or even striking him. I wouldn't put it past the man to pay off someone to smack him around and to then blame me for it.'

'This is awful, Jimmy,' Chandler said. 'Just truly awful.'

'I wasn't stressed about it before, when the IOPC paid a visit. I knew there was absolutely nothing they could have on me when it comes to Hazel's murder. But seeing Nevin today convinces me that something has been planted or tampered with, evidence altered, a bogus eye witness suddenly uncovered. Something that puts the focus back on me. And in doing so, away from him, of course.'

'But if they had all that already, why would the pair from the IOPC not have acted formally? Why the warning shot?'

Bliss had given that some thought as well during the journey up from London. The more logical approach would have been for the IOPC to keep their powder dry, then come at him with the full weight of an official investigation behind them. Initially, the tactic they had employed seemed to be the wrong one. But the more Bliss thought about it, the more he found sound reasoning.

'I think they were told there was fresh evidence, but maybe not what it was. I think they were given some assurances over a new approach, and that while they were waiting for whatever it is to be either produced or verified, they couldn't resist coming at me and taking a peek for themselves.'

'That sounds feasible.'

'Maybe they even suspected I might get wind of it from old Met contacts, and wanted me to think they were going for low-grade stuff instead, like ignoring regulations, or possibly even taking back-handers when I was younger and still coming up in the Met. A distraction, of sorts. Whatever the reason, my guess is they were preparing the groundwork because at that time they didn't have everything they needed.'

'And you think this Nevin arsehole will be feeding it to them via Gary Pemberton, the boxing trainer.'

'I do. And next time they come, they'll have it all. It'll be a full-scale disciplinary hearing, which will see me desk-bound or even suspended. If it's as bad as I suspect it is, then I'm in for the suspension and worse.'

'Worse?'

'There's no getting away from it, Pen. They'll be looking at me for murder.'

'Jimmy, I don't know what to say.' Chandler looked wounded by the conversation, as if hearing him lay it all out caused her physical pain.

'There really isn't anything *to* say. Also, I don't know how much more time this gives me on operation Cauldron.'

'Sod that, Jimmy! That's one case. The IOPC issue is the rest of your career if it goes tits up.'

'No. I refuse to look at it like that. In fact, quite the opposite. Finding Jade Coleman's killer is now my priority. She is my case, not just an operation name. If it's to be the last thing I do as a copper, then I want to get it right. I owe it to the victim, Pen.'

Chandler shook her head vigorously. 'You're thinking short term, Jimmy. I understand how you feel, but if you concentrate on Jade Coleman rather than yourself, then you risk not being around to solve dozens of more cases in the future for the sake of one right now.'

'That may well already be out of my hands. The investigation isn't. For now, at least.'

'Do I need to remind you that you are currently signed off on sick leave?'

'Not at all, Pen. That's the first thing I have to address. I'm cancelling my appointment with the Occupational Health doctor tomorrow. As for the note I got from my GP, I'll simply rip it up. I called in for two absence days, and I took them. But that's it now.'

'And we both know that's not what the Super told you to do.'

Bliss nodded. He had known he would meet with some resistance from his partner on this. Yet he was determined, and with that came a stubbornness that was so much a part of his character.

'I understand that. But at the time that agreement was made, we thought this IOPC thing was something I could get ahead of and deal with. It isn't. Not easily, anyhow. So I need to go back to work.' He held a hand in the air, palm facing his colleague. 'No more arguments, Pen. My mind is made up.'

'Then your mind is wrong. You're not thinking clearly.'

'And I said no more arguments.'

Her gaze narrowed. 'I'm not on the clock. This is my private time, and I'll bloody well argue all I like. Jimmy, I honestly understand why you want to see this one through. But you're wrong. This time, you are not playing with a full deck.'

'I've made up my mind,' Bliss said dismissively. 'It's my decision. Mine alone. You can argue all night long, but it won't change a thing. So don't waste your breath.'

Chandler had been draining her glass. Now she slammed it down on the table, drawing a disapproving glance from an elderly man seated nearby. 'You can be so infuriating at times, Jimmy Bliss. Why will you not listen to reason?'

'Has it ever occurred to you that you could be in the wrong, Pen? That I *am* listening to reason – my own?'

'Honestly? No. If you put all your efforts into the investigation, then you'll be caught unawares when the IOPC comes back at you.'

'Not entirely. And I won't ignore it completely. I'll work both still. The only difference will be that Jade Coleman gets more of my time from now on. That's my job, and murders like hers are the reason I do it. In terms of my private issues, I don't know where things stand in that regard any more. I can't approach Pemberton again if he is the man directly communicating with the IOPC, or even if he's going through a third-party contact. It will only count against me.'

'That doesn't mean we can't.'

Bliss shook his head. He raised his eyebrows and put a hard edge of finality into his voice.

'No. That's taking a step further than any of you should go. You were already putting yourselves in a dodgy situation just by helping me. I won't allow you to approach the man directly. Not a chance.'

'Won't allow? Did you really just say that to me?' Chandler leaned back in her chair as if shocked by his outburst.

He grinned and tried to throttle back a little. 'I know that's like waving a red rag at you, but we're not talking caseload here, Pen. This is not a professional development. Not yet. It's personal.

It's my problem, and yes, I do get to say what you can or cannot do in this matter.'

Chandler toyed with her empty glass, catching shafts of sunlight on its surface. 'What if the roles were reversed? If it was me, Mia or Bish in your position, you'd not only offer to do the same thing, you'd stop at nothing to make sure you confronted the man and got the answers you needed.'

'Not if doing so was entirely the wrong move.'

'Rubbish. This is me you're talking to. We both know what you would do. Why deny it?'

Bliss tilted his head back. The fading sun caught his face in its glow and he was glad of its warm touch upon his skin. He closed his eyes for a few seconds, disparate thoughts assaulting his senses in the darkness. When he looked back at his partner, he did so with real affection.

'The thing about people, Pen, is we're all different. We have our own reasons for doing things our own way. You can't just think to yourself that if Jimmy Bliss does something then it's the right thing for Penny Chandler to do as well. It doesn't work that way. If I am sometimes considered to be reckless, with little regard for procedure on occasion, then maybe the reason for that is because my career has stagnated since I made DI. I'm constantly on borrowed time, no matter how many cases I run that get solved. You're not. All three of you have promotion ahead of you if you want it badly enough. None of you should step out of line the way you'd need to now to help me. I'm grateful to you all, for both your friendship and loyalty, but you have to rein it in.'

'You think the others will buy that?' Chandler asked.

Bliss sighed. 'I doubt it. But, like you, they'll have no choice in the matter. I'm not throwing in the towel, Pen. As I reminded my new foe earlier, I don't have one to throw away. I will still spend some time with this, trying to find a different approach, using whatever limited resources I can afford on it. But the simple fact is that we are five days into the Jade Coleman murder case and with most of the information in, we're no closer to solving it. We may know who didn't do it, but that's not the same thing at all.'

Finally relenting, Chandler offered to get them another drink, but Bliss declined. Instead, he reached for his mobile and made a call.

'Mia, it's Bliss,' he said when it was diverted to voicemail. 'I'm cancelling the meeting at my place later. I'll explain tomorrow. Let Bish know would you, please. Thanks.'

Bliss slipped the phone back into his jacket, which was draped over the empty chair to his right. He looked back up at Chandler. 'It's done,' he said. 'And I can't tell you how relieved I am about that.'

She lowered her eyes and said on a sigh, 'I just hope you don't come to regret your decision, Jimmy. I can't bear the thought of you no longer doing this work. Can you?'

'No. But I promise you I won't be going down without a fight. And as we're on the subject of the investigation, what were you able to get done while I was visiting the old manor?'

Chandler gave him an outline of the items the team had picked up on in his absence. She had personally contacted Lucy Lancaster, confirming her previous statement that Jade had spoken about having a close female friend who was somehow affiliated to CAWED. She could offer no further help on the woman's name, however. The neighbour, Baldwin, had been spoken to and he was able to shed light on Jade Coleman's habit of throwing open her windows and doors when the weather was warm.

'So even early on that Friday morning, Jade could have felt the temperature rising and left her back door wide open,' Bliss said, mulling that over. 'It may not have been too difficult a proposition for someone to hop the back fence and find their way in.'

'Especially if they had been watching her and had already noted her behaviour.'

'Which brings us back to our stalker. Any joy there?'

Chandler shrugged. 'It's a work in progress. We're looking at a few of the names in the task force database, and will set up visits. There's nothing more coming from the recanvas of the neighbourhood. There will obviously now be a close focus on this cyclist in the hoodie. The difficulty there being, you see someone dressed like that on a hot day and you lower your eyes because you automatically think they might be a dealer. CCTV footage is being revisited as well. We discussed the crossing points you mentioned earlier, and when the forensic team go into Mandy Vickers's place tomorrow, I'm also sending Hunt and Ansari to speak to her more about where she and her stalker might have first crossed paths.'

'Good. Baby steps. I'm leaning heavily towards the stalker angle. We have to, especially now that we strongly suspect he's struck before. We'll cover all our bases, but that's our priority for sure.'

'There was one more thing I wanted to tell you,' Chandler said. 'It would have come up later, but you cancelled the meeting. Bish has taken a quick look back through your cases here in the city. He agrees with your own assessment that the areas of weakness are thin, and nothing more than procedural lapses. Slap on the wrist stuff. He's yet to dig deep on the two obvious investigations from your previous posting here – and by that I mean the one that got you suspended, and the one that resulted in you having to leave the city – but his impression was that because investigations into your actions had already been carried out, and you already served your so-called leave of absence time, as well as following up with psych, there's nothing they can touch you with again.'

Bliss blew out a deep breath. He was a man of few regrets, but there were times when he looked back on investigations and questioned both his motives and their subsequent actions and results. The case that led to him moving back down to London had begun with unearthed bones and ended with him burying the careers of several fellow officers due to their involvement in either murder or corruption. Or both in some instances. In his mind, the end sometimes justified the means. Bliss believed Chandler was living proof of that. He was convinced that had he not acted the way he did the previous autumn, when Malcolm Thompson abducted Chandler and used her as bait, his colleague and friend would no longer be around to chastise him and, in her own way, try to keep him on the straight and narrow.

His partner had become silent and appeared a little gloomy. Her gaze wandered across to the rippled water of the lake, pale sunlight glinting on its surface which was more reflective than he had ever seen it before.

Bliss understood her anger and frustration with him. He would feel the same in her place, because his decision had made her feel helpless. But he was convinced it was for the best. Nick Nevin's appearance at that gym had changed everything, and he had to roll with it or go under. He would do whatever he could to protect himself, but Nevin's shadow was vast and cold, reopening a wound much deeper and wider than Bliss had anticipated.

He could not fully explain it, not even to himself. Initially, he had been confident in taking the IOPC on, believing that whatever they had could only ever be circumstantial at the very worst. But somehow the fact that Nevin was behind the new attack on his integrity felt like the haymaker punch he had sworn he would never open himself up to again. It had subsequently caused his determination to falter, his confidence to evaporate, and the only way he could cope with what was happening was to immerse himself in his work.

As he had always done.

And the first job on his list when he got back home was to go through the files Sandra Bannister had mailed him.

Chapter Twenty-Six

There was still some light and plenty of heat left in the day when Bliss pulled into the Bill Fen Marina for the second time in less than twelve hours.

He had decided to drive out there within minutes of obtaining what he believed was evidence that Marvin and Ellie Cooke had lied during their interview. The questioning could have waited until the following morning, but Bliss thought it would be good to have made some progress on this before the team briefing at which he was going to be a surprise guest. He was not sure where this aspect of the case was headed, but he was not willing to let it go at this early stage. If it led nowhere, he would at least take comfort from the fact that he had taken it as far as he could.

The moment he had got back home after the drink and chat with Chandler, he made himself a cheese spread and peanut butter sandwich, and washed it down with a cup of his favourite Earl Grey tea. Over the hastily prepared snack, Bliss sifted through the material he had received from the *Peterborough Telegraph* journalist. Ignoring the documents, investigative notes, and other written files, he went straight to the photographs and online articles containing images. He wanted to take another look at these people when they were in their pomp and so full of themselves.

The article that captured Bliss's attention was one reporting on the trial of prominent CAWED member Diane Locke. Though identifying as a female at that point, Locke had been born Stephen Robbie. Robbie was a thug who spent much of his teenage years behind bars, got engaged upon his release, but a year later declared himself a woman and pretty much dropped out of society, reappearing at every protest gathering for whatever cause there was going on at the time. As Diane Locke, the woman claimed to have been turned by her experiences inside – both away from being a man, and towards anything remotely anti-establishment or cause worthy. In the media, the spokespeople for CAWED had consistently proclaimed themselves to be peaceful campaigners. Yet Diane Locke was a known agitator who was eventually arrested for affray and her role in aggressive strikes against suppliers to Whittlesey Energy Disposal.

To Bliss, this was evidence enough that CAWED openly consorted with the kind of people for whom terrorist activities were deemed acceptable methods of protest. Although they had always denied being party to such atrocities, and had rigorously defended their claims to be a movement without leadership, the more Bliss read about them the more their culpability took shape.

After reading the report, Bliss studied the accompanying photographs of CAWED protestors demonstrating outside the local Town Hall building. One depicted the banner-wielding group standing on the pavement directly in front of the entrance. At the front – as they always seemed to be – were the Cookes. To the left of Ellie Cooke stood two other women. Bliss did not recognise one of them, but his breath caught in his throat when he saw that the other was Jade Coleman.

A further search, now with a clear focus, resulted in three more photos in which Marvin and Ellie Cooke appeared with both the mystery woman and Jade Coleman. And in two of the photographs, Jade was either holding hands with the unidentified female, or had an arm around her shoulder. It was not proof that there was anything more than friendship between the two, but it was evidence that Jade was not quite the occasional hanger-on she had been painted as.

The Cookes were neither receptive nor antagonistic towards a second interview when Bliss arrived at their home unannounced. Marvin did ask whether they ought to be consulting with a solicitor, but when Bliss declared himself ambivalent to the suggestion, the man backed off. Once again, the two sat together on the same couch, though this time, Ellie was at least fully dressed while she attempted to project the same kind of sultry allure she had been aiming for that morning.

Bliss took out his mobile, opened up the photo app and brought up a folder which held four images he had downloaded off the website links he had studied earlier. Then he sat forward in his seat, held the phone out and showed the glowing screen to the pair, who were now casting anxious sidelong glances at each other.

'First of all,' he said. 'I would like you to take a look at these and then explain to me how they relate to your statements in which you insisted Jade Coleman was a mere irregular hanger-on. It seems clear to me from these images that she was at the forefront of your support.'

To his question there was no answer. Only silence from the Cookes. Neither so much as glanced at the other, their attention remaining fixed upon him. Bliss nodded once and continued.

'And secondly, I would like you to tell me who this woman is that Jade seems so friendly with, despite your earlier assertions that she had no friends at all within your group.'

This time, Marvin Cooke took a deep breath before admitting that their previous denial was less than honest. 'The woman in the photographs is Tessa Brady. And yes, you're absolutely right, Inspector, she and Jade were friendly.'

'Yet you not only failed to mention this earlier, you specifically denied it. Why is that, Mr Cooke?'

'Because we wanted nothing more to do with that hateful bitch!' Ellie interrupted, venom in both her tone and the flare of her eyes.

'You were not a fan, I take it?'

'You could say that.'

'How come?'

'I would rather not talk about it, if it's all the same to you. Tessa is a part of our lives we would rather forget.'

Bliss knew he could force the issue by making the interview formal and under caution. However, they had not yet clammed up completely, nor had they requested the solicitor Marvin had previously mentioned. He thought it better to get from them what he could before either or both of those things happened.

'Do you know where I might find Tessa Brady now?' he asked.

There was a lengthy pause before Marvin snorted and jabbed a stiff finger towards the wooden floorboards. 'She's down there. Where she belongs.'

Bliss frowned. 'You mean dead and buried? Or dead and in hell?'

The man spread his hands. 'Either. Both. I'm beyond caring.'

'So you don't actually know. Is that what you're saying, sir?'

Ellie Cooke leaned forward, brushing her hair back behind her ears. She wore unflattering casual clothing and was no longer looking to flirt. 'Inspector, that woman left one of our meetings after a furious argument, and never returned. She took with her all of our finances, because she was the organisation's accounts manager. We set your lot on her, but they were hardly interested because of who we were and what we represented. They gave up trying to trace her after only a few days. If they even bothered at all, that is. We were hardly flavour of the month with the police.'

'I see. So she stole from you. Anything else? It's just that the antipathy associated with these recollections is coming across as rather more personal for you than your husband, Mrs Cooke.'

If the photographs were anything to go by, Tessa Brady was a good-looking woman. While she certainly seemed attached to Jade Coleman, the photographs also suggested an intimacy of sorts with Ellie Cooke. Bliss wondered if there may have been something between the two women.

'Is theft not enough, Inspector?' Marvin demanded. He shifted forward in his seat. To Bliss the movement and aggression in his voice felt false. As if he were behaving this way to deflect attention away from his wife.

Nodding, Bliss said, 'Of course. I was simply thinking out loud. But you and your wife were convicted of fraud, Mr Cooke. So you're no strangers to making money disappear yourselves.'

'We were convicted despite our innocence. We were set up, and I think we both realised later by whom.'

'Ah. I see. You're saying Brady committed the fraud and framed you two for it. She sounds like quite the criminal talent. So what makes you think she is dead? Presumably the police never told you she was. Nor anyone else for that matter. I'm wondering why you concluded that she died as opposed to simply having fled and never returned.'

'Because she was just that type of woman.' This from Ellie Cooke again. She seemed incapable of staying out of the conversation, and that was fine by Bliss. 'Manipulative. Dishonest. Always doing whatever was best for Tessa Brady. Besides, her parents were desperate to find her, and I believe they attempted to put pressure on the police to re-examine her disappearance. Her passport was never found, money was withdrawn from her personal accounts as well as ours, and in her home they found clothes and personal items had been removed as if she had left willingly and quickly.'

'Which brings me back to the same question,' Bliss said. 'If the signs are that she packed her bags and skipped, why do you two think she is dead?'

'Oh, we also think she left. Possibly even to move abroad. But you see, a woman like that is incapable of switching it off. Wherever she landed, she would have done the same thing to someone else. And worse. The bitch was poisonous. You know that story about the scorpion and the frog, Inspector?'

Bliss frowned. 'Remind me.'

'A scorpion tries to convince a frog to carry it across a river on its back. The frog is unwilling because it believes the scorpion will sting it and kill it. The scorpion argues that if it did so, they would both end up dead because the scorpion would then drown. This convinces the frog. Halfway across the river the scorpion stings the frog, dooming them both. When the dying frog asks the scorpion why it stung him, the scorpion replies that it's in its nature to do so.

'Well, Tessa Brady was one of life's scorpions. It was in her nature to lie and cheat and be cruel. The fact that nobody within the group has heard from her or seen her since, suggests to me that she is dead. And I, for one, have never lost a moment of sleep over believing that to be the case.'

Bliss paused. He was excited that he now had a name to work with. Equally, he kept in mind that this pair had deceived him and Chandler earlier, and he was uncertain as to how to proceed. Tessa Brady might well still be alive, and if she was the ugly person the Cookes described, that would bring her into the frame when considering the murder of Jade Coleman. His instincts insisted the stalker was responsible. Could Brady be that stalker? It did not fit with the stalking and beating of Mandy Vickers, but Bliss did not want to rule out the possibility entirely.

'There's a lot to digest,' he said eventually. 'Even more to uncover, I suspect. I think it's likely that we are going to have to ask you to come in so that we can speak at greater length, and in much more detail.'

Marvin Cooke gestured towards the narrow steps leading up onto the deck of the boat. 'Anything else you wish to know you can ask with a solicitor present,' he said. 'Right now, I think my wife and I have been more than accommodating, but I am tired of all the questions. Please show yourself out.'

'You're not about to threaten me again, are you?' Bliss asked him, wearily. 'Only, there's a lot of that going around and you're going to have to wait your turn.'

Cooke looked him up and down, his lips twisting dismissively. 'That over-confidence might prove to be your undoing one of these days, Inspector. In my experience, nobody is untouchable. Just ask those people who worked for and supplied goods to WED. Drive carefully now.'

'You're a real nasty piece of work,' Bliss said, his gaze hardening.

'Oh, Inspector, you have no idea just how nasty I can be.'

'Actually, I think I do. Be seeing you,' Bliss assured him.

He chose a route home that took him through Yaxley and the Hamptons. As he drove, he selected CD three on his multi-player unit and listened to the Walter Becker solo album, *11 Tracks of Whack*.

Bliss track-hopped his way to 'Book of Liars', which was his favourite tune on the album. The lyrics mentioned having stars by the names of people written inside the book of liars, and he was certain he could add Marvin and Ellie Cooke to that list. Ellie's hatred of Tessa Brady appeared genuine enough, but Bliss would trust neither of them to reveal the entire truth. For so many years as part of CAWED they had grown comfortable living their entire lives as a lie, so it was hardly a stretch to think of them continuing that deceit outside of the organisation.

Bliss owed a call to his mother, as she had been out when he tried previously, so he took care of that. As usual she made him laugh. At seventy-six she still had all of her faculties as far as he could tell, and her overall health was pretty good. On his most recent visit out there he'd had to have the talk with her. The one about arrangements and wills and bequests. His mother was an open book on the subject, completely blasé about her own mortality. She had set herself no targets, though admitted that it would be nice to make it into the upper eighties provided she was neither bedridden nor completely gaga. Bliss steered clear of the subject this time around. His mother's death was not something he wished to dwell upon, although he was acutely aware that such topics could not be ignored forever.

As the skies darkened and night replaced evening, Bliss took his usual place in the back garden. He was exhausted from all the miles he had travelled, and his ribs reminded him that he had ignored orders to rest. Over a couple of chilled bottles of lager, he turned his thoughts away from the investigation and back to his personal dilemma.

Declaring himself fit for work was the right thing to do. He was not so egotistical that he believed the team were incapable of solving the murder without him. In Chandler, Short and Bishop, there was good, strong leadership and sharp, intelligent minds. All three of them commanded respect from others inside the team.

The aim of any good leader was to provide their team with the tools necessary to be successful in their absence. Bliss was confident in the squad he had pulled together, although he felt they still benefitted occasionally from having his steady hand on the wheel. The reason he wanted back on the inside was a selfish one – on Friday he had been tasked with finding Jade Coleman's killer. Irrespective of anything else that had happened since, nailing the vicious bastard responsible remained his job.

As for Nick Nevin, Gary Pemberton, and the IOPC, Bliss had to accept that no matter what he did now to intercede, he was never going to alter the final outcome. If they decided to come for him in the case of his murdered wife – and he was convinced they would – he could rely only on the one thing people should be able to rely on in such circumstances.

His innocence.

So focused was he on Pemberton and Nevin that his phone rang and went to voicemail without him even being aware of it. An hour went by before he checked the device and noticed he had a message waiting for him. He pressed the three digits required to listen to his voicemail and was surprised to hear DCI Edwards speaking.

'Inspector, I'm aware that you are currently absent due to the recent trauma you suffered. I would not normally bother you like this, but I thought you would want to know as soon as possible. I received an official request today from the IOPC. They want copies of all of your interview tapes and any accompanying footage. Every case you ever ran here in the city. The odd thing is, they have not prioritised the request on a case-by-case basis, nor by date. I don't know how you will see it, Inspector, but to me this suggests it's a continuation of their fishing expedition. Perhaps even a second warning shot. Anyhow, we have no choice but to comply and send them everything we have. I will inform our admin staff that they should abide by the request in chronological order, and not to be in too much of a hurry about it. Good luck with it, Inspector Bliss. I hope it turns out alright in the end.'

He stared at the phone as if it had grown fangs. Bliss had come to get a good feel for Edwards over the past seven months, and if his judgement was sound then she had been genuinely sympathetic and concerned about his current plight when leaving that message for him.

Bliss agreed with her assumption. If they had actually required evidence based on his interviews, the IOPC would have specified particular cases or interviewees. Instead they had gone for the lot, and that told Bliss they were messing with his head.

Trying to, at least.

Bliss smiled to himself. Pemberton had ruffled a few of his feathers, and Nevin's appearance had given him genuine cause for alarm. The IOPC now moving through the gears was designed to keep him on the back foot.

It was not going to work, though.

He would not yield.

Quite the opposite, in fact.

He would turn it around on them. Every one of them. All he had to do was keep faith in his own abilities, knowing that should he even look as if he was about to break beneath the strain, his friends and colleagues were there to bolster him.

Chapter Twenty-Seven

It was with no small measure of trepidation that Bliss stepped into the incident room the following morning. During the night he had felt a vertigo attack coming on, but he had taken some anti-nausea tablets, reclined fully in his chair, closed his eyes, and waited it out. It passed without fully taking hold, and although when standing to go upstairs to bed he felt as if he had slipped his moorings, he was able to quickly stabilise himself and go to sleep with a clear mind. By then he was so fatigued that he slept through the heat and stickiness and awoke to the alarm for the first time in over a month. Given the stress he was under, feeling unwell was to be expected; something he had to step on and manage until he was in a position to take a break.

Arriving minutes prior to the scheduled morning briefing, Bliss was glad to observe the entire team sitting there. In their faces he saw they were still keen, their enthusiasm obvious from the way they sat leaning forward, the room reverberating with intense discussion.

There was a genuine look of surprise from everybody who glanced up as he entered. Chandler had not forewarned them, which he was pleased about. He wanted no fuss. By now the rumours concerning him and the IOPC would have circulated throughout the entire building, but this was his team and he expected nothing less than their very best as operation Cauldron continued.

'Good morning, everyone,' he said, walking front and centre as usual. He caught Chandler's eye and nodded his appreciation. 'I know my appearance today will have caught you all on the hop, but for the time being I'm here and fully invested in this case.'

'It's good to see you back with us, boss,' Ansari said. There were nods and mutterings of agreement around the room.

'Thank you. I'm going to start proceedings with some new information. Yesterday evening I went through some CAWED links on the Internet, and there were a number of them archived. I paid particular attention to photographs. Now, when DS Chandler and I spoke to Marvin and Ellie Cooke, they insisted Jade Coleman was a hanger-on whose attendance at meetings was irregular. They implied she was a nobody whom they barely knew. Yet, my search online uncovered a number of photos at different rallies where Jade was standing shoulder to shoulder right alongside them. In those same photos, Jade was also standing beside another female, and they appeared to be extremely close.'

'You thought it was the unnamed friend Lancaster told us about?' Chandler spotted immediately.

'I did. To my mind it was obvious. Anyhow, I then went back to see the Cookes and showed them the photographs. They had no choice but to admit knowing her. They also gave up the name: Tessa Brady. First thing this morning, I sent a text to DS Bishop and tasked him with digging into Brady. Let's hear what he has to tell us.'

The DS hauled himself to his feet and gave a cheery smile. As usual he looked as if he had got dressed in the dark. Hands in his pockets, Bishop revealed there was no trace of Tessa Brady in the system since her days with CAWED. The investigation into allegations of theft and fraud made by Marvin and Ellie Cooke at the time was an open, unsolved case. As such it merited an annual review and no more. Bliss knew it would only ever be a cursory re-examination at best. According to her financial records, Brady had disappeared off the radar two days before the allegations against her were made. Checks against her passport revealed no foreign travel in more than a decade, and it had now expired. If she had fled the country, she had done so using false documentation.

'Well done,' Bliss said to him with a nod of appreciation. 'Good work, Sergeant. Impressive for less than an hour's rooting around. So, we now know that Tessa Brady was a fully-fledged member of the group, and she was also a good friend of Jade Coleman. The Cookes lied to us. The more I learn about these people the less I like.'

'That all sounds like positive news, boss,' Short said, beaming at him.

Bliss winced. 'It is, and it isn't. I knew that CAWED gave up its campaign against the disposal site in Whittlesey and then fractured as an organisation. What I wasn't aware of until last night was that the main reason it all fell apart was because the Cookes and Brady fell out in a big way. Brady quit, but as Bish just told us, when she left she apparently did so with the contents of the organisation's bank account. The main reason for their case being unsolved and still open is, I suspect, that Tessa Brady was neither seen nor heard from again.'

'Off to join the Marbella mob, probably,' Hunt said, shaking his head in frustration.

Bliss knew precisely what he meant. The coastal Spanish town of Marbella was the centre of what the UK police and journalists dubbed the Costa del Crime back in the 1980s, where ex-Krays' henchman Freddie Foreman held sway. These days it played host to villains from the UK, Ireland, and eastern Europe. Its pivotal location so close to Africa made it the ideal spot for drug runners to do business. For some, it was also the most likely place to be found tortured and murdered if you were a villain crossing another villain.

'I don't think she's quite in that league,' Bliss replied. 'But it does look as if she fled abroad under an assumed identity. She appears to have simply disappeared off the map. Marvin Cooke expressed the view that he believed Brady was dead, and his wife was even more certain. So, we need to dig into that open-unsolved, get whatever we can find plus photos to Interpol and various national agencies. I won't hold my breath, but it would be nice to track her down.'

'That was a bit risky going back there on your own, boss,' Chandler said. Her voice was light, but the look she gave him suggested he would be hearing more about it later. 'Especially after they threatened you the first time around.'

He shook his head. 'Marvin Cooke is all mouth. For a short period, he ran a cult-like organisation in which whatever he told people to do they would do. Some of those activists were little more than thugs looking to take us on. Anarchists desperate for a ruck. Cooke hid behind them. He was nothing on his own then, and he's even less now. His threats don't bother me.'

'Even so, boss,' Bishop said, a worried frown on his face. 'A threat against a serving police officer is surely worthy of dragging him in.'

'It was a vague threat. Impossible to prove, and really not worth our time and effort. Our focus now has to shift to Tessa Brady. She had to have been this close friend of Jade's that Lancaster told us about.'

'How much time are we devoting to this, boss?' Short wanted to know. 'I mean, now that it's looking odds-on that Jade was murdered by this hooded stalker, where do these CAWED people even fit in any more?'

Bliss spent a few minutes laying out his thoughts on how Jade's murder and her involvement with the campaigners might possibly converge. As he spoke, his left thumb automatically worried the small scar on his forehead.

'You're not seriously thinking this stalker is Tessa Brady, are you?' Bishop asked when he was done.

'Not really, no. But we'd be wise to ask ourselves the question. We always talk in terms of unknown murder suspects being male, but we all understand that's only our shorthand. We can't rule out a female at this stage, so therefore we can't positively exclude Brady from the debate.'

'But she and Jade were close friends.'

'They were. Doesn't mean they stayed that way. Brady did a runner, remember. When she left CAWED, she left Jade behind at the same time. Maybe that mattered in the scheme of things. I genuinely doubt it did to the point where it resulted in Brady killing her, I'm just asking the question at the moment.'

'Fair point, boss,' Chandler acknowledged. 'It's worth running down.'

'What I do think more likely is that Jade took that job at Esotere because of Tessa Brady. I don't yet know why, can't say whether she did so off her own bat or was somehow persuaded into it. But when I look at it dispassionately, I think something happened that year that sparked everything that followed. Is it connected to Jade's eventual murder? I don't know. But the more we find out about Jade the closer we get to finding out more about her killer. This was a significant time in Jade's life, and I think it deserves our consideration.'

The discussion opened up to become more general once again. Short had been responsible for communicating with Jade's previous employers, but she had come up against an immoveable stumbling block.

'There is no record of Jade Coleman ever having worked for the Peterborough City Council,' she announced. 'When I got knocked back from there, I contacted the county council on the off chance, but got no joy with them, either.'

'So she was lying to her parents all that time,' Chandler said, squinting in bemusement. 'I sort of get why she failed to tell her parents she had changed jobs and gone to work for Esotere. Given her anti-nuclear stance, they would have found that difficult to comprehend. But why would she lie about her original job?'

'Especially as that job was just about the only firm ground her parents felt hadn't been whipped out from beneath their feet,' Bliss observed. 'They will be devastated when they learn of this.'

'There are a lot of questions left unanswered where Jade Coleman is concerned, boss,' DC Ansari pointed out. 'Do you think we need to drill even deeper into her background?'

With a reluctant sigh, Bliss said, 'Yes, actually I do. I've not felt happy from the moment I assessed the crime scene. There is a lot of white noise, and I think it may be obscuring the bigger picture here. Speak to DS Bishop afterwards and he can advise on further actions.'

It was then that Bliss remembered something. 'Who is going out to interview Mandy Vickers later?'

Both Ansari and Hunt raised their hands. Bliss nodded. 'Good. As has already been discussed, the feeling is that the crossing points between her, Jade, and their attacker, may be critical to this investigation. It's vital that she recalls the very first time she laid eyes on him. We can't ask Jade, but Mandy has that information somewhere inside her head. You two need to somehow squeeze it out of her.'

'Yes, boss,' they said in unison.

Bliss grinned. He imagined the pair were extremely keen to have another crack at a victim of the stalker who was probably responsible for Jade Coleman's murder. Neither had done anything wrong, but both would be feeling some guilt nonetheless. They would now be doubly determined to find the key to unlock this case.

He allowed his mind to drift back over the meeting. One of the items discussed was bothering him. He had almost skipped past it again when it came to him. 'DS Short. It's probably a long shot, but check out Hunts District Council, and Northants while you're about it, see if Jade worked with either of those local authorities instead. We all imagined it was this city when we were told she worked for the council, but she might easily have travelled to work in another adjacent county.'

Bliss turned back to the whiteboard. The lack of connecting arrows between Coleman and Vickers worried him. He understood the vagaries of a stalker's mind; they were prone to being unpredictable, lacking reason when it came to selecting their victims. It was possible that no connection between the two existed, but he felt his team had to take that line of enquiry as far as it would stretch. Bliss shook his head, drew a deep breath then turned back to his team.

'That's it for now. We need only one thing to go our way. One thing to turn this case right around. Today's the day, people. Have at it.'

Before leaving the incident room, Bliss gathered together Chandler, Bishop and Short. He held them back as the room gradually emptied.

'Before any of you fire questions at me, let me just say this: I'm here today because there's nowhere else I'd rather be. The idea of protecting myself at the expense of this investigation didn't sit well with me. Yesterday, I discovered who is at the root of the IOPC interest, and because of that I have decided there can be no more involvement from any of you.'

'But, boss–'

Bliss cut Bishop off with a firm raised hand. 'Be pissed off at me if you must. I understand your frustrations, and I am genuinely appreciative of your support. From each of you. But understand this, there will be far greater scrutiny of this matter than I could possibly have imagined. I still have hopes of emerging from it intact. But what I will not put at risk are your careers. Now, I know we had this out the other day, and the three of you won me over against my better judgement. That was then, this is now.'

'Can you at least tell us who is behind it?' Short asked.

'The same man who murdered Hazel.'

'What? The man who killed your wife is now forcing the IOPC investigation against you?'

'I believe so. Behind the scenes they are still playing the long game. They are gathering up all of my interview audio tapes and any video footage of me in the room with suspects. They are still going to look into other areas of misconduct. By now they must be aware that I know the truth, but they have to be seen to be going about this in the right way. The more they come at me with, the easier it will be to bury the one thing they really want me for.'

'Then I will say it again, boss,' Bishop insisted. 'This is surely a time to ask for more help, not less.'

Short agreed. 'Bish is right, boss. We can still work behind the scenes on your behalf. In our own time. The four of us can achieve far more than you alone.'

'Let me be as blunt as I can be about this,' Bliss said, meeting each gaze in turn. 'If I am found guilty, I go down. If I'm not, but I'm not found innocent either, then I lose my job. They'll find a way of using such a verdict to push me out. What you have to be aware of is that anyone caught in the blast radius of that will suffer. So, when I say we are done, we are done. I have one or two things up my sleeve. And I'm certainly not lying down for these pricks. The very best thing you can do to help me now is solve this case. The moment it's over, I go on leave and I focus solely on me. So, get your heads in the game and if you have time to spare then use it to find some justice for Jade Coleman.'

Moments later when he entered his office, Bliss was startled to find Detective Superintendent Fletcher standing by the window, staring out at the sun breaking through the early morning cloud cover. She turned as he came through the door. Her features were rigid, but Bliss did not sense they were entirely unsympathetic.

'I thought you and I had an agreement,' Fletcher said, putting her hands behind her back as if to prevent one of them from launching something at him.

Bliss remained on his feet. 'We did, ma'am. But we also said the less you know the better it would be.'

'That's when I thought you were going to be working off book while absent, Inspector. I would like to know what's changed in that time.'

'I've just spent the past few minutes explaining that to the senior members of my team, ma'am. The fact is, I now understand that I have to continue this on my own, or run the risk of severely impacting on the careers of my friends and colleagues. And I also realise that the fight needs to come to me; that the IOPC need to make the next move. I'm sure you are aware that Nick Nevin is the man I hold responsible for murdering my wife. I'm sure you also know that a savage beating put Nevin in hospital many years ago. Now ex-DCI Nevin is after my blood, and while I don't currently know what new evidence he has against me, I do know he has something. The thing is, I reckon I can lure him out. If I do it properly, he'll take the bait.'

'And what then, Inspector? What is your end game?'

'I haven't thought that far ahead, ma'am.'

'And that's your great plan, is it?'

'It is. And in the meantime, my team and I are working hard to resolve the murder of Jade Coleman. I would be grateful to you if you allowed me to get on with that.'

Fletcher tilted her head as she weighed him up. Bliss hoped she understood. He was telling her that the best way for her to now offer support was to turn her back on him and allow him to run with it, scissors in hand.

Hands off.

No taint.

'If you think it's for the best,' Fletcher said reluctantly, 'then I wish you good luck, Inspector.'

As she moved to walk past him, Fletcher paused and laid a hand on his arm. It was a compassionate and tender gesture. 'And I mean that, Jimmy. I wish you all the very best.'

Bliss could only nod, too choked by emotion to relay his gratitude with anything other than the look of appreciation in his eyes.

Chapter Twenty-Eight

The first breakthrough came less than an hour after the briefing ended. DS Short burst into Bliss's office, her face split by a wide grin of satisfaction.

'I've found Jade's old employer,' she said, flapping a printed sheet of paper. 'But that's not even the best news.'

Bliss pushed himself back from the desk, immediately caught up in his sergeant's enthusiasm and excitement. 'Well go on then. Tell me. This is your moment in the spotlight, Mia.'

'Jade did work at Hunts District Council. Score one for you there, boss. I spoke to the HR manager myself, and she confirmed it. Then, on the off chance, because we'd had no real insight into the woman, I also asked whether a Tessa Brady had ever worked there as well. And guess what?'

Bliss shot to his feet, propelled by the adrenaline that ripped through him. 'Outstanding!' he said. 'Great job, Mia. That's one piece of initiative to really pay off. I take it you made arrangements for us to interview them.'

'Of course.' Short flapped the sheet of paper once more and slapped it on his desk. 'Nine forty-five. I put the details on here for you and Penny.'

Scooping up the hard copy, Bliss scanned the printout. Then he turned his attention back to Short and shook his head. 'This is excellent work. I think you've earned yourself a road trip. Tell Pen I'm taking you. Let's see if we can move this bloody case on a pace or two.'

Bliss accepted he would lose Short to a promotion within the year. He loved the way her mind worked, and she was so well-balanced. She had an enviable marriage, doted on her twins, but equally she was devoted to the job and everything that came with it. He thought it would be interesting to spend some time working more closely with her.

Curved and angular modern council offices had replaced the old T-shaped building close to the A14 and river Great Ouse in Huntingdon town centre. It was there that Bliss and Short met with Human Resources manager Alice Graham in her glass-walled office on the third floor, after a tortuous slow drive through roadwork delays. They got down to business as soon as the introductions had been made and they had seated themselves.

'I knew both Jade and Tessa quite well,' Graham admitted, her eyes downcast as she recalled them. 'We heard about poor Jade, of course. Such a terrible tragedy. It came as a huge shock here, I can tell you. Jade was a popular colleague and was much missed when she left us.'

'Tell us a bit about that if you would,' Bliss said. 'Jade was happy here, would you say?'

'As far as I can tell, yes.'

'But still she quit the job. Was that also a surprise, Mrs Graham?'

Alice Graham was somewhere in her mid-forties he guessed. A pleasant-looking woman in glasses with thin purple frames that matched the highlights in her hair. She dressed conservatively, but wore several beaded bracelets, bangles and wristbands to add a splash of colour and character.

'I suppose it was. I was aware that she had taken a day off to attend an interview. Esotere was still known as Whittlesey Energy Disposal at the time, but the takeover was already underway and several more jobs being created as a result. I actually recall asking Jade what drew her to the job, but she was reluctant to tell me. I have to say that it was probably more of a shock than a surprise. Jade was keen on nuclear disarmament, and you'll be aware, of course, about what goes on at the Esotere-UK site.'

This same discrepancy had been bothering the investigation team as well. Bliss thought back to his own previous lines of reasoning and asked his next question as a direct response.

'Did it occur to you that Jade might have seen herself as an anti-nuclear campaigner taking up a post on the inside, as it were? Perhaps looking to ensure that the clean image the company were portraying was actually genuine.'

Graham smiled. Nodded. 'You know, Inspector, it actually did. Her taking that job was so at odds with everything I knew about Jade, who was one of the most non-confrontational people I've ever met. But yes, I did wonder whether that was behind the move. Jade had changed a lot by then, or else the idea might never have dawned on me.'

'Changed?' Short said, leaning forward. She had been taking notes, and now paused, with her pen poised above her leather-bound notebook. 'How so?'

'She had always been a quiet person, timid even, but became even more withdrawn when Tessa left us. Their friendship was regarded as… odd, I suppose you could say. A case of opposites attracting. Tessa could be opinionated and loud. On occasion even brutal, in the way she raged against certain issues. She was actually reprimanded for it on two occasions, following complaints from her colleagues. I'm pretty sure it was the waste disposal link that drew the two women together.'

'You say Brady left you. Did she also leave for another job?'

Shaking her head, Graham looked pensive. 'Tessa left one night as usual to go home, and simply never returned to work. We had a phone call from her to ask for her salary to be sent as usual and that she would notify us of a change of address. To my knowledge we never received that.'

'Did you send her salary as requested?' Bliss asked.

'We did. Tessa should, of course, have provided us with a month's notice. We decided not to bicker, and her final salary was paid in full at the end of the month as usual. I think we even paid for a couple days of holiday she was owed at the time.'

Tax payers' money is so much easier to spend, Bliss thought. A hard-nosed corporation might well have made different decisions. What Alice Graham was telling them tied in neatly with the team's own observations and discussions.

Brady disappeared in August 2014. Shortly afterwards, in the spring of the following year, Jade quit her good job to go to work for a company she would previously have avoided like the plague. It only made sense if you made the reasonable assumption that Jade started working at Whittlesey Energy Disposal because she believed she might find out something. It had to have concerned Tessa Brady's disappearance.

So had Jade believed WED to be responsible for her friend vanishing? Or someone working on behalf of the company, at least? If so, the implication was that Jade believed her friend had come to some harm at their hands. Bliss wondered where that particular notion might have come from. Whatever the reason, whatever its origin, it was enough for Jade Coleman to leave one job and take another in the hope of finding answers.

'What possible connection does any of it have with Jade's murder?' he asked his companion as they headed north back to Peterborough.

'Maybe none at all, boss. There doesn't have to be a link. It could be that what we're seeing unfold is really just Jade's life. The threads we're interweaving might all relate to each other in terms of Jade, CAWED, what is now Esotere-UK, and Tessa Brady. But her stalker and killer could be someone entirely unrelated to any of it.'

'Then why does it grate so much?' Bliss asked. 'Why does it seem to be so important?'

'Because perhaps it's about Jade's life towards the end. She was trundling along just fine, then a wheel comes off, and in the middle of that she is for some reason targeted by a twisted individual. I think we now have to push the rest to one side and find our connections between Jade and Mandy Vickers. That's where our answers will be found, boss.'

Short was spot on, and Bliss knew it. When you step into a stranger's life the way they had done with Jade Coleman's, it was only natural to pick at the frayed edges to the point where you either cast them aside or continued to worry at them. This business with the waste disposal company, the protestors, and Brady, was its own individual story, which could be entirely separate from whatever got her murdered. There was no other reasonable conclusion, given the facts to hand.

Bliss valued logic; reasonable theories developed along rational pathways, based on hard facts and evidence where it could be found. The stalker connected Jade Coleman to Mandy Vickers, so that was the most logical route of enquiry. Yet still he felt a nagging doubt inside – the instincts which he also had faith in pulling him towards the connection with the anti-nuclear activists. Shaking it off, Bliss realised he had to put those doubts back in their box and seal it tight. There could be no more following instincts on this one.

As he checked his rear-view mirror, something snagged. About four cars back there was a scruffy-looking silver Rover 75. The reason it had caught his attention was that he felt sure he had seen the same vehicle during their drive down to Huntingdon. If he was being followed it made sense for it to be the IOPC. He wondered how long someone had been tailing him, and what they might have witnessed over the past few days.

Bliss shook it off. There was no point in speculating. What was done was done. He would be more cautious and observant from this point on, but for now he had to find a way to get his mind off it. As they neared the Norman Cross junction, Bliss asked his colleague for her thoughts on where things stood and what their next steps might be. He valued Short's precise mind, and decided he could do with her particular brand of clarity.

'It's been slow progress so far,' she admitted. 'But that's not due to a lack of effort or intellect. This is simply one of those operations that becomes bogged down to the point where you start to feel stifled by it. We've yet to discover the one special lead that causes the lightbulbs to flash inside our heads.'

'Any suggestions as to how we turn it around? You know I can take criticism provided it's justified. If there's a move I've failed to make, tell me about it.'

Short shook her head. 'It's like I said before, our lack of progress is not through want of trying. None of us have come up with any bright ideas, either. It'll change, though, boss.' Short glanced across at him and smiled. 'Somehow it always does.'

'Not always, Mia. Not always.'

'Okay, well mostly, then. More often than not. We may not be perfect, but we're damned good at what we do.'

'I'll drink to that,' he said, nodding his agreement.

Bliss admired her resilience. He realised he had not taken a great deal of time to get to know Short on a personal level since his return to the Peterborough Major Crimes unit. Her life had changed in so many ways during his time away, and something that had occurred to him a while back crossed his mind again.

'Mia, I hope you don't mind my asking, but why was it that you decided not to take your husband's name?'

'Boss?' Short's eyebrows angled downward in a deep frown of bemusement.

'It's just, Hazel and I had that exact conversation. It was at a time when a lot of women were keeping their own family names when they married. Deep down, Hazel was a bit of a traditionalist, so she was happy to become another Bliss. I wondered why you decided to keep your maiden name'

'I'm still not sure I quite understand.'

'Well, during my lengthy absence from the city, you got married and had a couple of nippers, but you were Mia Short when I left and still Mia Short when I returned. It's not a big deal, and probably none of my business, but I've always wondered why that was.'

Short laughed, putting her head back, her long blonde hair spilling over her shoulders. 'Of course. You weren't around so you don't know. The fact is, boss, I actually did take my husband's surname. Sort of. His name is Paul Short.'

Now it was Bliss's turn to frown. 'Really? What are the odds?'

'In this area, quite good. It's a popular local name.'

'If it's a Fenland name, you might well be related.'

Short slapped him on the arm. 'How did you know that? We're first cousins.'

'You are?'

The second slap was harder still. 'No, of course not. We're not all inbred out here.'

Bliss laughed. It felt good. Better than it ought to.

'At least I now know. I can rest easy in my bed tonight.'

'Strange question to ask at this particular point, if you don't mind my saying so.'

He nodded. 'I was thinking about you earlier, that's why. I realised we'd not spoken much on a personal level, plus I was considering the job you did and the way you handled it. How you seemed to have it all together, the balance between family life and your work. It's a healthy approach to the job, and one I'm sure you know will see you go far.'

'I appreciate you saying so, boss.'

'You deserve it, Mia. The next step up is a big one. It's a massive shift in accountability, but it's also the point where your career path splits. The divide was less obvious in my day, so there was room for me to carry on pretty much as I had when I was a DS, only with that added pressure of running a team. Don't let anybody tell you that the DCI runs things. They are the figureheads. These days, when you move up to my rank you are expected to run the team from behind a desk. That's the point at which you have to decide what kind of a DI you want to be.'

'And which type do you see me as, boss?'

Bliss sensed the question was loaded. Short wanted to know what kind of person he thought she was, not just what kind of inspector she would make. He glanced at her and smiled.

'You've got it in you to become either. If I've read you right, Mia, you'll want to lead from the front, which means getting out there and grafting alongside everyone else in your team. That's still possible even in this modern service, but it does add to the pressure because your admin workload increases massively when you move into your own office. If you want to be proactive, then you'll need to find the extra hours in your day. Which makes the juggling act between family and the job a great deal more difficult.'

'And if I choose to be the other type?'

'Then there's really no limit to how far you can go.'

'So, you're saying I can't have both. I can't lead from the front and continue with my career ambitions.'

Bliss nodded. 'That's the way it is, Mia. The job has changed out of all recognition, but nobody has yet discovered a way to give us more than twenty-four hours in a day. You can become a DI and move up the ladder as well as keep that family balance, provided you don't add the burden of doing so from the front. You take that on as well, and suddenly the numbers don't add up. Something has to give, I'm afraid.'

'And what gives for you, boss?'

'Late nights. Early mornings. Broad shoulders and a thick skin to protect me when I don't deliver on the admin side of things. Which is often. But I don't have a family to worry about.'

Short chewed on her bottom lip for a moment. Then she turned to Bliss and said, 'Thank you for your honesty, Jimmy. I do appreciate it. I think I always knew the choices I would have to make. I've seen the different styles from various DIs, and none of them seem entirely happy with their lot. I suppose I have a lot of thinking ahead of me.'

'You do,' Bliss agreed. 'But either way you still have a great future ahead of you. It really is about striking the right balance, and whatever you do, don't use me as a baseline.'

Short laughed. 'No fear of that, boss.'

'Good. See, you're learning already.'

The moment Bliss got back to HQ, the new man, Gratton, told him that DCI Edwards had been on the prowl looking for him and requested his presence in her office as soon as he returned. Not so long ago he would have ignored the request and made sure he stayed well clear until he had firm leads to provide. This time, Bliss decided his mind games with Edwards were no longer either useful or relevant in the wider scheme of things.

'Good morning, boss,' he said as he entered her office, which was every bit as neat and uncluttered as he had found it every other time he'd been inside over the past seven months. 'I heard you wanted to see me.'

Edwards got to her feet, so he remained standing also. He thought back to his earlier chat with the Super and wondered if there was a new edict whereby all meetings were now to be held unseated. If so, he had missed the memo.

'Yes, thank you for dropping by, Inspector.' The DCI nodded and even smiled at him. That made Bliss nervous. 'As soon as I heard you were back with us, I thought we ought to catch up. In your absence I have allowed DS Chandler to get on with the job in hand, with help from Short and Bishop. Chandler knows where I am and that the door is open, but I felt it better that I remain in the background so as not to usurp her authority.'

Of course, Bliss thought but did not say. *And your decision had nothing whatsoever to do with you wanting to keep your distance should it all go pear-shaped.* He let the thought go and quickly brought his boss up to date.

'So the focus now switches fully to the stalker,' Edwards observed. 'I think that's the right call. And where do things stand concerning your own… misfortune?'

Bliss narrowed his gaze. 'My misfortune? Oh, you mean the IOPC investigation. Well, yes, I suppose them looking at me for murdering my own wife could be seen as a tad unfortunate. Personally, I regard it as something a little more worrying and sinister.'

The DCI took a breath and fixed him with a tight glare of her own. 'It was just a word, Inspector. I didn't mean to make light of it. I really didn't know how to refer to the matter. I meant nothing by it.'

He saw that his tone had offended Edwards. In her own way she was attempting to discuss the issue with him, and he had shot her down because she misspoke. Bliss closed his eyes for a second before spreading his hands and apologising.

'I'm on edge,' he explained. 'This investigation is proving troublesome, and I really don't need this disciplinary action hanging over my head at the same time.'

'You must feel as if you are just waiting for the moment when they decide to pounce.'

'I do. I sense it gathering momentum, but I can't yet get a feel for when they will slam the hammer down.'

'If it's any consolation at all, the Super will be informed before they pull the rug from under your feet. She will of course then inform me. That may buy you a little time to gather yourself. Maybe enough to decide you've not yet fully recovered from your concussion.'

Bliss smiled. It was perhaps the kindest gesture Edwards had made towards him since he had moved back to the city. 'I guess I'll play it by ear, boss. Thank you, though. Anything else while I'm here?'

'No. Just make sure DS Chandler is kept current and knows what needs to be done should you have to take that sick leave after all.'

'Of course.'

'And Bliss…'

'Yes, boss?'

'I do genuinely hope things turn out okay for you.'

'Thank you, boss. Me, too.'

When they were done, Bliss was confused as to which version of Edwards he trusted more.

Or less.

Chapter Twenty-Nine

When he returned to the Major Crimes unit, Bliss sat between Chandler and Bishop, lowering his voice to engage them both. 'I understand the need to concentrate all of our resources on the stalker,' he said. 'But you know me, and you know I can't easily let go of any strand while there is still something left to unravel. I'm not asking either of you to do anything, just to spare me a minute considering one final aspect.'

Bishop leaned back in his chair, clasping his meaty hands behind his neck. 'Fire away then, boss.'

'Okay. So, we're now pretty certain that Jade left her council job and started working at WED because of Tessa Brady's disappearance. I don't see her arriving at that decision alone. I believe somebody talked her into it.'

'You're thinking Marvin and Ellie Cooke,' Chandler said. She sat with one leg crossed over the other, her foot jiggling and her mid-heel shoe hanging off the heel.

'I am. I think they persuaded her somehow that WED were responsible. That perhaps they had acted against Tessa because of her connection to CAWED.'

'But to what end? Jade Coleman was no corporate spy. She could never have pulled that off. What could they possibly hope to gain?'

Bliss shrugged. 'I don't know. But forget it for a moment. If we accept that was perhaps why she started there, then can we also assume she left because she found some answers?'

Chandler glanced at Bishop before turning back to Bliss. 'That's an interesting theory, boss. If you join the dots, then I can see how you might end up there. But what has any of it got to do with her being… Oh, I see where you're going with this now. You think Jade discovered something that got her killed. Really? Who by? Are you saying WED got rid of Tessa Brady, and then years later Esotere did the same with Jade?'

'No.' Bliss shook his head. 'No, that's not what I'm saying at all. But your mind led you there. It led me there, too. Is something along those lines really so implausible?'

'Yes,' Bishop responded evenly. 'I think it is. The bad days for WED and Esotere are long gone. They weathered every storm that came their way. Seriously, what could either Tessa or Jade have discovered subsequently that would have a company that large bump them off? That's reaching, boss. And in a major way.'

'I'm not really thinking along those precise lines,' Bliss said, unable to fully explain himself. 'But you see how the train of thought reacts to the stimulus of new information. Something happened to Brady, and Jade was murdered in her own home. These two women are connected. No, I don't actually believe anyone at either Whittlesey Energy Disposal or Esotere was responsible. But I do think they are somehow all linked together. I just don't know how.'

Bliss hung his head and huffed in frustration. Blowing out another troubled breath, he said, 'Time for some honesty. Clearly, I'm off my game at the moment. In your view, would it be better for me to stand aside now and let you two run with this investigation? I feel as if I'm just getting in the way, clouding the judgement of us all.'

The two colleagues exchanged looks once more. Bishop was the first to react. 'Speaking personally, boss, I'd rather have you inside the tent pissing out. You've got this other notion wrapped around inside your brain. It's like a vacuum cleaner head when it sucks up a sock or something. It's all tangled up and you're finding it hard to unravel. That's fine so long as we stay focused on the stalker, because that's our man.'

'I agree,' Chandler said immediately. 'A DI Bliss not quite at his best and a little bit distracted is still better than me and Bish working separately or even together. But you asked for honesty, so there is one thing I feel I need to say.'

Bliss nodded. 'Go ahead.'

'You're our leader. If you are sticking around then we're pleased to have you, but you must lead. Either you're absent or you're running operation Cauldron. There can be no half measures.'

'That's a fair point.' Bliss smiled, realising it would have been hard for Chandler to express herself so openly. He admired her for raising the matter. 'And as I am running the operation, it's time to come down in favour of a single line of investigation. So let's hunt that bloody stalker down, shall we?'

Moments later, Hunt and Ansari returned from their interview with Mandy Vickers. They brought news with them that the crime scene investigators had pulled up the usual range of prints and fibres from the bedroom that you would expect to find in any room, and had returned to their base to begin the process of logging and checking each item. Regarding the windows probably used to gain access, a few dark fibres had been picked off the catch, but there were no prints on the edges where errant hands would linger when climbing through.

As for Vickers, it took her a while, but eventually she had recalled where she had first spotted the stalker. It was her habit on a Friday evening after work to detour through Boongate and to stop for petrol at the BP station on St John's Street. From there she would cut through the centre by the lido, swing through Rivergate, across the river before hanging a right on Oundle Road. As she struggled to think about the cyclist, it came to her quite suddenly that she had actually seen him twice on the same journey home.

As she had pulled into the petrol station, the cyclist had circled the pumps once before setting off again, a peripheral dark figure that barely rubbed against her subconscious. Then, as she crossed the town bridge over the Nene, she caught a glimpse of him sitting on the bike, stationary on the pavement. To the best of her recollection he was looking away, staring north along the river.

Later sightings included the Sainsbury's supermarket car park off Oxney Road, the riverbank close to her house in Woodston, and the previously mentioned glimpse close to the quarry.

Bliss felt disheartened. There was no definite crossover with Jade Coleman. A sighting somewhere the two women frequented would have been something to work with. It just wasn't there to be found. He left his team to get on with their workloads. Back in his office he placed a call to Lucy Lancaster.

'I'd like to run something by you, Mrs Lancaster. Over the past few weeks, did Jade ever mention anything to you about a man in dark clothing, specifically someone wearing a pulled-up hoodie, and possibly riding a bike?'

There was a moment of pause before Lancaster replied. 'Not to the best of my recollection, Inspector. And I have to say, I've given some thought to our previous conversation and something did occur to me. You asked me if Jade had mentioned being stalked, and I said she had not, but that it did not surprise me if she knew about it yet had not told me. The thing is, I've changed my mind about that. I think she would have, had she been truly frightened by it. Jade had become increasingly aware of her surroundings, less naïve and innocent of the world. I now believe Jade would have mentioned something to me if she believed it to be a serious threat.'

'Thank you for sharing that with me,' Bliss said. He wasn't sure how it helped, but at least the woman cared enough to still be thinking about it. That spoke a lot for the last relationship Jade would ever know. 'So, I also take it that this figure on the bike means nothing to you? No memory of seeing anyone matching that description at the gym, perhaps? Or even at the hotel you two visited in Stamford?'

'I'll think about it some more, Inspector Bliss. But I can't honestly say I recall anything like that, no.'

'Fair enough. One final thing. Does the name Tessa Brady mean anything to you?'

This time the pause went on longer. Bliss recognised the silence of someone shaping a response. His chest constricted as he waited for the answer.

'Tessa was the name of someone Jade was once extremely fond of. I sensed an unrequited love.'

'How come you failed to mention this to us when you told us about Jade's friend at CAWED?'

'Oh. Tessa was *that* friend? I'm so sorry, Inspector. That's a little unsettling, actually. I always had the sense from Jade that they were two entirely separate people. It genuinely never occurred to me.'

Bliss thanked Lancaster and ended the call. Having Jade and Brady confirmed as being firm friends made a strong lead even stronger. By the time the evening briefing came and went, the team had taken things little further. Bliss had requested some digging into CCTV footage at the BP garage going back two months' worth of Fridays between 4.30pm and 5.30pm. Any additional surveillance of the stalker was worth looking at, even if he was still wearing the hoodie. Every potential sighting could offer up something new and potentially vital. Even so, it was with a heavy heart that he drove home, his thoughts in turmoil and his mood dark.

Chapter Thirty

That mood did not improve.

When Bliss arrived home, Gerry Quinn was parked on the street outside the house in the same Rover with faded silver paintwork that he had spotted on two occasions earlier in the day. As Bliss swept his Insignia onto the driveway, Quinn seemed to ooze out from behind the wheel of his own car before lumbering around to stand by the front door of the house.

'Whatever you're selling, I'm not buying,' Bliss told him, as he negotiated his way around the side of a ragged hedge. He made sure he stepped right into Quinn's personal space. 'And don't ask me if you can come inside, because I hear a smack in the mouth can sometimes offend.'

Quinn held up both hands defensively. He shook his head. 'I'm not here for a barney, Jimmy. I know I played it wrong the other day. Maybe we could start again from scratch.'

Bliss nodded. 'I like that idea, Quim. Can we go back to the day before I met you for the first time? Start over from there.'

'You always did think you were a cut above the rest of us, Jimmy.' The DI's chest puffed out. 'You was a London copper just like us, you was a London detective just like us. But you always looked down your nose at us. I always said you got that misplaced sense of superiority from your old man.'

Bliss's eyes went cold. He actually felt them react to the ice that had blitzed his veins in the moment before he responded. 'That's the second time that same sentiment has been expressed to me recently. It was bollocks then and it's bollocks now. There are a lot of things you can say to me that I'll let go, Quim. Even here on my own front porch. But you mention my old man again, and you and me are going to fall out in a big way.'

'Is that so?' Quinn started rocking on his heels.

'Yeah. I would say things could turn ugly, but you're already here so we've got that covered.'

'That gob of yours is going to flap its way into more trouble than you can handle one of these days, Bliss. And believe me when I tell you that day is just around the corner. I came here to apologise, and all you do is treat me like shit right from the off. I got it all wrong the other day, so I came over here to tell you I was sorry, and to explain that coming to see you at that boozer was my dumb way of fucking things up for Batty and Lee. It was deliberate on my part. It meant they couldn't use me no more, which was how I wanted it. But you ain't the sort of bloke to give anyone a second chance, are you?'

'That's where you're wrong. I'm fine on second chances, Quim. In fact, I'm a big fan of them. It's third, fourth and fifth chances I'm not willing to tolerate.'

'That's because you're looking at it all wrong, Jimmy. Obviously, my loyalties can be bought. I'll hold my hands up to that. But instead of kicking me out on my arse, use it to your advantage. You and me do a deal here this evening, I could be in the Batty and Lee camp tomorrow working for you. Wouldn't you like to know what they have lined up for you?'

Bliss took a moment to weigh the man up. He was lying, because his mouth was moving and words were spilling out. And it was so blindingly obvious that Bliss had to wonder yet again how Quinn had ever made it as a detective.

The truth was, the man was a good copper in his own way. He had a nose for sniffing out trouble. Plus, he could be determined, when he wasn't wasting his salary in shops of the betting and knocking variety. But he was completely useless when it came to subterfuge, which was one of the most precious tools in a good detective's armoury.

'I sort of believe your story, Quim,' he said. 'Only, I have to say I think you're working it the other way around. I reckon you told your boss that you could make it up to him for jumping the gun and revealing yourself to me too early. You told him you could talk me round, get your foot back in the door. Then, under the guise of you feeding information back to me, you could find out from me what I was doing about the IOPC visit and feed it back to them instead.'

Quinn shook his head all the way through that observation. 'No, no, no. You got it all wrong, Jimmy. Arse backwards, mate. They treated me like scum for stepping out of line the other day.'

'And I suppose my calling you Quim all the time is a sign of respect for you, right?'

Now the man was starting to look confused. Bliss was unsurprised. He had never known Quinn to be able to hang onto a story for this long without it all unravelling inside his head. The man heaved a long sigh and seemed to arrive at a decision.

'Fair enough, Jimmy,' he said, his tone less certain now. 'Give me a couple of minutes to make a call. You want to let me in? I could do with a beer, mate.'

Bliss stared at him evenly. When he spoke, there was no edge to his voice, 'Quim, you make all the calls you want, but you won't be doing so in my house, drinking my beer. Got that?'

'I can always go and get my own booze, Jimmy. That's not a problem.'

'It's not about the fucking drink, Quim!' Bliss immediately regretted the loss of temper. One of his neighbours was bound to complain about the language. He lowered his voice before speaking again. 'It's got nothing to do with the beer, and everything to do with the fact that I don't like you, and neither do I trust you. Never have, and never will.'

Quinn kept his eyes fixed on Bliss as he drew out his mobile, dialled a number in full, and then spoke as his call was answered.

'It's me. What? Me. Gerry Quinn. Yeah. Look, he's not going for any of it, so I thought maybe you'd just have a word and then I can have it on my toes back down south.'

Quinn nodded as he listened to the reply, started to say something, but then clammed up tight. Whoever he had been speaking to had said something and then abruptly ended the call. Just as he disconnected, the phone rang again. This time Quinn nodded at what he heard before holding the phone out to Bliss.

'He wants a word with you himself.'

Bliss took the phone from him. He gave it a moment of thought, then said, 'How are you, Gary? Well, I hope.'

It could only have been Pemberton. Quinn was being used as a convenient go-between, his friendship with the old boxing trainer and ex-copper going back a long way. As Bliss had considered who might be on the other end of the line, he knew it would not be either Lee or Batty, as neither man would be foolish enough to speak to him at this stage of the proceedings. That left only two possibilities, and Pemberton was the most obvious candidate.

'You bottled it yesterday, Jimmy.' Pemberton's voice was dry and harsh. 'You never came back for that chat like you said you would. Funny, you were a lot of things, but I don't remember you being a coward.'

'I stuck around for just long enough, Gary. I was sitting out in my motor when Nevin arrived.'

'Ah. So that's when your bottle went.'

'If you say so. What I say is that it took all of my willpower and inner strength not to get out of my car and fuck that prick up. Some people would say I've matured, Gary. Me, I reckon I've turned saintly. I wished so much pain and torment on that man over the years, and yet I passed up on the opportunity to smack him around.'

'Yeah? And why would you do that, Jimmy? You turned bandit on us? You come out the closet, you old fairy? I always thought you might be a nancy shirt-lifter, as it goes.'

'Gary, your childish comments are wasted on me. I'm immune to them after all these years of doing this job. What do you want? I assume you called back for a reason.'

'He still wants to meet with you, Jimmy. Face to face. This time with other faces around, just in case you reckon you're still a bit handy. Know what I mean?'

'I think I can work out your code on that one, Gary.'

'Of course, if you bottle it again, he asked me to give you a message. Said to tell you that this place ain't the same place you grew up in. There's nobody around these days who even knows who you are, let alone gives a fuck what happens to you and yours. But they know who I am, and they know who he is. Bung them a bottle of Scotch and they'd do anything for either of us. And I do mean anything. You get the picture now, Jimmy?'

'Yeah, you're not exactly being subtle, Gary. You're making a threat against me.'

'It's not a threat, Jimmy. It's –'

'Please don't say "a promise".'

'– a promise.'

Bliss actually gave it some thought this time. Nick Nevin had crawled out from beneath whatever rock he'd been hiding under, apparently with some fresh evidence on the murder of Bliss's wife that got some IOPC cocks very hard. Pemberton was the cut-out man in the middle, doing the spade work. Back in the gym he had briefly alluded to the fact that he was being forced to act this way. It was not much of a stretch to imagine that the leverage consisted of a file a foot thick containing all of Pemberton's misdeeds while he was still working in the Met. Actions which could not only impact on his pension, but might very well lead to charges being made, a custodial at the end of it. No way was Gary Pemberton going to sit and twiddle his thumbs if there was even the slightest chance of him ticking away his empty days and nights in a three-man cell built for two.

'Tell Nevin I'll think about it. But if I go ahead, the time and location will be of my choosing. Anything else and he can stick it where the proverbial shines. Got that, Gary? Am I making myself clear?'

Bliss decided there and then that he and Pemberton now officially had unfinished business. When this was all over, penalties would have to be submitted and paid.

In full.

Chapter Thirty-One

Bliss was treating himself to the Cantonese buffet at the Beijing Rendezvous Chinese restaurant in Orton Wistow when a call came in from Chandler. It had been a pretty awful day, and after the conversation with Quinn he needed not to be sitting around at home dwelling upon everything and drinking himself to sleep. He had not eaten Chinese food in anything other than takeaway form since moving back to the city, and Wistow was only a five minute drive west.

Having munched his way through a couple of spring rolls, and a dish of prawns cooked in ginger and onion, he was about to tuck into some sweet and sour pork when the phone rang. Bliss recognised the Pavlovian response as the ringtone sounded off, his instinctive reaction in pressing the receive button.

'Where are you?' Chandler asked without preamble.

'I'm having dinner. Is that okay by you?'

'Sure. I'll go and visit our new potential stalker subject on my own, shall I?'

Bliss lay his fork on the plate. 'Okay. You have my undivided attention.'

He heard his partner chuckle and imagined her chalking one up alongside her name on an imaginary scoreboard. 'The report came through the system. Last night a Deborah Crighton made a statement claiming she believed she might be being targeted. She mentioned seeing a stranger on three occasions over the past couple of days.'

'Don't tell me. This stranger wears dark clothes, a hoodie, and rides a bike.'

'You're a mind reader. A black bike, at that.'

'Okay. Where are you?'

'Standing outside your front door.'

'I'll be there in five minutes.'

Bliss threw down fifteen pounds, which was enough to cover the buffet and his bottle of Peroni, which was only half empty. He rushed back outside and jumped into the car, fired it up and left long streaks of rubber on the blocked paving surface of the generous car park. Impatient as ever, he got snarled up behind a line of cars adhering to the speed limit. As he drew up outside his house, he motioned for Chandler to join him. He made a turn using his own driveway.

'Where are we going?' he asked.

'Hampton Vale. Right opposite the primary school.'

Bliss knew where his partner meant. 'So this may be something,' he said, feeling the urgency in his own voice.

'Could well be. We could do with the bump here. That briefing felt so flat earlier.'

'Yeah. I wasn't at my best.'

'You can only sell it so far, boss. There are no idiots in the room. They knew we had little to work with.'

'I know, I know. It's still my job to gee them up, keep them in a positive frame of mind.'

Chandler nodded. 'Yeah, but it would help if you were feeling that way yourself. We've come up short so far. All of us. As a team. Maybe this will be the break we need.'

Bliss came off the parkway at the first junction, threaded his way through Hampton Hargate and into the Vale area. He clocked the school on the right just as Chandler gave him the house address. She pointed at a three-storey apartment block on the corner of Vale Drive.

Like all the houses and flats in the Hamptons, it looked clean and functional. Metal railings defined the property boundary, and as they approached the junction, Bliss saw a black bicycle leaning up against them outside a ground floor flat. Just as he raised a hand to point at it, the door to the apartment flew open and a hooded figure blasted through it at speed, threw himself aboard the bike and set off along the street.

'Get in there!' Bliss cried out, as he screeched to a halt outside the block. 'I'm going after him.'

Chandler was already unclipping her seatbelt. Almost before he had come to a stop, she opened the door and jumped out, slamming it closed behind her. Bliss turned to look back up the street, the cyclist now on the road and pumping the pedals furiously from a standing position. Bliss floored the accelerator and the Insignia's long bonnet surged forward.

The cyclist took the first turning on the left. Bliss braked hard but jumped right back on the accelerator as he made the same turn. It took him wide on a narrow street, but thankfully nothing was approaching him. He knew he might have to give up the chase if his driving grew more dangerous in pursuit of the suspect, but for now he remained focused. Ahead of him, the bike jumped the kerb and started moving at speed down a path that ran alongside the park and stretches of open land beyond. Bliss cursed as he noticed that, although the path curved to the right in order to follow the shape of the lake that lay on the far side of the slight rise, so the road curved the other way.

What now?

Quit the chase?

Get out and run?

There was no way he was giving up so easily, not now they had got this close to their suspect. And Bliss already knew he was in no condition to give chase on foot. That left him with one more option.

Uttering a single low growl of frustration and rage, Bliss threw the car across the road. It slammed against the kerb, and as the two came together at speed the nearside front tyre popped and shattered with a soft explosion of air. Immediately he felt the rumble of torn rubber slapping against the arches, and the steering wheel juddered in his grip. Rather than allow this to slow him down, Bliss pressed harder on the pedal and his car swallowed up the ground behind the bike.

Sensing his rapid approach, the cyclist veered off further to the right on the upward slant of the hill. Bliss went with it, fighting with the steering all the way. He saw the ground ahead of him become instantly less flat, more densely overgrown, and a long line of trees stood before him, like a formidable and unpassable barrier.

As they entered a patch of knee-high parched grass, the car dipped into a hollow that was far deeper than Bliss had anticipated. He was thrown forward and bucked sideways, causing the side of his face to smack into the window. Despite the subsequent ferocious surge of pain, he shook his head from side to side to clear away the dizziness and confusion caused by the heavy bump. Bliss somehow kept his eyes on the prize all the while.

He felt warm and sticky blood run down from his right temple but ignored it. As the bike swept through the treeline, Bliss saw there was no way of making it through without ripping out the bottom of the car along the way. Instead he spun the wheel hard to the right and aimed for a narrow gap between two of the younger, less established trees. He realised when he was too close to stop that he would not make it through the gap unscathed.

Unyielding branches tore along both sides of the car, and Bliss was buffeted once more. He swore as he hit his head again in exactly the same place. He thumped the steering wheel in anger and dropped down two gears, before planting his right foot one more time. Bliss saw he was now back behind the bike and gaining on it, the rider struggling with the huge effort of making his escape over such uneven and overgrown turf.

The car powered over the domed rise, and Bliss looked on in horror as he saw the bike picking up speed on the downward slope and heading directly towards the lake. He shifted gear again and stamped on the throttle. The bike began to weave in a zigzag across the ground. Bliss was peripherally aware of people standing both on the hill and by the lakeside, gawping at the sight of the car spewing chunks of rubber tyre and clumps of soil as it gouged a furrow in obscure patterns in pursuit of the cyclist.

With the lake looming all too quickly in his windscreen, Bliss knew he had to end it now. Anticipating the direction the hooded figure would follow next, he angled the car towards where he guessed the bike would turn, and as it did so he was right alongside it. Foot to the floor now, Bliss shifted the wheel through his hands, detached the auto lock on his door and threw it wide open.

There was a fierce clatter and the door slammed back almost immediately. Bliss was unsure whether it had struck the bike or its rider. As he stood hard on the foot brake he caught a glimpse of both scything across the ground in a bone-juddering descent.

That was also the moment when Bliss realised he wasn't going to make it, either.

Struggling with his belt at first, he managed to unfasten it, and at the last moment before his car flew into the lake, Bliss opened the door again and rolled out of it, smashing his right hip against the bodywork as he emerged through the opening and struck the ground just as the rear wheel flew past his head. Momentum caused him to roll and flip over several times. His head bounced back off the grassy surface, and his ribs stabbed his chest with every somersault.

The final thud on the baked hard earth blasted all the air out of his lungs, and Bliss lay on his back like an upended turtle gasping for air. Pain sliced through his body as if he had landed in a field of razor blades. Chest heaving as he struggled to breathe, Bliss looked up to see what had become of the cyclist. The bike itself had ended up in the lake, but its rider lay sprawled out at the edge of the water, his legs hanging below the surface from the knees down.

Body aching all over, head still swimming from where it had struck the side window, Bliss felt blood continue to leak from the hairline close to his right ear. Ignoring the piercing whistle cutting through the pain in his temple, he managed to pull himself first onto one knee, before finally managing to struggle to both feet. He felt his body waver, as if it might topple and collapse straight back down again, but he righted himself and staggered across to the man in the hoodie, who was lying still.

'Fuck!' he said, noticing for the first time that the entire front end of his car now sat deep inside the lake, the water bubbling and frothing as it sucked the vehicle further down. Swearing forced Bliss to cough and splutter. His chest felt as if it were on fire, and every joint ached as it had never done before. He was not yet close to sixty, but at this moment he felt ancient and way past his sell-by date.

Hoodie was now groaning and holding a hand to his back. Bliss guessed he had been winded and had only now found his own breath. That at least meant the man was alive, which was good enough for Bliss. He eased himself back down into a sitting position on the grass, plucked his mobile from his pocket and called Chandler's number. He was pleasantly surprised to find that the mobile had survived his ordeal. There wasn't even a crack in the screen.

Between ragged and painful gasps, Bliss told his partner where he was and who to send. He said nothing else as the phone fell from his tenuous grasp. Instead he hung his head between his upraised knees and continued sucking in precious air while he waited for the pain to dissipate and his thoughts to clear.

This time he guessed he might have a long wait.

Chapter Thirty-Two

The paramedic was still checking Bliss's breathing function with a stethoscope by the time Chandler had cleared her scene back at the flat and arrived at the lakeside. Her mouth fell open in shock as she surveyed the carnage caused by the chase, the car half submerged beneath water, and Bliss stripped to the waist holding a bloodstained wad of gauze to the side of his head.

'How is she?' he asked fearfully, looking up as his partner jogged towards him.

Bliss noticed Chandler's eyes soak him in for a moment before she responded. 'Battered and bloody, a bit like yourself, but other than that she's fine. I made sure she was in capable hands before leaving her side. She got lucky. *We* got lucky. What the fu… what happened here?'

'He was getting away, so I slammed him with my car door. After which I had to bail out as I was about to misplace the car.'

'You can say that again.' Chandler looked beyond him, where on the edge of the lake their suspect was also being treated by a paramedic, a uniform now in attendance. 'So how's he doing?'

The assailant's neck had initially been immobilised by the second paramedic in case of a cervical spine trauma, but that no longer appeared to be a risk factor. His airway had been checked, and as with Bliss, the paramedic had also ensured there was an equal rise and fall of the chest.

'He'll live,' Bliss said, his voice a snarl of dismissal. 'He took one hell of a fall after I clobbered him with my car door, but it seems like there's no serious damage other than a suspected broken collarbone and a few bumps and bruises.'

'Bit like yourself, then. As if you needed any more.'

The paramedic attending Bliss glanced up at Chandler. 'He told me about the ribs,' she said. 'I don't think there is any more damage, but it probably didn't help, taking the kind of tumble he did on such hard ground. Pupils are equal and reactive. The inspector seems lucid, his oh-two sats are ninety-six, which is fine.'

'What are you checking for now?'

'Kelly here is a little concerned about my breathing,' Bliss interrupted.

'Did you explain to her that you were just really old?'

'No need. She said that much was obvious.'

The paramedic shook her head in disapproval. 'This is no laughing matter. You can continue to ignore me if you want, but my advice is still for you to go to hospital. That cut needs looking at. You banged your head hard, and just a week after being concussed. You need a full assessment, Inspector Bliss. For all I know you may have fractured your skull.'

He regarded the paramedic with what he hoped was his most disarming smile. Kelly had a wicked glint in her eye, and mischief played with the corners of her mouth. She had a pleasant way about her, with a gentle and soothing voice. Her thick black hair was cut stylishly short, and she had not needed to tie it back on such a warm evening. Bliss imagined she would be a bundle of fun off duty, but she was taking this seriously, behaving professionally. Nonetheless, he was determined not to spend any more time in hospital.

'Kelly, I know you're only doing your job, and you're probably right to be cautious. But rather than sit in A and E only to be given the all clear in four or five hours' time, I would rather get on with my job because time spent with our suspect is of the essence. I did not lose consciousness, my head has cleared, and I'm thinking straight. I hurt like a bastard, but I'll mend. In all honesty, I am much more concerned about my car.'

'Well, right now you are my patient and I couldn't give a shit about your car. That said, and though I hate to admit it, your breathing seems to have settled and is no longer causing you any distress. Your BP is fine, heart rate good and skin tone reasonable, considering what you've just experienced. I'm sticking to my recommendation, but if you are determined to ignore it then, at the very least, I need to make sure that head wound of yours is temporarily sealed.'

'Take him away with you and check for brain damage as well, will you,' Chandler implored her. 'Or can I sign something and have him committed for psychological evaluation?'

This time Kelly laughed. A low, deep chuckle at the back of her throat. 'I've already completed my capacity assessment, and he clearly understands the consequences of everything I have told him. I take it you two know each other well.'

'Yeah, this is my mother,' Bliss told her.

'And this is my backward son,' Chandler countered.

'Can we stop this now?' he complained. 'I confess to being in some discomfort here. I need my cut fixing and a few tablets to dull the pain. When you two are quite finished, we have a witness to question and a suspect to beat with a baseball bat – sorry, I mean interrogate. If the cut doesn't need stitches, I'd really rather crack on with the job.'

Chandler raised her eyebrows at the paramedic. 'Over to you, Kelly.'

Less than five minutes later, Bliss was pronounced fit to continue by the paramedic, provided he did not drive. As she said it, all three glanced across to where his car lay like a beached metallic whale.

'Not that I think that's going to be an immediate issue,' she finished off, putting a hand to her mouth to stifle a chuckle at Bliss's expense.

It didn't snuff out Chandler's, though. She snorted and wept tears of laughter, hands pressed against the pit of her stomach. Despite himself, Bliss wanted to join in, but he knew it would only exacerbate the agony drilling through every single one of his pain receptors.

Because the cut on his temple was neither jagged nor shaped, Kelly was able to apply a wet dressing in the form of a strip of gauze soaked in saline. 'Check for leaks and change the dressing later on. I'll give you two spares and some saline for tonight and tomorrow morning. Keep the wound as dry as possible otherwise. If you are on your own for any significant amount of time over the next day or so you need to be aware of your own health. You've recently been concussed, so you know what to look out for. But I'm concerned about that cut, so if it's still oozing in the morning then get yourself off to A and E. Apart from that, you're good to go, Inspector. Though I will ask you to sign a form for me to say you are leaving against my advice.'

Bliss thanked the young woman and stood as she packed up her bags. After he had scribbled his name on the form she handed him, Kelly then moved across to see if her partner needed any assistance. The stalker was also now on his feet, hunched over in pain and glaring across at Bliss. He said nothing, other than to answer questions thrown at him by the ambulance crew. Two uniforms now stood close by, preparing to arrest and cuff the man at the appropriate moment. Bystanders filming the entire show on their phones were being backed up by more police officers.

As he studied the stalker's features more closely, Bliss had the unnerving sensation that he recognised the attacker. That he knew him somehow. Taken out of context, a name wouldn't come to him, but his mind remained busy searching for the answer.

Bliss was relieved that after leaving the restaurant he had jumped into the car wearing his jacket. Otherwise it would be lying ruined under water on the passenger seat of his car right now. The paramedic had managed to remove it without causing him too much distress, but his shirt had been cut length-ways, so that would go the way of his blood-soaked gauze and the wrappings from the butterfly Steri-Strips Kelly had used on his head wound. The jacket helped cover his modesty, but his chest remained mostly exposed. Chandler walked by his side back to the apartment block, and he felt her scrutiny all the way.

'I had no option other than to use the door to stop him,' he said defensively as they approached the flat.

'I don't doubt it. Frankly, I couldn't give a toss about him one way or another.'

'Yeah, but I can already imagine the excessive force charge, can't you?'

'You could have run the arsehole over and saved us all some time and future expense. He got off lightly as far as I'm concerned.'

'Let's hope the brass see it that way. The IOPC will have fun with it, no doubt.'

'He's taken a hard knock. He's in a better condition than he left Jade Coleman. Don't worry about it.'

'I'm not. The way you were looking at me just now, I thought you were.'

Chandler shook her head. 'I'm worried about you. I know you've not looked in the mirror, but let me tell you, it's not a pretty sight. Not that it ever was.'

'Do you ever give up?' Bliss asked her.

'Give up what?'

'Taking the piss.'

'Oh. That.' She grinned and shook her head. 'Not a chance.'

Deborah Crighton was sitting in her living room, still being attended by two paramedics. Bliss saw immediately how badly she had been punched; she had cuts on her mouth and left cheekbone. That whole side of her face was swelling and already highly discoloured. But she appeared to be talking normally to the two men treating her, and the grim look of determination on her face told Bliss she refused to weep and break down because of what had happened to her. This woman was strong, and Bliss knew she would make a terrific witness.

As they walked into the room, the victim looked up and her forehead creased as she took in his appearance. He smiled and said, 'You want to see the other bloke.'

'You caught him?' Crighton asked, her resolve starting to crumble.

'I did. Well, my car door did. But we have him in custody, and as soon as he's been given the all-clear by a doctor, we will be interviewing him.'

'A doctor? He's hurt? Good. Fuck him!'

Bliss nodded. 'No argument here, Deborah. We'd obviously like to speak with you before we get him in the room, so when you're feeling up to it I'd ask that you to take us through what happened here today.'

The woman's eyes flickered, and her chest started to heave. Bliss raised a hand. 'It's okay. Settle down. If it's too much for you right now then we can wait. I realise you've had a traumatic experience, Deborah, and I don't want to add to that by forcing you to relive it so soon afterwards.'

She nodded, but Bliss saw the fear in her wide-eyed stare and knew shock was settling over her like a heavy shroud.

'We have time before his clock starts running, as he is not being questioned while undergoing treatment either here or at hospital. We have arrested him and can charge him with the assault on you at any time during the first twenty-four hour period excluding his time in treatment, and of course that charge will stick. But in all honesty, I want to charge him with more than what he did to you here today. What you can tell us will be helpful, of course, but unless the assault is all we end up with, then your evidence is not crucial.'

'It isn't?'

'Not if we can charge him with something worse. So please, don't fret. I'm going to have a couple of our officers stick around until everything settles down around here, after which a Family Liaison Officer will stay with you. Our CSI crew will do their thing, and we will continue to communicate with you all the way. Please, don't feel under any pressure to talk to us about your ordeal. Concentrate on yourself for now. We'll speak to you again tomorrow.'

When he and Chandler were back outside the flat, the crime scene having been cordoned off and the various teams working around them, Bliss huffed his exasperation and shook his head in anger.

'This isn't right,' he said urgently. 'I didn't want to say anything in front of Deborah, but it just isn't right.'

'What do you mean?' Chandler asked. 'What's not right?'

'Think about it. Our stalker was already running when we arrived. Not *because* we arrived. He was already done and making his escape.'

'So?'

'So, why? Not only is there no further escalation this time, Pen, he's actually taken a whole step backwards.'

His colleague was now nodding. 'I see what you mean. With Mandy Vickers he settled for a few blows. Jade he stabbed several times. This should have gone the same way at the very least.'

'Exactly. Why would he backtrack like that with the third victim? It makes no sense.'

'Hold on, though. We've covered this ground before. We wondered if he had stabbed and killed Jade only because she came at him with the knife first. Perhaps he never intended to kill her, and had no desire to do so this time, either.'

Bliss thought about the man on the bank by the lake. Again there was that flash of recognition. Where had he seen him before? He took a breath and let it go. It would come to him in its own good time.

'You think he wouldn't have got a taste for it, Pen? He not only stabbed Jade several times, he was pretty brutal about it. If you're him and you intend causing no harm, and all you're doing is reacting to Jade having the knife, then maybe you use it a couple of times on her. Three at most. Just to fend her off. Seven thrusts of the blade tells me he enjoyed himself. And with his next victim he would be far more likely to increase the brutality. Settle for the same at a minimum. But definitely not less. Not this much less.'

'Or maybe you were right when you suggested Jade and he knew each other.'

'Maybe I was. But I'm sure about this, either way. It just feels wrong.'

Chandler puffed out her cheeks and pulled her hair back with both hands, holding it up at the nape to allow the slight breeze to cool the back of her neck.

'So what are we saying here, boss?' She pointed back towards the flat. 'We know it's him. This is our man. So what's wrong with the picture we're seeing?'

Bliss thought he knew.

'Motive,' he said softly. The night was cooling around them, but even so Bliss felt the lining of his jacket sticking to his back. 'He wanted or chose to beat Mandy Vickers. He wanted or chose to stab and kill Jade Coleman. Tonight, he wanted or chose to again only beat Deborah Crighton.'

'But that's deliberation. That's not some psycho losing it and unwinding even further with each victim. That's not the continued escalation driven by compulsion that we see with such cases.'

'My point precisely. So what are we still missing here, Pen?'

Shaking her head, Chandler said, 'I haven't the foggiest idea.'

Bliss glanced down at the ground, then looked back up again. He felt a stillness creep over him. A certainty that felt solid and grounding, prickling his flesh. He let out a soft gasp.

'I have. I know the answer. Or at least, I'm pretty certain I do.'

'Well, don't stop there. Tell me.'

He shook his head. 'This is one of those teachable moments people talk about, Pen. I could explain my thought process. That way you'll know the answer and how I got there, but you won't be able to replicate the sensation as the pieces come together unless you try it for yourself. Ask yourself the same questions, only this time put them together with everything else we know, every lead we have been following so far. Why would such a man first beat a woman, then murder another, only to beat a third victim days later?'

Bliss saw her eyes gleam at first. Then a cloud passed across them as she went from sheer excitement to deep thought in an instant. He had absolute faith in his partner. At the conclusion of their last major case together he had told Chandler that she was the best of them. Including him. And she was. He envied her talent. At her age he doubted he would have been able to work this out on his own. But Chandler would.

A few seconds later, her gaze narrowed and a smile crept over her lips. Bliss knew in that moment he had been right about her. He saw for himself all of that potential emerge like a beautiful butterfly from its chrysalis.

Speaking slowly, Chandler said, 'He beat Mandy because that was what he was supposed to do. He killed Jade because that was what he was supposed to do. And tonight, he beat Deborah because that was also what he was supposed to do. Just as instructed. He's not a stalker because he's driven to be one by his psyche. He's a stalker because it's his cover. He was paid to do all this. He takes money or favours to do whatever is asked of him.'

Bliss felt a huge surge of pride threatening to overwhelm him. His partner was correct. The man was nothing more than a mercenary, stalking his prey before pouncing. It was now obvious to Bliss that the two beatings were carried out in order to deflect the police investigation, to obscure the fact that Jade Coleman's murder was planned. Someone had wanted her dead, and decided to use the cover of a stalker to disguise the true purpose of the central attack. The man who had carried out the acts was merely the marionette. His strings were the most important factor now. Who was pulling them? Who was manipulating the man...

Bliss allowed his thoughts to trail off. Something about a word or a phrase he had used when thinking it all through now bothered him. He replayed the sequence of thoughts, not spotting the anomaly. There was nothing there. Nothing obvious. Their killer was the man who carried out the acts, but he was not their orchestrator.

He...

Bliss felt it then. That familiar tug inside his gut, deep down in the hollow pit of his stomach. The sensation that began there slowly, before starting to wind itself upward, grasping at his chest and causing his heart to thump and blood to pound in his ears.

'*He* didn't do it,' Bliss heard himself say out loud.

Chandler turned her head towards him as if she had somehow misheard or misunderstood what he was trying to tell her. 'What? He… he what?'

'*He* didn't do it. *She* did.'

'She? She who?'

'Him.'

'I'm sorry, boss. But are you feeling okay? You want me to see if Kelly is still there? You may need to get to hospital after all. You're not making any sense.'

He raised a hand. 'No. No, I'm fine. Really.'

'With respect, boss, you don't sound like it. You were rambling. I couldn't understand what you were talking about.'

'Sorry. I was still working it through inside my head. See, when I saw our stalker without his hood up for the first time, I thought he looked familiar. I couldn't place him for a long while, but I knew I had seen his face somewhere before. Then moments ago it just came to me.'

'But you mistook she and he, boss. It still made no sense.'

'But that's just it, Pen. That's what I'm trying to tell you. He is a she. Sure, he can clearly make himself look like the man he once was. This stalker, this man, once went by the name of Stephen Robbie. Except that he's no longer a man, and for many years now has gone by the name of Diane Locke. Pen, this is why Jade's link to her friend Tessa Brady and the whole CAWED thing wormed its way beneath my skin. It's why I couldn't let it go. Diane Locke was a member of that organisation and was very close to Marvin and Ellie Cooke. She was the fiercest and most combative activist of them all.'

Chandler was stunned by his pronouncement. 'You are shitting me,' she said, catching flies as she absorbed the information.

'No.' Bliss shook his head. 'I shit you not, Grasshopper. In amongst the clips sent to me by Sandra Bannister, was the "before" photo of Diane Locke, in her Stephen Robbie days. I knew I'd seen that face before. I just had to wait for it to come back to me.'

'So Diane Locke reverted to looking more like the man she had once been in order to carry out these attacks. She wasn't known to either Mandy or Deborah, but Jade knew her and recognised her. But if we're now saying he or she only carried out these attacks under orders, then are we also saying those orders were given by the Cookes?'

'One of them, at least. Yes.'

'But why? Why would they want to kill Jade?'

'That I don't know. But I plan to find out.'

Chapter Thirty-Three

Bliss was feeling trapped. A patrol car had dropped him and Chandler back at his place. He needed a shower or to soak in a hot bath in order to soothe his aching muscles, but all he did was change out of what remained of his clothing into casual wear. The first thing he noticed when he walked into the living room was how parched and neglected his garden was looking. He and Chandler chatted while he watered everything, taking particular care with his five different species of Acer plants. Bliss also studied the Koi for a few minutes to ensure they were behaving healthily. They moved around the pond in their usual languid style, neither hurrying nor acting lethargic, so he was happy the fierce heat had made none of them sick.

Outside in the back garden their discussion was led mainly by Chandler and focused almost exclusively on him and his injuries. She was about as happy as the paramedic had been that he was ignoring medical advice and had chosen not to have his head wound looked at in the Accident and Emergency unit.

'Christ, boss,' she said without any venom. 'You've been in a few scrapes before, but I don't think you appreciate how bad a condition you're in at the moment. We won't get to interview Diane Locke or Stephen Robbie or whoever she or he is until at least tomorrow morning. You have time to get yourself looked at.'

Bliss shrugged it off. 'Kelly did a great job. She was saying what she has to say, but given I'm still recovering from my previous head injury, believe me I know the difference. I'll be fine. I am fine.'

Chandler let it go this time. When they moved back inside, his plants now dripping water and spotting the patio floor, the conversation turned back to the investigation itself.

'Now that we think we know the who, we're still stuck with the why,' Chandler reminded him. She sat on the very edge of his second recliner, sipping water drawn straight from the tap.

Bliss also drank water, having buckled beneath the weight of his partner's stern admonishment that he avoid alcohol in his condition. 'We were supposed to be sucked into the whole stalker con. To think of them as random selections, driven by a warped desire. Whoever is behind this killed Jade because she was the ultimate target, and they must have believed that the beatings were enough for the other two victims to keep the stalker theory going.'

'If they'd limited it to only Mandy and Jade, their ruse might well have succeeded.'

'My guess is their initial plan was not to carry out a third assault. I think it may have been prompted by our interest in CAWED and the Cookes themselves. I feel a bit guilty about that, because it may have been my poking about in their lives that caused this most recent attack. They probably got scared by my visits and decided to steer us back towards the lone stalker theory.'

'If so, then it was their undoing.'

'Maybe. That all depends on what Locke tells us tomorrow. If she refuses to point the finger at Marvin and Ellie Cooke, then we may have to rely on breaking them in their own separate interviews.'

'When do you intend bringing them in, boss?'

Bliss paused to consider. His preference was to interview Locke first, but he was a little concerned that as soon as they heard about her capture, the Cookes might pack their bags and flee. There was no point in requesting the couple be put under observation, because it would be refused due to lack of funding. However, even though he could put out an all ports notice on their names, Bliss did not want them slipping through his fingers.

'I'm going to order their arrest for first thing in the morning. I think conspiracy to the stalking and murder will be enough for the time being.'

'Having met them, I doubt they'll go quietly.'

He grinned. 'It'll be just like old times.'

'I wonder if we should arrange some off-books observation on them overnight. I'm sure we could get a few volunteer pairings.'

'I like the way you think.'

Chandler looked at him for several seconds, and Bliss noted the concern still written in her expression. 'Tell you what,' he added. 'Why don't you get it done for me? I'm cream-crackered, I feel about a hundred years old, every single part of me aches, and I reckon I could sleep for a month. I'm going to call it a night if that's okay by you.'

'That's more than okay by me, boss.' His colleague brightened. She hesitated for a moment, then said, 'Look, Kelly thought you ought to be under observation. That was a nasty cut, and you're clearly shaken and not at your best. I could sleep here on the recliner tonight. I won't bother you, I'll just be here if you need me.'

Bliss regarded Chandler with the same affection he had felt towards her ever since the first time they met. He reminded her of that meeting now. 'Do you remember when we first worked together, Pen? I was fresh up out of London, the dark clouds following me north, my card marked by you lot from the moment I arrived. I was treated with suspicion and everyone was more than a little wary of me. Apart from you, that is. You marched across the room, pumped my hand and told me how much you were looking forward to working with me and learning from a Met detective. I was so relieved I was actually lost for words.'

She smiled at him, the recollection removing all the sharp edges of concern from her face. 'I was as nervous as anything,' she admitted. 'But I felt the chill in the room, saw the way the others were looking at you, and I knew I couldn't let you walk out of there feeling as if you'd drowned a litter of puppies.'

'And I've always been grateful for that kindness.'

'You know, despite the fact that you're still a bit of an old troglodyte, I've never regretted working with you, Jimmy. And I have learned from you. The good, the bad, and on occasion the downright ugly. But it's all helped me shape the career I have now.'

'A career which ought to develop even further. I do understand why you're dwelling at your current rank, Pen. But one thing you must surely have learned from me is that you don't necessarily have to end up being desk-bound when you become a DI. As I told Mia earlier, there's a shit-load more responsibility, no question. More admin, more meetings, more political bullshit. But you can still be your own person if you have no other ties.'

'Can you?' Chandler looked hard at him this time. 'I mean, do you really think the brass would allow the likes of another Jimmy Bliss to flourish these days? I don't. I think they'd cut me off at the knees if I started to go my own way. You know it's all about being target-driven right now. You're immune because you're… well, with the greatest respect, you're a fossil. But even you have to work under enormous pressure to survive doing what you enjoy. Being at the sharp end of things. You didn't break the mould, Jimmy, they broke it around you. They want automatons, drones who know the rule book inside out and stick to it. I'd be a fledgling DCI Edwards, and frankly I'd rather quit than be that.'

Bliss knew she was right. The service no longer had room for the likes of him. Barely tolerated, he had existed this long because he got results and helped tick so many boxes when it came to crime figures. But Chandler had their measure, and he felt aggrieved that she would never know what it was like to command a team in the way he had enjoyed.

'You think Mia will take that step up in your place?' he asked.

'She made sergeant before I did. She's an obvious choice. Maybe with the kids in mind she might settle for another few rungs on the ladder. I don't think she's that way inclined by nature, but I think she could adapt better than I would.'

Thinking back to the conversation he'd had with Mia on their return from Huntingdon, Bliss thought his partner had that about right, too.

'So, you want me to stick around overnight?' Chandler asked. 'I can pop home, grab some things, be back inside half an hour.'

'Thanks, but no.' Bliss shook his head. 'I'm going to stand under a hot shower for ten minutes, and then collapse into bed. There's no concussion, so nothing to worry about or any need to monitor me.'

Chandler slapped her thighs. 'Fair enough. You're the boss. Before I go, where do things stand with you and your IOPC issues? Have you decided what to do about this Nick Nevin character?'

'Not yet,' he said. Which was only partially true. He believed he would follow his instincts, no matter where they led him.

They made arrangements for her to pick him up at seven-fifteen the following morning. 'You think the DCI and Super will leave you be tonight?' she asked, pausing by the front door on her way out. 'There's a lot of mess to sort out back in Hampton Vale.'

Bliss nodded. 'I told Bish and Mia I'd speak to them tomorrow, so I don't expect any more calls for the rest of the evening. Not unless the Cookes try for a moonlight flit.'

Barely twenty minutes had passed before he was proven wrong on that. He had settled down with a cup of tea and a DVD showing highlights of Chelsea's previous season – in which they narrowly missed out on a Champions League slot, but had won the FA Cup by beating Manchester United in the final. Bliss hit pause on the remote before taking the call from an unknown number.

Initially there was only silence. Bliss wondered if it was a prank call, maybe even a scammer about to launch into a desperate story aimed at fleecing him. But the moment he heard the voice he knew exactly who had called him.

'Been a long time, Bliss.'

'So it has.' He jumped out of his chair, needing to be on his feet and moving. His body protested, but Bliss ignored it.

'Long enough for me to think about how you had me feeding through a tube. How you managed to turn people against me. Every day that I climb into my crappy old van to do some odd jobs or make deliveries, I am reminded of you and what you did to my career.'

Bless felt his throat constrict and his body becoming stiff with tension.

'Well, you did murder my wife, Nevin.'

'I have no idea what you're talking about, Bliss. We both know you did that yourself.'

'You think I might be recording this? Or that maybe someone is listening in? Is that why you won't admit what you did? There's just you and me on this line, Nevin. No need for the old *Jackanory* bollocks.'

'Still don't have a clue what you mean, Bliss. I'm starting to question your sanity. You had it in for me after I shagged your wife, even though you were in the same room at the same time shagging someone else. You killed her because you were jealous, blamed it on me because I was banging her.'

Bliss closed his eyes and clenched his right fist. He bumped it gently against his forehead, bile rising in his gorge. 'If that's the way you want to play it, Nevin, then you can go fuck yourself right now. I've got no time for games. Tell me what you want.'

'What I want is to make you pay for my shit life.'

'Why now? After all these years?'

'Just a question of timing. Things unexpectedly falling into place. Karma, I call it.'

'Smells more like bullshit to me.'

'I just reached a point where I couldn't take it any longer. It was chewing up my insides. You must know how that feels.'

'Oh, I do. The fact that you're still breathing tells you I've never acted on it, though.'

'Then that's your loss. Hopefully you'll feel the bite of cuffs around your wrists very soon, Bliss. And when they put you away for murder, I hope you get arse-raped every day you spend inside. Although there won't be too many of those. In the tougher places they feast on coppers who get themselves banged up.'

'Never going to happen, Nevin. I may not be able to prove that you murdered Hazel, but I'm not going down for it, either.

Whatever evidence you say you have now, we both know it's a pack of lies.'

'We'll see about that, won't we? One way or another, you're going to pay for ruining my life, Bliss.'

'That sounds like a threat. You no longer worried I might be recording this conversation?'

'Bliss, if I had my way you would suffer unimaginably before you were finally offed. Me, I wouldn't touch you with a barge pole, but I bet there's a very long list of people out there who would like to take a blowtorch to you for a few hours before cutting you up into tiny pieces and disposing of you in the sewers where shit like you belongs. Maybe if this IOPC thing doesn't work out, that's something you might want to keep in mind.'

'And let myself feel threatened by you or a worm just like you, Nevin? You actually believe I would spend the rest of my natural looking over my shoulder waiting for some tripehound to come sneaking up behind me? Don't waste your breath or your imagination. You don't have enough of either to spare.'

'The day they put you away I will be in court. I swear I will stand up and cheer when they send you down, you tosser.'

Bliss bit down on an immediate retort. Fuelled by anger and an obvious overflow of testosterone, he had been venting and knew it was pointless and puerile. It lowered him to Nevin's level, demeaning him and Hazel in the process. Shame burned his cheeks. When he next spoke, his voice was calm and measured.

'All she did was cut you off, Nevin. Spurned your advances. She did it quietly and respectfully. She did not deserve to die for that. You didn't have to murder her.'

'Once again, Bliss, I have no idea what you are talking about. I've never murdered anyone in my life.'

'Okay, okay. You want to discuss this in person rather than on the blower? Just you and me, no recordings, no listening devices. Is that why you called me tonight, Nevin? You want one final crack at me before the IOPC come knocking on my door?'

'Yeah. That's exactly what I want. To look you in the eye while there's still time. Once they start on you, Bliss, they won't be happy until you're behind bars. I won't get this chance again, so bring it on. Bring the best you've got.'

Bliss looked down at himself, felt the pain shift throughout his body. The best he had was sadly inadequate at the moment, but while he was many things – had been many things – he was never one to quit.

'So let's meet then,' he said defiantly. 'Saturday morning. First thing. You know my case history, and if you don't, you have friends in high places now who will look it up for you. The site of my first murder investigation. Scene of crime. I like an early start, so let's make it seven o'clock. I see anyone else around and I'm gone.'

'I'll be there, Bliss. You can bank on that. And I don't need anybody else to back me up.'

I might, Bliss thought. 'I want to know one thing up front. I want to know what you have on me.'

Nevin laughed, a harsh sound containing not a scrap of humour. 'I have someone willing to confess to the murder. A murder you paid them to carry out. Not only that, I also have someone who will confirm that they paid you in hard currency to look the other way when there was a raid due, and that you used that cash to pay the man who killed your wife. No names. Those you get when the IOPC come through your door, Bliss. But you are nailed. You understand? Nailed!'

Bliss felt the first injection of shock flood his veins. His balled fist squeezed tighter still, nails digging into his palm. His stomach clenched. He wanted to smash his way through the brick walls of the house and keep bullocking his way south until Nevin stood before him.

'How the fuck did you swing that?' he demanded. 'We both know it never happened.'

'I didn't have to swing anything. And it must've happened, because two honest citizens are now owning up to past mistakes. See you Saturday morning, Bliss. Be lucky.'

Pulling back his hand, Bliss had to choke off his anger and quell the urge to hurl the phone at the wall, as if smashing it to pieces might in some way divest himself of the rage he felt towards Nevin.

If the intention of the call had been to dangle bait in front of him, Bliss had snapped at it. Greedily. Obsessively, even. He was not yet reeled in; only his appearance in London on Saturday morning would see that happen.

But he knew he was going.

He had one day to get Diane Locke to talk.

At that moment, as his mind swirled and became enveloped in a blood-red mist, he could no longer see beyond the meeting with Nevin. He found himself not giving a damn about what might follow, because on Saturday morning his torment had to end.

Whatever that meant, and however it had to be achieved.

Chapter Thirty-Four

Before leaving home on Friday morning, and with the investigation into the murder of Jade Coleman now a week old, Bliss put in a call to Gareth Wigg. He told his friend about the conversation with Nick Nevin the previous evening, after which the two debated the merits of the fresh witness evidence.

'First of all, I never took a back-hander,' Bliss assured Wigg. 'Second of all, I never paid anyone to kill Hazel. So these two men are being paid off in some way.'

'That would be the most logical conclusion, yes.' Wigg was the epitome of reassurance in the face of stress, and his soothing voice worked its magic. 'The first character could be doing this for any number of reasons, from receiving a payoff himself to perhaps a free ride on something for which he is awaiting trial. I'm sure you will have already worked this out, but your second man will almost certainly already be serving a life sentence. A lengthy one, at the very least.'

'That was my assumption, Wiggy. What I could use from you are the names Nevin refused to give me.'

'As usual, dear chap, I will do my utmost. People are getting a sense of something in the air and are starting to close ranks, but I think by presenting what I now know, I can obtain the information you want. Don't do anything hasty, Jimmy.'

Too late for that, Bliss thought as he ended the connection. Less than five minutes later he was in Chandler's Focus heading to HQ. His partner made no comment about his appearance, but the look of anguish on her face revealed the depths of her concern. That same look was on the faces of everyone he saw upon arrival. Bliss knew he was a sight, despite the fact that he was wearing his best suit, shirt and tie, had showered twice and applied a fresh gauze strip. The clothes were merely his adornments, the lacerations, swelling and bruises his badges of honour. But to Bliss they also felt like stark warnings of his own mortality.

After fending off a few clumsy jokes about his next vehicle requiring amphibious qualities, and the odd mention about him bearing all to the pretty paramedic, Kelly, the briefing room settled down as Bliss laboured to the front of the room. He raised both hands, then swept them downwards as if presenting himself for their inspection.

'Yes, I am a bit of a sight,' he admitted. 'Two vehicle-related incidents in just over a week is not something I would advise, nor recommend. I'm battered, but I'm still standing. All of which is irrelevant, because yesterday evening we got our man.'

A loud spontaneous cheer went up, and there were raised hands, triumphant clenched fists, wide beaming smiles of pleasure, and the welcome release of laughter and back-slapping. Bliss regarded his team with pride. There were still one or two scruffs, the odd misery, complainer, shirker even, but as a team they gelled. Hard work was not an anathema to them. Quite the opposite, in his opinion. Chandler had told him that they were a team taking on the better qualities of their leader, and Bliss could not have asked for more in his name.

When the euphoria had subsided, Bliss thanked them for their efforts. 'We still have plenty of work to do, of course. It would be nice if we could get our suspect to cough, though we still need to piece our case together for the CPS. Moreover, I want to tie Locke in with the couple I suspect were her paymasters. I won't be looking at anyone other than Marvin and Ellie Cooke. And I do mean the pair of them. They were woken from their blissful slumber just after dawn and are currently sitting in separate holding cells, still waiting for their solicitor to make his way across from Birmingham. I'm hoping Locke will give them up, but be prepared for that not to happen.'

'We are putting together a warrant application to search their boat,' Bishop said, standing alongside his boss to deliver his update. 'We are also trying to tie down whether they still own or rent any CAWED-related properties, in which case we'll want to search them as well.'

'What are we looking for?' Short asked. She appeared perfectly relaxed, her feet up on a chair. It was one of her black leather days, and she gave off a vibe that suggested she would not be screwed with.

'Anything that links them with Locke. I'm not expecting to find a financial paper trail. No receipt for services rendered. But whatever we find may be helpful. I'd also be keen to see if there's anything connecting them to Tessa Brady since she supposedly disappeared. Something bugged me about their insistence that Brady was dead.'

'And the state of play with this Locke person?' Ansari asked. 'Where are we with that?'

'Being released from hospital as we speak. She will be taken directly into interview room one, where a duty brief will be waiting. The break in her collar bone was not so severe that it required surgery. Locke is wearing a figure-of-eight clavicle brace. It was that or a sling, and they settled for the brace. But she is fit to be interviewed, and that's all that counts.'

'The Facebook keyboard warriors and Twitterati are up in arms about what happened to him,' Hunt said gruffly. 'Another example of police brutality, according to them. And they are really overplaying the whole transgender thing as well. As usual with the fake news machine, overnight it turned from striking the bike with the car door to mowing him down and running right over him.'

'Her,' Short said, flicking her eyes at Hunt. 'Mowing *her* down.'

'Way I heard it she was back to looking and behaving like a man at the time, so take your pick, love.'

Short slowly removed both feet from the chair, placed them flat on the floor and leaned forward. 'Never call me that again, John. Not even in jest. Not if you want to keep all your teeth.'

'What's wrong with "love"?' Hunt looked around the room for either guidance or help. He received no support whatsoever. Not even from Bliss, who cut them short and moved on.

'Whatever form Locke presents herself to us in, we can expect a complete lack of co-operation. She clearly felt aggrieved when I sent her flying down that hill, and will undoubtedly play on that as much as possible. If my continued presence in the room antagonises her, well, all the better. Meanwhile, when that warrant comes in, get busy. I can maybe play this lot off against one another, but let's prepare for an evidentiary-based case anyway. Good luck. And thank you all again.'

Bliss returned to his office and waited on his own until Locke arrived at the station. His plan was to spend an hour in with her at most, before turning his attention to the Cookes. He felt the first stirrings of excitement in his stomach. It was going to be one hell of a day, and Bliss was determined that if it was to be his last in the job, it would also be his best.

***

If the previous day had been all about the Stephen Robbie reincarnation, then today Diane Locke was truly back in favour. The brunette wig was sleek and long, with a centre parting and a fringe that cut off in a straight line just above the eyebrows. Heavy make-up concealed many of the bumps and bruises and minor abrasions she had acquired, though not all of them by any means. Some swelling remained around her left eye and cheekbone. Locke wore a deep blue silk blouse and a tight black skirt that fell just below the knee. She was bare-legged and wore open-toed sandals with a wedged heel. She was swathed in costume jewellery, both wrists jangling like wind chimes each time she moved. The detention officer clearly had no idea what to make of the person he had brought along from the cells.

Every inch the woman she believed herself to be, Bliss thought. And determined that was who everybody should see. The poor, defenceless female, brutalised by the big bad policeman. Bliss thought it might work with the media and some of the public, but not in here. Not with him.

They went through the usual rituals and protocols required by the Police And Criminal Evidence act. Bliss was a little surprised that Locke had not focused her anger on him from the moment he and Chandler entered the room. Instead, the woman sat rigid and upright, staring straight ahead directly between the two detectives.

'How did you enjoy your night on the Green Mile?' Bliss asked.

'The what?'

'Surely you noticed the hideous green vinyl flooring along the corridor where the cells are. We call it the Green Mile, after the film of that name. Only, you won't end up with Old Sparky – sorry, the electric chair.'

Locke shrugged her shoulders as if to suggest she had no idea what he was talking about, and did not care, either.

Bliss nodded and got into it. 'Very well, that's enough of the chit-chat, eh? Let me begin by saying that no matter what is discussed in this interview, Ms Locke, you are nicked for what you did to Deborah Crighton yesterday evening at her home in Hampton Vale. I will ask you about that incident, and the one at Woodston in which Mandy Vickers was also assaulted by you. However, my early focus will be on the murder of Jade Coleman. Is that understood?'

'No comment,' Locke said. She blinked once and remained still.

'You knew Jade Coleman, didn't you, Ms Locke?'

'No comment.'

'Hmm. While it's your right to blank us with the "no comment" defence, it's not exactly the brightest thing to do when presented with facts rather than conjecture. Let me ask you again. You knew Jade Coleman. Yes or no?'

'No… comment.'

Bliss smiled. 'I see what you did there. Tricky, that one. Never been done before. All right, so let me tell you what I know rather than ask you. You did know Jade Coleman. You attended many meetings and events with Miss Coleman when you were both supporting the Citizens Against Whittlesey Energy Disposal organisation. We have photos of you two together. This is all a matter of public record, so why not add your own voice to this, Ms Locke? Juries regard "no comment" answers in different ways, and tend to find those in response to indisputable facts to be suggestive of a person who has something to hide.'

Bliss was glad to see the duty solicitor leaning across and whispering something to Locke behind his hand. Bliss knew the brief, though not well. He was a stickler, but also a realist. Hopefully he was advising his client to speak up when the easy balls were lobbed over the net, reserving the no comment form of defence for the trickier stuff.

Locke sat upright once more, blew a stream of air through her nose and looked at Bliss for the first time. 'Yes, I knew Jade. Just as I know you attempted to kill me yesterday, Inspector Bliss.'

'Let's stick to fact and not speculation, shall we? Tell me, Ms Locke, when did you last see Miss Coleman?'

'That would have been around four years ago.'

'When CAWED closed its doors, is that right?'

'Yes. Around then.'

'So you never kept in contact afterwards?'

'I've just said not.'

'That's right. Only, I'm a little confused by your answer. You say you haven't seen Jade since 2014, yet you were actually inside her home last Friday, the eighth of June. You had to have been, and you had to have seen her that day, because that was also the day you stabbed her seven times and murdered her.'

Locke frowned, then raised one eyebrow. She glanced sidelong at her solicitor. 'I think we'll go back to having no comment to make to that question,' she said.

Bliss paused. He decided to lay it all out for the woman, see what she made of it. He would concentrate on her reactions throughout.

'Very well. If you refuse to admit to what we already know, I will tell you in order to refresh your memory. And please, do correct me if I'm wrong about any of it.

'Ms Locke, we know that you stalked Mandy Vickers, and then broke into her house and punched her three times, leaving her battered and lying on the floor. We know that you stalked Jade Coleman, though less overtly, before entering her home last week and stabbing her to death. And we also know that it was supposed to end there, except that whoever paid you to murder Miss Coleman then asked you to do another little job for them.

'Which is why, yesterday evening, you were in the home of Deborah Crighton, whom you beat viciously, before escaping on your bike as you did on the two previous occasions. At the conclusion of the ensuing chase, you were bumped down a hill by my car door. As you have so far not corrected me, I'll assume that you agree with my version of events, Ms Locke.'

Folding her arms beneath her fake breasts, Locke looked up at the ceiling and shook her head. 'No comment. To all of it.'

'Are you sure that's the way you want to go?' Chandler asked, speaking up for the first time since the introductions were made for the recording. 'These are pretty severe allegations being put to you, Ms Locke. It's one thing to "no comment" your way through an interview where you're being accused of stealing a bike or handling stolen goods, but murder requires something a bit more effective.'

'That's right,' Bliss said. 'For example, despite you having no option but to agree with us as to exactly where you were yesterday evening when Deborah Crighton was getting beaten up, you might consider providing us with an alibi for the times when Mandy Vickers was beaten, and Jade Coleman stabbed to death.'

In Bliss's experience it was unusual for those unfamiliar with the routine of such interviews to stay the course without responding. The desire to protect yourself, even when guilty, was instinctive. Diane Locke was not exactly a novice, having been spoken to several times down the years about her actions relating to various protests and activities. But to Bliss's knowledge she had never been accused of murder before. It was much harder to sit back and fob the police off when what was at stake was a significant chunk of the rest of your life. Even the guilty sought some form of justification. Locke proved to be every bit as vulnerable as the majority.

'I was with somebody when this Vickers woman was smacked around. Same when Jade was killed. Last night was nothing more than a squabble between two people that got out of hand.'

The room started to feel larger to Bliss, though he knew the exact opposite would be true for their suspect. He leaned across the table as if to consume even more of that empty space.

'Leaving the events of yesterday aside for one moment, I'd first of all be keen to know how you are able to tell us you were with somebody else when Mandy Vickers was assaulted, when in fact I never informed you when that assault occurred.'

This was why people were advised to make no comment at all. Because every time they opened their mouths they played Russian roulette with their own lives.

'Didn't you? I thought you did?' Locke looked to her solicitor, who shook his head. 'Well, then I must have read about it somewhere.'

'Where?'

'I'm not sure. The local rag, probably.'

'It wasn't reported on.'

'The radio, then. I listen to Heart a fair bit. You know, the local station? It has regular local news items.'

'When I say it wasn't reported on, I mean not by any media.'

Locke shrugged in an exaggerated manner this time. 'Well, then I must have overheard someone talking about it.'

'And they happened to mention the precise date and time.'

'That must be how I heard, yes.'

Bliss nodded. 'And that date and time would be?'

Few people were capable of preventing panic from revealing itself in their eyes. Diane Locke was not one of them. 'I… I'm not sure now. I've forgotten.'

'But just a few minutes ago you told us you were with somebody on that date and at that time,' Chandler said, scoffing at the woman's excuses. 'Are you now saying that you are unable to recall the facts you were so clearly able to recall only minutes ago? Ms Locke, I think you know that simply will not wash.'

Flustered now, rather than leaning back on the original plan to make no comment, Locke continued digging a hole for herself. 'No, no. I remember thinking at the time where I was when this poor woman was beaten, but I've subsequently forgotten when that was.'

'That's really not an improvement on your last statement.'

Bliss decided this was the right time to take a chance and force the issue. 'It's not easy moving in a straight line when that first wheel comes off,' he said. 'One well-rehearsed lie leads to one less considered, and on to one never even thought of at all. Before you know it, you're tying yourself in knots and making yourself look guilty. Which, of course, you are. But in many ways, you're also a pawn. That's another thing we know, Ms Locke. You didn't wake up one morning and decide to stalk and beat and kill. No, you were asked to do all that. Perhaps even told to.'

Bliss paused as Locke glared across the table at him. There was less conviction in her eyes now, though. The set of her chin was less obdurate. He decided to continue without waiting for a response.

'I won't pretend there is any way around what you did, Ms Locke. The beatings aside, the very least you are facing is a charge of manslaughter, and only then if your legal team can find a way to convince the Crown Prosecution Service that you murdered Jade in self-defence or lost control of your temper. But murder is still very much on the cards, and if you continue to piss me about then that's the way I will be leaning. You can do yourself a big favour here. You can really help yourself out. Now, I know you had your code of silence back in your protesting days, Ms Locke. But that was small-time. This? This is the big league. This is the Premier League, and silence is not going to work in your favour.'

'But something else might?' Locke asked, definitely interested now.

Bliss explained to her how back in the day when instructions for leniency were issued, they were slipped into brown envelopes. Now it was all done electronically, as were so many key elements of the procedure. But it was the same thing in all but name – lenient charge, lenient sentence, in exchange for worthwhile information.

He thought he had judged it just right. There was more to say. Other ways to try and convince the woman, to browbeat her into giving up the Cookes. But there was also a time when silence worked so much better than further words. In the silence there were whispers, insinuations, the echo of words eating their way into your brain. Bliss knew that a suspect could spill their guts merely in order to break that silence, fearing they might otherwise go insane.

Alongside him, Chandler did not need to be told to bite her lip. Bliss fixed his gaze not on Locke, but on her solicitor instead. *Say nothing*, that look was insisting. *Keep your counsel. Yes, you want to represent your client. But don't you also want to see justice done here? Let the absence of sound work its magic. That's all you have to do here. Be quiet and earn your fee.*

'What do you want to know?' Diane Locke said eventually, the mask she had worn now crumbling to dust.

Bliss kept the triumph from his face. He cleared his throat, laid his gaze upon the suspect, and told Diane Locke precisely what he wanted from her.

Chapter Thirty-Five

For ten years from 2004, Roger Maypole had been on a lucrative retainer, his services paid for exclusively by the CAWED organisation. Interviews, cautions, and arrests were frequent occurrences while the war being waged on the waste disposal company was in full swing. The police intervened regularly, and each time it was Maypole who drove over from his home in Oundle at the time to appear for his clients, whether at Peterborough or on the first floor of the Queen Street station in Whittlesey. Bliss had encountered the man on two previous occasions, and had enjoyed neither.

'About time!' Maypole stormed as Bliss entered the room, making a show of checking the clock on the wall. Interview room two was compact and functional, providing no frills and sombre, dilapidated décor. Certainly no distractions. 'Keeping my clients waiting for this length of time is absolutely outrageous.'

'Stick the bluster where you tend to your haemorrhoids, Maypole,' Bliss countered, taking his seat at the table. 'You've only been here for fifteen minutes yourself, so get over it.'

The solicitor smoothed down his tie and shook his head as if at an unruly child. A large, portly man in an ill-fitting grey suit and sporting a ratty-looking goatee, Maypole's cheeks burned as he gathered himself.

'If that is the way you intend conducting yourself with a member of the legal profession, Inspector Bliss, then you had better believe a complaint will be lodged with your Chief Superintendent.'

'Fill your boots, Mr Maypole, but take a ticket and wait your turn. If you kept your trap shut I wouldn't need to talk to you at all. Mr and Mrs Cooke waited two hours for you to drive over here from Birmingham, so the additional fifteen minutes – which you would have demanded in order to consult with them on your own anyway – really made no difference. Now, can we please crack on? I'm sure you don't want Mrs Cooke hanging around on her own in that holding cell any longer than necessary.'

The charges had been read and the interview sanctioned. Bliss pushed ahead without waiting for Maypole to respond. He leaned across the table to press the record button on the tape device.

'Interview with Marvin Cooke, who has been advised of the charges and his rights in accordance with PACE. In attendance is the solicitor for the Cooke family, Roger Maypole, myself, Detective Inspector James Bliss, and my colleague, Detective Sergeant Penny Chandler. Interview begins at 9.17am.'

Bliss cleared his throat a couple of times before continuing.

'Mr Cooke, when you were arrested earlier this morning it was on the suspicion that you and your wife, Ellie, conspired to stalk and assault both Mandy Vickers of Woodston, Peterborough, and Deborah Crighton of Hampton Vale, Peterborough. Also, that you conspired to stalk and murder Jade Coleman, of New England, Peterborough. We now have evidence provided by a third conspirator that you and your wife instigated all three attacks, and that you both intended paying that conspirator to carry out the crimes on your behalf. Do you have anything to say in your defence to the charges I have put to you here today?'

Bliss knew this was where his case against the pair was weak. Not only was it based on the common 'he said-she said' type of evidence, but what he had also learned from Diane Locke was the bad news that the Cookes had yet to hand over a penny to her for the work completed on their behalf. With Marvin and Ellie Cooke in custody, there was no option but to run with it, but Bliss knew that with Maypole in their corner they would most likely walk away from their interviews and continue right out of the station.

Locke was going to be remanded because the police believed that she might commit similar crimes, not attend trial if bailed to appear, and specifically was more than likely to attempt to interfere with potential witnesses. None of those options were available to Bliss in respect of Marvin and Ellie Cooke. There was not enough evidence against either of them, other than the statement provided by the admitted offender.

'Let me get this right,' Marvin Cooke said, squinting at Bliss. 'A supposed co-conspirator, someone you have arrested for carrying out these awful offences, is now claiming that my wife and I asked this person to do so and that we paid them to. Am I understanding that correctly?'

'Essentially.'

'Then in my defence I have to say their story is utter nonsense. This sad individual has clearly become unravelled and is, for reasons I can only begin to guess at, trying to curry favour with you by implicating us. I suspect they realise how much you personally dislike us, Inspector, and so chose to lead you to us by way of a false statement. At such a trying time for you, with your own career currently under investigation, you might be forgiven for being taken in.'

Bliss glanced across at Maypole. The man had been busy during his journey over from the West Midlands. 'So you're denying the allegations, Mr Cooke?' he asked.

'Of course. Because they are asinine.'

'But are they unsubstantiated?' They were, but Bliss wanted to plant a seed of doubt in Cooke's mind.

'They have to be,' Maypole interjected. 'My clients are innocent, so these baseless allegations will remain unsubstantiated. I do hope you have more than that, Inspector Bliss. A lot of time and money is being wasted here.'

'Nonetheless, those allegations have been made. I hope you're not suggesting we ignore them without first asking Mr and Mrs Cooke for a response. Without allowing them to defend themselves against what has been said about them.'

'Not at all. It is why we are here, after all. I am merely pointing out that these claims are false, that you will find no evidence to back them up. I wonder, then, what else you might have up your sleeve.'

'You will have your answer as and when we reach that juncture. Right now, I have put the allegations to your client. Mr Cooke has denied them. I will shortly be putting those same allegations to Mrs Cooke. It's possible that she might have a very different story to tell us.'

'No, it's not,' Cooke said immediately.

'It's not what?'

'Possible. These allegations are nonsensical. Why on earth would my wife and I want Jade murdered?'

Maypole sighed and put a hand on his client's arm. Bliss grinned. No good brief would ever ask a question without already knowing the answer, and they were never happy when their clients did so.

'Why indeed?' Bliss asked. 'That's a good question, and I'm glad you brought it up, Mr Cooke. I was hoping you might answer it for me also.'

'Don't be absurd.'

'So you did not wish Jade Coleman dead? You had no reason to have her murdered?'

'Of course not.'

Bliss thought it through. He reasoned that it was time for another gamble, because he had nothing to lose by taking it.

'Only, the truth of the matter is that you did have reason, Mr Cooke. We do have motive to discuss. Two of them, in fact. Firstly, you previously admitted to me that you hold Brady responsible for your own conviction of fraud. Doing time for someone else's crime is a pretty good motive to begin with.

'Secondly, it is my belief that Jade was asking too many questions about Tessa Brady. You originally fobbed her off by suggesting somebody in an official position at the waste disposal place had either caused or been involved in Brady's sudden disappearance. You got into her head so much she even took a job there. You convinced her she might act as some sort of spy, when in fact all you wanted was for her to be out of your hair. But when nothing came of it, she headed straight back to you two. I strongly suspect that Jade eventually became suspicious of you both. Perhaps she even discovered something. Something more than your wife's personal relationship with Brady, Mr Cooke.'

Marvin gave an almost imperceptible shake of the head. But Bliss noticed it. He also thought he saw a moment of doubt pass like a cloud across the man's eyes as his tongue licked out to moisten his now obviously dry lips. Bliss had thrown out that bomb in desperation, but it had struck a nerve of some kind. He now began to wonder whether Ellie Cooke and Tessa Brady had actually enjoyed some sort of fling together, and if so, it seemed to be coming as a genuine shock to Marvin Cooke.

Bliss was not the only one to spot this. Chandler had scribbled something on her notepad. When she showed it to him, he read: *not sure where this is going but he is rattled.* He flicked her a sidelong glance and nodded. But Maypole had clearly also seen for himself that all was not well, because he elected to step in.

'I think it may be the right time to pause,' he suggested. 'My client needs a toilet break, a drink, and a brief consultation.'

Bliss rose to his feet. 'Interview suspended at nine thirty-two,' he said. 'DI Bliss and DS Chandler leaving the room.'

Chandler stopped the recording. For a moment the room was in complete silence. Bliss thought of a way to fill it. 'Once your client has peed, taken a drink, and consulted with you, Mr Maypole, you might try convincing him to tell us the truth about Jade Coleman. One way or another we'll be finding out all about it. Better it comes from him now than from his wife later on. If there is a deal to be had, it will be offered to only one of them.'

'This is an extremely unpleasant room,' Cooke complained, wrinkling his nostrils. 'No doubt designed to create unpleasant experiences. Being this close to you is certainly one of them.'

'You're lucky you have one with glass bricks to allow natural daylight to bleed in. Our smallest and dingiest room has no windows at all. You'd be right at home there, I reckon.'

Cooke was shaking his head at Bliss, eyes mocking the DI. 'Hardly conducive, though. Not if you want a happy suspect in the room.'

'They don't,' Maypole told him as if speaking to a child. 'They just want one who will tell them exactly what they want to hear.'

Before the solicitor could rebuke them further, Bliss took Chandler by the arm and walked out of the interview room. In the corridor he stopped, stood with his back to the wall and hung his head.

'You think they both had something to do with it?' Bliss asked.

'He gives me the creeps, and Mrs Cooke is a hard-faced bitch capable of anything, boss.'

'That's not what I asked, Pen.'

'In that case, yes, I do think they are both involved. I think she knows what happened, even if she didn't have the nerve to do it herself.'

Bliss had struck a blow; the possible relationship between Ellie Cooke and Tessa Brady causing her husband some pain. But he knew it was not enough. It might bend the man, but the betrayal was not yet sufficient to break him.

***

Bliss began the interrogation of Ellie Cooke by asking about her relationship with Tessa Brady. It was not what the woman had been expecting, and the tack unsettled her.

'I… I don't know what you mean. We were friends at first. Then we weren't.'

'That's right. It's the period in the middle I'm interested in, Mrs Cooke.' Bliss paused to smile and nod his head. 'The small matter of what turned your friendship into the kind of hatred I witnessed the other day. There are a number of potential causes for that degree of falling out, but one of them is most definitely the ending of a relationship. Particularly an intimate one.'

'You're suggesting Tessa and I were lovers? That's absurd.'

'Really? Your husband didn't seem to think so. In fact, it seemed to me he thought it entirely possible.'

'Now, you know very well that is not what Marvin said,' Maypole snapped. His eyes locked onto Bliss's. 'He suggested nothing of the sort, Inspector. I must object to that outright lie.'

'I wouldn't call it a lie.' Bliss persisted with the line he had planned to use after calling a halt to the previous interview. 'Mr Cooke might not have uttered the words, as such, but his body language spoke for him, and it was written all over his face. He believed it. And he was shocked by it.'

'You are making assumptions not in evidence.' Maypole turned to his client. 'Ellie, don't listen to this man. Detective Inspector Bliss is basing his whole line of questioning on unfounded assumptions, and you should not respond to his spurious claims.'

'You don't have to respond, Mrs Cooke,' Bliss said. 'I just want you to keep it in mind. Your husband very much minded even the thought of sharing you with another woman. Right now, he's sitting in his own little room with that new and unpalatable concept churning around inside his head. By the time I next speak with him he may well have decided to make you pay for your treachery.'

'Inspector Bliss!' Maypole threw his arms up in the air in exasperation. 'I really must insist you either continue this interview by asking my client valid questions pertaining to the charges laid against her or call a halt to it altogether. This is unseemly, and I won't have it.'

'I'm coming to the questions, Mr Maypole.' Bliss was not at all fazed by the solicitor's outburst. 'I simply thought your client might like to know exactly how things stood, and that she too ought to be made aware that only one deal will be offered here, and that her husband is already considering his own position as we speak.'

'Once again, that is not an accurate statement of events, Inspector.'

'Well, it seems we have a difference of opinion. In my view it reflects the conversation I had with Mr Cooke, and his response to it. If I were Mrs Cooke, I might be seeing the conflict of interest here and wondering who you were really working for.'

It was a calculated risk. The moment Bliss made that statement, he knew Maypole would call an end to the interview. Furthermore, he would register his complaint at the tactics being used, the breach of PACE guidelines, and would demand Bliss was replaced as the interviewing officer.

Bliss did not care. Not even a little. He had weighed up the evidence against the Cookes and decided it was not anywhere close to being enough, not when Diane Locke had admitted so much and was already in custody. So, he had opted to toss some kindling on the floor, start a fire, and then throw petrol all over it.

There was no time to dwell on any immediate reprimands, the effect on his career, nor his standing in the eyes of the IOPC. The only thing that mattered to Bliss was obtaining justice for Jade Coleman by not only putting away her killer, but also the two people responsible for ordering her murder. And the only way to achieve that objective was to have one of them turn against the other.

'Would you leave us please,' Ellie Cooke said, her head tilted downward.

'Don't worry, Ellie. Inspector Bliss and DS Chandler are leaving right now.'

'No, Roger.' Cooke raised her head, turned to face him. 'I meant you. I want you to leave. Go and sit with Marvin. He may soon be grateful for the company.'

'Ellie, you can't do this.'

'Yes. Yes, I can, Roger.'

'I really must advise against it. I can't allow you to continue without representation.'

'You what! You can't allow me? Who the hell do you think you are? I'm sick of men like you telling me what I can and can't do. Now, I'm not asking you to leave, Roger, I'm telling you to.'

'DS Chandler, would you please show Mr Maypole the way out,' Bliss said, eyeing the rotund figure as he sat bewildered and disconcerted by Ellie's Cooke's decision.

Chandler stood and turned to the room's only door. 'This way, Mr Maypole,' she said, cheerily. 'It would seem you are no longer wanted here.'

'He's such a creep,' Cooke said when it was just the three of them. 'I never did take to him.'

Bliss nodded. He had no response. Excitement raged inside his chest. It caused minor shivers to trickle their way along his spine, like the soft whisper of insects scuttling across his flesh. He was close now. So close he could feel it, breathe in its odour.

The woman gazed around the room, taking her time about it. When she spoke next, it was a diversion. 'Are those alarms on the wall?' she asked.

Bliss turned to look, nodded as his head swung back. 'They are. Panic strips.'

'I've seen them on TV shows and always wondered if they were real. Has anyone ever leaned against them accidentally?'

He was happy to play her game if it kept her talking. 'Happens all the time. That corridor out there echoes to the thunder of heavy boots as every copper within earshot of the alarm bears down on whichever room it's coming from. It's quite a sight when they burst into the room expecting the worst, because they do come mob-handed.'

'Looking to give someone a good hiding, I suppose.'

Bliss shook his head, smiling. 'That would go against PACE guidelines. If there was anything going off, our officers would gently escort the person out thinking only of their health and safety at all times.'

'I'm sure.' Cooke rolled her eyes.

'Shall we crack on now,' he said, leaning forward across the table. 'It's time, don't you think?'

'I suppose you want to hear my story,' the woman said finally. Her eyes became hooded as she looked at him, toying with her hair and pouting, putting on a show for him once again.

'Of course,' he replied. 'This is your opportunity to give us your version of events, Mrs Cooke.'

'Ellie. Please.' Cooke shifted sideways and crossed her legs in an obvious gesture designed to snag Bliss's attention.

'Ellie. Of course. In your own time.'

The woman took a deep breath. 'I confess, Inspector Bliss. I did have a sexual relationship with Tessa Brady. And no, my husband was not aware of it. You can't imagine what it was like having all that power in an organisation like CAWED. An entire coterie of supporters followed our lead and did our bidding. It was how I imagine the first flush of the sixties to be. All that free love. I was so turned on by it, I would have slept with anyone at the time, man or woman. It was intoxicating, and I wanted to indulge myself in every experience imaginable.'

'That's understandable. These cult-like groups often end that way.'

'All that heaving, sweaty sex, Inspector. Can you imagine it? I bet you can, actually. I bet you even want to imagine it right now.' Again, she purred and preened.

Bliss shook his head and flooded his eyes with contempt. 'It's of no interest to me whatsoever, Mrs Cooke. But the rest of it is.'

'The rest of what?'

'The stalkings, the beatings, the murder of Jade Coleman. Tell us about your role in those actions, and the role your husband played.'

With careful deliberation, Ellie Cooke raised both hands and clasped her face. It reminded Bliss of the painting by Edvard Munch: *The Scream*. Forming a circle with her mouth completed the mental image for him.

Cooke began to giggle.

It was exactly that.

Not a chuckle, not a laugh, nor a snigger. It was a childish giggle. A toddler playing a game as her shoulders bobbed up and down.

'Oh, Inspector. Is that what you thought I wanted to talk to you about on my own? Stalkings, beatings, murder? No, no, no. I wanted to clear the air about my affair with Tessa, that's all.

Without that pompous fool Maypole in the room. I thought you were keen to learn more about the sexual depravity, and I was more than happy to oblige. You seemed to be interested in that aspect of my life. I assumed the thought of two naked, glistening women coupling was turning you on. Actually, I was just bullshitting you in order to get your motor running. I had no interest in Tessa that way. But you thought I… how absurd. Why on earth would I confess to things I have no clue about?'

Bliss felt a chill emanating from somewhere inside the room. Bile threatened to coat his oesophagus with its noxious flavour.

'Perhaps to tell us what you know before your husband does,' he shot back. 'I don't think he's happy with you right now, Ellie. My money is on him sitting with Maypole at this very moment cutting a deal that puts him in the clear and you very much in our crosshairs.'

The smile never left her face. 'You do? Inspector, if you don't mind my saying so, you look as if you've had a hard time recently. You appear to be beyond exhausted, and a little rough around the edges. Actually, more than a little. I don't think you are quite at your best. If there ever was a best in your case. I feel I have to point this out, because if you genuinely believe my husband would betray me over a brief affair, then you clearly don't know a great deal about the human condition. Believe me, he knows that although I am a sexual free spirit, I am not in the least bit interested in women. Even if he had something to say about these dreadful attacks – which, of course, he does not – Marvin would never contemplate making a deal with the likes of you.'

Ellie Cooke sat back in her chair and folded one arm across her midriff, the other resting on it as her index finger played with her pouting, glossy red lips, still forming a wide smile. Her eyes, dark and cloudy earlier, were now bright and glimmering.

'And neither would I, for that matter,' she added. 'Now, would you like me to talk more about the sex, Inspector? The things I did and had done to me over the years. I'd be happy to… educate you.'

Bliss swallowed and pulled moisture into his mouth. They had been had. No, *he* had been had. His over-confidence had led him to believe he was toying with Marvin and Ellie Cooke, yet he now realised they had been playing him all along. They had known their tame predator might one day sell them out, and they were prepared for it. Their thirst for power now included taking him on in his own back yard.

And winning

His mind circled around the evidence, and nowhere did it alight on the Cookes. There was no money trail. No impartial witnesses. No known contact between them and Jade Coleman in several years. No known contact between them and the other two women at all. There was only Diane Locke and her tale of mitigation.

Marvin and Ellie Cooke had taken him on in a battle of wits. And for once, he had been unarmed.

Chapter Thirty-Six

Bliss had never been one to accept defeat easily. In his sporting days he would shake his opponent's hand whether he won or was bested. That was a matter of honour and respect. In life he embraced the vagaries of fortune, understanding that the rub of the green mostly evened out across a lifetime. But when it came to the life and death of his investigations, the injustices were impossible to swallow.

Dawn was still creeping across the east coast when Bliss travelled south in the taxi he had ordered. It was a hefty fee to travel the eighty-five miles from Peterborough to Leyton in east-London, but there was a part of him that thought he might not be making the return journey. As he slumped into the back seat, he told the driver he did not want to be disturbed until they reached their destination. Bliss closed his eyes but did not sleep. Instead he thought. About what was to come, but also what he had left behind.

Citing dizziness and pain, he had left Thorpe Wood the day before fully intending to drink himself into oblivion. He had said nothing to his team, leaving Chandler to explain to them what was happening with operation Cauldron. Marvin and Ellie Cooke had been bailed to reappear in fourteen days' time, at which point they would either be discharged or re-interviewed. Bliss knew that, provided the couple stuck to their story, his case against them was hopeless. They were too clever to have left evidence on their boat, so he put no faith in the search of it turning up anything of use. He had been unable to force a wedge between them. Instead, they had taken him for a ride, laughing all the way.

It wasn't the ridicule that Bliss wanted to blot out in those dark hours that followed. It was the harsh stench of failure. The next morning he would confront a man he wanted to kill. Had wanted to do so for seventeen years. He had no clue what he might actually do when the moment arrived, nor what might in turn be done to him. But between Nick Nevin and the IOPC investigation, Bliss was convinced his time was up as far as the job was concerned. And if his career was over, what else was there? It wasn't right that his last action as a DI was to fail in achieving justice for Jade Coleman. The fact that her actual killer would be charged was of little consolation to him.

Bliss had got a cab to the Windmill. There he could drink for the rest of the day and stagger his way home afterwards in less than ten minutes. It seemed as good a plan as any. He was two pints in when he called Wigg.

'Wiggy, my old mucker,' he said, aiming for carefree and missing by a mile. 'I was wondering if you'd managed to get hold of that info I was looking for.'

'I'd intended calling you tomorrow, old boy.'

Bliss thought it best not to mention that by then it would no longer matter.

'Then you have something for me?'

'I do. You sound as if you might be in a hurry, so let's look at the money side of things first. You remember an old lag by the name of Monty Chadwick?'

'Yeah. Little Jewish bloke. Had a factory out by Weavers Fields in Bethnal Green. Back of the railway line.'

'That's the chap. Apparently, his story is that a week before Hazel was murdered, he paid you ten thousand pounds not to raid his place on a night when he was putting together a shipment of arms out of his factory.'

'Ten grand was a lot of money back then. Any idea why he's coughing to this now?'

'No. But I can tell you that he's not entirely out of the business, so it may be that Nevin has something on him. Something rather more current and possibly a lot worse.'

'And the geezer who is supposed to have killed Hazel. You get anything on him?'

'John Fitzpatrick.'

'Iron Paddy?' Bliss pulled the face out of his memory. A tall and wide brute of a man, who earned his nickname both due to his love of West Ham football club, and his preference for using a hot steam iron when torturing people. Bliss had heard the tales of how, when an iron got to within a whisker of flesh, the skin seemed to rise to meet the heat, singeing the hairs first. Iron Paddy's expertise was prolonging that moment to create the utmost terror in his numerous victims.

'The very same. He is of course serving life in Belmarsh. However, there has been talk of him being moved from south London up to Wakefield, in West Yorkshire. Now, apparently, Fitzpatrick is on his last legs. Emphysema. His sister, who is struggling financially, is his only visitor, and has been for the past decade. My guess is, Nevin has arranged to put some cash his sister's way in exchange for Fitzpatrick's testimony. It makes sense, because he's never coming out anyway. What's one more murder charge against him when he won't see out the year?'

Bliss nodded to himself. It also explained why the IOPC were in so much of a hurry. They would need to get Fitzpatrick's testimony on record and even hope to have him around to be questioned in a courtroom while there was still time.

Two witnesses. Two statements. One to put the money in Bliss's hands, the other to explain what he did with it afterwards. Neither could be verified by a third party, but both together could be enough to convince others of his guilt. It was all the IOPC would need to proceed against him. Monty Chadwick's statement alone could cost him his job.

Three pints in and on his first scotch, Bliss looked up as the pub door was thrown open and Chandler stepped through the entrance, her head swivelling as she sought him out. He was at a corner table looking out at the rest of the bar, and her gaze lasered in on him. He saw her chest rise and fall before her shoulders dipped. As she made her way over, Chandler was shaking her head. She plumped herself down with a heavy sigh at the table's only other chair.

'You're an easy man to find,' she said. 'You weren't at home. You have no car to go driving around in. This place was second on my list. How tragic is that?'

'I'm not hiding myself away,' he said with a shrug. His eyelids felt heavy, and he had to blink slowly several times to keep them from sliding fully closed.

'But you are getting bladdered.'

'That I am. Fortunately, I'm a happy drunk. Not one of those snarling and spitting angry types.'

'Mostly. But you didn't start the session happy, so I'm not so sure where it might end up. Why are you here on your own?'

'Who else would I be with?'

'Thanks.'

Bliss was not so far gone that he could not recognise the fleeting look of pain that crossed his partner's features. He shook his head and waved a hand in the air.

'Now, don't take it personally. You know I always enjoy a drink and a natter with you, Pen. All I meant was, I knew I wouldn't be good company tonight. I didn't want to inflict my mood on you.'

'It's not just me, though. What about your team? You don't think they are hurting tonight? On the one hand they want to celebrate nailing Diane Locke. On the other, they know the Cookes have slipped through our fingers. Instead of being elated, they're despondent. Every single one of them. That's your influence, because like you they are an all-or-nothing team these days. They could have done with their leader standing up and telling them what a great job they did. That it wasn't over. That the Cookes would slip up eventually. Anything really. Anything other than you storming out and sulking on your own.'

Bliss blew out his cheeks. 'For fuck's sake, Pen! You're not my bloody mother. I'm your boss, remember.'

'Well fucking act like it then, Jimmy.'

The two glared at each other across the table. Bliss bit into his bottom lip. Chandler sat upright and defiant.

'You haven't even offered me a drink, you ignorant bugger,' she said after a moment that threatened to linger far too long.

Bliss dipped a hand inside his jacket pocket. He pulled out his wallet, took out a ten pound note and tossed it on the table. 'I'll have a double Famous Grouse while you're up there,' he said. Chandler did not smile, but he knew the moment had passed.

He hated it when she was right, but yet again his partner had made her point perfectly. He had sought to lick his wounds anywhere other than with his team, not wanting them to be exposed to the dark thoughts twisting and writhing inside his head like a poisonous knot of snakes. It had not occurred to him that walking away and leaving them to their own misery was far worse.

He and Chandler sat talking for another three rounds.

At some point, Bliss had managed to convince his colleague that he was sorry. He promised Chandler that he would apologise to the rest of the team on Monday morning. Bliss had known at the time he said it that he might not be in any fit state after the weekend, but he felt he had to say something positive in order to pacify her.

After that, the evening got a little murky.

As his cab eased through the relatively quiet streets of Woodford and Snaresbrook on its way to Leyton Jubilee Park that morning, Bliss tried to distinguish reality from drunken stupor the night before. After emerging from the pub, Chandler had accompanied him home. His gait was laboured, and he recalled a few occasions where her hand or arm supported him. When they reached his house, she called for a cab. They waited together by his front door, Bliss leaning against the frame, Chandler leaning against him to keep him upright.

Had he told her anything about this morning? He didn't think so. But his mind kept flashing on a moment shortly before her cab arrived when Chandler stepped towards him, holding onto his hands, her eyes beseeching him about something. All Bliss could recall now was a conversation that may or may not have even occurred.

'*Tell me what's wrong, Jimmy. I know there's something going on with you. Something much more than simply losing the Cookes. I'm seeing something in you tonight that I have never seen before. Jimmy, it frightens me.*'

'*It's all good, Pen. All good. Things turn out the way they were meant to. It's the way things have to be. How they needed to be.*'

'*I don't know what you mean!*'

'*It's time, is all. My time. I'm tired. Tired of fighting the tide. It's time to set things straight. I had a life all mapped out, Pen. Me and Hazel. Together. As one. We both had our lives stolen from us. All that… promise. Gone. Snatched away from us.*'

Tears slipping from the corner of her eyes, Chandler saying, '*Oh, Jimmy. Please tell me what's happening. Please. I can't help you if you won't tell me.*'

'*There is no helping me now, Pen. It needs to be over. I need to be at peace.*'

'*Don't say things like that!*'

'*It's all right. Really, it's all right. And you'll be all right, too. There's nothing you can't achieve if you put your mind to it. Don't let anyone steal your life away, Pen. Nobody. Especially not me.*'

It was a blur from that point on.

Except for one more rolling image which had to be the drink playing tricks with his mind.

The cab pulling up outside his house.

Penny unwilling to leave him on his own.

Him insisting she go. And then…

Had he leaned in closer first, or had she?

Had he kissed her, or had she kissed him?

Bliss could not remember. Only that their lips pressed together and lingered.

'*I love you, Penny Chandler.*'

'*I love you, too, old man.*'

'Whereabouts do you want dropping off?'

Bliss jerked his head up. His eyes flew open. It was morning and he was in the back of the taxi. He recognised Church Road in Leyton. It had been a while, and it seemed narrow and smaller somehow, the buildings larger and looming, more oppressive than before.

'Just up here opposite Marsh Lane, please.' Bliss could see the driver was using his phone as a SatNav. They were less than a hundred yards away. His destination lay at the end of the lane, but he felt like walking the final part.

Dagenham Brook did not run anywhere near Dagenham, which was an east London town in Essex. Instead, the brook ran through Walthamstow and Leyton. A minor tributary of the river Lea, created for drainage purposes, and the brook ran alongside what had once been Marsh Lane playing fields, but was now celebrated as Leyton Jubilee Park. As a youth, Bliss had played many games of football on a Sunday morning at Marsh Lane. It also happened to be the site of his first ever murder investigation.

An eighteen-year-old black kid found with his throat slit. He was a known dealer, but rumour had it that he was straying on someone else's territory. Three days after finding himself leaning over the dead body on the overgrown bank of Dagenham Brook, Bliss arrested a kid just one year older than his victim by the name of Daniel Butcher. By the time he was thirty, Butcher was back on the street and to Bliss's knowledge never did a deal or took a life again.

You always remembered your first.

Factory walls in red brick had once run the entire length of Marsh Lane on both sides of the street. To the right, as he made his way down towards the playing fields, much of the wall had been retained. Where it had been removed to make way for newer buildings, similar brickwork had been used to maintain the historical feel.

It was just after 6.30am, and Bliss was walking towards an uncertain future. Danger lurked there, of that he was certain. Before entering the park area, he made a call to a number given to him by Gareth Wigg.

'DCI Batty,' said the Met detective now working for the IOPC. 'It's Bliss.'

'Inspector. I don't recall giving you my number.'

'I think you slipped me your business card.'

'I did. But it doesn't have this number on it.'

'Well, then I guess I got it some other way.'

'What do you want, Inspector? This is highly irregular, and I will have to report this conversation.'

'You know something, Batty, I'm really hoping that is precisely what you will do. Tell me, is it me as a person you detest, or is it the things I am supposed to have done that make you lick your lips at the thought of breaking me?'

'I don't know you as a person. Does that answer your question?'

'It does. So you only want the truth, right?'

'That's correct. Are you about to confess everything, Inspector?'

Bliss laughed. 'Not right now. Just do me one favour… keep off this line for a while.'

He disconnected. There was no way of telling whether Batty was a part of this entire set-up, but Bliss decided to roll the dice for what might prove to be one last time.

He thought about his wife, the lives they had forged at a time when everything remained possible. Fate had thrown them together, made two individuals whole again when they both needed it most. Bliss had known from the beginning that theirs was a love that would endure. Hazel had not simply stolen his heart, she had become his heart. That was why she still existed ethereally within its chambers. Every second beat was hers, and the knowledge that a piece of her survived within his own body was the main reason he had endured without her.

His mind conjured up the faces of his parents. He hoped he had proven to be the kind of son they had always wanted. That, as an extension of them, they had been proud to call him their boy. Their standards were impossible to measure himself against, but he had given it his best shot.

And then he came back to Penny Chandler.

He could not be certain which – if any – of those flashbacks from the previous night with her were real and which were the elaborate creations of a mind soaked in alcohol and reaching for an emotional life raft. But Bliss did know that today was the day he either took back his life or tossed it away altogether.

The next hour was not merely the passing of sixty minutes.

The next hour was everything.

Or nothing.

Chapter Thirty-Seven

Bliss waited for fifteen minutes at the scene of his first ever murder investigation before he heard the undergrowth rustling and somebody moving his way. He tensed and held his breath. Nick Nevin was not an honourable man. There was every chance that he would not have come alone.

If he had come at all.

Bliss knew it might just as easily be two men with pickaxe handles bearing down on him.

But then Nevin emerged between the overhanging branches of trees that lined the walkway running alongside the river. He spotted Bliss and carefully picked his way down the overgrown embankment, his eyes never leaving those of his enemy. Momentum forced him to jog the last couple of places and crab sideways as he came to stand just feet from the edge of the brook. He wore jeans and a lightweight windcheater jacket, old and grubby trainers on his feet.

Seventeen years was a long enough time, but Nevin looked as if he had aged a quarter of a century, or more. His once lean physique had gone, replaced by a doughy body with no muscle conditioning or tone. His face was bloated and sheened with sweat. What remained of his hair was slicked back and across the scalp to disguise the colour, texture and volume. He stood with hands on hips, gathering his breath. He remained a big man, but no longer as imposing.

'Why choose this place?' he asked.

Bliss glanced around. On the other side of the brook, beyond the steep bank, high walls and fencing separated the secluded spot from the factories and warehouses beyond. The trail had been cut back and tidied during the redevelopment of the area, but the spot had stood the test of time better than either of the two men now appraising it.

'I thought the site of my first ever murder case represented a fitting bookend, really,' Bliss answered. 'As a kid I played more than a few games of football at Marsh Lane. I used to like coming here to the brook as well, and I wondered what it looked like now with all that Olympic money poured into it.'

'To me it's still nothing more than a wannabe river.'

Bliss shook his head. 'You've got no imagination, that's why.'

'You think?' Nevin ran his eye over it one more time, remaining unimpressed. He shook his head, bottom lip curling. 'I've pissed more than this after a night out on the lash.'

'You have no soul. I would say the job took it from you, but I doubt you ever had one.'

'I've been waiting for what feels like half my life for this, Bliss,' Nevin said, cutting across the insult. His voice was deeper and harsher than Bliss remembered. A lot of nicotine and alcohol had washed beneath the bridge since the two men had last met. 'So spare me the dramatics and let's get on with it.'

'Of course. It's why we're here.'

'I actually didn't think you would show. Didn't think you had the balls.'

'You always did underestimate me, Nevin.'

Bliss reeled in his anger, but the feelings that bubbled beneath the surface were confused. The man he despised, the man he wanted dead for what had been done to Hazel, was not the man who stood before him now. This was a virtual stranger. The person Nevin had become.

'Perhaps I did,' the man responded. 'But you being here tells me one thing. It tells me I've already won. You wouldn't be within ten miles of me if that weren't the case.'

Bliss shook his head. 'We both have our reasons. You want one last pop at me before the IOPC get their hands on me. You want to see me at my lowest ebb. I get that. As for what I want with you, well that's simple enough: I want the truth.'

'What do you care about the truth, Bliss? Did you ever admit to anybody exactly what you did to me the night you gave me that hiding? No. No, you wouldn't have been too proud at having to mention the way you steamed into me when I was already down and virtually out.'

'And still you got off lightly. You've had seventeen extra years to walk around, breathe the air as a free man. My Hazel never got that chance. But you want some truths, Nevin? Try these on for size. I know Monty is in your pocket and you have him putting me in the frame for looking the other way for a payment of ten grand. And tucked up in his cell you've got Iron Paddy taking the rap for killing Hazel, when we both know he was nowhere near my gaff that night.'

'Like I told you on the dog, they're two men who found their way and decided to come forward with what they knew after all these years.'

'What you said on the phone means fuck all. And what about your truth, Nevin? You have me here. Just me. You want a ruck later so's you can have your own chance to have me sucking down hospital food, you've got it. I'm going nowhere until this is over, one way or another.'

'Really? Only, you already seem to be in a bad way, Bliss. Old and tired is to be expected. But you're well past it. A real state, to be honest with you. It's a bit embarrassing, actually.'

'We'll see what I've got left in the tank. If I'm being honest, I'm in the shittiest physical condition of my life right now, but if you came at me, I'd have every excuse to end things in the worst possible way for both of us. Anyway I can... by whatever means. You're fucking with the wrong man at the wrong time. But none of that is happening here and now, Nevin. And it doesn't happen at all unless I hear those words from your mouth.'

'What words would they be, Bliss?'

'You know what I want to hear.'

'Yeah, and you think I'll say anything about it with you capable of recording me?'

Bliss spread his arms wide. 'I'll show you I have nothing to hide. Nothing at all that could be recording our discussion.'

Nevin snapped his fingers. 'Phone,' he said.

Bliss dug a hand into his pocket. He stepped forward and passed his mobile across. Nevin snatched at it. As he did, Bliss held on and yanked the man closer still. So close each could feel the other's breath on their face.

'You see me standing before you in this condition and still decide today is the day you'll have your go at me, eh? You're a pathetic excuse for a man, Nevin.'

The two grappled for a second or two before Nevin shoved Bliss back. This time he was holding Bliss's phone in his hands. 'Behave yourself,' he said. Then instead of switching the mobile off and keeping it, Nevin flung it far into the brook. He looked especially pleased with himself at the explosive splash it created. A couple of birds rebuked him as they took wing in fright.

'What the fuck did you do that for?' Bliss demanded angrily.

'Just covering myself, Bliss. I know what a slippery fucker you can be.'

'There was no need to sling it. Happy now?'

'No. Not by a long way. Now you can strip down to your shorts. You do that and maybe you hear what you want to hear.'

'You want to humiliate me, is that it?'

'No. Just taking care of business. I have to make sure you've not got anything else on you to record me with.'

Bliss ran a hand over his face, the harsh stubble on his cheeks rough against his fingers. He stared at Nevin, but a moment later began removing his clothes. In a few short seconds his lightweight jacket, polo shirt, trousers, socks and shoes lay in a puddle on the tall grass by the bank of the brook. The area was shaded by trees, and the early morning sun was yet to warm the air around them. Bliss stood there with his arms spread wide once more, shivering a little in the breeze.

'This good enough for you, Nevin?'

'Not quite. Butt crack and groin. Don't be a pussy. I'll let you pull them up again, but be a good boy and yank your boxers down to show me there's nothing down there God didn't give you.'

Breathing hard now, Bliss slipped down his shorts, bent over and even spread his cheeks a little. He turned, to confirm he was hiding nothing in his groin, either. The shorts came up rapidly after Nevin gave the nod.

'Satisfied?' Bliss appealed.

'For now. I won't be totally happy until you're suffering physically the way I did. Mind you, by the look of your body, you're not exactly doing too good as it is.'

Bliss shook his head. Lowered his hands. 'Let's get on with this. As fucked up as I am, you won't walk away unscathed. But now it's your turn. Tell me what you did to my wife.'

Nevin took a breath and nodded. 'It was like you said all along, Bliss. I wanted what I couldn't have. I balled her at the party, I wanted to ball her again. She wouldn't have it. No matter how many times I asked. So I called around to your place that night, knowing you were out on an op. I convinced her to let me inside because I wanted to apologise, to explain myself to her. Believe it or not, that's what I was intending to do when I went over. But then sitting there, just feet away from her, and Hazel looking so good, I thought about what she and I had done together that one time, and I… I couldn't help myself. I tried it on again. She reacted badly. So did I. I lost it.'

'You killed her. Stabbed her to death.'

'Yeah. It wasn't my fault, though. She should've just let me screw her. It wasn't like she didn't put it about. I wanted her, and all she had to do was open her legs one more time instead of her mouth, shouting and screaming abuse at me. I had to shut her up. She was asking for it. Brought it on herself.'

That was enough for Bliss. With a primal roar that welled up from deep inside his stomach, he charged at Nevin and wrapped both hands around his neck. As big as he was, Nevin was slow and heavy. As the two men struggled against each other, Bliss felt the larger man's hands begin to prise his own apart. Bliss cried out again as he tightened his grip, and this time Nevin stumbled backwards and fell to the ground. Bliss fell with him, landing on top. He managed to wrestle his arms away and began clubbing Nevin with short, but powerful punches to the face. So filled with rage and desire to avenge his wife's murder, Bliss failed to notice what Nevin's own arms were busy doing.

As Bliss pulled back his hand preparing to slam his fist down into Nevin's face one more time, there was a blur of movement. Both of Nevin's hands came up and around at the same time. Only when they struck his head did Bliss realise each held a large stone. One had a sharp edge and it slashed his temple where the cut from Thursday's accident remained fragile. The wound immediately tore open and started to leak blood again. The other blow took him hard almost on the crown, the flat stone dense and heavy.

Momentarily stunned, Bliss found himself suddenly unable to coordinate his own movements. He knelt above Nevin and blinked down at the man. He could neither focus nor gather his thoughts. Below him, Nevin wriggled out from between Bliss's thighs, and heaved his opponent to one side. His senses reeling, Bliss felt himself twist sideways and then slump on his back.

Both men lay panting, gasping for air, their muscles burning and bone-numbing weariness sapping the last remaining dregs of their energy. Nevin's balding head was now a wild mess of thin threads of hair across the scalp.

'We're too fucking old for this shit,' Bliss managed to say, wishing he had a fiver for every time he had thought the same thing over the past week or so. Pain flared like a scalpel cut in his chest. He pulled moisture into his mouth and spat it out.

'Fuck this! The IOPC can finish you off, Bliss,' Nevin sneered at him.

Eyes locked, the two men drew themselves upright, and eventually to their feet, legs spread wide to help maintain their balance. Their arms hung low by their sides. The evolution of man unwinding in a few seconds.

'You so sure I won't finish you off first?' Bliss asked him.

'I'm safe here. I know you've not brought anyone with you.'

'Because you have, yes?'

'Too bloody right I have.'

'Which makes me the bigger man.'

'Which makes you the bloody fool. What d'you think this is, Bliss? Some cosy Sunday night drama on the Beeb? There's no such thing as honour. There's just winners and losers.'

'And you reckon you're a winner?'

Nevin laughed and spread his hands. 'Well, I ain't the one standing around in my underwear with my big plan lying in the bottom of Dagenham Brook, am I?'

Bliss smiled. 'Neither am I, Nevin.'

'No? Then prove me wrong.'

'Fair enough. Why don't you check the left hand pocket of your jacket?'

Nevin's brow creased. He eyed Bliss suspiciously, but dipped a hand into his pocket all the same. The crease deepened. When his hand came back out, his fingers were wrapped around two slim mobile phones. The gold-coloured one had to be his, Bliss knew. Because the black one was not.

'The fuck's this?' Nevin said, faltering as his confidence began to erode.

'That's my Samsung. The one you tossed away was my old Nokia. I dropped that phone there into your pocket when we scuffled over the other one.'

The concerned frown was replaced by a slow, uncertain grin. 'So you recorded me after all. Big fucking deal. I have the phone now, arsehole. What use is it to you?'

'Before you chuck that one away as well, Nevin, you need to understand that I never said anything about recording you. Before you react at all, put your ear to it and say hello. Somebody would like a word.'

Despite his exhaustion, Bliss felt elation gathering in his chest. From the very beginning, he had assumed that Nevin would toss the phone and demand he strip down. So, the moment he heard the man making his way through the trees, Bliss had redialled DCI Batty and simply left the call open. Bliss then looked for an outline of Nevin's own phone in his jacket pocket so that when the two grappled as planned, he would know which pocket to drop his mobile into; he didn't think his opponent would notice the slight additional weight.

Bliss looked on as the colour drained from Nevin's face while he listened to whatever Batty was telling him. The sound of distant sirens broke through the early morning bird chorus. He stood still, waiting for Nevin's eyes to lock with his own once more. When they did, he saw only acceptance and the stinging pain of defeat.

Slowly shaking his head, Nevin first looked at the phone as if still shocked by its treachery. Then he casually lobbed it underhand into the brook. The flabby curves of his face became taut, and lines gathered around his eyes as they became thin slits of rage.

'I could have my men kill you right now,' he told Bliss, spittle flying from his lips. 'And I'd laugh while they did it.'

Bliss shook his head. 'If they have any sense at all, they scarpered the moment they first heard those sirens, Nevin. They have nothing to gain, and everything to lose by hanging around.'

'I should have killed you myself when I had the chance.'

'Yeah. Or it could maybe have gone the other way.'

'Nah. You're in even worse shape than I am.'

'You could well be right about that.'

'You going to stop me from running, Bliss?'

'No.' He said this with a firm shake of the head. 'I'm close to collapsing as it is. As are you. Behave yourself and sit your arse down. It's over, Nevin.'

The big man stood there as if undecided. 'It won't ever be over between me and you, Bliss.'

Bliss gave that some thought. He stared along the meandering path of the brook, recalling the hours he and his friends had spent here playing cowboys and Indians, maybe even soldiers. Never cops and robbers. He could almost hear his childhood self calling out, the vague impression of a young Jimmy Bliss coalescing into the shadows away in the distance. Gone but not forgotten. Saw, too, the young adult he had become as he stared down at his first dead body, his voice breaking as he issued orders to those around him. He had come a long way since. Only to end up right back in the same place. Finally, he shook his head.

'You know what, Nevin? You're wrong when you say it won't ever be over between us. I've waited a bloody long time to make you pay for killing Hazel, and whatever happens now you'll do just that. The past can never be put back inside the bottle. So, whether you hang around and wait for them to slap the cuffs on, run and have them hunt you down like a dog, or you find some deep part of the brook to drown yourself in, either way suits me. Because you're done, Nevin. And finally, I'm done with you.'

Chapter Thirty-Eight

By way of a change they were in Chandler's kitchen drinking filter coffee. As Bliss sat overlooking the river Nene where it flowed beneath the old town bridge, he realised it had been thirteen years since he had last been inside his partner's home.

Almost a quarter of his entire life.

It was Sunday morning. He had hired a cab over to confess everything, and was now starting to question the wisdom of that decision.

For the past ten minutes he had waited for his partner's anger to burn itself out. Chandler's fury towards him was vented with no holds barred, full spleen let loose on him with both barrels. He took it on the chin, knowing she was more wrong than right.

'Are you done?' Bliss asked as Chandler paused for breath during one particularly withering diatribe about his mental and physical condition. 'Only you seem to be covering old ground now.'

'You're lucky we're not covering you with old ground.'

He nodded approvingly. 'Nice allusion. But a little over-dramatic.'

'You think so? Really? Jimmy, you had no idea what you were walking into yesterday morning.'

'No, that's not entirely true. I had a pretty good idea what I was walking into, actually.'

'So you knew Nick Nevin wouldn't be alone?'

'I was hoping he would prove to be the untrustworthy fuckstick I'd always considered him to be, yes.'

'And still you chose to go without back-up.'

Bliss held his hands up defensively. 'Pen, just hear me out. If you want to carry on with the bollocking afterwards, then you can do so.'

Chandler took a seat opposite him at the small bistro-style dining table for the first time since he had arrived at her door. She took a sip of her drink, set the mug down on the mottled stainless-steel top, and sat there with her arms folded. 'Go on then. Give it your best shot.'

He leaned forward, offering a tentative smile. 'For my plan to work I needed Nevin to feel comfortable. To fully let his guard down by virtue of the sheer weight of numbers in his favour. If he had so much as suspected I had back-up nearby, even just one person who might be able to overhear us, he would never have admitted to killing Hazel. I had to convince him it was just me, him and his distant henchmen waiting in the wings, no phone and no recording.'

'What made you believe he would cough at all after all this time?'

'Because he wanted to. He's always wanted to. I didn't know the man well, Pen, but I knew his type. He would have revelled in telling me. Rubbing my nose in it, all the while believing there was not a thing I could do about it, would have broken me and invigorated him. To force me to live with that knowledge would have been the worst thing of all. And I mean knowledge, straight from his own lips, not just the gut instinct I have always had. If it had gone down that way, it would have destroyed me. And that, allied to whatever the IOPC might do to me, was precisely what he wanted by way of punishment for what I had done to him. So yes, I was confident that if I gave him the perfect opportunity, he would snap it up. He really couldn't help himself.'

Chandler unfolded her arms and took another sip from her mug. 'Okay. I see that. I do. But even so, you could have told me. You could have let me in on it, let me travel down there with you but keep well out of the way, yet close enough to make a difference if things turned nasty.'

Bliss was shaking his head. 'But that's just it. To be close enough to make a difference, you would have also been close enough to be spotted or overheard. I couldn't risk that happening, Pen. I'm sorry, but I simply couldn't.'

'You could have been killed.'

'But I wasn't.'

'You could have been badly hurt.'

'But I wasn't.'

'You could have trusted me.'

He paused before responding. 'I always have and always will trust you, Pen. But I also know you. If I had told you what I was about to do, and then insisted you remain up here while I went down to confront Nevin, there's not a force on earth that would have prevented you from coming down anyway. Tell me I'm wrong.'

She couldn't.

'Being there on my own was critical to the plan,' Bliss went on. 'I had one shot, Pen. Just that one opportunity to get him to talk. I knew that if I did it the right way that I could get him to cough and also kill the IOPC investigation into me. But I also knew that if I screwed it up, that chance would never come around again.'

They were both silent for a few moments. Bliss watched a longboat go sliding by beneath the bridge and on its way past the Key Theatre towards the fork with the Black River. The sight of the boat nudged something in the back of his mind, but he was too wrapped up in the current discussion to pay much attention to it. He allowed his eyes to focus on the strong wake left behind, while his thoughts continued to twist like a kite in the wind.

'Penny,' he said, eventually. 'I know you're angry with me. I know you're not about to forgive me right now. But I am hoping you will come to understand why it had to be this way. Maybe then you'll stow the anger somewhere and let it die out naturally.'

When she spoke next, Chandler's voice was soft and attentive. 'When I left you late on Friday night, I was beside myself with worry. I thought you might be about to… do something stupid.'

'That's always a good bet to take where I'm concerned.'

'No, I mean–'

He reached out a hand and rested it upon the back of hers. 'I know what you mean. And I'm sorry if I gave you that impression. Pen, from time to time I might get myself into scrapes like this that take me close to the edge. But believe me when I say I'm never throwing myself over it. I might not always care too much about what happens to me, but I care enough about other people not to do anything to myself. I would never cause them that much pain and distress.'

Chandler nodded and squeezed his hand. A tear caught itself in the corner of her eye, glittering like a precious gemstone in the morning sunlight.

Still drained from his various ordeals over the past eleven days, Bliss cast his mind back twenty-four hours. With Nevin still standing and considering whether to remain or flee the scene, Bliss had slumped to his backside on the grassy embankment. He lacked the strength to even pull his clothes back on. Sirens wailed in the distance.

Local cops for Nevin, an ambulance for him.

Hopefully.

The fresh damage to the side of his head felt hot and painful, and this time he knew he would need proper stitches to hold the gash together. This time he would do whatever the paramedic told him to. He had no more energy. The fight was gone from him.

When he had next glanced up at Nevin, he thought he saw the same resignation in the other man's drawn features. The two remained in those positions until the sirens first grew louder and then died altogether, the emergency responders appearing through the treeline a couple of minutes later. While Bliss was attended to, Nevin was arrested and hauled away. He never said a word. Sometime later, with Bliss dressed and his wounds tended to, DI Batty arrived at the scene and the remainder of the day and evening had been lost to procedure and formal interviews at the

Leyton Custody Centre, a new building to Bliss, who had only ever known the old Francis Road station.

Batty later arranged for a fellow detective to drive Bliss home. Throughout the entire journey, Bliss replayed the incident with Nevin over and over again inside his head. The brutal words; the confession; the realisation from Nevin that he had been played; the handcuffs being locked in place around his wrists.

The ultimate acceptance of defeat.

'I got him, Pen,' Bliss said now. He drained his coffee and backhanded his lips. 'I got the bastard.'

'Yes, you did.' Chandler gave a thoughtful nod, and a flickering smile. 'Hazel would be so proud of you, Jimmy.'

He looked up into her eyes, his own glistening and welling. 'You think?'

Chandler cupped his chin and ran the soft pad of her thumb across his cheek to intercept the three lines of tears streaking downward. The gesture was intimate, but neither of them were embarrassed by it.

'I don't think, Jimmy. I know. You put everything you had on the line yesterday, including your life. You did that to make sure that everyone else knew what you had known for the past seventeen years. And you did it to make sure he was punished. You did that for her, Jimmy. How could she not be proud of you for that?'

'I didn't do it just for Hazel. I had to do it for me, too. I had to put an end to it, Pen. I had to make myself whole again.'

'I know. And you have.'

Bliss shook his head. 'No. Not yet. But now I know that I will. Eventually.'

'So, you think you'll stick around for a while longer?'

'You mean not retire after all? Thing is, if the county were using the A19 regulation then they could have pushed me out by now. I've got my thirty years in. That may still come back around if the budget cuts continue. But until then, I think I'll soldier on. If they don't chop me off at the knees, I reckon I'll know when the time is right to put in my papers.'

'How close did you come this time?'

'Not close enough to make the difference. I was feeling sorry for myself, that's all. So, yes, you'll have to put up with me for a while longer yet.'

Chandler smiled at him. 'I just can't catch a break,' she said.

Later, after he got back home, Bliss helped himself to a cold beer. He put on a Danny Wilson CD and stood by the open French windows looking out at his garden. It was in need of a bit of TLC. As was he. It was in need of a good drink. As was he. After a while, he turned to head into the kitchen for a second beer. But as he did, he caught sight of the bare room and realised something that momentarily stalled his breath.

He walked into the dining room, picked up a cardboard box and carried it back into the living room. He placed the box on his recliner and opened up the four flaps. He reached inside and took out the first item his fingers alighted upon. The framed photograph revealed him and Hazel caught in an embrace on the evening of their wedding. The shot had not been posed, and sitting around them were their parents, whose candid laughter and postures matched that of the newlyweds. The seal had been placed on their futures that day, a seal that would bind them together for the rest of their lives.

A life had since been lost. The promise of a bright future together now torn asunder.

But that seal remained unbroken.

Bliss used the hem of his T-shirt to carefully wipe away the dust that had accrued on both the wooden frame and the protective glass. His gaze lingered on each face, especially those of his father and, of course, Hazel. Later on he would track down Hazel's parents, neither of whom had ever completely believed in his innocence. He would call them, let them know that this part of their ordeal was finally over. They had not stood by him, but he owed them this. And he hoped they would feel as he did now.

The framed photograph was freestanding, so when he was done cleaning it, Bliss walked across to the small bookcase which he had filled with albums. He set the photo on top, stood back and breathed it in. What he had realised minutes earlier was that, at long last, he was ready.

The bloodstained chamber in his heart that would forever be the place in which Hazel resided, pulsed and fluttered momentarily. It felt as if something had been cast free; taken flight and set off in search of a new beginning.

A new life. Full of promise.

Chapter Thirty-Nine

Monday morning. Early. Bliss was sitting in a nine-foot by nine-foot square room at HMP Peterborough, located on the former Baker Perkins engineering site in Saville Road alongside the railway tracks that speared through the spine of the city. Diane Locke had been transferred to the prison from her Thorpe Wood holding cell on Saturday at around the time Bliss was getting pounded with rocks like a caveman. She would be held on remand now until either her trial date or her solicitor's appeal against the detainment proved successful. The room was generally used for meetings between prisoners and their legal representatives, but Bliss had persuaded Locke to meet with him on her own.

She was escorted into the room accompanied by two prison officers from the female wing. The clunking of the door lock broke Bliss from his deep contemplation.

'Bloody hell, you're looking even worse today,' Locke said as she entered the room and took in his appearance.

He had seen himself in the mirror earlier and almost laughed at the spectacle. There was a wad of gauze on each side of his head now, his bruises deeper and uglier, cuts and grazes harsh and red still. Fresh abrasions were spreading like a rash. A sorry sight indeed.

The officers left the room as previously arranged. It was just the two of them now.

'I could say the same about you,' Bliss replied. The woman's own bruises had darkened and grown larger, her face remaining swollen and flecked with tiny lacerations. The brace she wore to protect her collarbone was obvious. He knew he looked much worse, though.

'What am I doing here?' she asked.

'I wanted to speak to you some more about the Cookes.'

'I told you all I know. I gave you everything you needed. I heard they walked and yet I'm still in here. That seem fair to you, Inspector?'

'Not really. But then, you did actually murder Jade Coleman. I keep asking myself why. Why did you allow the Cookes to use you like that in the first place? I know they were supposed to pay you, but I don't believe this was all about the money for you.'

'You couldn't possibly understand, Inspector. To be a woman trapped inside a man's body, to keep all of those emotions locked away and to then release them into the wild.'

'Try me.'

'Okay. Take this place for example. I'm a woman. It may not be my biological sex, but it is my chosen gender. For a variety of reasons, I have never had any of the available operations, so I have no breasts and I retain the male genitalia I was born with. When my bra comes off at night, my boobs come off with it. So then in terms of physique and appearance, I'm a man all over again. Which poses a problem for this place. I mean, where do they keep a freak like me, right?'

'I assumed most people had the ops. Making life a little easier in such circumstances.'

'Oh, sure. Because prison people are well known for their understanding that way. But you see, I signed my forms as the woman I truly am, so they have to house me in the women's block. They have to let me wander around there in general population and do all the things the other women do. I mean, a woman with a dick? You might expect me to be torn apart by some of them, but they are wary, uncertain of what I am. Can you imagine it in the showers? They do draw the line there, allowing me to take mine on my own. It would be nice if it wasn't quite so pathetic.'

'Things are changing, so I hear. Not as quickly as some would like, but you have to admit it's not only your adjustment to make.'

'Oh, I do. But you think even today's society wants people like me? Imagine what it was like back then. That's why the years I spent with CAWED were the happiest of my life. I felt accepted, in a world that did not embrace the likes of me. And it was because of Marvin and Ellie. They were my friends, and they took me into their hearts when others refused. I felt… useful, rather than use*less*. I was allowed to be what I always knew I was. I felt safe among them. Secure. I felt free.'

'So what went wrong?'

'Reality, I suppose. When CAWED folded, Marvin and Ellie gave up the fight. In doing so they turned in on themselves, and away from us. Including me. I felt that, Inspector. Deeply. So, when Ellie and I accidentally bumped into each other in town – I now know, of course, that it was no accident – I was beyond thrilled when she invited me back into their lives. I felt complete again. You have no idea what those two can be like, how they can make you feel so special. They are so charismatic, especially when they are together. And, clearly, manipulative. The truth is, Inspector Bliss, I would have done anything to stay inside their inner circle. For their approval.'

'Even so. Beatings, murder… that's stretching the boundaries of friendship, isn't it?'

'At the time, I really didn't think so. I was completely under their spell. If they wanted something from me, I willingly gave it. Perhaps it was the ex-con in me, jumping to order. What can I say?'

'Okay,' Bliss said, nodding slowly. 'Let's say I understand all that. Why Jade? Why did Jade have to die?'

'That was… regrettable. Believe me, it was never supposed to happen so violently. But she got scared, and to my complete surprise she held out that knife. She tried talking me down, backing away all the time. When she couldn't back away any further, I made a lunge for the knife. We grappled for it, and I wrenched it away from her. The next thing I knew I was kneeling over her and she was dead.'

'There must have been a lot of blood. If there was not supposed to be that level of violence, then you clearly weren't prepared for all that bloodshed. But the one or two witnesses who caught a glimpse of you leaving made no mention of you being covered in blood.'

Locke winced. 'I turned my clothes inside out. It was horrible. Her blood was still warm and tacky against my skin. It seeped through the material eventually, but by then I was far away.'

'Out of interest, where did you go to that day?'

'My gran has a place in Walton. I stay with her occasionally, and have clothes there in the spare bedroom.'

'And the murder weapon? Jade's own knife?'

'Washed it and buried it out in the back garden.'

'So you murdered Jade, cycled home to grandma's house, cleaned yourself up, and just got on with your life.'

'You make it sound so cold. But yes, that was the plan. Then I was asked to carry out another stalking and beating.'

'Deborah Crighton. But back to Jade. Why did they need her to die and not just be beaten? Why was she their real target?'

'First, they never told me exactly why. All I know is that they needed the police to focus more closely on the stalker character I had created, so for them it made sense for there to be another attack. They had no desire to kill Vickers, though. When it came to Jade, all Ellie told me was that she and Marvin had already done some pruning of their own, and it would be too risky for them to handle the job themselves. They were very concerned about Jade's state of mind. She had been searching for Tessa Brady for years. She was initially convinced – or had been convinced – that somebody at the nuclear waste disposal site was responsible in some way. That they had done something to her. But I got the impression that in recent weeks, Jade had been looking closely at Marvin and Ellie, suggesting they knew more than they were telling, making some wild accusations against them.'

'So, Jade came to believe that the Cookes might be responsible for Brady's disappearance.'

'That was the gist of it, yes. She felt betrayed, and told them she was going to go to the police.'

Bliss's mind drifted back to his second visit to the boat on Tuesday evening. It was the nudge his brain had given him while he drank coffee in Chandler's kitchen and watched the longboat disappear down river. The discussion he'd had with the Cookes about Brady came flooding back. Marvin Cooke's immediate reaction when Bliss had asked where Brady was, both the comment and gesture he made, played across Bliss's mind.

Bliss had taken it one way.

The obvious way. The intended way.

But what if he was wrong?

What if the gesture had meant something entirely different?

What if that smug, arrogant and self-satisfied look on Cooke's face had signified a completely different story altogether?

Chapter Forty

'Nice to see you wearing some clothes for a change,' Chandler called out as she walked the short distance from her car to where Bliss stood on the bank overlooking the *St Francis*. She wore a grin that Americans might call 'shit-eating', but he was aware that his partner was breaking the tension circling around him like a swarm of gnats.

Marvin and Ellie Cooke were being held close by in the car park, Hunt and Ansari detailed to keep the two from either driving off or returning to their boat after Bliss and Bishop had insisted the pair leave their floating home while search warrants were executed. The Cookes had been rearrested and cuffed.

A diving team had been in the water for a little over ten minutes, but Bliss had grown increasingly restless as he paced back and forth on the grassy bank. Each second dragged to the point where it felt as if hour after fruitless hour had passed. Even after confirming with the marina owners that the *St Francis* had been dry-docked for hull blackening to protect the wood the day after Tessa Brady had been reported missing, still Bliss was riddled with anxiety. He vacillated between certainty that his instinct was correct, and the overwhelming shame of having mistaken a common combination of gesture and comment for something much more depraved. Bliss had been glad of the space in which to mope when Bishop wandered away to chat with the head of the dive team.

'Nice day for messing about on the river,' Chandler went on, when she got no more than a grunt from him in reply.

'Nice day for your boss to be carted off to the old folk's home or sectioned,' Bliss muttered. 'Either one of those is looking far more likely than me getting a result here.'

Chandler nudged him with her elbow and gave a sly wink. 'Cheer up, boss. Look at the positives. For once lately you're not taking a hiding off someone, the IOPC have crawled away with their tail between their legs, and the killer of Jade Coleman is banged up. You couldn't have asked for more than that when this all began.'

Bliss knew she was right. None of it helped. Not yet.

'I know what you're saying, and I'd usually agree with you. But I want these fuckers so badly, Pen. I accept that I may never get them for Jade Coleman's murder, but I want them for something equally horrific. I need them to do some hard time rather than be swanning about out here in their floating Utopia thinking they've got away with it.'

'And you really think Tessa Brady might be down there beneath that boat?'

'I do. Or at least, I did. At the time I ordered up this expensive and all too public wetsuit party, I was absolutely convinced of it. Now I'm feeling like I've made a prat of myself all over again.'

Chandler shrugged. 'You wouldn't be you if you didn't do that every so often, boss.'

This time she got to him. He smiled and huffed some air through his nostrils. 'Yeah, yeah. Okay. I deserve that. I'm being a little self-indulgent.'

'The main thing is we solved the investigation. Jade Coleman's killer is in prison and won't be walking the streets again for at least thirty years if the eventual court case goes our way. You also got your man. You did your team proud. You did Jade proud. You did Hazel proud. Enjoy the moment.'

Bliss sniffed the warm air. 'I suppose. It didn't bring Hazel back. But at least it didn't make her leave me, either.'

'She can never leave you, Jimmy. She's always going to occupy a special place in your heart.'

His mind rolled back to the previous day, standing in his living room admiring the wedding day photograph. 'Yeah. The piece with all the bloodstains on it.'

'That's what makes her presence there all the more real. But in nailing that bastard Nevin you not only did what you needed to do for Hazel, you also got something back.'

'I did? What was that?'

'One of those two lives he stole from you. I know you don't believe in that sort of thing, Jimmy, but some would say that by bagging the man who murdered her, you set Hazel free. To move on if she chooses. But you, you got that life returned to you. All you have to do is accept it and choose to take advantage of it.'

'That's all, eh?' He gave a humourless smile.

Chandler matched it. 'Boss, you don't exactly wallow in the past, but you do live in its shadow. The thing is, that shadow has a long reach, and it can find you wherever you go, no matter what you do. When you need it, I'm sure it will be there waiting. But for now, in fact especially right now, I think it's safe for you to come out of there.'

Again, his thoughts turned to the moment he had felt something shake itself loose as he stared at the framed photograph. Was that fluttering motion inside his chest the moment when Hazel finally found her freedom once more? And at the same time had granted permission for him to find his own way back?

He shook his head. 'You've read a lot into one simple taking down of a killer, Pen.'

'Ah, but this was no simple killer and no mere victim. The way I see it, you set Hazel free. And did the same for yourself while you were at it. I know it'll be difficult for you, Jimmy. But you won't have to do it on your own.'

Bliss looked at her and smiled. 'Speaking of which, you hear anything from the Foreign Office or Six yet about Mehmet or Hannah?'

'Actually, I did. I forgot to tell you. I got a call from your pal Munday.'

Now he was curious. 'Go on then. Don't leave me in suspense.'

'Well, it seems as if the FO are inclined to work a bit harder when under the MI5 microscope. There is now a tentative agreement in place between the FO and the Turkish version of the same department. They are getting together with representatives from both of our security agencies. Given the correct paperwork, which includes Hannah's birth certificate – on which Mehmet is named as her father – plus the police report I filed on the day he snatched her, the meeting will agree on the following strategy: someone from Six, together with an agent from the Turkish National Intelligence Organisation, plus local police, will visit Mehmet and Hannah to see what arrangements can be made.'

Bliss felt his face break out into a radiant smile. 'That's… that's incredible, Pen. I'm so thrilled for you.'

'It's wonderful news. It will all take time, but we're heading in the right direction. Munday asked me what would be the least I will accept. I told him that provided Hannah knows I am alive, and that I never gave up looking for her, the final decision will have to be hers and I will abide by it.'

'And if she chooses not to meet with you?'

'Then I'm prepared for it. Hannah has had seventeen years without me in her life to become the woman she is. If she is unwilling to step outside of that life, even for a few minutes, I'll understand. She's not the toddler Mehmet took from me, Jimmy.'

He nodded cheerfully. 'You're braver than I am. How could you cope with coming so close only to have her snatched away again after all this time?'

'The same way I had to when she was first taken from me. I won't deny I'll be heartbroken. But it will give me some peace of mind knowing that she is aware of my existence. Even just to know that she is alive and well. And there will always be the hope that one day she may change her mind.'

'You know what I think about hope.'

Chandler nodded. 'I do. You believe it can cause more harm than good. I prefer to focus only on the potential good. In some ways, it's what keeps me going.'

'Then I'm all for having a drink later and raising a glass to hope.'

'First round is on me.'

Bliss turned to her then, tearing his mind away from the boat and the search going on beneath it. 'Pen, I realise you have family and that if you need anyone with you when or if you get the word to fly over to see Hannah, then it'll be one of them who goes with you. But just so you know, if they can't make it, if there are any problems whatsoever, all you have to do is say the word. I'll take time off and come over with you.'

She smiled at him, her brow crinkling. 'You'd do that for me?'

'Of course. Why wouldn't I? You'll need support. It's a tough ask for you, and tougher still on your own.'

'Thank you. I appreciate it.'

'Don't mention it. You need me, I'll be there.'

Chandler looked down at the ground for a moment. When she raised her head, she breathed out some pent-up air.

'Well, I'm grateful to you. And boss… what happened on Friday night standing at your front door. Two drunks losing their inhibitions momentarily. Agreed?'

Bliss nodded and rolled his eyes. 'I'm glad you said something, Pen. I was mortified when I remembered. For a time, I thought it was all part of some hallucination, but then I finally understood it happened exactly the way I thought it had. And trust me to be lying there in my bloody boxers when I realised it.'

She laughed. 'You're making a bit of a habit of that. It's not something we want to see more of, boss. As for Friday night, what we said and what we did, it was just one of those things. We both got caught up in the moment, the emotion of it all. I know there was nothing meant by it on your part.'

'Yours neither, of course.'

'No. Exactly.'

'Good. That's settled, then. As I think I said some time ago, we don't want to ruin what we have. I'm glad it meant nothing to you.'

Chandler paused for a second or two, then said, 'It's not that it meant nothing. I didn't say that. The kiss was stupid and the length of it definitely induced by booze, but I do love you, Jimmy. I love you as a boss, as a colleague, and as my dearest friend.'

'Right.' He nodded. Shrugged. 'Me too. Just so's we're clear.'

'We are. I wouldn't want to spoil it and make things awkward between us.'

'Absolutely.' Bliss nodded ferociously. 'Let's never speak of it again.'

'Besides,' Chandler said, sneaking a grin at him and batting her eyelashes. 'You *are* way too old for me. There's no getting around that.'

'I am.'

'And falling to pieces if the past week is anything to go by.'

'This is all true. And you're a pain in the arse, of course. Not to mention completely insubordinate. Nothing could ever come of it.'

The two continued to gaze at each other. Something hung in the air between them. Something neither of them could bring themselves to say. Chandler opened her mouth as if to speak, but at that precise moment a shout went up and Bishop came jogging over to join them. He was beaming, a grin splitting his face from ear to ear.

'We got a thumbs up from the divers, boss. They found a body.'

Bliss clenched both fists and raised them triumphantly. He felt like weeping with relief. On Saturday morning he had done so much to turn his life and career around; yet, had risked ruining it all again with this escapade. His heart thumping, Bliss turned to stare across towards the spot where Ansari and Hunt stood with the Cookes. Marvin Cooke happened to be looking his way, and their eyes held fast.

Bliss made a show of uncurling a hand and jabbing a finger earthwards. He mouthed the words, 'Down there somewhere.' Then he smiled and turned away, the shadow of fear that passed across Marvin Cooke's face all he needed to see.

Tessa Brady was not dead and buried and gone to hell after all, but murdered and weighed down somewhere beneath the boat, cocooned in waxy adipocere and losing form as the body slowly disintegrated in the cold water, the softer parts nibbled at by fish and other aquatic creatures, the rest decomposing and becoming something less than human as time ticked slowly by. Bliss had no idea how much of her would remain after all this time, but it was her and they would prove it.

Bishop charged back across to the diving team's staging area, keen to learn the details and covering ground swiftly for such a large man. Bliss and Chandler remained where they were, staring at each other, hardly daring to believe what had just happened. Bliss, in particular, astonished that his punt had paid off. Diane Locke had mentioned that the Cookes had carried out some pruning of their own. The result of that lay beneath the hull of the *St Francis*.

Though not for much longer.

Bliss closed his eyes, leaned his head back and allowed the glow of the sun to fill his life with light and warmth. Two days ago, he had feared losing everything; possibly his life, certainly his career. All while the Cookes congratulated themselves, believing their continued freedom was assured. Now the pendulum had swung back his way. Bliss realised its momentum was pernicious at times, and wholly unpredictable. It would undoubtedly move away from him again at some point in the future.

But not today.

Today he was a winner.

Today the promise of his life was starting anew.

Today one of the lives stolen from him had been partially handed back. Battered. Scarred. Traumatised. But a life, for all that.

It was now a question of how he went about protecting it, nurturing it, making it the right thing to have survived when another had not. He turned to face his friend, his colleague. His future. Bliss wrapped his arms around Chandler, pulled her close and hugged her tight.

'Never let me forget this feeling,' he said softly.

His partner buried her head into the curve of his neck and told him everything would be all right. For once, Bliss believed it.

THE END

Acknowledgements

A couple of individuals in particular were extremely helpful during my research for this book. First of all, my thanks to Kelly Thompson, who provided me with the medical information. Almost a quarter of a century after I taught Kelly both IT and Business Studies for an entire academic year, she is now a qualified paramedic, and this time it was her turn to provide me with an education. Secondly, I would also like to thank Martin Shelbourne, a solicitor family friend who not only helped me with arrest and detention procedure, but was also kind enough to provide a genuine insight into the real Thorpe Wood police station in which the fictional DI Bliss plies his trade. Any errors you find are mine alone.

Additionally, I would like to thank the staff at the West Yorkshire Police National Database for responding to my queries. Not only were they surprisingly quick with their responses, but they also provided links to further information – I am extremely grateful to them.

As ever I want to thank the entire team at Bloodhound Books. This is my seventh novel, and I want to extend my gratitude to them for giving me a shot at reaching out to people with my work. Thank you Fred, Betsy, Alexina, Sumaira, Heather, and Emma (not to forget Sarah). And a big thank you to my editor for convincing me to make changes where the fine line between fact and fiction became more than a little blurry.

Thanks also to my family and friends for their continued support, especially my aunt, Dorothy Laney, whose patience with my scraps of first draft manuscript has helped me shape the last four books. And I am, of course, immensely grateful to all of the book bloggers and readers out there who have been so kind and supportive.

And finally, a huge thank you to my Facebook ARC group, whose good-natured support has helped inspire and promote my work. Thank you to: Clive Bickley, Livia Sbarbaro, Tony Millington, Anita Waller, Eve Jones, Yvonne Jordan, Carol Rogers, Diane Warburton, Theresa Hetherington, Nicola Dunsford-Evans, Cassie Mortimer, Val Spencer, Hilary Edwards, Sarah Muxlow, Jean Homden, Pat Kirkup, Liz Davies, Maureen Dickinson, Ella Watson, Jan Eadie, Jon Dayton and Aimee Webb.

I couldn't have done any of this without you all.

Thank you.

Lightning Source UK Ltd.
Milton Keynes UK
UKHW012126160519

342795UK00001B/15/P